THE MOUNTAIRY ROCK CITY CHRONICLES:

THE SERPENT CULT

By

Howard Night

The Serpent Cult
Howard Night

Howard Night can be contacted at Maxxpete@aol.com

ISBN 10: 0985560304
ISBN 13: 978-0-9855603-0-0

Cover art by Kenneth Moerti
aka: Blazin Asian
Blazinasiangraphics@gmail.com

For The first SuperHeroes...
...Bernice...
and Pete...

THE
SERPENT
CULT

PROLOGUE: TOO LATE

Her kiss on his neck sent reassuring warmth down his spine, quelling the shiver of fear. Jean relished in that heat as she pressed against his back and in her sweet breath as she whispered in his ear. She urged him to keep going, urged him to not to stop. Eager to please her, Jean kept his pace, his heart hammering in his ears.

He kept going despite the screams, the howls and the blood.

Thundering along beside him were his brothers, her other lovers, just as determined to satisfy her as he was. And because he was clearly her favorite they ran even harder, hoping to race their way into her heart.

As if she had one…

The corridor took a sharp turn and one of his brothers slipped trying, foolishly, to negotiate the twist in his blood slick sneakers. Jean leapt over him easily and continued up the hall, receiving a sweet kiss on the nape of his nape for his effort. He pumped his legs even harder with joy etched across his face in a mean grin. The others fell behind as he accelerated. He was first…in everything.

The corridor opened up a bit into a small but lavish lounge set before a huge wooden door. They were almost there, Jean knew, and his excitement increased even more. He flew through the lounge kicking aside the small furnishings blocking their path and grabbed a hold of the huge ornate brass handle set right in the middle of the door. The heavy handle lifted easily enough with a loud click.

But just before he threw his shoulder into the door she hissed into his ear and dug her nails into his shoulders. Immediately he obeyed, stopping with a grunt, his hand still on the handle but the huge door had begun to open a bit on its well oiled hinges. It was far too dark inside the room beyond for him to see anything. A smell, like thick burning wood and copper, rushed out at them. Jean was sure he could hear someone…or something… breathing just on the other side of the door. With a caress that was almost sweet she pulled him back away from the door. Too late, she whispered into his ear, they were too late.

Finally catching up, his brothers tore through the lounge behind them. That she gave them no warning was further proof that he was her First. Even as she pulled him back away from the door she let them rush on through and into the room.

After they rammed their way into the dark the heavy door swung back and nearly closed. Jean heard them begin to rip the room apart in their search for it. He drew a shuddering breath in anticipation; would they soon have it?

There came a bellow of a growl, so loud and deep that it vibrated through the door, across the floor and right up his body. His brothers screamed. Not the powerful, joyous screams that they had been shouting earlier. Now they were screaming in terror.

Jean heard a loud, horrid, tearing…crunching sound and one of his brothers screams were silenced. The sound of the others footsteps rushed back to the door. Jean saw the bloody hand reach through the narrow opening, saw his brothers terror filled face as he tried to escape. But something large moved through the room after him, its footsteps louder, heavier…quicker. His brother managed to get halfway out of the door before something caught him from behind.

His brother screamed for help as he fought to free himself although Jean could not hear him and no longer saw his pleading eyes or blood streaked face.

Jeans eyes were focused deep into the dark room, focused on the pair of huge gleaming yellow eyes and his ears were filled with the warning his Mistress was screaming;

RUN!

Chapter one:
NEW YEARS IN MOUNTAIRY ROCK

"Happy NEW YEAR!!!" The raucous refrain bellowing from his car radio was followed by the distant sound of firecrackers echoing through the cold night. Maximillion Madigan listened woefully to the loud, off key, singing of the traditional New Years song as he drove on. He had been forced to leave the festivities at King square because of a sudden and mysterious call from the Director and head curator of Haley Museum, Dr. Odom King. It was a call that ordered him to go immediately to the Museum that night.

"Damn!" He muttered to the empty passenger seat. His date for the evening had "declined" to accompany him to the Museum. Not that he blamed her; the party at King square was going to be the best one Mountairy Rock city had ever seen. When he left it had been so crowded that he could not even see the huge stage set in front of City hall. New City Ave was a sea of people standing shoulder to shoulder. Although that should not have mattered; with all the parties and other celebrations going on in center city, there was plenty to see and do. The huge snowdrifts lining the side streets from the past storm only packed the crowds tighter, but did nothing to stop them from growing. There were exhibitions, vendors selling just about anything, music coming from several open doors along the avenue, pop stars performing live, and women running around baring their chests for beads in this crazy weather.

It was New Years' Eve in Mountairy Rock City, a celebration that had been getting bigger and better every year. The city had a strong and well represented culturally diversity. That meant that tonight there was nowhere you could go in Mountairy Rock and not find a grand celebration going on... except for the Museum that is. For the past three years Dr. King had ordered the Museum closed during New Years', usually for inventory. Several key parties that had been held there had been forced to move, not without a little resentment, to other parts of the school or the city. Especially the huge Mountairy Rock countdown party which was both New Years celebration and the City's founding day celebration.

That was the real reason for the blow out. Mountairy Rock was an old city, officially two hundred and ninety-five years old, and as the city got closer to its official tri-centennial the huge end of year parties got ever grander. This year the biggest party was being held in King square, on the other side of the city and far out of site in Max's rear view mirror. Or rather it had been held in King Square; Max had already heard the count down and fireworks.

So that meant that he was going to get there a little late this year if at all. Hopefully, he could return to his date before she found another escort.

His cell had gone off about fifteen before midnight, and like a complete idiot, he answered even though he knew it was his boss and mentor, Dr. King. Max had recently become King's top researcher and aid and that meant the doctor was relying on him more than he had in the past. Even so; King calling him in the middle of New Years' Eve meant something big had gone down at the Museum. So Max answered his phone.

It turned out that someone had broken into the Museum and the Doctor wanted Max to be there, as he himself could not arrive for some time.

"Probably at the party he's hosting, having a ball!" He thought. While King was the curator of one of the largest museums in America, he was also one of Mountairy Rocks biggest politicos. The big man hobnobbed with the Mayor and every other major V.I.P. in the city. So that meant he could not leave his own New Years party, to which Max had NOT been invited, just to see what was going on at the Museum.

"DAMN!" The young man cursed his luck. Even with it being the holidays there was always a good number of staff and security at the Museum, so much so that he should not have been called no matter what the emergency was. But if something had happened in the labs or offices where they had been working then it was important that someone who was familiar with what was going on to be there.

"Dammit!" He had only been trying to talk with Rosette for a month and when she finally agrees to go out with him this happens. Hell, he had rented a Benz.

Finally the Museum came into view; the tall front walls and towers were bathed in red and blue flashing lights. The police were there in force when he pulled up. Max saw half a dozen squad cars parked outside among the huge piles of plowed snow as well as a few ambulances. The usual over kill response the Museum usually got for alarms and such. Money demands attention and the Museum and the University were the two biggest moneymakers the city had in the past century.

The lot was so filled that Max had to park the rental a good distance away from the Museums entrance. All six feet three inches of him stepped out of the car. The long black over coat blew impressively as he walked down the row of police cars and snow banks. It was his good one, and also his only one as was the suit beneath it. His good hat had been lost so he complimented his wardrobe with a black baseball cap, the number 76 emblazoned in white on it. It was as sharp a look as he could manage and he was going to be wasting it on cops and a stupid break-in. With any luck he would be able to get out of there soon, find Rosette and somehow salvage the night.

There were only two officers just outside the big double doors of the Museum's barbican; the huge medieval guardhouse, but he knew there would be more in the Museum itself. Careful of ice he ran up the steps, noticing that one of the policemen was bent over.

"Excuse me? I'm Max Madigan. Dr. King sent me over to see what happened." The officer who was bent over stood up and wiped his mouth, the mess on the ground was apparent. Max almost smiled. It looked like these cops took to the New Year's festivities early, and hard.

"Go ahead inside." said his partner, who did not even bother to look in Max's direction. "They're expecting you."

Carefully he stepped past the officers, through the barbican, and across the causeway that sat over the empty basin of the moat. Why the cop couldn't stop here to gag, instead of inside the barbican, Max did not know.

This was Haley Museum's main visitor entrance, still very much the old world castle for tourists. The moat was usually full and fed by an underground waterway originating from and flowing back out to Cobbs river but in winter it was blocked off and kept empty. From the front of the Museum, which sat on Germantown Avenue, this was the only way to gain entrance. Students, Professors and employees entered through the "Dock" along the side. The fact that the police and Ambulance vehicles were sitting out in front must have meant that whatever had happened, must have happened either in the Gatehouse, maybe in the Outer Bailey beyond or worse, in the Main building of the Museum itself.

In that case it could have been something that happened in the South tower where Dr. King's offices and labs were, and where Max worked.

As he passed through the Gatehouse door he spotted the broken glass on the floor. The glass front door that was cut out of the larger drawbridge, which had not been lowered since before the town was founded, had been broken open. Cold winter air blew into the Gatehouse behind him when he entered but that did not stop a strong acrid smell from making him wince as he took it in. What was it?

It was almost as cold inside here as it was outside. The Museum was always a cold drafty place anyway and the heating system never seemed to be able to compensate, but now it was so cold he could still see his breath inside. There was another officer just inside the vestibule standing there apparently waiting for the ill officer. The look on this officer's face made Max feel an even greater chill.

"What happened?" He could already see that the Gatehouse was in shambles. "You guys had your New Year's party here again?" He was joking, but the police man's face only grew tauter.

"Thought it was just vandalism, until we found the bodies." The officer stated flatly

Bodies? He knew everyone who worked at the museum and the thought of having to see one of his coworkers dead scared him. He tried to remember who was supposed to be working that night. The security rotation was vague to him and there were only a few guards he knew by name. Only the kids doing post graduate work were still in town he was certain. That would mean few students but any of the research staff could have worked tonight. If he had not been able to get a date he might have been here himself.

Far across the lobby just inside the Outer Bailey entrance there waited more uniformed officers and a couple of men and women he knew to be some of the Museum's department Heads. From their attire Max could tell that they had all been enjoying New Years parties themselves before they had come here.

But as he scanned the faculty and senior researchers he could find no one from administration or from Dr. King's personnel department. The only person representing the South Tower was Max.

Besides the uniformed officers and the paramedic there were a couple of people he did not recognize though. They were engaged with the other Department heads, some of whom Max noted were gathering themselves to leave. Sure enough, one after another the strangers seemed to be dismissing the faculty. Many of them walked out heading for the dock exit but one moved his way, toward the Gatehouse entrance. Dr. Pini was a historian, and a usually energetic man. Tonight as he approached Max his face was pale and drawn. One of those people who always had a good word for you some would say about him, but when he passed Max the man never even met his eyes. It was going to be bad. The faces of friends flashed across his mind as Max wondered who might have died tonight.

The strangers were now looking in his direction. They were standing with Dr. Eastman, head of Biology, and he was pointing at Max. The strangers, a man and a woman, nodded and shook hands with Eastman before he too walked off. They must be police detectives, he figured. The oldest one walked up and introduced himself.

"Sher… excuse me…Derrick Mann, Detective, Mountairy Rock police, 1st district. You're Madigan?" Max shook the detective's hand and nodded. The Detective was in his fifties at least and had a tired, worn look to him. Dirty gray hair that had not seen a comb this evening made Max think that on New Year's Eve, this man had been home sleep when he got the call.

He had yet to see any paramedics or bodies, so that must mean the main building. Not the South Tower please. If it wasn't the South Tower then maybe no one he knew was hurt.

"Yes. Ahh... I was called me just a little while ago to see if... um... to see if something happened... where we work... in the South Tower. What happened here? Someone tried to rob the Museum?" The whole thing was confusing. Sure Rock City had its crime problems, but for someone to try and hit the Museum...well it would have to be someone who knew nothing of the Museum. Despite its grandeur the Museum never really held anything of value, nothing that could be sold anyway. Maybe it was just...

"Or was it vandalism?" he thought, suddenly wondering at the amount of damage done in the Gatehouse.

"Vandalism is a possibility son. Let me ask you, has the museum or any of its employees been threatened in any way?" No, he could not think of any mention of threats. He had been working as an assistant for a little under two years and before that as an intern there at the museum so he pretty much knew everyone who worked there well. No one had given any indication that anyone was having any serious problems.

"No sir." he answered.

The detective nodded knowingly. "I didn't think so. Come with me please." and Max followed the detective through the mess toward the Outer Bailey. The female Detective followed them both, sandwiching Max in between the two of them.

Cold wind blasted at them as they stepped out of the Gatehouse. First thing he saw was the paramedic. The second was the still form she was standing over, lying in the snow covered with a white sheet that was stained bright red.

Max then realized what the acrid stench was; it was blood.

"Try not to look now...although we may need you to help us identify some of the victims." The Detective kept walking across the Outer Bailey. The sheet lying over the body was just thick enough that it hid the identity of the victim, just barely. Max did not realize that he had stopped walking to stare until the other detective gave him a shove from behind urging him along the shoveled path to the main building.

"Come on." She said making a poor attempt to sound comforting but Max could hear the irritation in her voice; it was New Year's Eve.

They were indeed going into the main building Max now knew. Detective Mann walked into the entrance to Rebel's Keep and paused a moment, waiting for Max and the other Detective to catch up. There was more broken glass here; sitting on the ground alongside streaks of what must have been blood. The blood lead into a service corridor that Max used almost every day, to get to the South Tower.

There were more people here, some uniformed officers, some

wearing police windbreakers over party clothes. A few were wearing latex gloves and picking through the debris on the floor. The service corridor door opened as someone with plastic bags on their feet walked out. Before it closed, and only for an instant, Max could see down the hall.

"Oh my GOD." There were at least three bodies lying on the floor of the corridor and the walls were splashed with blood. One of the bodies that Max could see clearly was wearing a security uniform.

"No son, we're not going through there." And Detective Mann pulled him by the arm into the West hall. His legs did not respond in time and he stumbled a little. They walked through and past the West Hall and, much too soon for Max, they arrived at the South Tower. Past the swinging doors there was even more evidence of vandalism, although now it looked to be more like signs of a fight.

The Detective stopped and pointed at some crates in the corner. Max recognized them even though they had been smashed into. They had arrived at the museum earlier that week but because of delays they had yet to be opened. Random violence beat them to it.

"See there? The path of vandalism leads right to this spot. Plus the amount of damage done to the rest of the walls and exhibits is small compared to the effort it must have taken to go through these crates." It was easy to pick up on what the Detective was leading up to.

"You mean whoever it was broke in here; they did it just for these crates?"

"Maybe. Nothing's sure just yet. After the forensics team finishes here I'm going to need you to go through this box with them and tell me what's missing."

"Okay but where the hell are the rest of the security guards?" Max asked. Again he wondered who might have been working. The Detective shook his head. Then he pulled Max to the side, and spoke in a low voice.

"Of the seven guards that were on duty here tonight, four are in the bathroom Mr. Madigan. They are all dead from several severe blade wounds. That's not the worst of it though; there are two more bodies in the office of the administrator. They seemed to have been attacked by some animal. The other guards are in the service corridor and in the Outer Bailey."

"What… happened?" The smell was not overwhelming but it was making him gag nonetheless.

"Until the lab boys get here I don't want to make any speculations, but between me and you? I think somebody killed them." The detective's sarcasm angered Max but he said nothing.

"The two victims in the rear office are apparently the vandals. One of them was still holding an ax which is what we think was used on some of the guards."

Again the smell made Max gag as he thought about the bodies he had already seen. He knew there were women who worked at the Museum as guards. Acid formed in the back of his mouth and he knew that if he did not calm down he would throw up. He clenched his jaw.

"Uh Professor…?" The Detective reached a hand out.

"I'm not a Professor… not yet. I started late…" he was stammering now, breathing deeply to stop from losing control but taking in more of the smell of blood at the same time. He could explain why he had not yet earned a Doctorate later.

"If you could tell us what was in those crates." The Female Detective said, once more trying to sound comforting at the same time but again Max could hear the irritation behind her words. Looking at her now he could see the dress she wore beneath the police windbreaker. Her short blond hair had just been styled so despite the weather she wore no hat. She had to be freezing, but maybe like Max himself, she had planned to be celebrating the New Year right about then.

"I'll get the manifest…" and he turned to the rear stairwell and stopped. "It should be in the upstairs office. Is it…" 'Safe' is what he wanted to say, clear of blood and bodies is what he meant. "…okay to go up there?"

The female Detective said that it was but she would go with him anyway. Her heels tapped up the stairs with the same impatient tone her voice had. The office door was locked but Max had his own set of keys so it was no problem. This was not his office alone but one he shared with a few other researchers.

This was where he would have been had he been working that night.

Everyone who worked there was careful to keep the place neat and clean usually. Now with most of the students and assistants gone for the holidays, work had fallen behind. The manifests were probably in one of a dozen stacks of papers scattered about the room that had yet to be filed.

The Detective's cell phone went off and startled Max enough that he jumped a little. Thankfully she did not seem to notice and she began speaking into it. Reminded now, Max decided to call his own boss and let him know what happened. The Curator had stressed to him how important it was that Max get to the Museum in his stead but he could not have known that there were deaths involved. With any luck he would come down here himself and Max could get out of here. But then what? Go back to the party and his date and try to pretend that nothing had happened?

Not likely.

There was no answer. As the head Curator of Haley Museum, the Dean of African Studies and the Head of the Lost Tribe research

Project, Dr. King was hosting his annual New Years party at his home. A lot of the Cities V.I.P.s would be in attendance and the party would be in full swing by now. If Kings Wife had come back to Mountairy Rock for the New Year then she would have had the house staff turn off the phones.

Max had no other way of contacting him so he went about finding the delivery manifest that was hiding somewhere in the piles of paperwork. He had not expected anything to be shipped to the South Tower so the crates probably were for some other department. But when he did find the manifest it was indeed designated for Dr. King. It had come from the research site in Africa, site one in Nigeria and it had been sent by Dr. Bazillion who had been King's previous top Researcher.

By the time he found the manifest the forensics team was done in the corridor and the Detective, Lynne by the way she answered her phone, was tapping her foot with the rhythm of machine gun fire. Like Max didn't have somewhere better to be himself!

Max had entirely forgotten about the New Year's party as he watched the crime scene in the South Tower being swept for evidence. The police scientists carefully picked their way through the entire contents of the crates. Max identified each piece and checked them off of his list. The going was slow and many of the pieces were damaged but eventually all was accounted for. Max had managed well enough, not gagging as much near the end as he had at the start.

The Detective was baffled. He had been sure that the supposed vandals had stolen something from the crates.

"Maybe there was something in the crates that wasn't listed in the manifest. What is all this stuff anyway?"

"Dr. King's big project is finding a lost African tribe. These are artifacts that could be evidence of their existence. They have to be examined and we gained permission to bring them back here to the Museum because our facilities are better. I didn't think this stuff was going to get here until late January but here it is." Max was beginning to doubt the detectives' theory. Even though he could not explain why someone would break into the museum just to trash it, he did not believe that the crates had anything to do with it. Why were the watchmen killed if all the killers wanted was to steal something?

He looked at his watch. The New Year's party in King Square was over by now so he missed seeing Rosette. She would have made her own way home or to another party. Now all he wanted to do was go home and go to sleep.

"Do you need me for anything else?" he asked. Scratching his head and yawning Detective Mann stuck his thumb out, motioning him to leave. Eagerly Max grabbed his jacket and headed for the door. On his way something crunched under his foot.

At first it appeared to be a piece of wood broken off from one of the crates but the way it felt when he stepped on it made Max look closer. Bending down he saw that it was a small rock. It was firm and coarse in his hands when he picked up the small object, which had broken into two pieces. There was some kind of design etched into it. A zigzag line set in a circle.

A symbol of mountains, or of lightning?

It was familiar but Max could not identify the design. He thought that the symbol was ancient. Maybe African in origin… from before the Slave trade…Ibo?

No… no he had not ever seen it before. It could not have come from one of the crates, Max had checked in everything against the manifest.

"Excuse me Dr. Madigan?" Max was startled by the quick appearance of another cop and did not correct the title. He dropped the small rock and promptly lost it among the rest of the debris from the broken crates.

The female police officer asked him for his home phone number in case they needed to contact him later. He grimaced as he gave her his information and hoped that he would not hear from them, he just wanted to forget what he had seen. Just in case he gave them his home phone number instead of his cell, which she then asked him for.

"And your cell number?"

"I don't have a cell." And naturally there was a loud buzzing followed by a very static filled ring tone version of "Touch My Body" coming from inside his jacket.

This has to have been one of his most memorable New Years.

"… yes…" Max answered, and then woke up confused. His house phone blared suddenly. The sleep had been a deep one, filled with dreams that were quickly fading from his memory. There was a bright sun, and dry sand…

The phone blared angrily again and he looked at it confused.

"Hello?" he said. The phone just rang at him again. Then he woke up a bit more and wondered why he couldn't hear the person on the other end of the line.

… the phone worked a certain way…

It rang again before he remembered how to pick up the receiver. Too late he reached and his answering machine beat him to it.

"Max? This is Rosette!" He groaned and pushed his face into the pillow. He had not been looking forward to that particular confrontation. His date from the previous night was calling to kick him to the curb, to tell him not to bother her anymore.

"I just wanted to say that I'm sorry for being so crabby last night. I heard that you had some trouble at the Museum. Is it all right if we make it up this weekend? Please call me." BEEP! Max shot up out of bed.

"DON'T CALL IT A COMEBACK!!" he exclaimed as he hopped out of bed and walked the two steps to the bathroom. He scanned himself quickly in the mirror. Sleep had collected in the corner of his eye but he barely noticed it next to the huge white slobber stain going across half of his face. Other than that all six feet three inches of him looked good for a twenty-nine year old just getting around to finishing his studies and about to earn his first Doctorate. Maybe he should let his goatee bloom into a full beard, to look more scholarly. Nah! He didn't run the faucet to clean his face because then he might not have enough hot water for a shower.

Max lived in a small apartment complex in the Ivy Hills section of Mountairy Rock just a few blocks from campus. Cheap rent and a bad view; he could not see the Great Lake because of the taller buildings surrounding his. He did not mind, however, as it was not in the plan to go on living there much longer. His Uncle was moving back to Virginia and leaving his loft. Max hoped to be able to sublet the huge warehouse apartment at a low rate, thanks to his father's older half-brother.

In the shower he thought of what he had to do that day. He knew that he had to check in with Dr. King to see if he was needed at the Museum because the break in last night. The thought of returning to the scene of the crime sickened Max. The image of the service corridor filled with the guards bodies came to mind. He did not know many of them but he did know one in particular, not very well but they had played basketball in the Bailey behind Wolf's Keep once or twice. Larry was the man's name, and Max was certain he had been on duty that night. With all that been said last night the one thing Max had heard that had chilled him was that no one who had been working at the Museum last night had survived.

Who could have done something like that?

Worse was the fact that Max could have been there just as easily as not. Last year the Museum had inventory the week before Christmas and it lasted through New Year's. Dr. King had ordered a few of his top assistants to stay on New Years to help finish counting. This year Dr. King postponed the inventory for early January, but that decision came late. Max might have been one of those few assistants left in the Museum that night, or any other night for that matter. With the exception of Dr. King, Dr. Bazillion, and Bazillion's his first assistant Fatima Douglas, Max had logged in more after hours, than anyone else in the Museum.

He dressed quickly and called the museum. Dr. Saul Collins, the head of the Astronomy department answered. "Hello, Collins here."

"Dr. Collins? This is Max. What's going on over there now?" The Doctor told him that the police were still there but that they were almost finished. Then he asked him to come down and help clean the place up. Hoping that the bodies were no longer there but unwilling to ask, Max agreed and was on his way. He left the long black dress coat he had worn the night before on his couch and grabbed another shorter black jacket from his closet.

The Museum was not too far from Max's apartment, which was convenient in a city this big and old. So old in fact that only half of the city streets were laid out, "grid-like" from German influences. The other half were twisting winding European-like roads and alleys, interspersed throughout the old city. The older the section the worse the roads.

Mountairy Rock city, built along a sheer rock peninsula jutting out into the Great Lake, was just under three hundred years old officially. Founded by an odd mix of settlers, mostly poor immigrants who found themselves unable to compete for land along the profitable shoreline, the land seemed to offer little for anyone wishing to start their lives. No access to the lake, ground too hard for farming and it's out of the way locale on the ridge placed it out of trade lanes. As a matter of fact the only attraction proved to be, at the time, another obstacle; the goliath Rockwood trees.

Rockwood trees, aptly named due to the incredibly dense wood, were the largest trees on the planet. It was their dense wood and great weight that allowed them to push through the topsoil and past the billion year old dense stone of the ridge to take root in the nutrient rich soil beneath the ground. City planners had long ago decided that no building should be taller than the tallest Rockwood and so they dominated the skyline giving Mountairy Rock its unique look.

The smallest Rockwood in the city by weight sat in the immense Inner Bailey of Haley museum, its long branches still rose high above the tallest of the towers. Haley Museum, once called Lupainvania castle, was itself a mammoth structure and sat at the high end of Ivy Hills, in the northwestern section of the city. It looked down on almost everything in Mountairy Rock and could be seen from across the Great Lake or from almost any point in the city.

That is except for Max's apartment window.

As he got closer Max could see that not only were there still police cars outside the castle, but several news crews as well.

He loved working at the Museum but he never like the political side of it. There was always some city function, council member, Mayor, or Governor coming through and it was at those times that the science took a back seat to the considerations of politics. Dr. King seemed to handle those situations well but Max had never liked dealing with it. While his understanding of history had given him a good respect for the need to understand motivations and points of view, he never liked dealing with those who used people's motivations as a means to garner influence. Many a gala at the Museum had seen him leaving early, or hiding in a stairwell.

So Max made sure to avoid the news crews. What happened the previous night was sure to be big news and he had no inclination to be asked anything. Better to let Dr. King handle that. The Barbican was covered but the Dock entrance on the east side would be open.

"Max?" Fatima Douglas, Dr. Bazillion's first assistant, met Max in the empty South Tower lobby. She was a fairly tall, thin woman. Her never styled hair was again pulled back in a tight ponytail exposing what Max thought was a huge forehead. Loose strands having escaped the severely tied knot stuck out and framed her face. She wore wide oversized glasses, as some sort of statement that Max had never bothered to figure out, on her upturned 'pug' nose. Fatima had been working here like Max had, first as an intern during her undergraduate days, then as a part time employee while doing her graduate studies. She was a few years younger than Max, like many of his peers here at the Museum and seemed to distrust him mainly for that reason. He had never liked her attitude and this past year she had been particularly irritating. They teased and mocked each other back and forth for most of the time they worked together. Fatimah would pick on his lack of seniority among the staff despite his age or his lack of much of a social life on campus. But Max knew how to get under her skin too. All he had to do was remind her that Dr. Bazillion, who did not like Max either, had left for Africa without her. Now she was working for Dr. King and Max loved to imply that King liked him better. She would get upset and flustered; partly because it was somewhat true. Or he would pronounce her name; Fah-TEEM-mah, even though she wanted it pronounced FAHT-im-mah.

The look in her eyes right at this moment, however, was fearful. He wondered if they had any more information on what had gone on.

"You..uh..., did they say who the guards were who died? Larry?" he asked. Fatima wrapped her arms around herself and shivered slightly.

"Yes. He...I knew him and the guy Jim… and… I think her name was Barb." Max looked at her for a moment, then decided that it would be all right to put his arm around her. After all he did not think she was a bad person, just irritating. Fatima did not flinch at his touch, but rather leaned against him. "Right here in the Museum."

"Did the police make an arrest yet?" he asked her. She shrugged her shoulders and shook her head as if she did not know.

"Mr. Madigan! Miss Douglas! We've got a lot of work to do." Professor Collins walked quickly into the room from the South Tower stairwell. The fifty-year-old astronomer and professor at M.R.U did not have the presence that Dr. King had but still got the people who worked for or studied under him to work without having to tell them twice. Maybe it was his fairness or his wonderful insight when it came to research. Max thought it was his breath. Hot ASS personified!

"I've called every assistant and intern that works here and you two are the only ones to show up! Looks like we are going to have quite a few jobs slots opening up this semester." Max flinched at that remark and chanced a quick breath. The Mountairy Rock Haley museum was one of the best museums in the country. Getting a position there was hell and if the Professor was serious then there would a stampede of college students running down Germantown Avenue from every college in commuter range. One had to sympathize with those who had not come. Though this was the last place he wanted to be during the holiday break, Max had his future to think of. He would need all kinds of grants if he wanted to continue his studies after getting his doctorate or get a good research position. Working at Haley museum for Dr. King would be a great way to get some of those things. Still he did not despair, figuring that there could not possibly be that much cleaning up to do because the police still had the damaged areas taped off.

Then Max noticed that Dr. King was still absent. "Hey where is Dr. King?"

"He called earlier to say that he won't be in today but that we should do our best to prepare the museum for the New Year. Hopefully the police won't get in our way" Collins said right into Max's face. He tried not to blink too noticeably.

Max thought that was odd that the Doctor would not be here after such an emergency. Who was going to speak to the media? Call the families? Whatever was keeping him away must have been pretty important.

"So what are we doing today?" he asked making sure to stand back a ways.

"We must inventory the damage and then write up applications and requests for the money to replace the exhibits. There were a large number of displays damaged and so a lot of paperwork. You'll work in the South Hall since the offices are closed off."

The Doctor drew a breath then. "I…will have the task of making calls to the families of victim."

Max clenched his jaw. He could not imagine having to give that kind of news to someone. "The police haven't done that?"

"Doctor King insisted that we make the calls. He's already made some but needs me to make the rest." With that Collins left them to go to his office. Solemnly Max settled in for a long day.

Whew! Max's hands were hurting not even a fifth of the way through his stack of paperwork. Insurance forms, permits, notices, and dozens of more types of paperwork had to be filled out not to mention the ton of data entry needed and phone calls to be made. Eventually some more of the graduate students filed in and helped out but not nearly enough to finish the job. It was Eight o'clock by the time a haggard Dr. Collins had decided that they had done enough for the day. He announced that they would resume in the morning and for everyone to get a good night's sleep.

Max waited while everyone slunk out, groaning about having to return in the morning. He wanted to talk with Dr. Collins alone but Fatima was not going to let that happen. So he saved his questions for later and escorted her outside. Sometimes he felt as though she was not really the kiss up that she played at. Maybe she did it to just to tick him off.

"I thought it was Eight o'clock." Max said when they got outside.

"It is Eight, almost half past." Fatima said as she headed off towards the lake, her house was in that direction.

"Then why is it so bright, Man?" He looked up and down the street. It was lit well enough to be midday.

"Stop calling me man!" Fatima stopped and burned a mean look at him as he stood on the steps of the museums side entrance. Max turned to the streetlight.

"AHHH!" Pain lanced through his eyes when he saw the streetlight the brilliance nearly blinding him.

"What's wrong with you?" Reaching back with his hands Max carefully sat down on the steps as Fatima walked back to him. He rubbed his eyes vigorously trying to ease the ache.

"Damn! That hurt!" When he could again open his eyes his vision adjusted slowly. Objects appeared to glow at first, blurring everything, then he could see just fine, very fine. What should have been a dimly lit street still seemed to be midday or late afternoon to him.

"Everything's so bright." he said. Fatima watched him for a few moments, and then left when she decided that he was just being weird. Max walked down the steps and to his car around the corner.

The city seemed strange now, even stranger than the fact that Max perceived it as midday. It was just brighter; the city seemed to just be… more there! There was high-pitched squeaking high above but he could not identify the source. As he looked around the very air seemed to vibrate with excitement. The hairs on his arms were standing on end. For a brief second he heard voices, people talking, someone yelling over the phone. He even thought that he heard Dr. King's voice, then Crash!

Max jumped at the sudden shattering sound. There was a couple arguing across the street. The woman had thrown something very breakable to the ground. She then stalked off toward the bus stop, her male friend picked up whatever it was and walked off in the other direction.

He watched the girl and the more he watched her, the easier it was to hear her. Even as she walked away he could hear her mumbling to herself. Whew! She sure was mad at her boyfriend.

Max sat down in the car. It was warm despite having been outside in the winter weather all day. He reached inside his jacket pocket to pull out his keys. Then everything returned to normal. Like someone shut off a light the street was just dark; Eight o'clock winter dark again. The sounds, the air, everything had returned to normal.

"What the hell?" He rubbed his eyes again and it was still dark. Max mused that it was probably some unique phenomenon that had something to do with his working and straining his eyes all day. Maybe there was a Museum light on that he had not noticed and it just went off. It took a little shake of his head to clear things and Max drove on home. "Weird." He muttered.

When he stepped out of the car he looked it over. He had to return it soon, to the rental place, so that meant riding the bus through two and a half more months of Montairy Rock winter. A winter that was famous for bringing the city to a halt many a year. Even so Max thought it would be a good idea to invest in a car as handing his dates bus tokens no longer played as sweet and romantic as it once had when he was in high school.

Speaking of dates, once inside Max hazarded a call to his New Year's Eve date, Rosette.

"Hello. Is Rosette there? This is Max." Some woman with a familiar voice, probably Rosette's housemate, answered the phone. After a few minutes his former date picked up the phone. To his surprise Rosette was actually pleased to hear from him. Spurred on he dared to ask her out for the next day asking if she wanted to see a play. This seemed to impress her and Max decided against mentioning that his ex-frat brother was starring in it and had given him free tickets. She asked if they were going to go to dinner first and Max said, "Of course." She then suggested a restaurant and Max agreed without hesitation even though it was rather expensive. They hung up a little while later when Rosette' explained that she and her house-mate were doing their hair and Max said good bye.

"Oh! Yea-yea-YEA!" Earlier he had thought that he was tired but now he felt charged up.

"So what can I do tonight? Terps is probably rehearsing right now so I can't hang out with him. Don't really feel like going to a club with Steve and 'em. Wait! The student center! All the undergrads are home for the holidays so it should just be filled with grad students." He showered quickly and dressed while listening to his radio for any news on what had happened the previous night. There was nothing about the break-in nor the murders; however, there was a report on a body found that had been mauled by an animal. He listened more closely then until he realized this was an old story. Someone, the news figured, was attacking male and female prostitutes with pit bulls or some such animal. But that had been going on since the Fall. Of the break in there was nothing so Max figured that they would come to it later, if it were not old news by now.

He walked into his front room and grabbed his good jacket off of the couch. As he pulled it on he was startled to see a big gray cat sitting outside his window.

"DAMN you scared me!" he yelled and caught his breath. "How did you get all the way up here?" The big cat was dirty gray with patchy fur and was obviously a street cat. It lay one blackened paw against the glass and just eyed him curiously.

"Fine." Max said. "You got up here by yourself; you can get down by yourself." Although he could not figure out how the cat had managed to scale the side of his building. His apartment was a good seventeen floors up! For a moment he thought to open the window and look down the side of the building to see how, but the way the cat was looking at him made Max uneasy so he simply left.

In the hallway he found himself waiting for the elevator with one of his neighbors. Mr. Alt eyed him suspiciously as they both stood there but Max tried his best to ignore it. 'Old Man' Alt would forever distrust him after what had happened with Max's fraternity of which the old man actually happened to be an alumnus. So he just tolerated the disapproving looks that Alt flashed all the way down the elevator ride.

Outside Max walked over to the car he had rented. It probably was not a good idea to take it to the student center. It had been one of Dr. King's connections that allowed him to get the rental in the first place, and he would have to pay for any damage done to it himself. But with the campus empty there would not be too much ruckus going on. In two more days he would be back to riding his old mountain bike or public transportation. He had better make the best of his date with Rosette' the next night, because after that the longest parts of their dates would be spent on the bus.

Just as he put the key in the lock the big gray cat stepped out from behind the bumper.

"Jeez!" Max jumped back and stared at the cat. Then he cast his eyes skyward toward his window, some seventeen floors up the alley side of his building, wondering how the big cat had gotten down so quickly.

"You're NOT the same cat." He said as though his voicing it would make the statement true. The cat looked up at him expectantly.

"What? What do you want?" Just then Max noticed the very attractive woman getting into the car parked behind his, eyeing him strangely. He was, after all, talking to a cat.

"Ah... damn." He just walked around the other side of the car avoiding the cat all together and got into the car.

The Mountairy Rock University student center sat in the center of the campus. The usually loud and crowded center was calmer now with the majority of students having gone home for the holidays. The inside was keeping up with tradition, Max discovered, as the noise level was appropriately deafening. He smiled as he searched the room for former classmates and friends.

"There is he is man." He heard someone say, but the voice sounded strange. He turned searching but he could find no one close enough to him that he should have been able to hear above the din of the crowd.

"… been trying…" Where? "… with my woman… punk-ass-mother-…" Max spun around and saw two men standing by a pinball machine leaning against the back wall of the room watching him. They looked away when he met their eyes.

"See? He know. But we got some somethin' for his ass…" Max was confused. He could hear them above the rest of the noise but they were not yelling. As a matter-of-fact they were whispering.

"Wha'sup Max?" a short, portly, deviled eyed guy with a mischievous grin came walking up. Steve Green. Max smiled nervously as he greeted his longtime friend. He had known Steve since high school back in the Philadelphia. Behind him holding two drinks was a tall, lean and very attractive undergrad. As long as Max had known him Steve had always drawn the attention of the most attractive women.

"Nothin' man. Just chillin'. What's going on here? I thought you'd be at Finleys." Max continued to listen over his shoulder but he could no longer hear the voices.

"Man have I got something to show you. Come on." Steve started to lead him back outside.

"Wha? Outside man? I just got here." But Steve continued to pull him out.

"Steve!?! It's cold outside!" the undergrad was pouting.

"Yea Steve, 'it's cold outside'. What's the big deal?" Also as long as Max had known him, Steve managed to find little "Projects" to get himself into trouble. That trouble usually found its way to Max as well.

"I got a bike man, you gotta see it." Steve laughed as they walked outside.

Snow was piled up against the sides of the student center. Max had not noticed the dirty white motorcycle leaning against the snow bank.

"Whoa… that's yours?" Max said not believing it. "I thought you meant a bicycle."

"Nope. No bicycle here baby." Steve ran his hands over the bike with pride. "Guess how much it cost me?"

"How much?" Max asked.

"Guess." Steve smiled hard.

"Steve!?!" the undergrad was hugging herself in the winter air and still managing to hold onto the drinks. Steve blew her a kiss but otherwise persisted in egging Max.

"Guess."

"All right, all right. It's used right? That takes the price down a lot. Plus you were able to buy it so that means it couldn't have cost that much. Finally ignoring the fact that you owe me more than I owe on my student loan I'd have to say...What? About a grand? And just where did you get a thousand dollars?" Max was really curious now, and worried. Steve was always prone to making careless mistakes that required constant bailing out. He took a deep breath, as he knew that he was not going to like Steve's answer.

"How much Steve?"

"A hundred." Steve smiled even harder now and started to snicker, then chortle, and then laugh out loud. His short body shook hard with every guffaw.

"A hundred dollars? Steve who did you buy this off of? You know it's stolen."

"It's not stolen! I got it off this crackhead." Steve's smile was fading.

"Oh! I see! Of course it wasn't stolen, 'cause crackheads always own twenty thousand dollar motorcycles!"

"It was his, damn! He brought it to school with him when he came here. I've got the pink slips and everything." Steve wiped some of the grease marks off of the side of his new bike. The undergrad laughed as he hopped on and made revving noises. Max allowed the words to sink in.

"He was a student? And you took his bike and gave him some crack money?"

Steve sucked his teeth at that. He said that if he had not taken the bike someone else would have. Max just turned and walked to his car. He did not feel like hanging out tonight after all.

"Come on Max!" Steve called after. "Wanna go for a ride?"

Max just looked over his shoulder. "No Steve."

"There he is."

Max stopped cold. Voices came from nowhere again. Except these were not the same voices. He looked around but he did not see anyone outside except for Steve.

"Did you hear that?" but Steve was paying so much attention to his new bike that he did not hear the question.

"Are you sure?" More voices again. Max scanned the area, unsure of where the voices were coming from. He wished for the great vision that he had experienced earlier that day. Then he saw, sitting on the hood of his rented car, the big, old, gray, cat.

"What the hell is going on!" The cat stared at him intently. Its eyes glowed brightly and when they met Max's, he saw intelligence there.

*DANGER*SHADOWS*

"GOD!" That came from the cat, he thought. The message was not vocal. He felt it inside his mind. It was an intense feeling that evoked pangs fear and dark shadowy images; Danger in the Shadows. Max turned away from the cat despite what it had just done. Behind him, in the shadows of the student center, something moved.

"He sees us master!"

"Kill him now!"

From the darkness leapt death.

STONED

The world whirled around him as he pin wheeled through the air and for one precious moment, there was peace. The winter night sky rolled across his field of vision, clear now and filled with stars. Then the top of the Douglas Hall building scrolled into sight, upside down, gently breaking that peace. Max became aware of the sound of the wind whipping past his ears as he watched the grass of Douglas yard roll around him until the Mercedes Benz he had rented slid into sight. His boots then slammed down onto the roof of the car with a resounding thud. Nothing broke the peace as much as the sound of an ax sinking into the car door or the mad frustrated cry of a crazed psycho.

"Jesus Christ!" Max exclaimed. What the hell had he just done?

Another few seconds of time passed as he stood amazed and confused on the roof of the rented car. He took in the sight of the crazed looking man with wild hair, dressed in black leather jacket and pants, ending in studded, black, steel-toe boots. The individual was frantically pulling at his weapon still wedged in the car.

Someone else was screaming and suddenly and there was a flash of blue metal light. It seemed as though a moment was lost as Max found himself in the air, realizing that he has propelled himself upward again, instinctively, to his surprise as much as his assailants. Easily he avoided a second attacker's ax blade.

Not spinning this time, his jump was one big hop, over the two axe-wielding attackers and in between them and the student center. He landed evenly, without stumbling or even dropping to a knee, and turned to face them.

Who the hell are these maniacs? He asked himself.

"YEEAARGH!" screamed the one still pulling at his trapped ax. Then cursed, at least it sounded like cursing, spit and ended his rant with something that sounded a lot like: "...Or DIE!"

Max could not control his breathing.

"No."

His hands shook and his eyes twitched.

"This... this can't be happening."

Strength seemed to drain from his heart.

"What am I gonna...?"

There was nothing he could do. There was nothing he could say. He had not prepared for this and now he was going to pay the price. A growl erupted from his throat, a mix of pain and anger.

"GRRR!… not insured! I have to pay for that you ASSHOLES!" That ax had punched right through the roof of the car.

"He mocks us!" said the Maniac who had attacked him second. His ranting was a lot more intelligible and Max turned his attention back to them. If it were not for the fact that the axes had almost hit him he might have thought this to be some prank, an expensive prank judging by the damage done to the rental car.

Hairs on the back of his neck prickled and Max turned around despite the danger he was facing. There still was something in the shadows, behind him, something far worse than the two Maniacs. His eyes began to adjust again and the entire area lit up. In that one corner there was an almost mystical flash of green light and, Max thought, the faintest trace of glowing eyes. Then there was nothing.

Except for the sound of metal ripping, quick and quiet whisperings with evil intent, pounding boots on frozen sidewalk…

…The Maniacs rushing up behind him.

Again there was no conscious thought to move, it was all instinct. Strange, it felt as though it was something he had been doing all his life. He ducked low, avoiding the lightning fast ax blades of the Maniacs. The clumsy first attacker missed and hit the second with his wild blow. The injured man fell holding the ax, which was jammed into his mid-section. Max had never taken his eyes off of that same dark corner where the "whatever it was" had been.

The two Maniacs stumbled backward together as he turned to face them. They looked to shadowy corner from where they had come running at him. Their eyes were filled with terror.

"Master? Where are you?" the injured one yelled.

"Run fool!" the other said and then took off, leaving his injured friend who slowly hobbled after.

Max watched them go, confused and stunned as he just stared at the trail of blood in the snow left by the other. It was so much blood that he thought that the wounded man would not survive if he did not get to a hospital. They had attacked him with axes; the guards at the Museum had been murdered with axes.

"What the HELL man!?!" Steve ran up beside him and looked after the two running would-be attackers.

"I…" where the HELL had HE been? "I don't know." Max answered. He looked to the student center and saw that a small crowd of people had gathered outside. They were murmuring and asking questions about what happened.

"Are you ok Steve?" The undergrad had dropped their drinks.

The large gray cat was nowhere to be seen and he wondered

where it had gone, hoping that he had only imagined it speaking to him. He looked to the Benz and winced when he saw the jagged hole cut into it by the ax.

How much was this going to cost him? He wondered.

"That's too much damn money!" The woman screamed at the Desk Officer. If not for the fact that he had to get up early the next day and deal with both the museum and the rental place Max might have found her amusing. It was about thirty degrees outside but this woman was dressed in high heels and a bomber jacket, complimented apparently by a thong.

This was the First District Police headquarters. The police who responded to the attack at the student center had "insisted" that Max come down and talk with Detectives at the station. Evidently that entailed a long wait for those same Detectives who were apparently busy with the alarmingly large number of hookers in the station that night.

At first he had not noticed them, but after seeing some of the more outlandish outfits Max began to realize that many of the women waiting in the station that night were prostitutes. From the bizarre to the exceptionally ordinary there were about twelve of them, all waiting or giving statements he supposed, being processed or whatever. There was one thing that he saw when he looked at them, that they all seemed to have in common; they were afraid. Funny, Max would have thought that being booked would have been old hat for some of these "ladies".

"Hey baby." The voice had an island accent to it. Max turned to see a brown skinned woman with long curly hair sitting on a bench just behind him. Another prostitute from the way she way dressed, which was not as garish as some but more provocative than others. She was holding a cigarette out.

"Can ya light mey?" She had strong yet soft eyes and was pretty; enough so that Max stared for a second longer than he should have.

"Ahh… no I'm sorry." His thoughts drifted to Rosette. With his studies and trying to get his professorship he had not dated much in the past few years. Now with his scholastic career winding down he had been finding more and more time to get out and have more of a social life. Not that it had been easy, what with his history on campus and everything. Max thought that he…

"…make him wait just a little longer. I want him to see us bringing in his boss." This voice came at him from nowhere, like before at the student center. He panned around the room quickly, his ears prickling up.

"Whatcha' doin' here? Ya see da ting too?" the woman behind him asked.

"What thing?" he asked. Her eyes were intent on him but Max could see that she was nervous. She shook her head and looked away, dismissing Max.

"No'ting." And she went back to her cigarette. Her nervousness became his and Max felt the hairs on the back of his neck stand up. It came on like a sudden panic attack. His breathing became shallow and his body rigid in the chair. His hands grasped the arms ready to spring him up if something… happened.

He looked around the room again as his panic rose. Why was he suddenly so nervous? Something in what the woman had said maybe? The "Thing"? Something to do with the murders at Haley?

There were offices at the far end of the room. Blinds covered their huge picture windows so there was no seeing inside. Now one of the doors opened and out walked a man Max thought he had seen before. He was a small, white man with bright white hair crowning his head and lining his jaw. This man's name escaped him now but Max was sure he had seen that hair at the museum. Without meaning to he stood to get a better look and unintentionally drew the man's attention.

The white haired man spied him and then immediately turned back into the room. A second later he walked back out and Max then knew where he had met him because before the door closed behind the white haired man he had gotten a good look into the room.

Standing behind a desk in that room was Dr. Odom King, the Head Curator and Administrator of Haley Museum, the man who was teacher, mentor, and employer of Max Madigan.

So that meant the white haired man was… "something"… Tragan, King's lawyer. Max only glimpsed the huge man who was the head administrator and curator at Haley Museum but was sure that it was he. Tragan walked across the room toward Max.

"Mr. Madigan?" Max had only met King's lawyer once before. He had barely recognized the man and was surprised that Tragan had recognized him in turn.

"Mr. Tragan." It then took Max a second to realize that Tragan had not been greeting him so much as demanding to know what he was doing here. "Oh… uh… some guys attacked me on campus. Police think they were the same guys who… uh… from the Museum… thing." The nervousness Max was feeling was not going away and it was making him stammer. He had to take a breath.

"This happened tonight?" Tragan asked surreptitiously. Tragan was asking him questions like he suspected that Max would lie or was lying.

"Yes. At the student center."

"And they were attacking you specifically?"

"Maybe, I don't really know." Max looked past the man to the room where he had seen Dr. King. "I need to talk to Dr. King."

"Exactly what time did this occur?" Tragan pressed him, ignoring his statement.

"Late evening," Max knew the time was actually closer to nine p.m. but he was becoming increasingly combative with Tragan. "Some time after I got out of the Museum. That's what I need to talk to Dr. King about." Although Max was not sure he really had anything to report, he knew he had questions of his own.

"Did the police make an arrest?"

Enough of this! Max pushed past Tragan as politely as possible. "I don't know." He said on his way to see King.

He was almost to the room when another man stepped into his path stopping him.

"Professor Madigan." It was Detective Mann who was flanked by that female Detective… Lynne, who must have been his partner, although she seemed more formally dressed than the slightly rumpled Mann. "Heard you had a little trouble tonight?"

At the sound of his voice, Max realized that the disembodied voice he had heard earlier tonight was Detective Mann's. He just had not recognized it.

"Yea, I've been waiting to speak with someone about it. But I just saw Dr. King and I…"

"Well you can tell me all about it." And Mann placed his hand on Max's shoulder to steer him away from the room King was in.

Max Madigan is six foot three inches tall, and about two hundred and twenty pounds. When Mann pulled on his shoulder he did not move, at all. It immediately became aware to everyone standing there that there would be a problem.

Mann left his hand on Max's shoulder realizing that he had missed the opportunity to remove it gracefully. Now there was a second of awkward silence as everyone waited for Max's response.

He simply looked at the hand placed on his shoulder until Mann finally, simply, removed it.

"Professor we need to go over…" he began but it was finally Max's turn to interrupt.

"I'd like to talk to Dr. King." He tried to say as if nothing tense had transpired. The panic that he had been feeling was still there, still rising. It made him anxious and fueled his combativeness, but he still managed to keep his composure.

"We'd like to talk to you first Professor. We have some questions about what happened tonight." Mann said. His voice was a little harder in response to Max's.

"He isn't a Professor." Tragan chimed in. Max watched the exchange of looks between the two police officers and the lawyer and realized that there was some game being played between the two groups to which he was not privy. Was King in some kind of trouble?

Was Max?

"I've already been waiting to talk to you Detective, for two hours. Now you can wait until I talk to my boss." But Detective Lynne was shaking her head with her arms folded. Mann answered;

"I'm sorry Doc… Mr. Madigan. But Dr. King is being held for questioning. He can only see his lawyer. So please come with us." Max stood shocked at the words: 'Being Held'. What the hell!

The room that Mann led them to was not as clean nor comfortable looking as the one he had seen King in. The desk was older and well worn and there was no picture window; although, there was a huge mirror that Max guessed was a "two way" mirror.

"Wanna tell me what happened at the student center?" Mann asked. There was that tone again, the one he had heard earlier with Tragan that made Max think there was a more subtle game being played here. Whatever it was, he did not want to play.

"No."

"What?" Detective Lynne took a side step and placed her hands on her hips. Her hair, which had been styled the other night, now was a bit disarrayed.

"I've already told everything to the police who came to the Student center. I've been here all night waiting for what? To tell you the same exact thing? No. You wanna know what happened, you should have come to see me sooner. Otherwise just read the report, but I'm not going through it again."

"I have read the report Professor, but I'd still like to hear it from you." Mann was trying to smile. Detective Lynne did not even attempt it.

"No. I've already said all I've got to say. I hope your officer got it all down 'cause I'm tired." Max was tired, and still agitated. His speech patterns were becoming more guttural, more street as the tension grew. He knew this was not the way you talked to cops.

"Fine, then I won't ask you about the attack." Mann motioned for Max to sit, and then took a seat himself on the opposite side of the table. After they both settled into the wobbly chairs Mann spoke again. "I'll ask instead what you were smuggling into the country in those crates?"

"What?" Max nearly stood up.

"The crates that were broken into that night at the Museum." Mann leaned back confidently. "You said nothing was missing."

"Nothing was missing! Everything that was listed in the manifest was still there." The agitation that Max had been feeling jumped another notch. He had an overwhelming urge to run, but he clamped down on it. What the hell was that? It was making him look guilty!

"Of course, you and King wouldn't have listed drugs or

whatever it was, along with everything else in the manifest Professor."

Wait a minute. "Drugs? What makes you think something was smuggled in anyway? And if it was, why do you think I had something to do with it?" Maybe he should call a lawyer.

Lynne handed Mann a sheet of paper. "This crate's weight at customs was fifty-six pounds. After we placed everything back into the crate and reweighed it, lo and behold it seems to have lost six point one-five pounds." He slid the sheet a paper across the table to Max. "So what was in the crate Professor?"

He looked at the sheet, which was an incomprehensible police form with no sense of order. "Yeah," he said and tossed the paper onto the table. "Whatever THAT says… Look, so there was something in the crate. What makes you think it was ME who was smuggling something?"

"Why were you attacked tonight?" Detective Lynne asked, her tone just evil. Which one was good cop?

"I don't know!" Then a thought occurred to Max. "You think that those guys at the student center were the same guys from the Museum break in right? So if they attacked me why would you think I was in on whatever it was?"

"Maybe the deal went bad somewhere. Maybe that's why the murders happened at the Museum. You and King double-crossed them."

Max took a breath. "There was no deal. There was no smuggling… that I know about. And I don't know why those guys came after me at the student center tonight." Max felt his anxiety rising even more. Why was he so nervous? He had done nothing wrong!

"Well they disappeared. Those men who attacked you…" Mann said. "…must have had some help. There was entirely too much blood for the one to get away alive with just one other guy to help him."

Detective Lynne leaned forward. "Your friends at the student center said you used some kind of martial arts on those guys. You've studied self-defense?"

"You've already been to the Campus?" But they just stared at him, the woman, Lynne, particularly hard. "No. No self-defense." He would not count the Tae-bo DVD he used to do. "I just ducked pretty much. They were sloppy… you know? Like they were on somethin'."

"Or maybe desperate to get high?" Lynne said accusingly. The look in her eyes and her tone, Max had seen them before too many times and the fear that had been riding up his spine was forced back down by sudden anger. Jaw clenched he looked her directly in the eye and answered her.

"I wouldn't know." Was all he said but he maintained the eye contact. Lynne read the challenge correctly.

"What am I supposed to be scared?" she stepped forward and their eyes remained locked together. Her gaze was fierce and uncompromising but Max was sure of one thing; she was scared. It was something in the air like jasmine but it had a sour smell to it; fear. He could… smell it.

She was not terrified, but definitely unnerved. Mann stood then and placed a hand on her shoulder.

"Back off, Lynne. He's just a lab jockey, remember?" Her partner got her to lean back and Max could read the strain in her eyes as she tried to maintain eye contact. "Maybe we read you wrong Doc." Mann said somewhat contrite. He was good cop then, but Max kept his eyes on Lynne, the accusation she implied still fueling his own anger.

There was the slightest waver in her eyes.

Maybe it was because of the unexplained fear that had been feeding on his heart, the anger felt better than the nervousness, or his almost natural dislike of this woman, or even something deeper, but on one level Max enjoyed seeing her flash of unease. He allowed the smile he felt to come.

"WHAT?" Lynne yelled, but she knew just like he knew what he was smiling at. "You think you're some…"

"All right Lynne!" Detective Mann could see things had gone wrong. "Let me talk to him alone for a minute." When neither would stop the stare down Mann stepped in-between them. "I said go." And she left slamming the door on her way out.

"Look, I'm sorry if we came on strong but we're just trying to do our jobs. Sheriff Lynne is under a lot of pressure to resolve this case."

Sheriff? Mountairy Rock's police departments were run with a primary law officer for each Neighborhood. The man or woman who held the position was, in some of the small and somewhat less affluent neighborhoods, much like a one-person police department. In District 1 the Sheriff would actually have the support of the local precinct. Most of Rock City's Sheriffs worked in the poorer neighborhoods that were cut off from the rest of the city due to geographic boundaries such as the park or the ridge wall. Lynne had to be a pretty amazing cop to have gotten the position. Either that or she was connected to someone who gotten her the job. Max did not remember hearing about there ever being any female Sheriffs but he had not really been following things like that. If she was the Sheriff for District 1 or probably just the neighborhood around the Museum itself then she was indeed going to be held accountable for whatever the police response might be. Maybe that was why she was coming at him so hard. It would be real convenient if this whole thing turned out to be a drug deal gone bad. Sorry lady!

"You've got no proof of drugs, no proof of smuggling. I was attacked tonight, ME, and you accuse me of a crime that you have no evidence of what so ever. Seems to me that you don't know how to do your jobs." With that Max stood to go.

"I want to see Dr. King now."

"Sure. I'll go with you." He conceded but Max was sure that the Detective only agreed because he thought it would help him solve the case.

Mann walked into the room first. Seated already were Tragan and some woman Max did not know. Standing reading the same shipping manifest that the police had shown Max earlier was Dr. Odom King. He was a big man, at least four inches taller than Max. A big mane of black and gray hair that did not end, until it became a pair of sideburns stopping just below his lips, framed his face. The square gold rimmed spectacles that sat on the edge of his broad nose were so thin and clear that Max had always joked that he wore them just for effect. Not in front of King though, as he was pretty sure that the big man never laughed. And he was big around as well, with a barrel chest, and arms as thick as Max's thighs and thighs as thick as tree trunks. As always, or as long as he had known the man, King wore a suit, this one black, an "Orendai" tailor made to fit him. On his arm he wore a ceremonial cloth tribal band, like a memorial or tribute to signify the death of a loved one. In this case it was worn for the tribe that may not have even existed. The man had dedicated the past seven years toward proving this "Lost Tribe" did in fact exist and he had been obsessed with them long before that. If they ever proved the tribe was real, Max thought that the armband might come off.

All in all King was an impressive and somewhat intimidating sight to most. However, after knowing him for more than six years and having been guided and helped by the Man, Max had come to see him as somewhat of a father figure. Now he was among a select few who worked at the Museum who was not scared of Dr. Odom King. At least he said he was.

"Dr. King?" he asked and King looked up from the paper and for the first time in a long time Max felt a little fear of his mentor. King was obviously furious with what was going on. His eyes spoke volumes of anger and now he was directing his fury at Max.

"Mr. Madigan…" and King paused, his eyes searing into Max's for a moment, no doubt trying to figure out if Max had been guilty of something. "It seems as though there was a hitchhiker aboard one of Museums deliveries. Did you get a chance to check the crates?"

"N-No sir. The manifests were pulled but not inventoried. We weren't expecting anything from Dr. Bazillion until late January." King could not think that Max had anything to do with what was in those crates. Could he?

"The police feel that my changing the inventory and security schedules is somewhat suspicious." He was still staring hard at Max, who managed to look away, up, down, wherever and whenever it was possible.

"Yes sir. They implied that you and I are smuggling in drugs."

"No sir we just wondered what was in those crates and asked the appropriate questions." Mann chimed in.

"I'd very much like to see a transcript of what was said at Mr. Madigan's interrogation." Tragan said.

"We did not interrogate anyone." Mann defended himself. "Madigan was attacked tonight at the student center. We were just getting his account of what happened. Could be that it's related."

"At the student center, on campus?" King asked, his eyes having never left Max. "But not at his home nor at the Museum?"

"But similar weapons and dressed pretty much the same as some of the other victims from the Museum the other night." Mann countered.

"If Mr. Madigan were involved in anything with those men they would have followed him from the Museum to his home, not waited until he went to campus." King finally looked away from him and back to the paper but still he addressed Max.

He had to admit he loved the way King just decided for the room why Max could not be involved in anything. Just like that he put it on the table and did not invite any counter argument. It was not an ability that Max possessed, nor would he ever he figured. Oh he could be stubborn or resolute, but he never had the gift of dealing with people in such a way as to govern their assumed points of view. It was more "politics" and Max knew that was why he never bothered to develop the skill. With one sentence, that may or may not have been accurate, King decided for the room that Max was innocent. Now if only it would hold up long enough for it to be backed up by real facts.

"Mr. Madigan, when you return to the Museum, please help Dr. Collins complete the inventory. I should return before the King Day celebration."

And that was that. The dismissal evident, Max turned and walked out, past Mann, past Detective (SHERIFF!) Lynne, who was waiting just outside, and finally past the cute hooker with the Island accent.

The next day could not have been worse. First thing he had done wrong was to call the car rental place and inquire about the insurance. After being on hold for half an hour he had been told that his insurance only paid partially for the damage. Despite the police report stating it as a mugging he was going to end up paying for the damage to the roof for a long time. This bit of bad news would sit like a cloud over the rest of his day if not the year. He still had the car, but by the next day he would have to return it. The depression made it difficult to concentrate on the paper work that needed to be done. It was not until late that afternoon that Max realized that he had planned to work on his research this day.

His part of the project on Dr. Kings "Lost" tribe would have to wait now but any further setbacks would put Max's chance at a Doctorate in jeopardy. That realization depressed him even more. King was really very little help to Max, offering no information nor incite. Despite his needing a team to help find this tribe, King was very secretive and protective of the information. That, along with the armband, gave Max the impression that King had a more personal stake in the tribe's existence. His protectiveness seemed almost like he thought that if the information was gathered the wrong way the rest of the evidence would crumble and blow away. That had made researching it a daunting task, as King was one of the few experts on the Lost Tribe in the country. Of the few others the prevailing opinion of the Lost Tribe was that it was little more than a myth. He would have to look elsewhere for information and guidance. As it was King had not shown up to the Museum that day and so they were on their own trying to put everything back together. The police still had a section of the Museum blocked off, namely King's rear offices, making their task that much more difficult. What could have happened back there? How bad could it be? Was there still some danger? Would King give him an advance on his salary?

Still though, at least he could salvage the remainder of the day. He would not miss his date.

Max checked his watch again. No he was not late, so why was there no answer. He hesitantly knocked again. This was not looking good.

"Of course," he thought to himself, now his day was complete.

Then the door opened. On the other side however, was not Rosette but another girl who looked familiar, but Max could not place her.

"Hi. I'm here to pick up Rosette?" He asked, but now he was more focused on where he had seen this girl before. She was tall for a woman, about 5'7" with soft brown skin and light brown hair that was drawn back into a single braid that went far down her back.

Couldn't be real.

She looked at him with a slightly annoyed expression and he felt even that was familiar.

"She'll be right out. Come on in." Her voice had just the tiniest rasp to it, almost as though she had a slight cold. Max watched her as she led him in. Maybe he had seen her on campus before, or subbed for one of her professors. Their apartment was small, but nowhere as small as his. It was decorated with faded pendants and posters with M.R.U. logos on them. The front room had a large old couch that was littered with papers and notebooks. That was where the girl who answered the door sat down. She placed an open notebook in her lap and looked up at him.

"Have a seat. She'll be a little while." The only other place to sit was a big green bean bag. Instead he just looked around the rest of the room. As many signs and posters as there were Max noticed that there were many open spaces on the walls where something had been taken down. The sun bleached walls showed impressions on the wall where they had been. He wondered if maybe someone had not just moved out and he looked back to the young woman on the couch to see her quickly look away from him. She folded her legs up underneath her on the couch, sat Indian style, and began gathering the papers and notebooks. Maybe she was going to study at the library. One of her papers held the course name at its heading.

"You're in the post grad program?" he asked. She looked back at him, the annoyed look gone from her face and replaced with one Max thought seemed a little disappointed.

"I'm doing post graduate work in botany. You?" This surprised him; she did not look old enough to be in a postgraduate program.

"Uh... yea. I'm just finishing up for my doctorate. Hopefully by the end of this year. My name's Max."

"Amanda Allen." She then looked at him as if contemplating whether or not to ask him her next question. "So, you stood Rosette up on New Year's Eve." It was more a statement than a question.

Max inhaled deeply. He had been hoping all was forgotten but it seemed as if he wasn't going to catch a break today. Not today.

"There was a break in at the Museum." He could say 'the Museum' because every student at Montairy Rock knew of it, and probably had a few classes there as well. "In the South tower where I work. A couple of guards were murdered." Maybe more than he should have said, but damn it was not like he wanted to miss the date!

"Oh. Right. It's been all over the news." was all she said. He had avoided the T.V. himself, not wanting to hear the news hype.

Just then Rosette called from the back room, saying that she would be only a second. Max smiled, something was finally going to go right today. In a few minutes he would be spending pretty much his whole check on a night out in downtown Mountairy Rock with one of the finest...

He could feel Amanda staring at him and got the sudden feeling that something was about to go bad. He looked back at her and wondered if maybe it had something to do with the fact that she seemed familiar to him. Amanda looked into the back room quickly, checking for Rosette, and then she looked back to him. Then slowly, deliberately, she raised the sweater she was wearing up to her neck. Max's jaw dropped open.

Beneath the sweater she was wearing was a tee shirt.

Embroidered on that tee shirt was a Greek symbol, a symbol of a Greek sorority that had a chapter on campus. He stared at the symbol until the girl pulled her sweater back down. She did not look back up at him. Slowly Max looked back around the room. The sun bleached markings on the walls now made sense to him. He had been set up, again and turned to leave immediately but stopped short of the door. Amanda was watching him.

"Why?" he asked, not sure if he was asking why the set up or why did she let him know. Amanda looked back again to see if Rosette was coming. She then turned back to look down at her books, not meeting his eyes. All she did was shrug and Max left.

Fatigue forced him to lean against the back of the elevator as he rode up to his apartment. Sweat on the back of his sweater chilled him horribly when he pressed against it. After getting back from Rosette's he had decided to work out in the basement of the apartment building. No longer dressed for a date he wore the same black sweats he always wore whenever working out or jogging, which was rare and infrequent. The basement was usually chilly in the winter so he wore a black skullcap to keep from catching cold. Now he was overheating so he reached up to pull it off. The forty seconds of inactivity had been enough time for his muscles to stiffen and an ache flare across his shoulder. He may have gotten a little carried away with the workout and was beginning to feel it.

He rubbed his eyes trying to rub away the pain. So Rosette was a Beta Gamma; the sister sorority of Max's ex-fraternity, Rho Phi Gamma.

"At least I know they haven't forgotten about me." he mumbled. It had turned out to be the perfect day after all. Now if only he could get some sleep, maybe tomorrow would be different. Out of the elevator and down to his apartment to find Mr. Alt waiting for him at his door.

"Madigan! There are no pets allowed in the building! You know that..."

"Hey! Mr. Alt, today is not the day." Max was slightly surprised at the way he snapped back.

"Don't you raise your voice at me boy! I'll..."

Max waved his hands. "Mr. Alt I am not in the mood for a lecture all right! I don't have any pets. I can barely afford to feed myself much less anything else. Okay?" But Alt continued yelling even as Max moved past him and opened the door.

"Damn thing has been howling all night! And another thing..."

And Max closed the door. He closed his eyes and leaned down hard with his hands on his knees. Things were getting bad again, piling up just like before when he let the pressure force him to make one bad decision after another. Reckless...impulsive choices that got him kicked out of his frat and out of his school. If felt like he needed to catch his breath.

"Please GOD, let that be it."

"mrrr" and Max opened his eyes and looked down. The big gray cat sat there in front of him, with a patient look on its soft furry face. He just stared for a moment and then he looked past the cat to the window beyond.

It was open.

"I did not open that window. Not in the middle of winter. How did... who let you…" He shut up as the cat walked over to his couch and leapt up. The feline then pulled Max's jacket off the couch and let it fall to the floor. Out of the pocket fell the small stone.

"What?" Max whispered. The cat then walked away from the jacket but not far. It sat about a yard away and waited... staring at him. Max stared back,

then stared at the stone,

at the cat,

then again at the stone and then walked over and took a closer look. It appeared to be the same piece of debris that he had stepped on back at the museum, but it was not broken. Slowly, watching the cat all the while, he bent over, picked up the stone, and looked at it. Exactly like the stone he had broken at the museum the night of the murders. How had it gotten into his jacket?

His thumb rubbed over the etching on its face and suddenly the hairs on his arm stood on end. The cat leapt to its feet with an excited, alert look. Max snapped his head up.

The room was lit up, like midday. As the street outside the museum had been. Max looked to the window to find that light poured in from outside.

"What's going on?" Looking down for the cat he found that it was gone. He looked around the apartment until he saw it on the windowsill looking back at him framed with sallow but bright moonlight. When he started forward and then the big cat leapt from the window.

"Crazy son-of-a..." Max ran to the window but did not see the cat anywhere. The entire city, however, screamed at him. It was bright and alive in a way Max had never seen before. He could see clearly everything in the alley below his window. Dozens, no scores of voices, resonated up the alley in between his building and then from all around. There was a couple arguing somewhere in his building beneath his window, and another making love somewhere above, there were children laughing down on the street, and sirens in the distance. Then there was a kaleidoscope of sounds: tires screeching, someone listening to their radio, a dog barking, birds flapping their wings, wind scrapping across the rooftops, the smell of cooked vegetables, slight flowery fragrances wafted every so often, cigarette smoke, spoiling garbage, and the smell of the Great Lake over all.

"WoW." He was squeezing the stone tightly and had to force himself to relax.

"mrrrrr" To his right there was big gray, sitting on the neighbors sill. The cat's eyes shone clear silver, and were rectangular. They peered into Max's own and then...

COME and the big cat leapt down into the darkness until Max lost sight of it against the building. Farther down below he could see the gray shape moving on some structure he could not make out. How had it gotten down so fast? There was nowhere safe for it to leap from Max's windowsill for about four floors. That's when he saw the air conditioner sticking out of a window about three floors down and two windows over. How had the cat made a jump that far though? How had it landed without breaking its neck? Why was the air conditioner getting closer?

The shock hit him like a bolt of electricity as Max realized that he had thrown himself from the window. Icy wind ripped across his body as he fell toward the air conditioner. Just as at the student center he found his body acting on instinct. His legs came forward, feet framing the air conditioner in his line of sight.

Strangely he was not afraid. The cat was somewhere down below and moving.

CLANG!

Max hit the air conditioner and bounced off, flying across the alley toward the other building. His body tumbled in midair and, in the split second that he was facing his old building, upside down, he thought he saw the air conditioner falling out of the window. Instinct straightened out his body and he flew feet first into the neighboring wall where he coiled against it shedding the momentum. He pushed off at an angle back toward his own building and turned, again in midair, head over feet.

Max could see the fire escape; saw that he was going to over shoot it by about a foot. Instinct slowly merged with conscious thought as Max turned his head ever so much. This caused his body to rotate away from metal frame. There was no time to glance but he could see the roof top of the smaller building next to his own in his peripheral vision. There was movement along that roof top; the cat. His muscles tightened as he past the outside railing of the fire escape then in one burst his body exploded outward, his legs slamming against the rail. His feet hit the rail squarely and pushed him off toward the rooftop.

Muscles contracting along his body caused him to twitch and jerk. Somehow this kept his feet under him and aimed his body at the roof. It was not until a second before he landed that Max felt anything resembling fear.

THUD! The gravel flew when he touched down and he skid a few feet in his sneakers. But his legs held him and he only had to touch one hand down to keep his balance. Slowly he stood and looked back up toward his building. Almost ten floors down he had fallen, but he was not hurt… …breathing hard yes, but hardly winded.

What the hell was he thinking?

What made him jump out that window?

Cold freezing wind slid across his calves and up his legs chilling him horribly and freezing the sweat on his body. Everything was cold, save for his hand.

The stone! It was warm. Hot really. What was this thing? The symbol etched into it seemed even more familiar to him now than before. It was rough on the face but smooth along the edges. This, all of this, had something to do with this stone.

It felt like bone.

Somewhere far below and behind him, the air conditioner smashed into the ground.

Another cold gust and Max was ready to go in. How the hell was he going to get off of this roof? Maybe there was a door to the… whoa.

It was musky and spicy at the same time and it was carried by the cold wind. Max turned to see the big gray cat sitting ponderingly atop a heating unit, regarding him. Then when their eyes met the cat stood and started to turn.

COME and with that it turned and jumped out of his line of sight. And then came the surge.

It was powerful, the urge to chase; it was so strong that he could not resist. It was like being pulled in a current of hot rushing water, except the water ran through his body as well. It surged out of his heart and through his veins and burst out of his muscles.

His hand closed over the stone in a fist and gravel flew out from under his feet as he gave chase. With little wonder at himself Max leapt to the top of the heating unit and quickly scanned for the gray cat, straining to hear some sign of it above the wind and the blood pounding in his ears. But the cat was nowhere on the roof. It could not have moved that fast but never the less Max looked past the rooftop to the adjoining building. There it was and it was still running, across that rooftop and heading for the next building. He leapt to the chase again and ran after the cat at full speed.

But the gray cat was fast and Max could not gain on it. Even though the next adjoining building stood a full story higher than the others still he could gain no ground. It was moving so fast the thing simply ran up the side of the wall, scraping and clawing as it got to the top and springing itself over. Again with a strange confidence Max simply lengthened his stride as he approached the wall and with a bound he kicked off and planted a foot on the wall about head high. Then he pushed himself up planning on grabbing the ledge and hauling himself up. To his astonishment, his own strength and momentum carried him almost over the top, all he had to do was step onto the edge of the roof, and he was there.

All of this had not helped him gain on the big gray cat but neither had he fallen farther behind. It was still well out in front and moving fast but it was coming to a dead end. This building marked the end of the street and the next building was not close enough for the cat to jump to. Soon he would have some answers.

But the cat never slowed. It still flew across the rooftop, pumping its legs for all it was worth and when it came up on the edge it did leap. A high graceful leap it was but it started to come down well before it was even halfway across the gap. Max skidded to a halt sending gravel flying over the edge and watched as the cat began to fall. But it did not fall. He could see it tense to land and then in midair the thing stopped falling and continued running as if it had hit the ground.

"Oh SHIT!" Max stood jaw agape for a second until he saw that the thing was not flying. No it had landed on a telephone wire connecting the building with the one across the street. Still he stood amazed, because the wire was narrow and the cat, big as it was, ran along it as though it were running across the ground.

He looked down and saw that there was a truck parked on the mostly deserted street only about two stories down. There was no hesitation as he stepped off the roof and landed with a thud leaving a dent on its top. He sprang off in the same motion and flung himself in the direction of an alleyway behind the building across the street. The angle in which he jumped brought him down in the middle of the street where he was immediately lit up by headlights.

Legs tensed then sprang in an instant sending Max up and over another parked car as tires screeched and horns blared behind him. Now he could hear even his own heartbeat, not the blood pulsing through his temples but his actual heart beating against his rib cage. He landed, stumbled a bit and slammed into the side of the building knocking the wind out of him. Time to stop this crazy chase!
COME

And he was up again darting into the alley. With the car horn blaring behind him Max ran through the alley, around the dumpster, under some broken scaffolding, over the bum and through the broken fence. He ripped through the alley knowing the cat was still moving and had probably pulled out to a bigger lead. But the alley continued on for more than a street block and Max could not be sure that the cat had not changed direction up above. Finally the alley opened onto the next street and Max came to a halt looking up and searching the next roof. Nothing. No sign of it and no crazy quiet voice ringing in his head.

But there was that spicy, musky smell again. Close this time. Max inhaled deeply, his head turning until the smell grew definitive. There! Across the street at the edge of the next alley he saw a flash of gray and again he gave pursuit.

Into the next alley and then he was sure as the smell was hot and fresh in his nostrils. The cat was still moving somewhere ahead of him. Leaping piles of refuse, Max charged after.

Still the cat stayed ahead of him. Block after block, alley after alley, and past some construction site, he could not close the gap on the big gray cat. The chase took him halfway across Mountairy Rock all the way to the park. The scent had him running across a small section of clear parkland leading him into the park itself. Into and past the tree line he ran as his vision picked up the moonlit earth easily and keeping him from stumbling over roots, fallen branches or uneven ground. Then the smell of river water hit his nose moments before he could hear it moving and scraping along the bank. He followed up along a steep rise and ran alongside the road which a small bridge running over a ridge that sidelined the river. That was when he finally caught sight of the cat again. It was well past the road and still hauling. Here was a chance to close the distance. Instead of taking the path he figured the cat must have, he leapt across the road and then sprinted up the muddy hill, getting to the top rather easily. It worked! Big Gray was less than twenty feet away and now Max had the angle.

Next thing he knew the ground came out from under him.

The entire bank fell and slid down toward the river carrying Max with it. On his back and floundering he rolled over quickly, pulled his knees up under him, and kicked but found no purchase in the sliding mud. Once again with more force this time he kicked and his feet dug deep into the mud and found enough resistance to launch him back to dry ground. The landing was awkward, and mostly on his head, and he tumbled to a stop. The mudslide was loud, with big chunks of mud smacking into the water.

Damn! The park was having problems with mudslides he suddenly remembered, but he thought those problems were up by the Highlands, the most western section of the city.

His body ached terribly all of a sudden. Max stood slow and looked around. It was dark, he could not see where he was and the spicy scent he had been chasing was gone. So tired! Max braced his hands on his knees as his legs cried out in pain and… The ROCK!

It was gone! He had dropped it when he fell. It was too dark to see anything because the nearest streetlight was almost thirty yards away. The damn thing could be right in front of him or down in the river for all he knew. Still, Max dropped to all fours and began feeling across the ground. Oh there were plenty of rocks here, but not the one he wanted. Slowly he tried to retrace his movements but as he searched he got the sinking feeling that it was gone. At best he would have to come back during the day and find the damn thing. Almost to the riverbank Max worried about another landslide. If he had not been able to jump clear the last time he would surely be drowned by now. Damn. He would have to come back.

"mrrrr" The soft call came from behind him. Max turned but still could see nothing in the darkness. Not really expecting anything he began to search the ground going in the general direction of the sound.

"mrrr!" closer now. Max could feel the air growing warmer on his fingertips. Letting that guide him now, he slid his hands along the ground, following the warmth until...

The park lit up again as the moon and stars shone like they had just been turned on. The stone rolled under his hand and Max picked it up and held it firmly in his fist.

"Whew." But when he looked about the cat was still nowhere to be seen and the scent was still gone. The pain in his legs gone now Max stood feeling clumps of mud fall from his back and legs.

"Incredible." He was breathing hard. "Is this real?" Opening his hand he looked at the stone. It was still warm, like a living thing. It was the stone that had done this to him.

Whatever THIS was. Rooftops, he'd run along rooftops like kids playing hopscotch.

Twenty to thirty foot leaps without really even gathering himself first.

The musky, street smell of the gray cat had led him, as easily as if he had been following street signs. And that was not all he could smell. The mud, the water, the choky car exhaust from the nearby bridge all came past his nose on the cold winter night's air.

And he could see in this night's darkness as if it were simply twilight. Even the nearby park, with foliage so thick that it held shadows at midday seemed brighter and more open than ever. He could see quite a ways into the underbrush. Night vision...

...like a cat's.

It was something to do with the cat and the stone. Max looked at it again but the strange jagged lines in the half circle was no more familiar now. He had to find out what it was, where it came from. That meant using the research tools back at the Museum.

Looking around Max wondered where the cat had gotten to. It had led him to the stone but had vanished after that. The musky, street scent was very faint in the air. He knew that it was gone. But why? What had this run been all about?

Then he wondered where it had brought him. Relaxed now, Max walked towards the bright streetlight and looked for a street sign but there was none. Finally he saw that it was not a street at all but part of a highway, an exit ramp. So he looked up and panned until he saw the exit sign.

"Lincoln's Pass? Jesus! I'm halfway across the city!"

He was walking up Germantown Avenue, the main street of the Ivy Hills section of Rock city, on his way from the park to get home. The chase he had been lead on had brought him from his apartment all the way to the Lincoln Pass on ramp which crossed the Park to the southwestern section of the city; West Oaks. With no money, dressed as he was, and filthy from mud Max had no choice but to make the long hike back to his apartment. Walking the long distances between places in Rock city was something that he was used to by now. He usually enjoyed it, as it gave him time to think. But his wet, mud splattered clothing made this hike particularly hard. So he tried to ignore the discomfort because right now he had a lot to think about. The stone was tucked in his sweatshirt front pouch pocket. There its effect on him felt minimal and he could concentrate. It was obvious that the stone must have been part of what the break in at the Museum had been about. And it was also the reason he had been able to avoid being hit by those maniacs.

Only why all the death and the damage just to leave the damn thing on the floor? Then again after seeing how clumsy the maniacs were with that attack at the student center he could believe it. So what should he do first? Talk to the police?

"Ahem." It was a familiar rasp. Max started at the sound and looked behind him to see the young woman whom had warned him off from his "date" earlier that night.

"Amanda right?" he asked, sure that he was.

"Hi Max. Don't tell me they caught up to you?" She had a sincerely worried look on her face, sincere enough that Max was not so quick to tell her to leave him alone. Plus he was still curious.

"No. I went for a run in the park." NOT a lie. "Slipped in some mud, took a fall." STILL the truth, although he actually hated running and avoided it by doing almost any other exercise instead. Oddly he felt an aversion to lying to her. Probably had something to do with his feeling that he owed her for her warning him earlier. "So what did you tell Rosette?" He asked.

"Just that you had found out that she was a Gamma." She actually looked relieved. "She's pretty pissed; they had done a lot of planning to get to you." Unfortunately that made sense; the Phi Gams had attempted to get him fired from the Museum the year before with some phony radio contest scam.

"Yeah well it's good to hear they're still thinking of me. So why did you help me out? Won't they kick you out if they find out? Should you even be talking to me out in public?"

"They can shun me all they want, I'm not a Gamma." She said

this with a laugh that had the same slightly hoarse rasp to it. Max was surprised. He had assumed that since she was wearing the tee shirt that she was Greek. Then again it kind of made a sense; none of the people involved in that long ago incident save maybe one or two, would consider him anything less than public enemy number one.

"Still, for people who know, I'm not the most popular guy on campus." he said. It was a big school, but among the Greeks, the name Max Madigan was a curse, and he had found that at times they could seem to be everywhere on the huge campus at once.

"That's just it. Nobody really knows what happened to you guys that night but you guys. I'm sure that all the stories that were told around school were exaggerated and I have a feeling that the rest of your frat weren't telling the whole story anyway. I mean, they were all expelled, and you're still here."

Max wondered what she was getting at. For a hot second he wondered if he was being set up again. "It's a long story."

"Well, we've got a long way 'til we reach campus." Amanda said and started walking, then stopped and looked back. "It's late, mind walking me back?"

Max thought for a second, he did not need this right now what with everything that was happening that night. Besides he did not want to have to relive what had happened again.

"That was over four years ago. I try not to think about it." But he still fell into step with Amanda and the two walked down Germantown avenue together. Instead of Greeks and scams the two found themselves talking about their respective histories. While Max was from Mountairy Rock originally, Amanda was from Virginia. Both of their families were far away, Amanda's were of course in Virginia and Max's lived in Philadelphia where he had spent his high school years. Amanda had two little sisters and was surprised when Max said he had no siblings. His uncle still lived here in the city and Amanda had a cousin who was going to school here. She was still debating law school; while, Max was hoping to get sponsorship and funding for his own research. The Museum was still the best way for Max to...

"Whoa..." Max said as they finally reached campus. They had just been passing the Museum when he spotted him; a Maniac. There, in the alley between the East Dock wall and the Admin building. The Maniac was ducking in and out of the shadows there. Where were the police?

"I hooked up with Rosette' cause we had the same major and it was good to have a partner to study with for a while..." Amanda went on, not noticing Max's preoccupation. He reached into his jacket pocket and grabbed the stone. Nighttime became a bright twilight to his eyes and he could see the Maniac clearly. The dark dressed man seemed to be searching for a way in. Max got excited. He could tell the police about this now and have this guy caught, and clear Dr. King and himself at the same time.

"So far it's really been working out for me as I'm getting all the experience I need to..." but would the classic Madigan luck show up again? The entire day seemed to have been set against him. Should he just go ahead and tell the police about the stone? Would they believe him? Or would they implicate him? Besides he wanted to study the stone first, find out its origins and what it was made of, but to do that he would have to get into King's office and see what the police where hiding. There had to be something there that could give Max a lead on this thing. He did not think that the Doctor had any information himself. Something about the way he looked at him when Max saw him at the station. It was like King thought Max might have actually been involved when he first looked at him.

And Max felt a rising surge of adrenaline…and a strangely familiar confidence. No… he would go back to the Museum and search through King's office and the crates again to be sure. Tonight… while the Maniac might still be there.

"I enjoy being naked whenever I can, and so do all my girlfriends." Max turned back to Amanda.

"What did you say?"

"I thought that would get your attention. You drifted off there for a while." Amanda didn't seem upset, but Max felt bad anyway. Almost as if to reassure him she then asked, "You seem cold. Are you?"

Along their walk Max had indeed gotten colder. The heat of his cross-city run had bled off and his hands had found their way underneath his sweater. With a little smirk Amanda pulled off the scarf she was wearing and gave it to Max. When he hesitated she moved close and tied the scarf about his neck for him. It was black with stylish red "A"s crisscrossing its length.

"Thanks for walking me back." They were indeed in front of her apartment building. They said goodbye then and Max found himself unsure of where he stood with her and more importantly, where he wanted to stand.

This late at night there were still a few joggers braving the cold, so Max did not look out of place. On his way he formulated his plan. Years of arriving late and having to sneak into the museum after hours had given Max more than one way to get into the building. Tonight he knew that the best way would have been to enter the museum from the North Tower which was always open but there were too many cameras between the North and the South towers. There was a better way and Max was confident that he could do it. At the south end of the now empty moat there was a huge gutter cut into the side of the south end outer wall tower. It was old, left over from when the Castle was first reconstructed here in Mountairy Rock. Still made of large stones Max guessed that he would be able to climb it all the way to the top of the outer wall and then use one of the service bridges to reach the first level of the South tower without being seen. Then climb the repair scaffolding to the roof, and in through the skylight above King hall. No problem.

Max crept up to the edge of the moat and peered over. For a brief second the bottom was filled with blackness. Then his eyes adjusted and the smooth gray bottom appeared. There was an access ladder about forty feet further down the edge of the moat but that would bring him into camera view if he remembered correctly. On a thought he pulled his skullcap down low near to covering his eyes and drew the hood of his sweatshirt up. Then he pulled the scarf Amanda had given him over his mouth and nose. If he was seen now he would definitely be looked at as a criminal but he knew that he could now out run any pursuit. So he slid his body over the edge until he was hanging by only his hands. A deep breath and he let go.

It was a noiseless slide down to the bottom. The basin was rounded so Max slid until he reached the center without any problem. Looking up Haley Museum never looked so imposing. Just a different angel but Max felt a little daunted. The climb he was planning seemed a little crazier now.

Looking down along the moat wall he saw the gutter-way just ahead. He got to his feet and padded down the basin until he was directly beneath his goal. The bottom of it was about twenty feet above him but now that should not be a problem. Okay… one big jump, just take a deep breath and…

With a sudden prickling of his ears and Max turned about sharply. He had not heard anything but suddenly he was sure that he was not alone. Why? Max took another breath this time through his nose and he felt it now more clearly. There was a familiar smell down here. He snorted again, once, twice, before he was sure it was coming from somewhere further down the moat. The smell was faint but unique and Max thought that he could even taste it on his tongue.

What could be down there?

He looked down the basin following it until it rounded the corner going toward the front of the museum. The odor grew fainter and within moments Max was not even sure he had smelled it in the first place. He shook his head and without the deep breath this time leapt to the edge of the gutter and caught hold.

Once in the concave curve Max found easy hand and foot holds in the large stonewall and pulled himself up with no difficulty, but he never dared to look back down. That strange familiar confidence was still running through him. Here he was climbing the side of the Museum and he was more worried about not getting in than he was about not getting caught…or falling. The thought crossed his mind briefly but quickly was forgotten as he neared the top.

Once atop the outer wall, crouching low to avoid the casual observer, Max studied the first level of the South tower, which was covered with construction scaffolding from the Museum's ongoing restoration. It would prove an easy climb once he got over there. Looking down into the outer bailey, Max saw only one person walking about on this side of the Museum. Must be a student, by the look of her, who was probably just doing some late research in the museum tonight? She would not see Max up here, and the Museum security would not either. Their cameras did not include the tops of the outer walls. So he crossed the service bridge that was not a part of the castles original construction, over to the South Tower. It was amazing how easy this all was and Max's confidence grew.

The South Tower was topped by a parapet, which was one story above the main roof. There was a door here, which would allow him into the building, but he knew that it was armed with an alarm. He also knew that the skylight was not. So, staying low, Max crept the long way toward the middle of the South Hall and the huge skylight. Looking down he could see pretty well through the dim light. There were more scaffolding and construction materials inside the Great Hall, but there was no movement. The hall was empty.

Unfortunately the skylight above the South hall was shut from the inside and his every attempt to open it only threatened to crack the window. Crap!

What about the door? He had ignored it earlier not considering it only because he knew there was an alarm on it and that it was locked anyway. Still though, he walked across the roof to the South Towers Parapet. Not only was it not locked the door was wide open.

"Yes!" someone must have forgotten to close the thing.

This was going to save him a ton of time climbing back down and finding another way in. Max leaned into the doorway and stared down the steps. He did not hear nor see anything, but there was something faint in the air. The same familiar smell and … feel he had at the bottom of the moat. He started down the stairs.

The museum was empty. Max expected to see, at the very least, some police officers. The only staff that should be here now would be the main security contingent that would be watching the South Towers video monitors with special interest. Let them watch thought Max, he knew where all the cameras were and how to avoid them. Not that it was hard to do, they were fifth largest museum in the World and they were too cheap to buy a real security system. They would not place cameras in the back offices anyway. He had worked at the Museum for almost five years and every once in a while he found himself sneaking about trying to avoid this Professor or that Administrator but never had he been trying to avoid the entire Museum. Dressed in black with a scarf for a mask, he would feel like a fool if he was discovered by a coworker.

Max stepped onto the South Hall. It was the main center for exhibitions and congregations for the South tower. Right now there was a display on medieval armor and weaponry. He slid through the hall with ease, heading for a service stairwell that would lead him to the below offices. Carefully he turned the knob on the stairwell door, each click sounding like gunfire to his now sensitive ears. When it opened he peeked through, to find someone waiting for him.

"How did you get in here?" Max whispered to the big gray cat. Those silver eyes looked back at him and then it reared up on its hind legs.
TRAP the thought shot through Max's head like a bolt of fear, images of shadows closing in on him from over his shoulder.

He backed away from the door and heard something behind him. Then there was a screeching, inaudible scream and he turned to see the wild man running at him, ax in hand.

Then Max understood what he was screaming. "DIE!"

COPS and MANIACS

Knees, elbows, shoulders, and head all knocked along the hard marble floor of the Museum's South tower hall as Max tucked and rolled. He escaped out from beneath the attack of the Maniac who brought down a double-sided battle-axe and it rang loudly on the floor. He rolled to a stop a few feet away and stood quickly. The axe was from one of the many displays here in the South tower hall. The Maniac lifted it up and charged at Max again.

So clumsy was his attack that he easily sidestepped the screaming Maniac who then fell into a display of a model of an English castle. The attacker floundered and Max could not help but to smile. He felt in no way threatened by this man who was attacking him, as a matter-of-fact he almost reached to help him up.

Then there was the sound of metal sliding against leather, a quick inhale, and a hesitant step. Max turned around, his eyes easily penetrating the dark hall, and searched for the new threat. From behind the center display of an armored knight stepped another Maniac, wielding a short sword taken from that very same display. Max noticed the crazed look in his eye, the same barely controlled rage in the Maniac's shaking hands, and he smiled again. Raising his left hand he motioned the attacker to come at him.

Infuriated the Maniac screamed and rushed at him. Max prepared to sidestep this charge as well when there came another rustling from just to his left. A quick glance and he saw yet a third Maniac leaping at him from over a display case. Still confident he reached up, grabbed the leaping man in midair, and redirected his flight into the attacker rushing at him with the sword. The collision was satisfyingly dramatic as they both screamed and went down. Max grinned again as he sensed the first Maniac moving again, coming at him from behind.

He whirled around to find, however, not one but two more Maniacs swinging blades at him. To get away Max hopped backwards and dodged behind the display case. Glass flew everywhere when the Maniac with the battle-axe missed him by hair's breadth and hit the glass case. A table against the far wall came up against his back as he backpedaled away.

"Don't think I can take four of them." he mumbled to himself and quickly looked around the room. The four Maniacs now gathering themselves to attack again blocked the way to the roof. There was the service stairwell but that only led deeper into the Museum.

Wait! The skylight!

It was only in the adjoining corridor behind the two large doors on the other side of the hall. If he could get to the roof he could defend himself a whole lot better, or at least he could run away.

The Maniacs screamed in unison and rushed at him, running around the shattered display case to get to him. Max screamed in return and rushed back at them, but slid under the display case instead and climbing to his feet on the other side, he ran for the double doors.

Their pounding boots filled his ears as the Maniacs rushed up behind him as his hands grasped the door latches. He pulled both doors open at the same time and leapt through the doorway closing them behind him as he came through. Without a thought Max turned and grabbed the door latches on that side of the double doors to keep the Maniacs from getting through. The doors held as they rushed against it and he finally let out a long loud breath.

"Ahem." someone said in the corridor behind Max. There was a twang and then a loud whistling sound behind him.

THWACK!! Something slammed into the door just in front of his face. An arrow.

Dammit! Another Maniac!

He turned to see where the arrow had come from.

There, standing in the corridor, were over twenty Maniacs.

The four maniacs on the other side of the door were bowled over as Max burst through the double doors. It was a good thing too, as several arrows followed him in and would have struck them if they had not been on the ground. As it was they were simply trampled by the stampede of their friends coming through the door.

Max did not stop in the South Tower hall, he made such a sharp turn after he rammed through the doors that he fell and slid along the floor back under the display case. From there he scrambled to his feet and bolted for the stairwell. Cries of rage erupted behind him as they saw his escape attempt. His sneakers squeaked on the marble floor when Max skid to a halt in front of the door. The clicking of triggers being pulled, several sharp twangs from catgut being snapped tight, and the snake-like hiss of arrows in flight alerted him to duck. Three arrows sprouted up out of the door like branches. He pulled the door latch down, pushed through the door, and slammed it shut from the other side. There were several more hits against the door and Max watched the arrow tips emerge through the metal.

"Jesus!" He just held the latch and felt it and the whole door shake as the Maniacs rushed against it. The door latch was being pulled on the other side but Max held it tight so it would not move. The cries of outrage seemed to vibrate the door with their own power.

"FREEZE!!" came from behind him and down the stairwell. Still leaning against the door Max turned his head slowly to see a security guard leveling a flashlight at him.

"Call the police!" He shouted.

"What the hell are you doing?" The man called back with obvious fear in his eyes. Max recognized the guard, Phillip... something, but knew that the guard did not recognize him with the scarf covering half his face. Why the hell would he have investigated anything on his own and unarmed after everything that had happened less than a week ago?

Then the pushing and shoving on the other side of the door stopped and it became strangely quiet. Max listened intently. Soft footsteps on the stairs as the guard advanced from behind, heartbeats were pounding like thunder, breaths came in and out from twenty something lungs, and someone was counting.

"Oh shit." Max slowly backed away from the door. The guard continued up the steps behind him.

BOOM! Twenty-five Maniacs slammed through the doorway almost all at once. The door broke off its bottom hinge and swung up. The corner caught Max under the jaw throwing him backward down the stairs and on top of Phillip the guard. The two tumbled to the bottom of the flight of stairs together, Max ending up on top.

He looked up to see the Maniacs pouring down the steps after them. Without a thought he stood, grabbed Phillip by the belt and pulled him down the next flight of stairs, kicking open the door at the next level. Not even noticing that lifting the guard was extremely easy, Max tossed him through the doors ahead him. He then followed and slammed these doors shut as well. Behind them he could hear the Maniacs coming after them.

They were in the South Tower laboratory, an extensive and inclusive facility used by the Museum and the University for any and all archaeological and anthropological Studies and experiments. While most of the Museum maintained its medieval castle motif with stone walls and tapestries, the Tower Laboratories were strictly high tech and state of the art.

Max knew that even now, with the lab deserted for the night, there were critical experiments going on. Disrupting anyone of them could push back months of research for students and researchers… even his own. A lot of kids could fail out of the Post-grad program.

"What the hell is going on?!?" a rough and exasperated voice wailed. Max looked back down; he had forgotten about the guard for a split second.

"Hell with it!" and he grabbed the guard by the belt again and hauled off through the lab searching for the exit into the East wall hall. By a few seconds the maniacs broke through the door and rush into the lab.

Only by running could he limit the damage to the equipment in the room. If only they would chase him straight through the without firing off those crossbows or throwing those axes. The guard complained with every herky-jerky motion as Max ran them around the lab stations. They could hear the Maniacs smashing and crashing behind them. More arrow shafts whistled through the air but none in danger of hitting the two. He winced as he saw them sink into a couple of computer hard drives. This was going to be expensive.

Finally they reached the exit to the East Hall or rather to the service corridor beneath it. Again Max tossed the guard through first and then closed the doors behind them.

"Quick!" He said, not noticing how deep his voice had gotten "Run down the service corridor to the East Tower and call the police. I'll lead the Maniacs up into the East Hall, it should be deserted so..."

"What the hell is going on!?!" Screamed the guard. Max did not have time for this.

"There's no time. GO!!!" his voice came out in an animal growl. The guard screamed with a new terror in his eyes and then hopped up and fled down the East Hall service corridor.

The guard's reaction confused him for a second but he had no time to wonder at it. Max ran for the small door that led to the stairs to the East Hall. He knew that the Maniacs were close behind and that he had better haul ass...

There came a scream from the lab. Not like the crazed blood thirsty screams of the Maniacs but a fearful cry from a woman and it stopped him in his tracks. The cry came again, and Max recognized the voice.

"Oh my GOD. That's Fatima." Rising in chorus behind her cries was the laughter of the Maniacs. Something welled up in his chest, his jaw tightened and his fists clenched.

If they harmed her...

With a growl, Max slammed himself back through the doors into the mist of the Maniacs.

They were all over the lab, standing on top of desks and file cabinets like animals. All of them had some kind of wicked bladed weapon... save for the few with the crossbows. Their dress was all similar, black leather, studded spikes, wild hair, and black boots. Fatima sat in the middle of them, on her knees with her hair being pulled by one of the bastards to keep her still and in pain. Max looked around the room to see that all of the Maniacs were staring at him with an insane hunger in their eyes, all of them even...

"Jesus... Jean?" He knew one of them, a former student at Rock

University. Jean looked bad; his face was covered with sweat and grime, his hair was matted and full of debris and his eyes peered back at Max from deep shadowy sockets. He was dressed the same as the other Maniacs, dirty worn black leather jacket, stained dark jeans, but he was carrying something on his back that Max could not make out. He called his friends name again.

There came no response from him however as Jean seemed not to know him at all, or maybe it just did not matter. Still they had not yet attacked him so maybe there was a chance he could talk his...

"KILL HIM!!!" said the Maniac holding Fatima captive and they all charged him from several different directions.

Instinct took over as Max sprang straight up to the ceiling and burst through the insulated paneling. The Maniacs came to a halt beneath him as he pulled himself through the paneling and into the dark shadows. They quickly lost sight of him and another chorus of outraged screams erupted. A few of the bowmen began firing into the ceiling trying to guess where he might be.

Then all was quiet for a moment as they listened for any sound that might tell them where he was.

They finally heard it but there was nothing they could do he moved so fast. Max came crashing down out of the ceiling above the Maniac who held Fatima hostage. One swift blow and that Maniac went down then up came Fatima over his shoulder.

The power and balance he felt was amazing. He had hit the Maniac with his fist on his way to the ground. At the same time he spread his legs wide almost in a hurdlers leap, using his fore leg as a wedge that pried the Fatima away from her captor. Still he landed evenly without, stumbling, having to use a hand to break his fall, or even knocking Fatima down. With one hand he shoved the Maniac over to keep his unconscious body from falling on him, and he wrapped his other arm around Fatima's waist. His feet had not hit the floor for more than an instant before he hopped back up. Fatima's legs swung and kicked wildly as he swung her up onto his shoulder. One of her shoes kicked off and landed smack in the middle of a Maniac's face.

Then Max threw a growl from his throat so loud and deep that a few of the Maniacs in his path jumped out of his way. This became his only clear path but it was not back toward the service corridor. It led back along the lab wall where the only exit was another small service corridor that led to King's rear offices, to where the real slaughter occurred. With Fatima over his shoulder Max bounded through the clear path toward the door.

The door was closed and crisscrossed with police tape. The tape proved to be the only resistance when Max pulled it open. Ducking through with Fatima he tried to close the door behind him but the latch did not catch and the door just bounced back open. He did not risk pausing to try to get it the latch to catch. Instead he turned and again faced a spiral staircase. Here, however, in the middle of the landing, was an old wooden door. King's office.

There was dried blood on the floor just outside that door. He sniffed on reflex, catching only a hint of it now and swallowed with a grimace.

There were footsteps and cries just behind him so Max hurried up the few steps, pushed open the door and ducked inside. He dropped Fatima to the floor, turned and slammed the heavy oak door closed behind him. This time the latch caught and he turned the lock, sealing the door. It was covered in dried, black blood, like someone had flicked a wet paintbrush at it several times.

The scent of the blood filled his nose and mouth through the cloth of Amanda's scarf. Hot and pungent it was, and he could feel it on the carpet beneath his sneakers.

Wham! The door shook as the maniacs slammed themselves against it. Numerous blows followed the first and then came a steady series of hits. From the sound Max knew someone was hacking at the door with an axe. The door was thick oak but the lock would not last long.

"Oh God…" came very faint and very weak from Fatima looking up from the floor and Max followed her gaze, knowing that the rest of the room would be a nightmare compared to the door.

It was worse. There was blood everywhere. Most of it still red. The smell seemed to get even worse as he took in the sight before him. King had decorated his office lavishly with alleged Lost Tribe artifacts. Hangings, weapons, wooden statues, and cloth covers, all of it had been smeared or sprayed in by blood. The walls, too, were crisscrossed by blood splatter and in some places horrible handprints. They gave the impression that someone had been pinned against the wall. There were white designs on the floor that stood out in the dark room. Police outlines marking the positions of two bodies. Except, these outlines were incomplete, neither of them marking the position of a head.

The banging and hacking went on behind him as Max gritted his teeth and searched the room. Where were the heads? There were no other police outlines that he could see. The smell became even worse. It felt like his nose was filling with bits of dried blood. He took a step. He should be running. He should be getting Fatima out of there.

The heads had to be here somewhere, this was the only place left off limits due to the police investigation. Once again he looked to the outlines of the bodies. If they had lost their heads there then maybe they fell in the direction… He wondered which guards they were. Had he known them? He had never bothered to find out.

Max's eyes slid across the floor to the side of King's huge desk. There was nothing there. But there was still dried blood that had slid down the side of the desk when it was still wet. Up the side of the desk there were two sets of dry blood patterns. It was at the top of the desk where he finally saw the outlines he for which he had been searching: two irregular circles, sitting evenly apart on opposite sides of King's ink blotter.

"Oh God." Max whispered.

Crash! The wooden door flew open and in poured the maniacs. Fatima screamed. Max grabbed her hand and swung her over his shoulder, then took off through the gore to the other exit. This door was unlocked as well but could not be locked from the outside without the key, of which Max had a copy of…

…on top of his dresser.

So he just swung it open and leapt through.

They were back into the South Tower stairwell. Once there he ran for the stairs and ascended to the East Hall landing. Fatima cried out in yelps as Max's shoulder bucked under her. The Maniacs had passed through King's office seemingly unaffected by the gory scene and gave chase but Max had them beat now. Even with Fatima over his shoulder he found that his speed was far greater than it had ever been. It was faster than the speed of his pursuers. All he had to do now was make it to the East Hall and he would be able to sprint the entire length to the East Tower where, he hoped, the security guards would be in force with even the police possibly.

At the top of the stairs Max reached for the door.

Almost there!

He grabbed the latch but it would not turn. The door was locked!

"Damn!" He set Fatima down quickly and threw his shoulder into the door, but amplified strength or not, the thick metal service door would not budge. Max kicked at the door, pounded on it with his fists, and threw himself into the door again and again. Grunts and curses burst from his tightly clenched jaw.

There was a retching and then a strong sick scent filled the stairwell. He turned to find that Fatima had thrown-up over the edge of the stairwells banister.

"Dammit!!" he thought of that set of keys that would open the door and knew that they were DEFINITELY on his dresser. Now came the rumbling of the Maniacs as they thundered up the steps.

"Here." came Fatima's frightened voice. Max looked to her again to find… Of course! …HER set of keys held out to him.

There was not time, however, for him to turn and open the door. The Maniacs were closing fast. He reached but grabbed Fatima by the waist and pushed her to the door.

"OPEN IT!" his voice came out in a growl and he met the tide of Maniacs with ferocity of his own. They found it hard to keep their footing on the slippery steps and a few fell causing them to log jam on their way up, nevertheless the more able bodied of them made it to the top and met him head on with their weapons.

Max dodged a spear, ducked an axe, and finally took a flying tackle in the mid-section. He was knocked back into Fatima and heard her drop the keys.

"NO TIME!" he shouted in frustration and kicked the tackler off of him to find another maniac armed with a dagger diving on top of him. Max grabbed the forearms of his attacker and then turned him over. He heard Fatima picking up the keys and praying to GOD. With another animal growl he slammed his fist into the Maniac's face and pulled the dagger out of his hands then turned just in time to block the swing of a long serrated blade.

He had never fought with a blade before, but the handle felt insanely familiar in his hand. Somehow he KNEW that the serrated blade would catch on his blade at each tooth, slowing the stabbing blow.

Sparks flew lighting up the dark stairwell briefly and Max could hear the key slip into the lock and push past the tumblers. One strong push and the serrated blade went flying away and Max broke the attacker's jaw by slamming the hilt of his blade into the Maniacs face.

An axe came down from another direction and he ducked, hearing it hit the Maniac on the ground. Max jumped to his feet and kicked that Maniac down the stairs into the arms and weapons of his friends who charged anew.

Light from the East Hall then poured into the stairwell and Max turned to see Fatima running through. He dove after her, half on instinct after hearing the stretching of catgut, knocking her to the floor just as arrows flew over their heads.

They had fallen away from the stairwell too far for Max to run back and close the door so he just picked up Fatima and keeping their heads low, ran for the East Tower.

The East Hall was not in use right now and was being readied for a future exhibit. There were scaffolding and construction materials everywhere. Max used these to cover them from being struck from behind by the bowmen but the ducking and weaving slowed them down considerably. He doubted that they would make it to the East Tower before the Maniacs over took them. Evidently the Maniacs could sense this too and their cries of outrage became more and more triumphant as they could see that they were going to catch their prey.

Max, with Fatima over his shoulder again, kicked a huge, cloth covered scaffolding down. It fell behind them cutting off a group of the fastest Maniacs from catching them and that bought them a few more seconds.

Maybe enough!

The East Tower double doors came into view.

There was a cloth-covered desk, table, or something ahead of them and he gripped Fatima tightly and leapt over it.

Too late in mid-leap he heard the hiss of yet another arrow behind his left ear…

…and Fatima was on his left shoulder!

With a cat like twist Max turned in midair and felt the arrow just whip past the right side of his face, burning his cheek as it passed by. The two of them fell hard onto the marble floor and slid several feet ending up about ten yards from the double doors.

The Maniacs rushed up behind letting out howls of victory. Max looked up dazed but aware.

So close.

The Maniacs walked up calmly now, readying their weapons to finish the hunt.

With a slam the double doors opened and the police stormed through.

"FREEZE!!" came the yell in unison. Max did not listen to the rest of the command about putting weapons down and neither did the Maniacs. Somehow the entire group of deranged black leather clad crazies switched their collective focus away from Max and Fatima. With anger in their voices they charged the police with their medieval weapons without hesitation.

Quickly Max reached out and shoved Fatima under a table near the door. She slid the several feet without making a sound, still too dazed from their fall to say anything. Max then crawled out of the path of the Maniacs battle path toward the police hoping that he could get away unnoticed.

No such luck, his movement attracted the attention of a particularly huge Maniac, who spotted him. After a second of indecision, as he pondered whether to continue after the police or go for their original quarry, he rushed to attack.

Max shook off the confusion and the dizziness, if one could do that, climbed to one knee, took the charge of the attacker and turned him into the thick table end of some sheet covered display. The Maniac fell unconscious, his weapon clattering across that display. Before he could be attacked again Max leapt up onto that table and saw the entire battle.

The room was now filled with Cops and Maniacs. Shots were being fired and the police were steadily winning the battle, as their weapons were far more effective and final. But the Maniacs seemed not to care about life or death, they fought on until they became either unconscious, too wounded to fight, or dead.

Fatima should be alright. No one seemed to notice when Max shoved her under the covered table and the police should have control of the situation before she was found.

However there was no way out though for Max. The police still poured in through the double doors, and there were still at least fifteen Maniacs between him and the South Tower lab. The only other way out was a window or...

The Skylight!

Max looked up and saw what he wanted. Each hall had a skylight and the East was no exception. Unfortunately the skylight was about a good two story climb above his head, a height that he was sure he could not jump even as amplified as his strength was. An arrow sank into the table at his feet and he dove for the ground.

There were Maniacs wrestling with police officers all over the place and so he crawled through the melee keeping his eyes raised skyward as he tried to get under the skylight.

THAT would not be that difficult. The East Hall skylight was a good sixty feet by forty feet of slotted window vents. It was above most of the hall. The problem was getting to it.

"DIE!" an axe slammed down inches from his head. The Maniac had missed because a policewoman had tackled him just as he swung. The cop and the Maniac rolled over each other a few times until the Maniac came up on top. He pulled a switchblade out of his boot and plunged it into the officers' midsection.

"Hey!" Max screamed and jumped at the Maniac knocking him clear of the wounded officer. He grabbed the hand that held the blade and the crazed man screamed in pain. Something warm and slippery slid between his fingers. A now familiar metallic smell reached his nose. The Maniac looked into Max's face and screamed again in terror. A quick look at the Maniac's hand and he could see it was bleeding terribly. Why? He looked to his own hand and stared in amazement.

On the tip of each finger was a smooth, curved, white claw. The tips of a few had blood on them. He could feel the muscle behind each one as he slowly retracted and extended them.

Another police officer slid up beside the wounded cop who lay bleeding and watching Max. Max then turned and looked back at them. The second officer called for GOD and then leveled his weapon right between Max's eyes.

The Officer hesitated only a second then…

The muzzle flash went off and the bullet flew but Max had already leapt clear. He bounded from table to scaffolding to table to scaffolding leaping over sword blades and dodging flying arrows and police gunfire alike. Finally he came to a rest against the far wall away from most of the remodeling and most of the fighting. He crouched behind an enormous tapestry of some 12th century origin. It was time to leave.

With no great effort he leapt onto the tapestry and after sinking his new claws into it, he began to climb the thing. He kicked and instinctively dug his toes into the tapestry, trying to use the claws he felt straining against the inside of his sneakers to catch hold.

There were shouts coming from behind him and an arrow shot into the tapestry near to his thigh but that was all. When he was high enough Max leapt from the tapestry onto a low hanging ceiling light that swung mightily from his weight. Then he climbed the support cable to the ceiling and the skylight. Two kicks and glass came down falling into the din below. Cold wind blew in as well as a shocking blast of snow that hit Max in the face. He looked up through the skylight to see that it was snowing and that it was snowing hard. Careful of the glass he pulled himself through his escape route and slid onto the roof.

It was a moment's peace. He stared up into the snowing white nighttime sky. Only a moment more perhaps had elapsed then he heard the heavy stomps of booted feet running up the stairwells. Cops or Maniacs, someone was coming up to the roof after him

Max stood at last, and listened to the air. There were sirens screaming in the distance, the sound of screeching tires around the Museum, shouts and screams down below, and the clomping of heavy boots on steps that led to his temporary haven…

…Oh, and there was the sound of snow falling, tiny tingles landing on the rooftop all around.

He jumped a bit as the Maniacs burst onto the rooftop almost all at once from the South Tower parapet, what was left of them that is. Wounded and frenzied they scrambled to the roof's edge and much to Max's horror, they began leaping from the South Tower into the outer bailey. He watched this insane display until the one maniac he had recognized earlier ran out onto the roof and sprinted for the edge carrying something pale and white slung across his back.

"JEAN!" he called. "Wait… Don't!" and screamed but his friend either never heard him or just did not care because he, too, threw himself from the Tower. Open-mouthed Max rushed to the edge and found that several of the Maniacs had managed to land or grab hold of the scaffolding that stood against the side of the South Tower. To his relief Max saw that Jean had, too, managed to land on the now swaying bit of metal. If he wanted to find out what the hell was going on, then he would have to catch up to him. But what were they doing? Why weren't they using the service bridge? Then he saw why. It was gone.

Someone had cut loose the support cables from the South Tower end and sent the thing swinging down against the outer wall. Oh crap, how was he going to get out of here?

There were careful yet quick footsteps on the stairs leading to the roof now. He heard rushed whisperings, the sharp smell of what must be gunpowder and finally the coppery smell of what he now knew was fresh blood.

The police were about to charge onto the roof.

He looked around quickly, searching for an alternative route, something other than joining the Maniacs in hanging from that rickety scaffolding that was beginning to lean dangerously over the courtyard of the outer bailey. The first thought that came to him was the courtyard with Wolf Den Tree, which was the giant, twisting, Queen Rockwood that stood taller than the Museum. Maybe he could jump to the tree and climb down?

Yes! The police would be busy chasing the rest of the Maniacs and he could...be trapped inside the Museum with however many other cops had stayed behind.

Because he had snuck in Max would not be on the log tonight. There would be no way to explain why he was there even if he could change his clothes. They already suspected he was involved. No, he had to get out.

There was the outer wall. How strong had he become? Could he make a jump that far? He felt strength in his legs and felt confidence growing that he could make the distance if...

"FREEZE!" was all Max needed to hear and he broke for the roof's edge. The adrenalin built up fast as he neared the edge of the South Tower and he imagined he could feel the police gun sights burning holes in his back. His foot landed in the center of the embrasure and he tensed to spring across when he got a good look at how far the expanse to the outer wall was.

"AH SHIT!" his attempt to stop was not successful, he was going way too fast and he tumbled head over heels down into the outer bailey.

Strangely, he wondered at how much spinning he had been doing lately.

In desperation he stretched his arm out, searching for something to stop his fall.

One rotation,

two,

three, then SLAM!

His hand caught hold of the construction scaffolding that lay against the building. It hit the rail with such a stinging force that he thought it was broken. Nevertheless he held on, but the momentum of his fall compounded with the stress that the Maniacs that had already slammed into the thin metal structure caused it fall away from the Tower. It grated loudly, and the Maniacs screamed in resounding echo.

Max found himself dangling wildly beneath the scaffolding as it fell. The ground was falling up at him and he was screaming along with the Maniacs. That screaming stopped as the scaffolding slowed and stopped its descent as the braces on its lower quarter held. Unfortunately a few Maniacs could not do the same, they were shaken loose and fell down to the courtyard of the outer bailey far below. The rest became quiet.

They all hung there, suspended for a few precarious moments, Max and the Maniacs who were able to remain fixed to the metal. With his heightened eyesight, Max could see the snow falling past them in the darkness but not the ground below. Looking around there were at least five Maniacs that he could see, hanging under the scaffolding as he was. The closest one seemed to be able to see him, and Max nodded to him.

" 'sup." Despite his predicament he was amazingly calm and confident again. He only began to worry a little as he realized this. Was the Stone doing something to his mind as well? No time for that now and so Max swung himself up through the scaffolding to the other side and perched on top of it. Here was another Maniac, murmuring to himself.

"master... master... master..." the disheveled boy said over and over. Again Max's thoughts went to Jean, the Maniac he had recognized, but he had not been hanging under the scaffolding nor was he here atop it.

The metal began to groan, quietly at first then louder as it again began to give way. Max looked around for something to grab onto when he saw an air-conditioning duct against the Museum wall. As lightly as he could he began to crawl along the scaffolding toward the duct. Not too far...

The groaning culminated in a horrible snap, and the topsy-turvy monkey bars began to fall again.

With a snarl, Max hopped up and leapt from bar to bar trying to get to the edge of the scaffolding to jump for the duct. One slip, a quick hop over a crying Maniac, and he was at the edge. Another snap and the scaffolding fell from beneath him. The step that would have propelled him to the duct came down instead on empty space and again he tumbled, and tumbled.

The castle wall could not be too far off. He reached out for it, hoping to catch a ledge, window sill, stone crevice, anything. Muscles jumped into reflexive action and his whole body twisted and quivered. Somehow, his body stopped its rotation and he could see the blur that was the castle wall. The translucent, white claws slid out of his fingertips. So close was the wall that he could feel the air push back against his hand. Just a little closer DAMMIT, he was running out of... WHAMM!!

"AAHHH!"

Did that hurt!

"OH GOD!"

It really did hurt!

"Oh I wanna cry, I wanna cry, I wanna cry, I wanna cry, I wanna cry, I wanna cry."

"Geyoff…" Something moaned beneath him. It seemed that he had landed on a Maniac.

His left foot hit first, along its side and then down came his left knee. Then his left hand extended to break his fall but landed on the Maniac's shoulder and he could not catch himself as his right arm came down on hard icy ground. Max's head came down on the Maniac's head with a clunk, and that Maniac must have been trying to get up because the impact was somewhat blunted. But his knee was swelling before he could even open his eyes, one of which had connected with the back of another Maniacs head during impact.

The first blurry image he saw was yet another Maniac lying just a few feet away from them, then another, and another. The courtyard was littered with them, some moving, some not, and a few others seemed to be up and running across the outer bailey. The fuzzy black figures were all running to the same place at the outer wall where they… disappeared?

Trying to lift his head brought on waves of dizziness and throbbing pain that made him want to lay it back down. Joints and bones cried out as he resisted the urge to stay down and pushed himself to his feet.

PAIN! It was something he was just going to have to endure because he did not want to be there, still lying on the ground when the police started rounding up the suspects. So across the courtyard Max hobbled and found that even as his body ached and his head swam, he seemed to be recovering faster than the Maniacs who took the same fall he did. The dizziness faded quickly and his blurred vision sharpened a bit, though his left knee was starting to swell to ghastly proportions. Soon he would lose full range of motion and that meant he would not be able to get away. Also his left arm was numb from his shoulder to his fingertips. He tried not to think about it.

As he neared the opening in the outer East wall Max began to hear the shouts of the police as they ran into the courtyard behind him. The sounds of sirens continued to ring in the air as well; he could hear them just over the buzzing in his ears. If he allowed himself to panic now he would just get himself caught so he knew that he had to just keep running toward the opening. Since he was in better shape than the Maniacs after the fall, he easily passed several of them on his way to the small opening in the ground. It looked like a drain, one that had been recently unearthed and then possibly covered up in one of the numerous reconstructions the Castle had undergone in the past couple hundred years.

Yes, the drain was definitely part of the original construction. You could tell by the size and shape of the stones used to angle the water.

But he really should not be holding up the line to admire this find right now.

"MOVE!" A Maniac grabbed him by his bad shoulder to spin him around. Max instinctively swung at the offender with his good arm… or rather, the one that hurt less. The blow sent the Maniac reeling several feet back into the arms of the approaching police.

"Jeez!" He did not realize how close the police were. Another second and they would be on him. There was a particularly fat Maniac jammed in the drain and several other Maniacs were trying to simultaneously push him through the opening and pull him out. A growl rumbled from between his clenched teeth and Max shoved the two fighting Maniacs pulling and pushing them out of his way. Then he kicked, (Damn! MY KNEE!) planting his foot right on the fat Maniac's rump and sent him through the hole.

The sounds of fighting were right behind him now as the police grappled with Maniacs. There was no time so he dove through the hole. The opening itself was a tunnel about ten feet long and Max slid all the way through and was grateful not to run into the back of the fat Maniac. Until, that is he came out the other end and landed hard on cold, wet stone.

It was dark for a second. Max listened intently as his eyes adjusted. Running footsteps were a ways off ahead of him, water was passing over rock, and another Maniac was coming down the hole.

So he moved as quickly as he could; his knee so bad now that he could not bend it more than a few degrees. The low ceiling of the tunnel cracked him in the head but despite the tight fit he realized there was much too much room here for this to merely be a drain. A long hidden secret passage that these Maniacs knew about but the Museum staff did not?

Feeling along now he limped after the echoing footsteps. A Maniac crashed to the ground behind him with a loud grunt and struggled to his feet but he appeared to be as injured as was Max if not more so. Those footsteps quieted behind him as Max out-limped them down the tight passage. The sounds ahead of him grew louder as he gained on them and he could now hear muffled voices, or moans.

The first Maniac he passed was crawling, dragging one leg that was nauseatingly bent at the knee. Another Maniac who hopped along desperately did not even acknowledge Max as he was passed by. Then there were more Maniacs scurrying down the tight corridor. There were a few who had stopped, obviously too injured to continue. Jeez! How many had been in the Museum? Twenty? Thirty?

He was still in the mix of these Maniacs when he felt the winter air hit his nostrils. They were getting closer to the outside. The fresh scent made him inhale even more deeply and he could almost taste the various scents of the Maniacs in the tunnel. There was something else there however, something a little more… oily?

The tunnel opening was hidden under the causeway and led out into the moat. So this was how they had gotten in. Max had scented them earlier down the moat basin but had not been able to identify them. The escaping Maniacs were running down the basin now towards the dock. One pushed past him as he paused at the secret entryway. The curved bottom of the basin caused the Maniac to slip, fall, and roll across the concrete. So Max treaded carefully out of the Museum, and then down the basin towards the dock.

The Police sirens still sounded through the air and there were flashing red and blue lights reflecting high off of the Museum walls. If the police were waiting for the Maniacs at the dock then Max would have to find another way out. He could not allow himself to be caught; he had not been seen entering the Museum so he would have no plausible way of explaining his being there so. But even if he managed to escape now if Fatima or any of the guards had managed to recognize him then they would just come grab him up later at his apartment.

He tried not to think about that now.

The dock rose high above the bottom of the dry moat but not as high as the castle walls. Fortunately there were step rungs here, laid against the wall of the moat that a few Maniacs were scrambling up. From the bottom of the concrete trench he could hear Cobbs River rushing along on the other side. It would fence him in once he got past the dock, forcing him to stay on its Southern bank where the police would be gathered in large numbers. His leg was getting better but he would never be able to outrun them, even to the bridge, which was less than a mile east. But if the swelling could hold off just a few more moments then maybe he could jump from the dock to cross gate on the other side. The dock was built at the narrowest point of the river. On the other side the cross gate had not worked in years and was connected to a store house that was no longer used. The distance was no more than fifty feet, if he remembered correctly, but his leg was getting increasingly tighter with the swelling.

The oily scent was heavier here as was a pungent… foul smell that was more like urine. It hung in the cold air almost like steam. What was it?

There were two Maniacs climbing up ahead of him and Max promptly pulled the first off the ladder and threw him back into the dark moat.

The second reached the top and leapt out of Max's reach. Not too long now…

He pushed off his good leg with as much strength as he could muster but he only made it to the second to last rung. With this kind of effort he would never make it across the river.

Plus he just banged his knee on a lower rung.

Okay one more jump would get him onto the middle of the

deck, but he was so tired, and his knee was no good. Even the sounds of police sirens somewhere behind him could not inspire anymore adrenaline. He was beginning to feel how heavy his body was on this ladder.

"Hurry!" the hoarse order came from just below him on the ladder. Max twisted and looked down to see the one Maniac he had recognized…with something entirely unrecognizable clamped onto his back.

"Jean! What are you…"

It was pale, its skin almost translucent in a sickly way. Its long thin fingers…no claws…clutched at the cracked black leather of Jeans jacket almost desperately. The face of the thing peeked out from just behind the wild locks of his friend's hair. Max could see one tiny bright green malevolent eye.

"Jesus, Jean, what the hell…"

"HSSSSS!"

Something clamped down on his arm from above with a strength behind it that could not have been human. The pain was so bad Max did not even notice that he was being pulled up onto the dock and swung high into the air until he was then slammed down onto the deck. There was more hissing and he looked up to see that another Maniac, this one a bit bigger than the others, was holding his arm. Before he could react the Maniac pulled his arm again, lifting him off of the deck and swinging him further down the dock until he crashed into some old equipment still stored there.

The landing was hard and knocked the wind was out of him. Not until they were almost on top of him did Max hear the running, slamming footsteps of the Maniac. Again the powerful hands grabbed at him, squeezing large knots of his sweatshirt and lifted him up again. The Maniac spun Max around to face him.

There was something wrong with his face, partially hidden as it was by the dark mass of oily hair. The Maniacs eyes were slits, like Max's own, but there was more. His nose was little more than two slender oblong notches under his eyes. And he was hissing with, (Oh shit!), two long slender fangs hung down from the top of the Maniacs mouth. His skin appeared strange as well. It was mottled, green in pallor, and slightly segmented into what Max immediately recognized as scales.

"Hsssssssssssssssss!" the Maniac drew him closer and those fangs suddenly seemed even larger.

"NO!" and his hand snapped shut into a fist and he brought the uppercut right into Maniacs jaw. There was a satisfying crack when the Maniacs mouth slammed shut but he did not release his two-handed grip on Max. Instead he pushed him to the ground and then straddled him. Once again the mouth opened and the fangs flashed at him while the Maniac hissed.

"GET OFF!" Max hit the Maniac again, this time his punch missed the jaw but hit the side of his face at an awkward angle. He swung again with his other hand ignoring the pain streaming down the side of his hand from the first try. That one caught the Maniac in the nose and shut that hissing up. Max did not stop swinging but the power of his own punches made it hard to control their accuracy and many hit at angles that did nothing to deter the Maniac. But the sight of those inhuman fangs was panicking Max and he did not stop throwing. His punches got wilder and more inaccurate until some missed the target entirely.

The Maniac was using these misses to draw closer to him, his yellow eyes staring intently at Max's throat.

Punching was not working. He gave up and simply pushed against the Maniacs chest with both hands, trying to hold him off. His sweatshirt stretched and tore but his arms did not give out. The Maniac drew no closer and, as a matter-of-fact, Max was able to fully extend and lock his arms.

"I'm! Stronger! Than! You!" he realized. Hesitation and fatigue let the Maniac get the drop on him but now Max knew he could at least hold him off. Maybe more if he could get some leverage.

Yellow serpentine eyes, narrowed into slits and framed with anger stared down into Max's own eyes whose lids were drawn near to closed, tight with renewed determination. Each snarled at the other, the Snake maniac flashing his sharp wicked set of fangs and Max gasping through clenched teeth.

The Maniac brought his full weight to him. But Max's arms were longer and while his claws cut into the Maniacs chest and drew blood, his own sweatshirt found itself being pulled upward, tearing at the seams. Still, the Maniac pressed and Max could not afford to change his grip.

Then the Maniacs face lit up white, blasted by a police cars mounted spotlight.

"Mountairy Rock P.D.! You're under arrest!" Both wrestlers looked up but Max, being on the ground could not see over the edge of the dock. Whatever the Maniac saw infuriated him and gave him renewed strength, but he relented on his attempt to rip out Max's throat with his teeth.

"GET OFF OF HIM!" Max chanced another look around and saw the Detective…SHERIFF Lynne standing just climbing onto the dock, gun pointed at the two of them.

She was not wearing the party dress tonight. Funny the things you notice.

Max took his hands off the Maniac and spread them wide. The Maniac with his fanged mouth agape had no such intention.

Two lightning punches slammed into Max's head while his hands were spread causing Max to see several flashes of light behind closed eyes. He felt the great relief of weight on his chest as the Maniac leapt off of him. Then he heard, eyes still closed, Sheriff Lynne scream, a gunshot and a crash at the other end of the dock.

When he opened his eyes everything was moving in slow motion.

Well not everything exactly, the flashing lights still flashed pretty quick, and that Sheriff was screaming at a reasonable pace, for someone who was facing a snake man.

Okay the only thing moving in slow motion was Max.

He tried to roll over onto his stomach but the going was hard and his body did not seem to be hearing his mind in a timely manner. Plus he apparently forgot to tell his legs to roll at the same time and when they finally got moving, they had no problem reminding him how terrible they were feeling. His hands moved slowest of all and as he rolled onto his stomach they responded too lethargically to stop his face from "thunking" back down onto the dock floor. Everything went dark again for a second.

The Sheriff screamed again and Max's now remaining one good eye popped open. The dock seemed to be spinning. The last of his senses to catch up was his vision; he could only make out the shape of the Snake maniac. Sheriff Lynne's legs were futilely kicking and pushing to get him off of her but if Max could just barely keep him at bay then she was going to be snake food. It would not be too long before it finished off the Sheriff and came for him. That thing was probably going to have him for dinner as well if Max did not run right this moment.

And he did not like her. Not one bit.

One good leg launched him across the deck. The off balance leap caused him to spin a little in the air but he landed right on top of the grappling pair and wrapped his mostly good arm tightly around the Maniacs neck.

"GET OFF HER!"

But he could not move the Maniac. It was all he could do to keep its fangs out of the Sheriff's flesh.

The oily smell oozing out of the Snake Maniac was mixed with the perfume covered fear flying off of the Sheriff. All three of their faces were within inches of one another. Max found himself staring directly into the Sheriff's eyes. So much fear, she had not been expecting this, and there was pain there as well. Max saw that the Maniacs hands were tightly gripping the woman's shoulders and drawing blood!

Despite his fear that the crazy nut would bite her Max switched his grip and grabbed both of the Maniac's wrists. Then he swung his legs to straddle the pair and braced them against the ground.

"GET OFF!" and he pulled and jerked… and PULLED! The

muscles in his fingertips pushed smooth ivory claws out and they bit deep into the thick rough flesh until they drew blood themselves.

"HSSSSSSSSSSS!" and the Maniac let go of the Sheriff then swung an elbow back into her would be rescuer's ribs. Max "oofed!" and let go. The Maniac bucked hard and sent Max stumbling backward.

Somehow he managed not to fall, which was good because the Snake Maniac was now advancing on him again. Now Max could see that the Maniac had claws of his own, longer than his own, sickly curved and dripping with the Sheriff's blood. Those claws were extended, the hands were open and clearly the Maniac was intent on using them.

"I thought… I thought we was boxin'!" and then those claws came at him. First Max hopped backwards but he forgot to favor his bad knee and it buckled nearly taking him down. The first swipe of those claws caught nothing but air but the Maniac was now on top of him.

Another swipe was meant to open up his throat but Max ducked fast and again the Maniacs claws could only whistle through the air. The quick dodge was good but the bad knee would not let him come back up. Instead he could only extend his bare forearm to protect his face even as he fell backward again trying to get away.

The slash burned hot and three nasty gashes opened up on his arm.

"AHH!" and he kicked trying to push the Maniac away but his foot hit empty air. Instead a nasty clawed hand dug into his chest, grabbing both sweater and skin alike. Max grabbed weakly at it trying to pull his flesh free as he watched the Maniac raise the other hand, claws splayed wide. Those narrow serpent eyes glared down in triumph at Max's throat.

BLAM!

The Maniac jerked and swung around dragging Max along the ground. Sheriff Lynne stood, obviously hurt, her weapon extended at the end of her one good arm, the other hanging limply at her side. She sighted down the gun's barrel snarling her own damn self, but her hand shook and she looked like she could drop it any second.

The Maniac hissed at her and seemed ready to attack again. He looked down at Max and bared those needlelike fangs at him. Then, with the one hand he lifted Max easily off of the ground and spun him round the dock once, twice, and then again. On the third time his feet left the ground and he was whipped hard into the air. The Maniac released his sweatshirt and Max watched the dock fall away from him.

Dock - police lights - starry night - North Hills skyline - the cross gate - black water.

SPLASH!!!

There was no sudden shock of cold water. If anything Max felt as if someone had thrown a warm blanket over him, thick and covering him from head to toe. So thick that he couldn't feel anything on the other side of that blanket. It was almost fascinating, how quickly his limbs had lost all sensation. If it were not for the slight feeling of rocking in his ears, he would not have known that his arms and legs were at least moving. Hopefully, they were kicking and paddling him toward the surface.

Hmm… his eyes felt hot.

It was not until his head broke the out of the water that he knew he had reached air. His hands had broken the surface first but told him nothing. He kept them moving anyway as well as his legs.

So tired…

Looking around Max could see that the dock and the cross gate were now far up river. The current was pulling him southeast toward the Falls and the Park. He was closer to the Northern shore so he clumsily paddled in that direction. His vision was so blurry… must have been caused by the cold, because his arms looked fuzzy as they cut through the water in front of him.

"… at an angle, then twist and pull…" said Jean. Max laughed as he listened to his roommate talk about swimming, like it was a religion or something. Whatever, the swim party tonight was going to be the…

His arms came down on a riverbank of fat white, snow covered stones and thick sheets of ice. The numbing cold kept him from feeling any pain as he slammed his fists into the shoreline which broke through the ice and sent those river stones flying. He tried to catch hold before the water pulled him back into its course. His arms shook as he hoisted himself out of the water, slowly, because he could not get them to move him any faster. So cold…

Ugh! There was some kind of film covering his arms.

Filthy ass water!

It would not come off when he tried rubbing it off. The cold made stiff rocks out of his hands and he could get no grip on the soft brown substance. "UGH!"

His body was still numb, it was shaking, and it was getting harder to breath evenly. He knew he would freeze to death if he stayed still. So he feebly pushed off of the riverbank and began to stumble away from the water. Without feeling in his legs or feet he found he had to watch every step he took on the uneven stones or he would fall over. Hopefully this movement would warm his body somewhat.

Frozen feet found their way up a snowy hill to and Max climbed over a guardrail to the main road. Where was he?

Behind the Museum on the other side of the river was Wadsworth Cemetery. Like most things in Mountairy Rock it was one of the largest of its kind in the world being over a mile and a half wide.

But looking across the road Max did not see the cemetery, he saw a burnt out old fire station. Behind the fire station he could see the tops of buildings falling away and downward into a valley. The buildings were old, an odd mix of Germanic, Roman, and old English architectures and they were laid out in mazelike fashion. It was a place that would be easy to get lost in; the Downhills.

The current of the river had swept Max farther downstream than he would have imagined. This was either a stroke of good luck, or a very terrible turn of events.

…there had been a party here… somewhere… a little while ago…

On the one hand the police at the Museum might not think he would have been pulled so far and might search for him elsewhere. On the other he was now even farther from home, or anyplace where he might get warm. Mountairy Rock winters were harsh; the night time temperature often dipped well below freezing. Dying of hypothermia before he could get home was a very likely possibility.

There was very little police presence in this isolated valley, not even a station, if Max remembered correctly. No cops… but then the people here were clannish and always took care of their neighborhood themselves. How would they react to an outsider running through their backyards in the dead of night?

So cold… Where was he? What was he doing? Someone's playing music…

Headlights flashed from the north and startled him into running. The road was slippery but he managed it with good speed and made it to the shadows of the fire station before the car drove past. Just a car it was, not the police.

…Just a car headed into the Downhills.

Had he been there before?

…Long ago, when he first attended Mountairy Rock U. as an undergrad.

The run did him some good he thought. Warm blood pumped down his legs to his feet, through his arms to his hands. Don't stop now unless you want to freeze!

So he ran again, into and through the hollowed out station, then into an alley beyond. The heat of his working muscles warmed his bones and for a few city blocks worth of back alleys it was all that he thought of. The pumping blood, his pounding feet, and the wind racing past his ears blinded Max to everything else. Even his surroundings became a blur, the dark alleys seemingly all the same as he raced along them. But as the numbness faded his head clouded over. The haze of passing alleys became the blur of softly lit homes and green yards. The walkways twisted and turned and Max was sure he was lost now but it did not matter. He had to keep running…

...keep the blood hot...

...fight off the cold...

But the air he sucked in was so cold, his lungs quickly went raw. Every breath pained him.

There were small lights in front of him now. Dancing and moving like lightning bugs. The light they cast grew brighter and as Max raced up to them, they took shape. He could see the little fluttering wings,

the soft curve of her swaying body,

the bright mane of her flame colored hair,

the large lupine eyes,

the slight warm smile...

EASY LIKE SUNDAY MORNING

The ache started somewhere between his shoulder blades and ended right behind his right ear. It was a muscle ache and Max had not previously been aware that there was a muscle behind his right ear at all. Apparently it was very instrumental in helping to turn his head. It hurt so bad that he dared not move the rest of his body because it might disturb just that one muscle. Best to just lay still and fall back to sleep.

But now another unpleasant sensation disturbed his slumber. A nasty bitterly cold wind shot across his cheek. Too cold and too insistent to ignore, the wind forced him to open his eyes. Blurry, sleepy eyes opened slowly and could see very little. In no hurry Max let his vision slowly clear, the details emerging from the gray background like it was a fog was settling to the ground. The vague but familiar patterns of his bedroom let him know where he was.

His window was open again. Cold Great Lake wind rolled right on through. Rightly he should get up and close it but he was too tired. So he just turned his head again despite the ache and tucked it down under the blanket where it had been.

Sleep came easily now.

The loud ring of his phone woke him up some time later. Even though his face was beneath his blanket, Max could still see the light that illuminated the room. The phone was right next to his bed and its ring demanded his attention, insisted there be some action. Shifting his legs told him something he had not realized when he woke earlier; he was still wearing his clothes. Why was he dressed?

What had he been doing last night? Was this a hang over? Couldn't be, he did not drink. The phone stopped ringing as the answering machine picked up.

It was Dr. Collins. He demanded that Max find his way in to the Museum because there had been another break in.

Another? The image of a man in black leather swinging a mace flashed in his mind.

More aches arced around his body as he rolled in the bed. Something was wrong with his knee,

and his arm,
and his ribs hurt.

He groaned but the aches did not stop him from sliding his legs off the bed and setting them on the floor. With another groan he pushed the rest of himself off the bed and wobbled. How bad was he? His arms were weak and his right one burned, his legs shook and threatened to drop him to the floor. But he still did not stop.

The blanket fell from him as he took a step. That's when he discovered his clothes were wet. Not soaked, but definitely damp and with a horrid mildew smell. Cold wind from the window ripped away whatever heat the wet clothes had absorbed from his body. Why was he wet? The shaking got worse. Max took another step.

The machine beeped as the Doctor finished his rant. There had been another break in and that meant more clean up. King would be furious if Max did not show up to help. How bad could it be? Bad enough. He had better get there. Nothing was more important right now.

Another step and he reached the window. The cold wind froze his chest and thighs but only for another moment. His shaking hands reached and pulled the old window down and closed. If he had more feeling in his fingers he would have locked it too. Now on to more important things.

The aches and pains were not so bad, he found, when getting into bed.

There was pounding at his door. Max's heart leapt. Police?
The police were here? But then a voice joined the pounding. It was Steve. Whew! That was close!

His eyes snapped open. The police were after him! He had been running from them last night! Cold memories and disjointed images returned to him; climbing the bank out of the river, being thrown in, and the twisted mottled fang filled face of the Maniac. There had been Maniacs at the museum. Police too. He had been running carrying a woman. A woman? Who?

Pretty, with a warm but slight smile, she...
"Max?"

He shot up in the bed. Someone was in the room with him. It was dark and his vision was clouded by sleep but he still turned to the intruder. Though he could not see him an outline of information surrounded the person. The breathing was familiar, nasal, and shallow. The feet shuffled across his worn carpet in a way Max also was familiar with. Then his nose, which cruelly was not stuffed shut with mucus, was assaulted by the horrible mix of sour milk and Brut cologne.

"Steve?"

"Where you been man? Why's your door open?" with that he hopped onto the edge of Max's bed and immediately began wrinkling his own nose. "What is that smell? You sick?"

"What time is it?" Max slowly slid from the bed and found that his legs were sturdier now.

"Quarter after Six. You weren't at the Library. You know there was another break in at the museum? Why is your bed wet? I hope this isn't what I think it is!"

"Was anyone hurt?" There was… a girl.

"Fatima was attacked. She hasn't been back since. It's freezing in here!"

"Fatima?" Now he remembered her screams. The maniacs had her by her hair. A wicked looking, black leather wearing, wild haired psycho had her on her knees. Max remembered the sound his fist made with it came down on that guy's skull. Then he had grabbed Fatima and they ran upstairs. What else had happened? She had not been back since? Steve couldn't have meant since last night. Uh oh...

"When was this?" he tried to sound unconcerned. Why wasn't he telling Steve everything?

Oh yeah, he was Steve.

"Thursday. What did you do this weekend? Help clean the Museum again?"

Max had made it to the bathroom doorway. It had been Wednesday night actually, when the Museum was ransacked again. Steve was talking like the weekend was already past. He could not have slept more than a day. Could he have? What day was it?

His clothes were filthy, still a little damp and smelled moldy. He remembered water, cold, unbelievably cold water that still lingered in his clothes. More pain fired down his back as he began peeling them off. A shower. A shower was all he needed to get back on track.

Off came the skull cap, which hit the floor with a wet smack. He could not have slept for day could he? His clothes were still wet... but it did not smell like river water. Was it sweat? No… couldn't be… it was freezing in his apartment.

Off came the gloves, with tiny holes at the tip of each finger and thumb. Then, painstakingly, his sweatshirt top came next, but his arms locked just as he had them raised above his head.

"Uhn!" he grunted. The sweatshirt was wrapped around his arms and head now and held them tight so tightly that he could not even lower them. So he stood there and struggled to free himself while the stabbing pain in his back was joined by fatigue pains in his shoulders and arms.

"HEH HEH!" Steve snorted when he saw Max's predicament. "Work out too much huh? I thought you chilled on Sundays… just watched the game. You're missing Wildcard Weekend?"

73

The Serpent Cult

"Sunday?" but his question was too muffled for Steve to understand him. He'd slept for almost four days. Four days and his body still ached. Four days and his clothes were still wet, was that right? Was it just the physical beating he took? Or was the stone doing something more to him? Why would he sleep for four days? Was it like an addict crashing after using speed? Max wondered what kind of damage it might be doing to his body. He could feel it against his chest. It was so warm he could feel it through in the sweatshirt pouch.

"Jeez man. Here let me help."

"No, Steve, I got it."

"What were you doing?"

"Ahh! I got it Steve!"

"Just relax your arms."

"Ughn! STEVE!"

"I hope you can make it to work tomorrow."

"AHH! I GOT IT DAMMIT!" and he pulled away and banged his hip into the sink. Steve apologized but Max could hear the laugh behind it. With a final frustrated tug the sweater came over his head.

"I gotta shower." …so get out.

"All right man, I'll be back in a few and we'll go downtown." Steve was already on his way out when Max got the sweater off. He stared in the mirror at his bruised and scarred chest, neck, face, arms, hands, then twisted a little,

back, shoulders, and then he pulled down his sweat pants, waist, thighs, knees, and legs.

What a complete mess! The bruises crisscrossing his body oddly matched the worn and battered Stone he had hanging from his neck. He should take the damn thing off before it killed him.

…hanging from his neck?

The Stone was not sitting in the little hand warming pouch sewn into the front of his sweater but instead was hanging from his neck by a thin braid of string. The string was a kind of fine thread, brown, red and not like anything he had lying around either here or at the Museum. It was wrapped tightly several times around the narrowest part of the Stone and knotted tightly. When the Hell had he done this? He made to grab the string and pull it from around his neck and then hesitated.

What if whatever had made him stronger, quicker, and able to see in the darkness was also keeping his body together? There were four jagged and scabby scars just beneath his left collar bone and three running halfway around his right forearm. Again the memory of the Maniac with the claws flashed in his mind.

If he took the Stone off now, could he die from the beating he had taken? Looking at the other bruises they did not seem so bad but then again he had been asleep for four days. How bad had they been on

Wednesday? Maybe he had been sleep for so long so that his body could heal itself.

Something about that thought felt right. The Stone had changed him, so could it be healing him? What kind of damage would taking it off do to him? He grabbed the strange string and pulled the Stone up off of his chest.

Nothing.

With a grunt he raised his arm and pulled the string over his head and then held the Stone out before him.

Again; nothing.

So he snorted a little laugh at himself and dropped the Stone into the sink.

He saw the bright red drops hit the not so white porcelain rim before he noticed the pain. Sharp and burning, the four crusty scabs on his chest were leaking blood. Fire arced over his arm in three lines and blood flowed down his arm which then went numb.

He reached out for the Stone with his other but the sink suddenly rose up over his head. In an instant it was too high for his hand to reach over the rim. He then saw his knees sticking straight up and realized that he had fallen to the floor. So much of his body had gone numb that he did not even feel the cold tile.

The Stone. He had to get the Stone. Only his left arm had any feeling left but it could barely reach the tip of the sink. He panicked and kicked out uselessly.

From beyond the bathroom door he could hear Steve mumbling something. He tried to call out to him but all he could manage were a few sharp breaths. Steve would freak when he saw Max lying on the floor with blood everywhere but he could care less now. *Just get in here!* he tried to will him through the door.

But Steve's voice only grew quieter and Max grew more desperate. The spreading numbness felt like a growing weight holding him down, pressing hard on his chest, squeezing the life from him. The fingertips of his left hand grew cold. He watched his swelling knees drop out of sight when his legs no longer had the strength to hold themselves up.

So cold was his hand now that he did not know it had reached the top of the sink until he looked back up. He clamped his hand down and pulled. His arm shook with cramps as muscles seized up but at least the cramping muscle was contracting. Slowly his torso came up off of the tile.

He grunted and snorted. Blood from his nose spattered his good arm and he could taste it, thick and metallic, on his lips. After a wet grunt he finally came up eye level with the top of the sink.

But he could raise himself no more. The crazy angle of his body next to the sink afforded him no more leverage. With his arm shaking he simply hung there, losing strength. He looked over the rim but could not see down into the sink, could not see the Stone.

A cold blast of air hit him square in the one spot on his back he could still feel. It was enough to drain the last of his strength and drop him back to the cold floor. Helpless, he gasped feebly, trying desperately to regain enough strength for another attempt. But with every breath the cold tile beneath him seemed to tighten its grip. Still he had to try.

With another grunt he pulled and reached into the sink grabbing blindly. His hand had become too numb to tell him if he has grabbed the Stone and his arm too weak to hang by the crook in his elbow. The bottom of the shower tub was particularly hard when the back of his head fell back against it.

Strength flowed back into his limbs. When the pain of the fall subsided and he could open his eye Max saw the Stone. It spun on the string dangling from between his pinky and his palm.

He was just touching the string, not the Stone itself. Why would that work?

Thank God it did.

The open wounds on his arm and chest were still open now but no longer bleeding. The realization that he could now die without the thing scared him. How long would he have to keep the Stone on his person before his body could get along without it? Forever?

And what would happen if he lost it or someone took it from him?

Well, he was not going to let that happen. Not at least until he was sure his body had recovered enough. Hopefully it would. He pulled himself to his feet; after three days in bed he still needed to get clean.

The shower was good and hot, though as usual the water pressure was terrible. It was probably for the best now because he was not sure his skin could take being beaten again. As it was his arms and shoulders hurt so much it was hard to wash with any real success so Max settled for letting the hot water burn away the residue from the river. God knows what was in that water.

Time to plan. First thing tomorrow he would head to the Museum and see what was happening. He would have to come up with a good reason he had not come in over the weekend. Hopefully King had not returned to the school and Max would only have to deal with Dr. Collins, a far more easy going man. There would be a lot of make-up work to do, so Collins would hesitate to be too hard on him. That work also meant that he would again have to put off his own graduate work for a little while. He might even have to take over one of Kings Classes. Hopefully it would be the undergrad class, which was all he could handle right now. Again all the extra work would mean that Max had to put off his own projects like getting to the computer lab and researching the symbol etched on the Stone. He looked down at it on his chest.

Oh God he was wearing it in the shower! But then he had swum in the river with it and it seemed no worse for wear. Maybe it was not actually made of stone. Could it be bone? He ran his fingers over it and felt its rough surface scratch his fingertips. It could not be too old he realized, the surface should be smooth from years of wear; unless it had been sitting somewhere undisturbed for most of its history. Was that likely? When had it been made? If the thing was recent then it might be easier to find a meaning behind the etching.

Tomorrow. He would look tomorrow.

The water went cold and Max reached with a moan for faucets and turned them off. Drying was just as difficult as washing but did not hurt nearly as much as taking off his sweats.

The shower had done him some good. Now he should probably go down into the gym and stretch some because he did not want to wake up stiff like that again.

Outside the bathroom he found that Steve had gone; although, his scent still lingered. He took in a deep breath through flared nostrils. The walls of his lungs and nasal passages were still raw and sensitive. The scent was strong and intermingled with it Max could smell the heavy carbon monoxide of motorcycle exhaust. What had Steve been doing? Standing behind it for an hour? There was more. The scent of the Great Lake was there as well, although it was much fainter. A quick glance at the window told him it was still closed.

Good.

The window had been open while he slept. Did he open it? He could not remember getting home last night... no, not LAST night; Wednesday night. That window had been mysteriously opened before when he had not done it. The night the big gray cat had led him on that chase. Had it been here again?

And after falling... No! After being THROWN into the river... how had he gotten back home?

And, again he wondered while looking at the brown and garnet colored string tied around the Stone, when had he done this?

Aches flared in his back as he sat on his bed. Another deep breath, and another, and one more when finally there came that musky scent. The cat had been here but not recently. It was connected to the Stone obviously but more importantly it was now connected to him. Finding out more about that cat might help him find answers to everything that was going on. If he could find it again.

There was another set of sweats in his dresser. Putting on his pants was a major workout in and of itself. When he finally got them up to his waist he fell back on the bed exhausted and out of breath.

Going to be hard to get downstairs.

SLAM! Max jerked awake. Suddenly it was freezing again.

The window.

"Jesus Max! Why was this window open?" it was Steve again and he was standing next to the window. He had said that he was coming back but…DAMMIT! Max realized he had fallen asleep again.

"The window was open?" Max sniffed. Big Gray had been here but it was faint. What time was it? Did he still have time to go stretch?

"Come on man. Let's go to campus. I'm gonna get some studying in since there's no more Monday night football. Are you ready?"

Oh God! It was Monday?

It had snowed again while Max had slept away the weekend. More snow was piled up against the street curbs and the old drifts were covered with fresh snow. But the air seemed warmer or at least not as bitter. The usually harsh Mountairy Rock winter was in a bit of abatement. That meant it would probably snow again and soon. Steve agreed.

"Yea maybe. Wouldn't know the weathers been this bad by all the activity up at the Museum. Been real busy this weekend." Steve said. It was noticeable even a few blocks from the great castle. There was a lot more traffic than usual. And people too, going into and out of the shops along Germantown Avenue. This was odd for this time of year and for this kind of weather. Could the recent events at the Museum have stirred up some kind of weird interest? Max wondered.

It was even more crowded at the Museum. There was still a heavy police presence with two squad cars by the dock and at least three in the parking lot across from the fountain. There were several cars too, SUVs mostly, and a couple of buses. It looked like someone had booked a trip to the Museum. With the number of people milling around he wondered if the Museum had known they were coming. After the murders Max had expected the Museum to close but it seemed as though that would not be the case.

The two of them made their way past the dock, which was now closed off with police tape. Steve thought they would be able to get by but Max was not willing to do anything to attract police attention. Not that staying below their radar would keep them from coming for him if they had known he was here last night (no last WEEK!). Of course if they had known then they would have already been to his apartment. So…

"Great… Gypsies." Steve muttered. The barbican was very crowded with people coming and going. Indeed quite a few visitors bumped and jostled them as they walked through the gateway. Max saw that many in the crowd were the people whom the student body typically referred to as "Gypsies". Although as far as he knew that term was born out of both stereotype and ignorance.

The "Gypsies" were not gypsy-like in any way really, at least not anymore. From what Max knew of their history the very eclectic peoples from the Downhills once were roving families who came to Mountairy Rock after the Quake of 1806. Being very reclusive and private, they held to their old world traditions despite the modernization of Rock city. The peoples of the Downhills had come to garner a very poor reputation as backwoods, hicks, and old world Euro-trash.

Max knew there had to be more to their history. The Downhills people were a strange mix. While a good majority of them seemed to be of European descent, there were many in their group with obvious African ancestry as well as those who had names that he thought were Native American. But if there was much of a difference between them, they never seemed to display it publicly.

Finally across the causeway and through the Barbican, Max and Steve found no relief from the crowd of people. Again he wondered at the great number of tourists who were shopping so casually, in the cold, among the small shops set inside the outer bailey. It looked like the Downhills were out in full force and Max had the feeling that he should know why for some reason. He observed them milling about as they were but he did not stop walking toward Rebels Keep, the main building of Haley museum. Their clothes were distinctive enough that he supposed that anyone would be able to point out someone from the Downhills, especially in the winter. The fur lined leather jackets and coats had an odd but definite frontiersman feel to them, almost as if they had hand made the clothing themselves.

"She's hot." Steve muttered, looking over Max's shoulder. "Not like most of their girls." When he turned to see whom Steve was speaking about the woman herself had turned away and was looking into one of the shop windows. Again like many of the Downhills people she was dressed in a fur lined leather coat, dark brown in color. Though her hood was pulled up Max could see that she had a huge mane of dark brown hair with burgundy highlights. It was too much to keep under her hood and it spilled out of the light brown fur lining. She wore a rather distinctive fur lined leather skirt as well. The pelt was a striking sable color making Max wonder what animal had once called it home. Another second and she would turn around.

"Oh! Excuse me!" a rather diminutive Downhills man ran into Max's midsection. Again there was that fur lined leather clothing though this man wore it rather conservatively for one of the Downhills folk. His face was fur lined as well, Max mused, looking at the thick brown beard this man wore in an unruly and uncut fashion. But his eyes were kind, like old paintings of Santa Clause, squinting at him through thin rimmed glasses. "Sorry young man." He said.

He could not help but to smile in turn. "S'Okay." He said, waiting a polite second before trying to turn to see the woman again.

"Do you work here?" the man asked. Okay, if he said no, he could move on and still get a look at the girls face, but he did not want to have to lie to the old man especially since he was just about to walk into Rebels Keep.

"Sure…"

"What do you do here?"

Oh crap. "I'm a researcher." Max answered.

"…oh."

Well damn!

"Would you know where we might find Wolf's Keep?" the little man asked.

"It's on the other side of the Museum. You can go through Rebels Keep, then across the courtyard, past Wolf Den tree, into the Great Hall, and then into the Keep." Max made a show of pointing it out so that he could turn away from the old man and chance a look back at the woman…who was now gone.

When he turned back to see if the old man had understood, he swore he thought he caught the old guy sniffing him! "Thank you so much!" he said with a little too much twinkle in his eye. Max expected him to turn and leave towards Rebels keep but the old man just continued to smile at him.

"Sure… excuse me." And he stepped past him into Rebels keep.

Steve was waiting there checking out some notices on the campus board. Curious if there was anything about the break-ins, Max joined him.

"Cute huh? I love those almond eyes, and those lips!" Steve was snickering.

"I didn't see her face."

"Too bad, she was fine. Sista too!"

"Shh…" Max warned as a small group of gypsies hurried past, including the old man and the woman of whom Steve had been speaking. Her hood was still up, and being silhouetted by the Keep's door, her face was hidden in shadow. They ambled past and he noted that none of them was taller than Steve, who was only five feet five inches tall his own self. As he watched the old man direct his small group through the Keep, occasionally calling out to stragglers to keep up, Max wondered if he had ever seen any of their clan who was tall. He supposed that was one of the things that helped to collectively make them stand out as different, which contributed to keeping them isolated from the other communities in Mountairy Rock.

Reflexively Max sniffed the air taking in the various scents they left behind then caught himself. The Stone was affecting him more and more every second he kept it on. How much of his behavior could the thing affect? Or control? The lab, he reminded himself. He had to try and find out what it was and where it had come from.

There was nothing on the board about the break-ins that he could see. The only new item was a meeting being held about something called Prop 615. Some Earth group was protesting something.

"Hey, are they still gonna have King Day?" Steve asked. That was a good question. The Museum held festivities every year for the celebration of Dr. King's birthday. They certainly could not be thinking of still running the events. The main reason the Museum was so crowded today was because of the heavy police presence, and those were just the uniformed officers. How many undercover policemen and women were there? Not too many as only a few of the tourists stood taller than the large Downhills crowd.

"I gotta go to work." Max said.

"All right. If you finish up soon, I'll be in the library doing some research." Steve said with not one book or note pad in his possession, but he left, continuing on through Rebels Keep toward the Inner Bailey and the Library.

Again the signs of the recent violence at the Museum were apparent; but amazingly, it was already in a state of repair. No doubt the Museum wanted to quickly put the ugliness behind them. Even though the service corridor was clear Max avoided it and headed for the South Tower through the South Tower Lobby. The lobby was busy now, during working hours. The repairs in this room were already complete and the room was given back its glossy yet warm appeal. The administrative desk in the center of the room was busy as usual, and there was a small group of people standing in line in front of it. He began to walk past and straight to the stairwell when his name was called out , rather rudely.

"Max? EXCUSE me but did I sleep with you last night?" Mrs. Dana had her hand on her hip again. This was Mrs. Dana's favorite line whenever someone came in and did not say hello. Max had seen it embarrass many a student, researcher, even Dr. King, which is why he had taken to using the service corridor and dock entrance. However the past weeks events had him off his game. He had always made it a habitual point to say hello to her, or at least make eye contact and wave if she was busy, lest he be the target of her ire. Now everyone had turned to look at him, as he appeared to be sneaking past. The worst part of Mrs. Dana's "line" was that if you were a stranger to the South Tower you might not know what it was that she meant. As it was at this moment several people were looking at Max wondering what it was that he had done just then that only someone whom had slept with Mrs. Dana would do. The snickering would start soon as he would stammer an apology. He knew the drill. When he came in tomorrow he would have to grovel and kneel when he said hello to her because he had better not sneak around to the East Tower because that would only make it worse. Or he could…

"Was that YOU?" he said with as much feigned surprise as possible on his face. "Then who was the midget? She was BEAUTIFUL!" and even Mrs. Dana had to laugh.

Any lift in spirit he might have had faded away as he entered the South Tower lab. It had been almost a week since the second break in but from what he could tell the recovery had not been as quick here as it had been in other more public parts of the museum. Many of the post grads had already returned from whatever little break they had been on and were now hovering over their projects and research. They were trying to determine how much had been lost and what could be recovered. Usually the room had a pretty good noise level whenever this many people were here. With many of the computers down and the equipment smashed, the background hum of the equipment with which Max was familiar was eerily missing. There were tech guys here as well trying to recover information from hard drives, while, students waited with baited breath hoping that their scholastic careers had not been set back a whole year. Most of the researchers backed up their files but Max thought that backing up was something many did not do frequently enough. The impatient, worried faces told him that he was right.

As he continued through the room he made sure to take a mental note of the states of some of the projects he himself had been interested in seeing finished. Joel Williams had been working on a virtual map of Mountairy Rock before the quake. Not that Max had any expertise on the computer side of it but he did not think that was the kind of thing you could easily back up. Erica Jordan, whom he had once dated, was attempting to trace the descendants of Haley Freeman, the escaped slave who somehow took ownership of the castle that was now Haley Museum. While he was pretty sure that most of her research was actually on paper he knew she would be screaming of a conspiracy to keep the rightful heirs from making a claim on the Museum. Then there was Chris Whites project, a computer program that could provide translations for a number of languages, ancient languages. There were plenty of translation programs online but Chris was trying to improve upon the methodology by, if Max understood it correctly, using a small handheld unit that was not only be independent of any server, but had the ability to read not just the keyed input but handwriting or even inscriptions on objects.

But his project was spread across many of the servers including his own impressively self-built computer system. That system was now, as Max reached the middle of the lab, just as impressively smashed into pieces against the wall. Chris himself sat on a stool slowly spinning himself back and forth on its axis. Despite his predicament he did not seem to be too upset.

"How's it lookin' Chris?" Although he was sure Chris had not seen him approach the younger researcher answered him without looking up.

"Like six more months of winter." He said sarcastically. "All my gear is smashed. And the geek squad is telling me that the program backups I filed are irretrievable. Someone took an 'Axe' to it." Max winced at that. "But the gear is the really bad part. There are components that are going to take a while to replace. When I think of the money it's going to take… Yep, another year maybe."

Damn. Chris had been using a lot of the equipment, and it was now wrecked. If the other stations in the computer lab were smashed too that would leave only the equipment in the North Tower labs. Max could not get access to that without having Dr. Gardener up his butt wanting to know what he was using it for. It was possible to go online from anywhere else in the school but it was the ancient languages database locked in these particular servers that Max was used to… was what would have been best.

DAMN. Even if the equipment in the other station was okay, he was sure he would not be able to get access to it for a good long while. That meant tracking the Stone solely by… what? The tracking records from the crates? That would raise suspicion from the police and Dr. King. Maybe he could just go to the library and dig in and find the damn symbol. That would be the worst and longest way to finding out about it.

Carbon dating? Testing it to see what it was made of? That might give him a time and very possibly a location of origin, a place to start when looking for the symbol. Unfortunately that could mean destroying the Stone itself just to find out. Max reached into his jacket pocket and ran his thumb over the rough edges. He told himself that there were other ways to find out about the Stone.

"Where's Dr. Collins?" he asked Chris who was still spinning.

"I don't know."

"Who's running the show? Who called tech?"

"I did." Came Dr. King's deep resonant voice.

There he was, filling the room with his presence, his frame, and only now did Max realize; with his scent as well. It was like burning wood… cedar. It had not been there a moment ago.

"Where were you this weekend Mr. Madigan?" Funny how everyone decided to get quiet right at this moment; they wanted to see Kings Protégé get ripped for not being there when he was needed most. If there was a pecking order among the research assistants, then Max certainly had been near the top of the list. He was ahead of Fatima but far behind Bazillion, who was in Africa at the moment. Nigeria sure sounded good right now.

"I had… personal business to take care of." This would never fly. "But it's done." He could not very well tell what had been happening to him right here in front of everyone. The worst thing about working for King was that you never really gained any footing with the man. He had fired top researchers, professors, Doctors, even teachers with tenure before, all with good histories at the museum. All of them were let go for infractions of varying degrees, some as minor as excessive lateness. It was not that the man was some crazed tyrant, because he also seemed to have mercy on others who did not have the strongest of resumes. Worst of all he did not play favorites. Everyone knew that King thought very little of Bazillion, but he had given him one of the most coveted research jobs. Collins was the new assistant administrator because King had fired a man with whom he had been working with for fifteen years. Max dared not look away from King's eyes because the man might interpret looking away as some basic character flaw that the Museum should do without. Another thing that he had learned was that when you messed up, keep your excuses and answers short and uncomplicated. Few others knew this method, and it gave the impression that Max wasn't afraid of King, but the truth was the shorter the response the less likely you were to stammer or stutter.

King stared back at him and the room was silent for a second longer. Someone closed the door to the stairwell and Max noticed that King's cedar scent drifted away as the airflow pattern of the room changed. Without burning cedar filling his nostrils he felt calmer. Another moment of King staring…

"Are you sure it's done Mr. Madigan? Perhaps you need more time?" The small crowd around them began to fidget. Surely King was going to get rid of him now they must be thinking. More time? He would soon have all the time he could ever need. Max could almost hear it in their thoughts. But on the contrary; he knew better.

King never played THAT kind of game. If you were gone, then you were just going to be gone. In his time here Max had been present at three firings and never had King been anything less than completely professional and cordial. That meant that he was absolutely serious about extending him more time.

"No sir." And then he realized that there could be an opportunity here. "I know there's a lot of work to do, and I don't want to fall behind on my own project any more than I have to." Out of the corner of his eye he could see a couple of hands going to hips. Surely he would be fired now; expressing selfish concern for his own work over the Museum as a whole.

"I'll extend the due date for your part of the project and thesis Mr. Madigan. We will evaluate compensating you for any excessive cost of the setback. Please feel free to put your own work on hold while you help the other students to get back on track." And that was that.

Then King gave Max his work schedule. That, along with whatever extra hours he would have to spend to help the others, would have him working all week. With no other recourse he accepted the schedule without complaint and then asked King about the extent of the damage, hoping to find out about the equipment he would need to research the Stone. It was not as bad as it looked but Max would be waiting a couple of weeks before he could even think about getting his chance. It would be at least that long he figured before he got any time for himself anyway.

Then King hit him with stark bit of news. "In a few days I will be leaving for Site one…"

Site one in Nigeria!

"…at Cameroon."

…Right! Cameroon!

"Dr. Bazillion has gone missing. I believe it may have something to do with whatever was smuggled into the Museum. Since there are no answers here, I will seek them there."

"I thought the police were still investigating…" whoa now. "…us? You can leave the country with no problem?" Careful… careful.

"I have convinced them that the trip is necessary. Bazillion is missing, probably kidnapped or worse if he discovered the smuggling. The police believe as I do that there may be answers there. They will send along some of their own people as an added security measure." Security? For what exactly? Site one was pretty much secure being deep in… but Site two…

Site Two was deep in the Congo. Well beyond any friendly or welcome area. There was no way…

"Sir?" Max asked. "Bobby wasn't at Site Two… was he?"

Kings eyes never wavered. "Dr. Bazillions guidelines were very specific. Site Two is clearly out of bounds."

"I know Sir." But Max could not let go of the train of thought that was rolling hard out of the station. "But Site Two was far more promising and now… Bobby's missing."

King was already looking back to the papers he was carrying, reviewing someone's progress. The noise level in the room had begun to rise again as the students and other researchers went on to their projects and conversations. Max kept his voice low.

"Was there any reason that Bobby might have risked taking a trip to Site Two?" The only reason that Max could think of was if King directed him to. How badly did King want to find his Tribe? King looked up from the pages in his hands.

"If there was," he said with a tone of finality. "I shall find out when I get to Site One."

With the Security contingent of local police, Max thought. Why were they going again? For King's safety or to prevent his escaping? It was hard to tell because of how much pull he had in city government. Were they protecting him or would rivals be looking to bring him down? Whatever it was it would be good to have them along anyway. If there was evidence that Bazillion had gone to Site Two then the Doctor would likely elect to head into the Congo himself. It would be very dangerous and illegal and Max was sure that the police who went along would have to be ex-military. There was a squad in the South Hills notorious for their military training whom undoubtedly would be the escorts. Again the power of the Museums importance to the city made itself known. Despite the 1st District's voicing suspicions that King was involved in the break-ins, they were allowing him to leave the country, albeit, under police protection. No doubt pressure from the Mayor's office as well as several of the City's special interest groups was already bearing down on them one way or the other. Max wanted to ask more questions but King brought their conversation to an end.

"I'll expect all the students' work to be up to date by the time I return Mr. Madigan." There was no way that was going to happen unless King was going to spend the better part of the year in Africa. King started to turn away but then stopped and set his gaze squarely back in Max's eyes.

"And I want the Department back up and running before then as well."

"I'll let Dr. Collins know." Max stated flatly, almost defiantly, meeting King's dominating gaze with a resolute stare. He was not going to take on jobs that belonged to other staff. This was what King had done with Bazillion, had tried to do with him, and had given up trying with Fatima. Max was not going for it. He loved working at the Museum but he was not trying to run the damn thing.

King's eyes never wavered. "I've already given Dr. Collins his duties." The huge man took a breath. "I'm leaving the Museum in your charge, Mr. Madigan. It's time you took more responsibility"

Before Max could object King placed a heavy hand on his shoulder. "Perhaps you feel that there is a place for you here that only involves research and casual tutoring. That assumption would be wrong. You have been an excellent assistant, an above average researcher, and a fair mentor to the students. However your position here is tenuous at best if that is as far as your career goals extend. My plans for you are far more demanding."

Max felt his jaw tightening as he held back saying; "Did these plans suddenly come up because Bazillion screwed up?" but King seemed to be able to read it in his eyes.

"You will see to the department." He said finally, deciding for them both that they were now in agreement. Max could not see any way to argue with King, not if he wanted to keep his job. He took a quick glance around and saw that King had discreetly moved them away from the rest of the students and staff while they talked. At least no one else had heard. So he loosened his jaw and tried not to look away as he nodded.

"Will you be back by King Day?" He asked though he was not sure why he needed to know.

"Most likely not." And he turned and left, stalking off into a side door that led to his inner office. The opening of that door caused the air to swirl about and Max was hit with the return of the fading smell of burning cedar, and then... jasmin?

"Mr. Madigan." Emphasis on 'Mr.'. It was Sheriff Lynne standing just a few feet away with her coat draped over one arm and the other in a sling. His breath caught in his throat at the site of her, the memory of her on the dock replaying in his mind. That night the injured arm had hung limp at her side and she held her gun high and straight with the other. There had been blood, her own, streaked across her face and in her short curly blond hair. The Sheriff had been hurt; although her tightly closed mouth had shown little fear and her eyes had been narrowed with determination as she pointed the gun. The shot had been off and though it had been enough to stop the Maniac from ripping Max's throat out with those wicked claws, it had not been enough to stop him from throwing Max into Cobb's River. She must have killed the Maniac after that, he thought; otherwise, how was it that she was standing here now?

And there was no recognition in her eyes. The police had not come to get him at his apartment, nor had they been waiting for him here, so Max supposed that she really had not seen him enough to recognize him atop the docks the night of the second break-in.

But...but she had looked right into his eyes.

"Detective Lynne. How's the case?" If he was MR. Madigan because he really was not a Professor, then she was going to be Detective.

Even if she really was a Sheriff.

She walked up to him casually, giving him the impression that she had been there for a while.

"Still going nowhere. Plenty of crazies in lock up but not a one of them seem to know why they came to the Museum." The Maniacs! Of course! They had caught some of them, probably a lot, and they must have also caught the one who had tossed him into the river.

"How could they not know?" He asked, playing it cool. Maybe she was still trying to get Max to 'slip up'. The Stone right? The Maniacs had to want the Stone.

"Mostly it's junkie talk. They were high on something. Severe withdrawal symptoms… They're still coming down. I wonder what they were on." She looked at Max pointedly.

He felt the accusation and it angered him but the implication of what she said struck him. They had been wild he thought, wild enough to have been on some kind of narcotic? Sure. "You can't test them?"

"Not legally no. Whatever it was, it was bad. They actually seem to be getting worse, not better. You should here the crazy, religious, cult-like talk. But in the end they'll tell us. They'll tell us what it was they were after in the Museum, and they'll tell us who gave them whatever it is they're on." Again the direct and accusatory look at Max with her solid, strong eyes. Her jasmine scent had no sour smell to it. He felt his anger rising as it had in the police headquarters.

Before he could respond the Sheriff pulled aside the coat she had folded over her arm and revealed a large travel case. One handed, she opened it up and pulled out a folder. She played at opening it up for a moment but she was still holding her coat and with her other arm in the sling it was too difficult. Seeing that, Max could not hold onto the anger that he was trying to let build.

"Here." He reached out and took the folder from her. Inside was a sketch portrait of what he thought was a man in a Halloween costume. He had seen masks like this one being sold at the malls last year. Beneath the first sketch was another. What did these have to do with anything? He thought as he flipped to the second. It was another man in a mask, but this one also had… WHOA! Long slits for pupils!

It was a very BAD sketch of the Snake-Maniac, drawn by someone who assumed that the Maniac had been wearing a mask; the kind that sat over your eyes and nose but left the mouth exposed. The fangs in the Maniac's mouth looked terribly fake and a lot stubbier than Max remembered. But the mottled, scaly skin of the mask was very close.

"What are these?" he asked her curiously but calmly. He wondered if he had any visible reaction to recognizing the Maniac.

"Those two characters were at the Museum last week. Tore it up pretty bad. We figure they were responsible for the deaths on New Years Eve." She was looking at Max evenly. He could tell that she was in fact judging his reaction.

"Some kind of cult we think," she explained. "…playing out some religious or Pagan holy war. These two nearly escaped from the docks, by way of the river."

These two? Max turned back to the first sketch.

"They're both probably dead," The Sheriff continued. "… but so many got away that we're sure there'll be two more to take their place."

The hood was wrong. It was drawn more as a turban, coming down around his face. That would be the scarf Amanda had given him. Part of the design was even drawn in but the artist placed red, animal-like stripes across it instead of little red "A"s. The scarf was supposed to keep his face hidden but the face on the drawing was still revealed quite a bit. And what it revealed was not good. It was drawn as a mask but that was not what worried him the most. First was the fact that just like the drawing of the Snake Maniac, the sketch of Max included a wicked set of fake fangs, drawn more canine-like, or feline he thought. Then the artist rendered the skin as if it were covered with fine hairs and tufts sprouting from his chin much like small mutton chops. The nose was raised more than it should have been, again in a feline like manner. Finally; his eyes, the pupils were narrow, cat like, and drawn in the most sinister manner. What was this?

How could anyone think that he looked like this? Maybe they all saw the Snake Maniac and somehow transferred the images onto him?

But then Max remembered the reactions of some of the police who had seen him up close. They were terrified, as was Phil, the guard. He had screamed at him in the East Hall and the guard had run off in what Max had initially thought to be fear of the Maniacs. And when he had pulled the Maniac off of one the wounded officers, the police's reaction was one of utter terror. At the time Max thought it was because of the claws that had slid out of his fingers but if this was what he looked like?

"Look familiar, Mr. Madigan?" Damn! He had been staring at the sketches too long. Sheriff Lynne was bound to be even more suspicious of him. At least she did not recognize him from the Dock.

"They got away?" he asked, trying to avoid her question. She kept her eyes locked on his, steadily searching for guilt. His mind continued to go over that night, trying to remember anything that would indicate that he had indeed been transformed into that monster in the sketch.

"They both jumped into the river. It's being dragged but no one thinks they'll be found. Bodies probably went all the way to Church Falls and are in the Park right now. Any idea what they're made up to be? Anything to do with something the Museum was researching or collecting?"

Honestly… "No." There was nothing Max knew of that the Museum was displaying that would have anything to do with…snake men. There had been…

"What is it?" Lynne had seen the hesitation in his eyes. Something from Cobbs River had gotten onto his skin, he had thought at the time. Something thin and brown that would not come off. Was it fur?

"I don't know of anything." But he could tell she did not believe him. "Maybe something that was in the crates. But nothing we have been working on."

"But you went through the crates?"

"Yea, but only to inventory it. I never looked at the pieces to see what they were." And maybe it was time he should.

"Well, maybe you could do that for me?" she grabbed the folder from him, walked away towards the other researchers in the room and began to show them the sketches.

Max tried to look busy, checking on the other research projects, but his mind wandered back to the contents of the crates. Nothing had resembled the Stone, not in the least. So it must have been hidden in the crates and not listed on the manifest. The police had said that the weight difference between what had been listed there and what was actually in the crate was something around six pounds. Six pounds? That would be a LOT of Stones! The one he had weighed only a few grams. What if the other Stones did the same thing for the Maniacs that the Stone Max had was doing to him? That could explain the Snake Maniac. Then why had there been only one of them? And why did it seem that Max's transformations seemed to favor a cat and the Maniac's a snake?

The Snake Maniac had jumped into the river after him. If Max had survived the swim surely the Maniac had. Though he had been wounded, shot in fact. Not that it had mattered; there had been at least six pound of Stones, probably intended to be passed out among other Maniacs. That meant there were more out there, a lot more.

Sheriff Lynne would look subtly over her shoulder at him every once in a while as she continued to question the other researchers. Once again Max considered turning the Stone over to the police and letting them handle it. But was his body ready? No. He was too scared to attempt to remove the Stone again. Besides, what would just giving the Stone to the police lead too anyway? Would they even believe him?

Worse, he would be totally unprotected without it. The Maniacs could still be lying in wait, waiting for him to show himself at the Museum. The fact that they had not come for him at his apartment meant that they, like the police, had no idea who he was. He hoped.

So for the time being he would keep the Stone and try to research it on his own. The Sheriff had already given him an excuse to look in the crates again for all the good that would do. Both the police and King had both found nothing.

King was going to Africa. Whatever Bazillion had found over there, King was sure to discover for himself. That would be great as long as Max could hold out that long. There was no telling when the Maniacs would attack again. There were a ton more police watching the Museum, but an attack, as Max knew, could come at anytime and anywhere on campus. He would have to keep his activities centered around the Museum, which would be easy enough considering all the work that he had to do.

KING DAY

One tedious and very unproductive week passed at the Museum. Once King left it seemed that the fire that had been lit under the grad students collective asses had gone out. Not that Max could blame them seeing how much of the progress they had made on their personal projects had been lost. Many of the setbacks were due to computer problems. Until the South Towers server was back up there was going to be a lot a waiting around to see how much information was really gone. Apparently Max had missed one of the Maniacs attacking the server station with as much enthusiasm as they had been attacking him. And since servers can't fight back, or run…

Convincing those in the program to start gathering their research again as if the servers were totally lost was not easy. Too many of them had not been as disciplined as they should have been in keeping their projects backed up while many of the rest needed the unique systems of the Museums isolated network to continue at all. And they all seemed to want to blame the Museum. It was almost as though they thought they should be passed by default because the Museum lost their work. Max knew their tune would change once King returned but that would mean that nothing would have been accomplished while he was gone. And that would come down on Collins and Max. So they came down on the students a little harder than was maybe necessary but if it got them hustling it was going to be worth it. Still it made for a tough week.

At least the police had kept the fact that both he and King were suspected of being involved in the break-in to themselves for the time being. This had more to do with City politics, he guessed, than any kind of courtesy.

Before Bazillion had left, Max had never really been asked to do much in the way of mentoring, teaching, or anything really to do with handling the daily responsibilities of the South Tower projects. It was not something that he was comfortable with. Despite his bitterness at having basically lost the competition of peers with Dr. Bazillion, Max had actually enjoyed the freedom the lesser role as assistant had afforded him. Now he was more involved with several projects of which he had no interest, rather than his own work. The researchers continued to come to him for help on their own projects. In the past, it had never been so frequent that he could not set them on the right path or defer them to someone who could help them. Now with the state of the Museum's computer system Max found himself having to give advice and instruction that had a bigger impact on the student's projects and their futures than he had ever had. To have that many people depending on him for things that so were important to them was becoming too much for him to handle. What if some bit of his advice ended up sabotaging someone's project? There was many an afternoon when Max found himself hiding in the library to avoid having to fix even one more problem.

Dr. Collins was very little help as well. Max expected to have the researchers to look after but the day-to-day administrative stuff was supposed to go to Collins and other support staff. Somehow painters, construction foremen, and the Heads of the other Towers were finding their way to him instead. As much as Max loved working at the Museum, as much of a home it had been to him, he would have done anything to keep from having to run the damn thing. Never-the-less Max tried his best, knowing that King would not accept anything short of what he himself would have done. Odom King could be a harsh judge, and Max had already used up his years worth of screw-ups. Even the upcoming celebration planning had given him several hours' worth of paperwork and a few nights of going to bed with a headache. At least neither that cat nor the Maniacs had shown themselves again.

And his attempt to find anything from the crates turned up almost nothing. There were no more Stones left behind, which could have meant that the Maniacs had the rest of them in their possession. But then why continue to come to the Museum? Just to get the one Stone Max had? He supposed it was possible that the Stone he wore was just a piece of a larger item. But again why would they still come after him? Could the one piece be more important? The only odd thing he found when checking the crates was that one of the artifacts had been damaged in a rather odd way.

There was a primitive axe, Max was unsure of its origin, which had been split into two pieces. The blade had come free from the handle. When Max felt along its length he found that there was an impression left from the thread or twine that had been used to keep the parts together. Searching through all the crates unfortunately, turned up no such wrapping. It could have come that way he guessed but then Bazillion would have been sure to wrap the blade and handle together with something else.

None of the items were hollow, nor was there a space in the crates that could have hidden a small cache of Stones. That could have meant several things. One idea Max had, was that the Stones had been added after Bazillion had packed the crates. Or…

Max thought of the Snake Maniac again. What if the Stone had not come from the crates but rather from one of the Maniacs who ransacked the Museum? Could they have already had the Stones? But then why did they attack the Museum? The sooner he could find out where it came from the sooner he guessed he would know.

January 15th, King Day. Traditionally this was one of the livelier events held at Haley Museum. It was an all day affair with visitors from all over the city joining in the programs. Those visitors included; community groups, religious organizations, and many of the elementary and high schools from around the city. The Museum was a packed house with people coming to celebrate one man's birthday.

On this day there was plenty to do. Several networking quorums and discussion groups were held in the Museum's classrooms and lobbies. There were prayer groups and services being held in the chapel. Anyone who could get a seat could watch plays and enjoy bands or vocalists performing in one of the auditoriums or the outdoor stages that had been set up. It seemed that nothing was going to dissuade the rest of the city from coming to the castle. Not a few homicides or assaults nor even a foot of snow could deter them. Every booth, and or stage was crowded with the visitors who were mostly school children. As a child Max had visited the Museum on King Day. His elementary class had performed a play in one of these auditoriums, though he could never remember which one.

It was a good day for King Day, the weather was quite warm for this time of year and the snow well shoveled. The clear sky held no threat of bad weather, as it had for most of the winter season. Despite his own problems Max felt particularly good as he walked around the outer bailey. Not a single person had bothered him today about Museum business whether it was research problems or administration nonsense. All the King Day preparations had been handled by another department entirely so he did not have to worry about that. And without a whiff of a Maniac in over a week Max could not help but to let his guard down a little and was able to enjoy the festivities.

The drama club from Sisters-of-the-Holy-Trinity High School was using one of the larger outdoor stages, set in the outer bailey. The kids from Holy Trinity had invited groups of children from the catholic elementary schools for whom they were patrons, to perform with them. With so many kids here it was also the most watched performance of the day. Parents and teachers laughed and applauded as the children reenacted sit-ins and retold speeches.

The children from the elementary schools wore their individual school colors during their play and all could see that plenty were represented. That included St. Peters, the grade school that Max had attended, who he saw were now wearing their burgundy and gold. That was a long time ago for him; still the memories came back easily. Though few of those memories matched what he now saw. The children on stage were all smiles even as they pretended to be oppressed and vigilant in their mock non-violent protest. There had been few outings like this for the kids at St. Peters when Max had been there. There had been very little fun at all and it was good to see it now.

"I haven't seen you at mass recently, Maxwell."

He laughed out loud. Karen Robbins was the only secular teacher at St. Peters during his time there and consequently the one he loved the best. She was also the first Black teacher to work there as well which had been a shame for a school full of Black students. Her hair was still colored amber, so Max saw no hint of gray and her skin was filled out with a little weight gain that comes with age so few telltale wrinkles were evident. If it were not for the fact that Max was no longer four feet tall he might have thought that no time had passed at all since she had been his teacher.

"Hey Ms. Robbins!" and he hugged her. "I WAS at mass. I was in the back!" and she laughed. The fact of the matter was that her greeting had been an old joke. The pastor of St. Peters, who told Max never to return after his eighth grade graduation ceremony, had never taken the time to know that "Max" was not short for Maxwell. Since then old man had seemed to forget his personal excommunication of Max whenever they encountered each other. Father Boyle always wondered why he never saw Max on Sundays.

"I see St Peter's on the stage there." He nodded to the stage.

"Yes. Things are different now. You should come back. These kids could use a good positive example of a St. Peters kid who made good." Ms. Robbins was always on him about mentoring some of the students. Most times he felt guilty about not finding the time to help out.

"If it weren't so crazy here at the Museum right now…" she was twisting her face up at him as he spoke. "…then I'd have to come up with some other excuse for why I can't help out."

"Why do I always have to beg you to come back Max?" That hurt. He had never thought of her persistence as begging and the fact that she felt that way shamed him a little.

"You know St Peter's wasn't my favorite place. Besides, I got kicked out."

"You got kicked out of M.R.U. but you came back to finish up."

"That wasn't the same thing…"

"St. Peters isn't the same anymore. And you can help to make sure it doesn't go back to that. Just come back and talk the kids. They need to see someone who's from where they're from, who is such a success."

"Ooh you're good. You've been working on your game." Max

breathed a sigh as she laughed. "Maybe after all the craziness that's been going on here has been settled. I'll set something up and you can bring a class or two up here for a program."

"Not a 'program' Maximillion, you're going to talk to them."

"Whoa, whoa, whoa!" he began looking around to see if anyone heard her use his full name. "Max! Just "Max" around the white folks Lady!"

While she laughed he spied a familiar sight over her shoulder. Fatima Douglas was walking among the booths. She had not been back to work all week and had not returned any of his calls. After seeing the police sketches he was not worried about her having recognized him, not really.

He excused himself and said goodbye to his old teacher. The play was winding down anyway and she had to corral her students.

With the exception of a slight bruise on the left side of her jaw, Fatima did not look any worse for wear. As a matter-of-fact she looked rather cheerful. Even though it was relatively warm today she was dressed for cold weather, with her scarf wrapped around her neck, a thick knitted hat and matching gloves.

"Fatima." He was hesitant.

"Hi Max."

Hmm… now was that a "Hi Max" Hi Max, or a "I know you're a Cat-Man" Hi Max?

"Heard you tore up the Museum again?" Was he never serious?

"Very funny." She said flatly but she smiled at him anyway, though not without a hint of gloom. "Was that Ms. Robbins?"

"Yup. She's here with St. Peters." It had been a bit of a revelation when Max discovered that Fatima had attended St. Peters as he did. Although she had been there some years after he had graduated, they shared a lot of the same teachers.

"So? When can I expect you back?" he asked with straight face.

"When can YOU expect me back?" she asked him back cocking her head and putting her hand on her hip with attitude. Yea… she was definitely feeling better.

"Yea. You do know King left me in charge? I've got plenty of work for you too."

"If you're in charge then how come you don't know I came back today?"

Uh… "I can't be expected to keep track of every minor employee. What have you been working on?"

"Dr. COLLINS had me tracking some deliveries to Dr. King back from site one. He's been talking him with all morning."

Max had seen Dr. Collins earlier and the man had said nothing to him about talking with Dr. King. As concerned as he was with finding out everything he could about the origin of the Stone, Max found that he was a little relieved that Collins had taken care of something without involving him.

"Did they find anything?" he asked.

"I don't know." Her pleasant demeanor was fading. "But he didn't look happy. He wouldn't talk to me about it."

That sounded serious. He knew he should go see what was up. His day would probably be spoiled, but he could not let anything that concerned the Stone pass him by.

"I'll go see what's up." He could not keep the edge out of his voice.

"I'll go with you." She said and fell in step with him. He was used to her making sure she was in on any Museum business that involved him on but that had been as a matter of competition. From the complete change in her body language Max knew that now she was more afraid of not knowing what was going on. It was an admirable quality he thought. Fatima could have tried to pretend nothing was wrong, or just left the Museum entirely. But she was here and she wanted to know what was happening and what was being done. Max loved the Museum and he was beginning to understand that she loved it too.

They entered Rebels Keep in tandem and Max caught the scent of the Downhills people. He looked around but they were not in the foyer, nor were they in the South Hall lobby. The scent began to fade as he and Fatima entered and climbed the South Tower stairwell. He wondered if the furry old man was here somewhere. Was the girl?

The door to Dr. Collins office was closed and there came no sound from within. At least none that Fatima could hear. To Max the sound of Collins' breathing was clear enough. He was taking strong shallow breaths. Something was bothering him.

They knocked but the Doctor did not answer, although his breathing changed.

"Maybe he went downstairs." Fatima offered. Max only knocked again, this time more purposefully.

"Dr. Collins. It's Max." he did not want to just barge in, but there was something wrong. He knocked again and again and finally…

"Come in Mr. Madigan." Collin's desk was a mess, the kind of mess that was made by someone who was searching for something. Not that the office was often neat anyway, but this was a little beyond the regular mess. "Oh, Ms. Douglas. Please both of you sit down."

Fatima took the chair in front of the Doctor's desk while Max cleared a stack of files off a smaller chair by the window and pulled it up.

It was bad. Collins was not even looking at the two of them. In all the time he had worked at the Museum, they had never really had a situation this bad. It was very unsettling to see the Doctor like this. He had been dressed for the day, which meant his good suit. Now the tie was pulled down and hung loosely about his unbuttoned collar and he did not even have his glasses on although he must have been reading one of the papers on that desk.

Fatima seemed to have run out of her determination to face the bad because she simply sat in the chair almost as if she were content to let Collins decide whether or not to tell them anything. Or maybe she had some reservoir of patience that she had not shown before.

"What's happened?" because that was what this was about; something had happened; not was "going" to happen, not "this turned out to be that" or "we didn't get the thing". Something bad had happened.

"Dr. Bazillion is dead." He said. This was probably the first time Dr. Collins had given this kind of news to someone. It came out a little abrupt and he kind of looked at them after he had said it as if waiting to see if he had done it right.

"Oh my God." The tears came from her eyes faster than the words from her mouth, still Fatima did not sob. Max became stone faced.

Robert Bazillion. Doctor Robert Bazillion, actually. They had entered Mountairy Rock University as freshman together. When Max returned to school after his brief exile Bazillion was just adding the title Doctor in front of his name. Despite the difference in their status they became immediate rivals. Bazillion fancied himself King's successor but Max was soon given as much if not more responsibility for King's projects. Still, in the course of their ongoing rivalry Bazillion had come out on top in most competitions. So when the opportunity to go to the Africa came up it was Bazillion and not Max who was given the chance. He had never liked Bazillion, not from the moment they had met. The useless rivalry between them may have been started by now late Doctor but Max was just stupid enough to buy into it. They battled over almost anything that lay in their collective field of vision and neither of them had won anything of any real value except for the position in Nigeria.

…and look how that turned out for Bazillion.

Max worried that he should feel bad. Not that the rivalry between them made him enjoy this in anyway. It was just that Bazillion's death was more than just another tragedy. It was an ominous warning.

"What happened? How did he die?"

"They haven't said." He could see the dread in his eyes. None of this was going to be over anytime soon.

King was not going to be coming back soon either. Apparently he was going to gather more information on the artifact shipments as well as the circumstances of Bazillions untimely death. It made sense; he was not going to go all that way without finding some answers. He should be safe enough Dr. Collins assured them, with the police escort there with him.

But Dr. King did not know what he was up against. Not really. What if some of the Maniacs had found their way to Site One? Could that have been how Bazillion died? Certainly if Bazillion had been the one who sent the Stone, or Stones, to the Museum then he should have been able to protect himself. Unless he just was not as lucky as Max had been so far. Or maybe he was not the one who sent them in the first place.

"I need…" Max caught himself. "I would like to talk with Dr. King."

"He won't be able to talk to anyone until he returns from Site One. The valley it lies in cuts off any transmissions. What's the problem?"

No one knew about the Snake Maniac being more than just a man in a mask. He should have talked to King before he left. But he could not just say that to Dr. Collins.

"Did they say when he died?" Max asked instead of answering.

"No. I assume Dr. King will let us know everything when he returns." If he returns, Max thought. Fatima's' eyes were dry now Max noticed; although she was still upset. He wondered at her strength now. Would she stay, or would she ask for time off? Not that he could blame her if she did. Looking at her now he did not think that she would. She sat upright in her chair; hands clasped tightly together, and listening intently to what Collins was saying. She only needed to wipe her eyes just once more. He wondered where she was drawing the courage from.

Max excused himself and walked to the assistants' office where he had kept his own research notes which was everything he had on King's mystery tribe. All the information he had found himself, which amounted to very little. Then he made his way back down and out into the inner bailey. It was very crowded here, as there was much less space for the visitors than in the outer bailey. At the moment then there was a large contingent of workers among the guests. They were busy tearing down a stage that had been used earlier that day in preparation for a social 'meet and greet' later that day. It was a sort of last second arrangement brought on because of the good weather. Someone wanted to take the opportunity to network with some of the city's elite under the starry sky. As such, and also due to King's absence, Max supposed that he was expected to be there.

They could forget that.

To avoid getting in the way of the workers, he walked the long way around Wolf Den tree. The Queen was exceptionally wide, even for a Queen Rockwood. So big that the knurled rolling roots of the tree tore up the ground enough to create a winding twisting set of tunnels along one side, known as the Wolf's den. It was roped off both for safety and to preserve the aged tunnels from undue wear and tear. The courtyard sat out in front of the big tree and the burrow, which was why the space in the inner bailey was so limited. While the Great Hall and Wolf's Keep sat so close behind it that the upper branches pushed up against the walls of the castle. There was a tight path behind it, uneven and rolling over thick roots, that Max negotiated to get past the tree. It was a little dark and shadowy, but Max had used it many times before when crossing the Inner Bailey to get to his preferred study hole.

The library, named Edward's Library for one of the founders of the University, lay across the small courtyard. It was one of Max's favorite places in all of Rock city.

The library was one of the first places in M.R.U. that had felt like home to Max when he started at the school so long ago. It was huge, but not daunting, complicated but not confusing, and Max had mastered its inner workings quickly, but not completely. That was probably the best part of the library. There were still little nooks and crannies, and surprising properties that it kept secret, waiting to be discovered. These hidden nooks always kept Max coming back here whenever he was stumped or reached a dead end. There would always be the chance that the library still had the answer hidden away.

Even in the Library there was an event. A lecture or seminar, Max had to guess having ignored the poster on his way in. There was a small group of people seated on the main floor. Before them, on a small platform, a small skinny man, the speaker continually referred to a huge map of Rock Park. On the map were several red markers, tags with little flags on them. Max noticed that none of the tags were in the center of the Park, no one went there.

"The third cause is an old one," the speaker was saying. "The attempt in 1920 to run gas lines through the Park. Though abandoned, many of the lines are still connected to the present system. Decades of minor bleed through have led to large deposits of gas that eventually find their way to the surface and…"

Oh… The Parks erosion problem. Max had experienced this first hand at the river. He did not think that the mudslide was from gas deposits but was a part of the overall dilemma. There was a tiny flag on the map at about the same spot where the bank had collapsed. This could be some kind of Park Commission meeting but why where they here at the Museum today? All the events were supposed to be King Day events, but this hardly qualified.

The floor study tables were all taken up by the gathering, not that Max would have wanted to sit among the group anyway. So he turned and made his way to one of the staircases located next to the entrance. The second level to the library held stacks and more study tables. Only a few of these were occupied, so it did not take him long to find a place to work.

Three hours in and Max had found nothing new. This meant that he still had virtually nothing at all.

Kings Lost Tribe. There was not much that Max really had on their history. Some symbols but no name even or any bits of language what so ever. There was the armband, which King wore, was a warrior's band, in theory, from that same tribe. Again Max had seen similar markings among the tribes along western shores of Africa but nothing that could identify them as the same tribe. That marking had only been found somewhere else once, that he knew of, and that was by Max himself. Engraved on the wall of a hidden tunnel that had, at one time, been a stop along the Underground Railroad it had been hidden behind some fungal growth. Max had kept the find to himself as the competition between he and Bazillion was in full swing. The combination of the competition and the fact that King was so tight lipped about his own discoveries made Max feel he had to keep the find a secret. Only King's best students and assistants were involved in the project but the man had kept his own discoveries mostly to himself. The fact that he knew far more than everyone else was a given. In meetings he never shared his own findings or theories. Occasionally he would tender more than a passing comment. It was almost as if he were testing them at the same time he was doing his own research. So Max was sure that pressing him about it would somehow lose him points while finding out information on his own might be a little different. As a matter of fact he was sure of it. King seemed to respect that kind of initiative or at least that is what Max told himself. Ever since seeing the engraving, a symbol shaped like a crescent moon cradling a smaller full moon, he had been obsessed with the idea of a small tribe of slaves having survived the Diaspora fully intact and yet somehow leaving no trace of themselves back in Africa. There had to be more to their story. They had to have done more. King's armband was proof of that wasn't it?

Now somehow their search for the tribe had lead Bazillion to stumble across the Stones. Or had it? King obviously had not known about them, or he would have grabbed the crates the moment they arrived at the Museum. It was very possible that someone had used Bazillion's shipment as a matter of convenience just as a way to get the Stones to Mountairy Rock. They may have been unconnected to the Museum or to the project. Still, the project was the only connection Max had right now.

So he had poured through book after book. For the better part of his post grad career, he searched for clues until every resource he could get to dried up. Only the Edward's Library continued to sporadically keep him going. He researched everything the library had on the Underground Railroad, at least until he found some more hidden resources and information in some previously lost book. Even so clues to the Lost Tribe were elusive.

The book he was staring at now he had read so often that it could no longer hold his attention. Despite himself... his mind drifted.

The Stone. Yet another symbol he would find himself searching for. This one should be easier he thought, if only he could get some kind of place or time of origin. A zigzag line, the kind that could signify water or lightning, placed above three diagonal slashes and all of it surrounded by an elliptical circle that was broken on both ends. Easier he thought, because it seemed so familiar. Like he had...

Then came a wonderful scent: a fresh, sweet, woman's' scent.

Max looked up to see Amanda sitting on the other side of his study table. "Uh? How long have you been here?" he asked laughing a little.

She had her own set of books and loose papers spread out along his/their table. She looked up and smiled back at him.

"You study HARD! I gave up trying to say hello an hour ago." Luckily she did not seem too put out. As casually as he could Max moved aside some of his stacked books to clear some space but she had already "captured" all the territory she needed.

"I'm sorry, lots of work and I'm getting nowhere." he said.

Her eyes were so clear and sharp.

"What are you studying?" he asked, seeing she had pulled some folders and books he had never bothered to look at himself.

She was really pretty.

"Case law. Do you know that hazardous chemicals are being shipped right through Mountairy Rock every month?" Most of the things that Max was aware of outside of his field of study fell into the "theme song from the Transformers" category. Oddly though; this was one of the few subjects that Max actually had some knowledge. He frowned. To his knowledge Mountairy Rock's rare and unique ecosystem was supposedly protected by law.

"It's supposed to be." Amanda told him. "But there are always loopholes. They drive the stuff right through the Park too."

Feign concern, and worry over the danger. "If there were an accident in the park..." and shake head ruefully.

"It's serious!" she said twisting her mouth at his words and the little rasp in her voice becoming a tiny throaty rattle. "That park has an effect on everything from here to Florida."

"Not to mention," Max added more seriously. "...that the park is home to many species of plants and animals that have yet to be seen by anyone. They could be extinct before we even get to know them. How are they getting away with that?"

"Lincoln's Pass is legally an interstate, so..." she and some of her friends were pseudo activists Max gathered. He had seen some things on campus about this but had never really paid much attention.

Even now, as he realized that he was becoming more and more attracted to Amanda; he was only half listening to the legal talk. Not that some company running dangerous chemicals through the Park was a trivial thing. It was just that Max was fairly sure that someone would put an end to it before something actually happened. Right now he was looking at soft brown eyes, listening to the sexy, throaty rasp of her voice, and being filled with her wonderful scent, like some kind of blossom.

"Heard there was more commotion here after I saw you running that night." She switched the subject. Max was sure that he had been wearing his best "I'm totally interested" look on his face.

"Yeah; another break-in. They ripped up the labs and research facilities this time." He explained some of the damage and how everyone had been set back.

"Were you there?" and Max thought there was some concern on her face. He could not tell her what had happened but he still did not want to lie to her... even though he did not really even know her... yet.

"I was off that night. But there were some research assistants here. The way I hear it, though, the cops got here just in time. They caught some of them. Shouldn't be too long before they know why they were breaking in."

"They weren't just stealing?"

"Nope. Just vandalism... well... and the murders. Nothing was taken. Although the police think there was something in the Museum that maybe we didn't know about."

Odd how easy it was to tell her about the problems at the Museum. She must be a lot better at faking her concern than he was. Still he was careful not to mention that the police were targeting himself and King as suspects.

"I haven't noticed any increase in security since then." Amanda said with more concern. There had not been an incident in weeks and it was getting late. She was looking across over the balcony and across the great room to the huge picture windows with the western view. The sun was setting in the clear sky and amber colored distant clouds filled the horizon just over the snowcapped City reservoir on the highest point of the ridge. The sun was sinking slowly and the view was growing darker.

"There really are more security people. Plus there's always a police car or two sitting outside... probably some undercover inside as well. They know how the vandals had been getting in undetected so it shouldn't be a problem anymore. More cameras too, so if anything does happen they'll come running."

"And where's my scarf?" oh jeez!

"Sorry. I was sick for a few days after that run. I have it at my apartment."

Good time to ask her how she was getting back to her own place. Walk her home… get her number…

"Max?" and they both looked up. It was Fatima. Why was she still here? Then Max finally noticed her scent. He could practically taste the acrid nervousness. The pattern of the circulating air flowed around and came at him from behind. That was why he had not noticed either woman's scent until they were right in front of him.

"What's up Fatima?"

"Cleaners need to be let into Dr. King's office and I lost my keys. Could you…?"

Max knew she did not want to borrow his keys; she wanted him to go up there himself. There was no way she should be walking around the museum by herself. She only just came back to work.

"Sure. Why are you here by yourself though? It's late as hell. How are you getting home?" She told him that she had a ride and was leaving just then. So Max begrudgingly said goodbye to Amanda but left his things where they were. This would not take long if he could help it.

The Inner Bailey had turned into a real party while Max had been in the library studying. It was getting darker but someone had set up lanterns over the entire courtyard. There were tables set up there now as well, almost like dining tables but that would be crazy. It was warm but not so warm that they could serve food outside. No one was sitting there anyway. Most if not all of the crowd were up and mingling. It was really a party atmosphere. Almost all of the Museum's Department heads were here and then he remembered that it was a 'meet and greet'. Dr. Collins probably expected him to attend. Max hurried across the courtyard and into the South Tower.

He could hear the cleaners arguing before he hit the landing. Sure it was late and they were ready to get on with the cleaning. King's office was just the first one of the night and they were being held up.

This was the office where the guards had been decapitated. Cleaners had already been through here but King had complained saying that he could still smell blood. It was true. The coppery odor still hung in the office. Max wondered how they were going to get it out.

He was going to find out. The cleaners could not be in the office by themselves because King had several very pricey pieces of art in this room. The cleaning company wanted no part of the blame if something came up missing. So Max slumped down in a chair out of the way and hunkered down for wait. How long would Amanda wait?

He had been in this office many times and had seen and had already examined all the artwork. Finally King had acquired something knew. Peering along his bookshelf it was evident that King had developed a fondness for knick-knacks. Ivory bracelets book-ended one shelf, he could not reach them because they had already shampooed that part of the carpet. There was a necklace hanging around a bust that King had already had and a flint dagger that Max really wanted to look at, but again; wet carpet.

Finally the cleaners were done and Max's head was spinning from the strong ammonia in the air. It was really late now and Max was certain that he had missed his chance to get Amanda's number. He had not seen her in two weeks so it could be another month before he caught up to her again.

Of course he still had Rosette's number.

They probably had separate lines though and Max did not like calling women who did not give HIM their phone number. Steve had the franchise on that strategy. Maybe she would come back to study again? Great. Max was pushing thirty and hoping for a study date. What a punk.

Sure enough she was gone when he eventually made it back to the library. The Parks meeting was going full force though with voices raised and fingers pointing. The most raucous among them was a group of mostly older gentlemen, a few of whom were wearing ceremonial sashes. Their senior member was shaking his fist at the small man at the podium and his voice boomed throughout the library.

"We're not willing to wait SIX MONTHS! Those buildings were condemned over a year ago! They must be demolished NOW!"

The rest of the men echoed him in loud chorus. The man at the podium had to yell to be heard.

"Six city blocks of housing and commercial buildings can't be queued for demolition just like that! There is also the erosion problem to…"

"Erosion problem aside," The older man cut him off with another chorus of angry shouting by the group behind him. Max took another look at those sashes and realized who they were; Masons. There were Temples all over Mountairy Rock but he could not tell which one these men represented. Not that he was all that curious. He sidestepped the gathering trying his best to pass by without disturbing them.

It was just getting dark outside, and there were a few more events that were going down after sunset that most would not want to miss. The Museum was a twenty-four hour research facility and that meant that the library was open twenty-four / seven, and even holidays during programs. So there was still a student librarian working and despite the racket from the meeting in the main room he was asleep.

The poor guy had probably been here most of the day and now had to chaperone the evening programs. So instead of just leaving them Max gathered and returned the books he had been looking through, which took him a good fifteen minutes. It was just as he was scooping up his notes that he saw it. On the top off his planned outline lay Amanda's phone number.

He was right; she had her own line.

Definitely in a better mood now Max hurried back out of the Library and waded through the still partying crowd. He had a pretty good idea of where to take Amanda. All he needed to do was to call in another favor and… There was that Downhills scent again.

Max stopped dead in his tracks. The smell bothered him for some reason. Everyone in the courtyard left some bit of scent in the air but the Downhills scent was very distinctive and a little stronger maybe. Why was this bothering him? There were people from all over the city here for King Day. Why would…

His ears twitched… he inhaled deeply the cold air through his nostrils. There it was; a heavy, heady scent that was so damn familiar.

Max looked around the courtyard of the Inner Bailey and the dark corners lit up to his eyes. There were so many people and they were everywhere. None of them looked like Downhills folk but then again he probably would not be able to see the typically shorter people through this crowd. So he inhaled again and began walking; Past Dr. Busby and that terrible Brute cologne… past Dr. Rowling, who had way too much to drink… past the fading scent of Dr. Collins' cheese breath…

Finally the Downhills musk grew stronger, nearer to Wolf Den tree.

It drew him around the tree, toward the back, then behind it before it grew weaker and he lost it. He had to retrace his steps until he found it again. This time it lead him up the steps into the Great Hall; the Administration offices. There was not supposed to be anything being held here Max knew. What were they doing inside?

"I told you he'd be here." The deep guttural voice seemed to whisper in his ear from just behind him. But Max immediately knew that it had come from farther away just like the night he had been attacked outside the student center.

"Yo this is crazy. My physics Professor is here man." Another voice joined the first. Max could hear breaths rising with excitement.

"I'm tired of waiting to beat this fool down! Now come on." Said the first. Yet another voice agreed.

"Don't be a bitch man. This is our chance."

As casually as he could Max turned away from the Office steps and looked around the Inner Bailey. It did not take him long to spot the rather out of place group of young men hunkering in the corner by the end of the buffet table. There were four… five of them that he could see but likely more were walking about the courtyard. The group watched him but Max kept his own line of sight vague and let his eyes drift across the crowd still keeping track of them with his peripheral vision.

"Nook, Jay; walk around the other side of the tree." He heard the first voice say. Now he recognized this as the same voice from the

The Serpent Cult

Student center, the one claiming Rosette as his woman.

Two blurry forms moved away from the rest. A month and a half ago Max would have been really worried. Now his only concern was that the party was going to be disrupted. One quick look around the courtyard and he did not see any Security people. It would be a disaster if he let a fight break out right here. But then maybe…

He turned, walked up the steps and pulled open the door to the Great Hall.

Without the winter night air to disperse it, the scent was very powerful once he passed through the doors. There were two distinct scents actually. One was thicker, fuller and musky… masculine. The other, lighter, but more heady… spicy? No, that was not quite right. The scent brought him to the foot of the foyers stairs. The Downhills folk were upstairs somewhere.

He turned and looked back through the glass pane set in the door to see the small group of men advancing through the crowd. Rosette's boyfriend was in the lead and walking at a pace that the others had trouble keeping up with without jogging a little. His eyes were intent and angry. He looked older than the rest, probably no longer a student but he certainly was not old enough to have been here when Max had been a member. This guy certainly seemed to be taking this vendetta seriously, almost personally. For Rosette? Maybe… but then what was her stake in all of this? She was not old enough to have been here then either. Max had only turned twenty-one when it all had gone down. Like bile, regret and bitterness welled up in him at the old memory.

Rho Gamma Phi.

"Let it go Max" he whispered to himself.

The group approached the steps to the doors. Max's muscles tensed and thoughts off throwing them around the dark lobby behind him for a few minutes played in his imagination. He could make sure they never thought about ambushing him ever again.

Or… he could just end up escalating the situation. They had been carrying this grudge for more than half of a decade; one beat down was not going to deter them. How could he burn them for this without making them up the ante? Rosette's boyfriend set a foot on the first step.

A twisted smirk crossed his lips and Max moved across the hall to a small panel and opened it. It took him a second to recall the code but soon the silent alarm was set for the front door. One last look and he saw the Gamma's silhouettes filling the glass paned door and he turned toward the steps intent on tracking that Downhills scent.

It was when he was halfway up the steps that Max realized that he was creeping, sneaking, on tip toe, up the steps as quietly as he could. What was it that made him so apprehensive? Something in their scent?

Or the fact that as quiet as he was being, they were being even quieter? He had not heard a sound out of them even though they were definitely in the building.

The scent got stronger farther up the steps to the third floor. Max stepped off the landing and peered down three dark corridors. Directly in front of him was the hallway that led into Wolf's Keep. To his right lay the staff offices and lounge and to his left were the human resources office and archive. The scent veered to the left.

Behind him and below the front door opened and the Gammas poured in. There were more of them now, at least seven, and they stumbled around the foyer. Max realized in must be pitch black in here to them. For a moment the thought of jumping down and doing to them what they had planned for him almost had him leaping over the banister.

Instead he just watched as they peered about and complained to one another about the lack of light or about being bumped into, and then finally about where the hell Madigan went. One of them kept trying to talk the others into just leaving Max the hell alone, but Rosette's boyfriend was particularly adamant. Yasir, they were calling him.

The front doors opened again and a bright light shone in.

"What are you all doing in here?" said the Security officer. He was flanked by three others and Max thought he saw another standing just outside. Someone yelled out; "Cops!" and another yelled; "Break!". The floor below was filled with the sounds of grunts, hammering boot steps and thumps of colliding bodies. It did not take too long for the Gammas to find their way back out into the courtyard by either running or by being dragged by the Security force. Luckily none of them tried to escape up the stairs and the Security did not seem to think any of them had either. They made such a commotion that the few snickers that escaped Max's mouth went unnoticed.

The Gammas were not sporting their colors so Max doubted that the Fraternity would suffer any more sanctions or punishments. They did not know it but they were lucky tonight; he would have been a lot harder on them.

The door closed behind the last guard and soon the offices were quiet again. Max turned and looked around.

The corridor was empty, his eyes could tell, but the Downhills scent was still very strong here. There were rooms on both sides of the hallway. Only one of them had an open door.

Max paused and listened to the silence.

No one had emerged to see what the ruckus was.

They had remained hidden.

The door lay open but there was no light on. As he drew closer Max was sure that the scents led to this room. No light on but… it

could still possibly be two Downhills kids just getting their freak on.
Max stepped into the doorway.

The room was hot with the lighter, heady, feminine scent. Max
saw standing against the far wall, a shadow, a woman.

"Are we not supposed to be here?" her voice was strong, low,
with a resonance that perfectly matched the headiness of her scent.
What little light managed to enter the room came in from the courtyard
but had to make its way past the thick maze of branches from the
Rockwood. As it was, her face was cloaked in shadow.

"What are you…" the faintest creak came from behind him.

Max snapped his head around. A dark figure emerged from the
previously closed office across the hall and ran at him at full speed.
Regardless of the darkness Max could tell the man was dressed all in
black and had wild ragged hair. Another Maniac? Hadn't he earned a
rep with these fools?

His book-bag hit the ground as Max shucked it and swung his
fist. The contact was satisfyingly hard and loud and sent the attacker
stumbling backwards… a few steps.

Then Max watched as the man shook his head a little, looked
back at him and charged again. This time the Maniac ducked to one side
as Max threw a haymaker and missed. There was a growl and then it
was Max's turn to catch one full on.

Good God the strength behind it! The ground came up fast and
Max hit the cold tile floor. Could this be the same guy he fought on the
dock? Max wondered as he scrambled to his feet. The smell coming off
him said no but…

The Maniac continued his attack and Max back pedaled wary of
the fangs he had seen that unforgettable night but this man seemed
smaller somewhat. The growling was… well growling and not hissing.
He wore all black like a Maniac but it was more like a body suit rather
than the black studded leather.

And no weapons. No mace, battle axe, or crossbow. Who was
this?

There were footsteps coming up from behind him. The woman!
A girl Maniac?

From the Downhills?

If he stayed where he was he'd be trapped. Without a thought
Max leapt backwards over the woman. But the room was small and his
legs hit the paneled ceiling so he came down hard onto what probably
was a copy machine against the window. There was no footing and he
could not right himself before the Maniac rammed into him with his
shoulder. The window did not break, it just popped out of its' frame,
hanging on by one hinge. Max fell out and into the arms of Wolf Den
Tree.

The same spot on his back that had landed on the copier was

the same spot that now came down on the thick curve of Rockwood branch. The branch itself was so thick that Max thought maybe he had hit the ground at first. The fact was he was still quite a ways up in the tree. He rolled onto his knees and looked up into the dark window from which he had fallen.

"I told you." a voice whispered. "He's one."

"Let's go."

"No. We take him!"

The two shadows popped out of the window one right after another with a quickness and grace that was very un-Maniac-like.

There was a fine thick branch to brace himself against and Max used it for the leverage to kick the first to attacker to get to him, the same one who had caught him in the jaw. He fell back into the wall beneath the window gracelessly enough but the second barreled into Max and took them farther into the branches of the Queen Rockwood.

The Queens were like oversized Oak trees and their branches became thick and maze-like the closer to the trunk they were. They were also as wide as sidewalk tiles and so being they were kind of hard to fall off of. Max and his new attacker rolled along one branch until stopped by another thick one crossing its path.

The scent of the woman filled his nose again and he felt how much lighter SHE was than the other. She twisted and got behind him locking her arms about his neck. Her breath was hot behind his ear and she whispered.

"So you're the new head of this house?" her voice was low and husky. Her grip was stronger than it should be. He grabbed at her arm and could not pull her off. "...not much to..." she started.

Max turned in her grasp before she could finish and found her face right up against his. Dark, wicked, feral, lupine eyes met his. She was smiling, and he could see the sharp canines. Lord was she... like him?

"Prya!?!" The other had leapt back up to the tree; his form was a shadow against the wall. They both turned when he called out what must be her name. He could not take them both.

"UNG!" Max threw his elbow into her midsection and her grip slackened. The other charged into the tree and met the bottom of Max's boot. Another elbow into the girl and then Max pulled her arm off of him...

RIP!

"AHH!" Fire tore over his shoulder. Claws! She'd ripped open his shoulder when he pulled her off. But he did not let go of her arm. Instead he gathered himself and tossed her over his shoulder right at her boyfriend. They both flew out of the tree and Max heard very satisfying smacks when they hit the administration wall and then the ground below.

Their running footsteps were quickly drowned out by the din of the crowd and music.

Max lay back in the tree, feeling strangely safe in its branches. His shoulder was not as bad as it felt; it was not even bleeding that much. Her scent was still on him, clinging just over his shoulder. It was still heady, still feminine… a scent he had smelled before. Like those eyes… he had seen them before too…

…in the Downhills…

Security must have been too busy with the Gammas to even notice the fight. There was no further commotion; no one seemed to have noticed the two darkly dressed individuals fleeing through the crowd. How had they managed that?

The party continued on and Max remained in the tree for a good while listening to the music and bits and pieces of conversations. It turned out to be a much better hiding place than a stairwell.

THE DOWNHILLS

Another dragon fizzed by. With blue and green fire spewing from its mouth, it turned and made another run at the front of the balcony before climbing higher as its wings caught the wind. It did not go far, the taught near invisible string kept it from flying free. Instead it looped again and traveled further up the street as the winds and the hands at the other end of that string guided it along.

Max had seen the celebration of the Chinese New Year a few times before but never from the balcony of the Emerald Forest Restaurant. One of the oldest eating establishments in the city, the Emerald Forest sat on the Northwest corner of the Emerald Forest Hotel. The Hotel itself was old enough that it had been built before the Rockwood protection laws had been put into place. As such it was one of seven buildings that were actually built onto a living Rockwood, this one a queen. It was built along, around, and in some places, through the tree but in such a way as to never inhibit the tree's natural growth. Nor did it harm the tree so far as botanists could tell. The Restaurant sat cradled in the bow of the largest branch. Not the highest point of the hotel but it was the highest point on the avenue it overlooked. From the balcony the entire three street lengths of celebration could be seen.

The street was filled with costumed revelers dressed as all sort of mythical figures in amazingly colorful costumes. There were jugglers and acrobats, stilt walkers and fire breathers, and several versions of the Gray Dragon of Mountairy Rock. Hanging between the buildings were not the traditional paper lanterns that were the norm for the Lantern festival, but rather sparkling and spinning lanterns that occasionally fired out green bursting fireworks of their own. Above that rockets flew and exploded sending confetti showering down in such amounts that it filled the air like a heavy green and gold snowfall. Rising out of the cloud of smoke and confetti were the flying dragons, eagles and hawks. The January winds that flew across the park kept the kites aloft even as many of them were supported by rocket powered wings that fired intermittently. There were those that breathed fire; while, others just trailed brightly colored smoke trails into the night sky. Some were held by invisible lines, lending the illusion of independence to their flights, while the other's lines were decorated with frills and tassels. It was quite the visual spectacle that Max had never seen from such a unique perspective.

He really was not seeing it now though.

The green, crimson, and gold lights from a flickering, blossom shaped table lantern played on her face in turn, each highlighting something beautiful. Whether it was the centers of her soft brown eyes reflecting the shining green fireworks, or the gold confetti caught in the red highlights of her hair, or even her smooth brown skin glowing in the warm light it did not matter. Max found nothing in the New Year celebration that was more pleasing than Amanda Allen.

The balcony was an open air balcony, exposed to the chilling winter air, but they were warm. The Emerald Forest owners had installed a system of fans that blew hot air across the dining area. Combined with seating that arranged people side by side, it made for a very cozy experience.

There was a vent somewhere in the rail and it made Amanda's' hair flutter softly. She had worn it out and it fell in supple curls down her shoulders and back, telling Max that the braid had been indeed her own hair. No way she relaxed all that hair he realized, it must be her hairs natural state. What was her ancestry? He wondered, to have hair like that. The anthropologist in him searched her face for West Indian, or Native American features but found nothing telltale. He knew there was no real way to know anyway. Her features marked her typically African-American but were general enough that they could be found in many cultures or ethnic backgrounds. There was software he knew that could help to trace her genealogy back about a thousand years whether through her genetics or her family tree. Maybe he could just ask her.

Instead he continued to listen to her voice. Even with the sexy rasp to it, it was clear. And as soft as it was it was still strong. The rasp gave it a rhythmic vibration that was almost warm. His own voice could come out a little squeaky he knew, when he got excited or even too relaxed. So he keep it low, trying to sound like he wasn't keeping it low, while she told him about her studies, or her job, or about living in Virginia with her Aunt and her family.

And she actually had a sense of humor, a real one, where most women would think that just laughing at his weak jokes counted as having a sense of humor, Amanda was making him laugh.

"There wasn't hardly any room back there anyway for three people in the first place." She was saying. "So every time we had to pass each other it was a tight fit. Now Angel and I would always pass each other butt to butt, you know. And it wasn't even all that often we had to pass each other anyway. I served drinks on my end and she served drinks on her end. But her old dirty ass uncle kept on sliding by me and I know he didn't need to come past me all those times. And never butt to butt, ALWAYS crotch to butt!"

"How do you know he was doing it on purpose?" Max laughed. "Was he… um…"

"You know he'd slide past all slow. And I could feel every last bit of what he was about!" He was laughing harder now as she continued. "And yes he was…UM! And I know he was because he wasn't the first couple of times he slide past!"

"Why didn't you just turn around then?"

"That would be WORSE!" she said as if the very notion was beyond her delicate senses. "I think he would watch for a chance to catch me facing that way so he get a little feel on my chest!"

"So you just let him get free grinds all night?" he could barely get it out, and his voice was squeaking but she did not seem to mind.

"There was a little section right next to the tap where if I jammed my hips into the corner he couldn't get at me without being obvious. So once I found that little space I would just watch for when he was heading my way. And when he was I would run for my little space and jam my butt right in there, I didn't care if I had customers drinks in my hands or whatever!"

"Did you tell your girlfriend about her uncle?"

"She already knew! She was laughing at me all night long."

Another round of drinks, Max noticed she did not order anything with alcohol in it and neither did he for that matter.

"A lot of people never come back after dropping out of school. Why did you?" she asked.

"I didn't really, drop out. I was suspended. For five years." He always grimaced whenever he said that, more from the memory of having to tell his parents that he had basically been kicked out of school than for the actual suspension.

"And…" he continued. "…with my scholarships and grants gone I had to work to get the money together to get even get registered. Took me another couple of years on top of that. But no matter how long it took, I always looked at it as though I was coming back."

"You couldn't just go to school in Philly?"

"Sure. But I got a chance to work at the Museum, you know, cut my tuition in half." But there was more. And Max found that he wanted to tell her. "Plus… I grew up here, in Brookhaven. Love Philly, but I always wanted to come home. Besides I have an Uncle here who helped me get a cheap apartment, made things easier." He took a breath. This was gonna sound corny. "Plus M.R.U. was really the first school I ever went to that I felt like I was a part of. Felt like home to me."

Amanda's smile at what he said was warm and genuine. Strange, it had never been easier to talk to a woman than it was for him right now with her. She was relaxed and seemed very comfortable with him. Almost as if she knew she could trust him even though they really had only just met. That took a lot of the "First date" formalness out of the evening. So he never even went into any of the usual game. No guile, no hard front, just a relaxed Max Madigan.

Not for long.

A scent found its way past the smoke below and was sucked into the warm air stream blowing from the vent. Damp, musky, it was a Downhills scent. Not just any scent, it was hers, the woman who jumped him at the museum; Prya.

"Even with your fraternity still here?" Amanda had not noticed his sudden tenseness. Somewhere down on the street the Downhills woman was about. Was she following him?

"They were supposed to be banned from the school for more than ten years but somebody got them back in early. Even though my scholarships and grants had been lost I still should've been able to get back and graduate without ever seeing them. But…" The scent was fading. Had she moved on? Was she able to smell his scent?

"Funny thing is all the members who are here on campus aren't even the people I went to school with. They're only mad because of the sanctions and probation the frat is still under."

"Maybe," Amanda suggested. "…some of your ex-brothers are still hanging around you know, involved with the fraternity?" She said it like she knew something.

"Maybe." Max inhaled deeply through his nostrils trying to find the scent again.

"AAACHOOO!" That was loud! "Whew!" Too much dust in those vents.

"THAT was loud." Amanda laughed. "Bless you." Pinching his nose was the only way to stop the inevitable second sneeze from busting loose.

"Thanks." That was a little embarrassing. "So, you left M.R.U. for a little while too. I don't think they suspended you."

"No. I started late, money problems. It took me a while to earn enough and get enough financial aid to get here." Max could tell that it bothered her, a little bit, to talk about it. She had told him that her Aunt and Uncle had raised her after her mothers' death. Whenever she talked about anything she hoped to do, it always had a lonely, isolated feel to it. It was almost as if she did not count on her family to help her out with anything. She spoke about that with some regret and anger as well.

They stood on the corner of the street where her apartment building was located. Amanda did not mind being seen with him but Max knew that she might catch a few problems from Rosette. So he would just watch from there until she had made it into building okay. She was a sight, with the gold and jade dragon confetti in her hair. Max leaned in…

"Thanks for remembering my scarf!" her mouth was a twisted smirk.

Oh yeah. "Oh yeah, I swear I'll bring it next time."

"Next time?" she asked with a cocked eyebrow but she was still smiling.

"Yeah, I had thought we had a good time." He said as innocently as possible. She laughed a little.

"Next time." She agreed and then started to her apartment. Then suddenly she turned and looked back at him.

"What year is it anyway?"

"Are you serious?" Max laughed.

"The Chinese New Year. What year is this?"

"Oh? The uh…" he thought for a second. He had no idea but then… "…the year of the Cat!"

"There is no year of the cat! You don't even know." And she laughed and walked to her apartment. It had begun to snow as she went inside. Max hardly noticed the falling flakes as he walked home.

There had been no mention of any problems in the Human Resources department the day after King Day; other than the whole corridor being as cold as a freezer because someone had left a window open. In case there was anything he missed or that his two attackers might have left Max toured the hall again. The cold night air had swept the offices clean; the Downhills scents were gone. Since no one seemed unduly concerned or alarmed Max guessed that the fight could not have caused as much damage or left as much of a mess as he thought it had. The week passed with no further incidents

Back in the South Tower Dr. Collins remained hidden in his office for days. The few times Max walked by he did not hear anything to make him think that there was more bad news. The Professor probably just wanted the time to himself. That was understandable but it did leave Max all alone to handle whatever came up.

"I don't understand. What's the big deal with filling the moat?" Steve had come by and decided to hang out. Something Max would not have allowed if King were still in the country.

"It's not supposed to be filled until spring." He explained.

"So? What happens if it's filled?" WHY was he so interested?

"I don't know… something to do with the reservoir."

"What?"

"I don't know, Steve! It's not my decision anyway."

"Then why are they asking you?"

He ignored at least four more questions from his friend while he scanned the paper in front of him. There had to be someone he could call about this other than Dr. Collins who once again was not answering his phone. The Administrative department had sent this over three days ago and they kept calling Max about it; apparently it was very important. The moat was never filled during the winter, not in all the time Max had been here. He slid the paper to the side when he felt the hint of a headache about to brew.

"Just have to wait." Then to Steve, "Haven't seen you on the bike recently?"

"It's too cold." was all he answered. There was more, there had to be. Steve may not have paid a lot of money for that bike but he certainly should be riding it like he had. Cold or no cold he was not the type of person who could delay gratification.

"Right. It broke down huh?" Max guessed.

Fatima walked into the room. Her desk sat cattycorner and faced his. As always Steve perked up, smiled that smitten smile and greeted her to which she frowned back. Max could count on one hand the number of women who had managed not to fall for his devilish grin. Fatima was one of the few. As always when she ran into Steve, she frowned her face up as if she smelled something bad.

And as always she moved her stapler back to the other side of her perfectly set desk from where Max had previously shifted it. This time though she tossed a package that she had brought in with her, across the room and onto his desk, scattering everything but not really making it any worse.

"What's this?" he turned it over.

"You requested programs for neighborhood schools. That's your package. Ms. Dana asked me to send it up."

The manila envelope was thick and heavy. He had not asked for all of this. Just a small listing of things he could take to his old school, not more work. He really did not need this on top of everything else that was going on. The envelope was so bulging that the edges were worn and ripped. He tossed it onto the "To Do" pile on his desk.

"No it did not break down. It's just…" Steve was muttering.

"Mrs. Dana said she needs to have some of those forms back by the end of this week." Fatima said gesturing pointedly at the envelope. "The whole process will be an even bigger mess if you wait." Her lips were twisted up and pouting. She knew this was for St. Peters and she was not going to let him put it off.

"… just that the guy I bought it from told me before he sold it to me that the Top Side was tryin' to take it from him…"

Max picked the thick envelope back up and considered it. "I don't suppose you want to run it over to St. Peters for me?" he said to Fatima. Her mouth twisted and pouted even more. He wondered if he could bluff her into doing it. "I guess I could just put a stamp on it." He said.

"Max you have to go through it with Mrs. Robbins! You have to take it there yourself."

"Mrs. Robbins is a certified Educator. I'm sure she has the ability to comprehend anything…" he pulled a sheet of stamps out of his desk. "…that could possibly be in this little thing." He made a small show of trying to turn over the heavy envelope over and began sticking stamps on it. Then ended the act by tossing the heavy envelope onto another desk where there was a small pile of outgoing mail. This got her up. She walked over to the desk and rescued the envelope.

"I can't believe you. After all she did for you when you were in school!"

Whoa! What was that?

"Whoa! What was that?" what did she know about THAT?

Fatima just cocked her head in that "ah ha" way. No way she knew about that! Max struggled briefly with the need to find out why she had said that and the need to allow her to process that packet. As she tore open the envelope Max could feel some of his stress drain away.

"You seen Terps' new play?" Steve was still going on.

"No time. I know he's pissed."

"Probably not. It's been really big. They've been selling out nearly every show." Steve told him. "I doubt he's even noticed."

Joe Navies or 'Terps,' nicknamed for a reason unknown to Max, had been one of the big brothers of C-Phi-G when Max had gone over. After the frat was disbanded and suspended from campus, Joe was the only member who had not held Max to blame. The only one with whom he had remained friends. Despite what had been happening this year, Max still felt guilty about not being there to see his friend's play.

"I'm going to go this week." He said meaning it.

"Sold out Friday & Saturday." Steve told him.

"Jesus. It's been running for three weeks now!"

"They've got a big church following. Those old ladies love a chance to get out on the weekends." He snickered. His snicker was always childlike and rolled in a way that had to make you laugh.

Unless he was snickering at you.

"Church crowd. I thought the play was about a group of hookers. …Hey!"

There was a loud plop as Fatima dropped the packet back onto Max's desk.

"Mrs. Dana gave you the wrong one. This packet is for somebody Named Forrest." She said and turned and stomped back to her desk. Apparently the bluff did not work well enough to get her to take the thing back and get the right one.

"Forrest?" Max opened the envelope and pulled out the top cover sheet. The sheet was a note to a Dr. Carey, who worked in the City history department Max remembered. It gave instructions for him to print an address on the label. The one that they had on file could not be used. He flipped through a few more sheets until he found one with a sticker attached to it. It read:

Dr. Henry D. Forrest

Forrests' Carpenters Shop

The Downhills.

True enough that address could not be used. The rest of the packet contained various books, pamphlets, and forms. One; Dr. Forrest, was asking for a position at the Museum.

Dr. Forrest from the Downhills.

"I'll take this back to Mrs. Dana." He said, but he grabbed his hat and coat as he got up from the desk. Steve took the cue and hopped up as well, disappointment showing a little as he glanced at Fatima, who paid him no mind.

"You remember Jean?" Max asked him as they walked out together.

"Who?"

"Jean… uh, Crap! I can't remember his last name. He was on our floor of Gentleman's Hall first year?"

"That's a ways back…" Steve looked lost.

"Jean? We used to call him 'Bam-Bam'? Watched Saturday morning cartoons with us every week in the lounge?"

"Right Bam-Bam! Yea 'course. Why?"

"You seen him around lately?"

"Naw. He an'… uh… Marc! Yea he an' Marc had a place in West Oaks last I knew but that was a while ago. Why?"

"Thought I saw him the other day."

It was not an easy place to reach, the Downhills. There was one bridge over Cobbs River if you were not willing to swim. Other than that you could go the long way around the Park's northern branch to come from the North Hills if you did not mind the hike. Even after you got over the bridge or around the Park, there was no major avenue in the Downhills. No one street that could connect you to every other street. There were, for the most part, no streets at all, just buildings. Buildings laid out, almost at random, from where they had initially been built by the first settlers here in Mountairy Rock. Plus the buildings themselves were not built to standard. There was no front or back to most of them. Few of them had anything close to a symmetrical shape. This added to the mazelike nature of the Downhills. It was so crazy and unplanned that a car could not fit down many of the streets, even those that lead to Lakefolk Fountain, the unofficial center of the Downhills. That was why there was no real address on the package. There were no real streets in the Downhills. The taxi stopped to let Max off in front of a large church.

It was actually one of the smaller buildings in the Downhills, but at least it appeared on Max's map, The Chapel Sylvain. He had picked the landmark because it was very discernable on the map and rather close to the Fountain. This way it should not be too hard to get there.

He paid the driver, remembered to grab the package and hopped out of the taxi. His foot came down into six inches of snow. He had not thought of this. The Downhills had not been plowed, and his plan was to walk around until he found this carpenters' shop. Good idea. Just as it had been a good idea to be dressed for the occasion. The long black coat was warm enough to be sure, though the bottom trailed in the snow. The black gloves were leather and comfortable but his head was going to be freezing soon. His baseball cap was not designed for this kind of weather, nor were his pants, which were going to get soaked stomping through this deep snow. At least his boots were calf high, which was high enough that the snow would be kept from slipping down his ankles. He tightened Amanda's scarf around his neck and watched the taxi churn its' way out of the unplowed street and back up to the bridge.

Dr. Carey had been in Mrs. Danas' office when Max brought the package back. He was glad the package was found but still did not have an address for Dr. Forrest or even a number to call. The whole idea of him taking the package to the Downhills himself went over very well with Dr. Carey. He only seemed to care that he would not have to resolve it himself. Thanks came in a mutter about it having been for King anyway. Might not be such a good idea to show his face down there but Max had volunteered before he thought of that.

Maybe with the legitimate reason for going down there and by being dressed in business attire (except for the baseball cap), he could keep any hostile feelings to a minimum.

Maybe. He HAD been thrown from a window.

It did not take long for him to realize that the map he had either needed to be updated or was just plain wrong. As soon as he walked around the church he ran into a building that should not have been there. It was an old stone building. No matter how Max turned the map it did not match the two buildings that were supposed to be there. So he walked around it as well and found two buildings that might be the ones reflected on the map. The alley between these buildings was narrower than the map seemed to indicate and the height of the buildings blocked out a lot of light. So Max avoided the alley and walked around the northwestern building.

Finally he saw some people, walking ahead of him along yet another tight road in what he hoped was the direction of the Fountain. There was that Downhills scent now, varied, but distinctive never-the-less. It looked to be a mother and two children, wading ahead, then an older gentleman crossed their path heading east or what he hoped was east. When Max reached the end of narrow road he came upon a small row of shops. There were a lot more people in this section, walking about, in and out of the shops. The ground here had been plowed, and Max saw a few cars parked along the street. They certainly had not gotten here the way he had so there must be more accessible roads on the other side of the Downhills.

Though most of people he saw were completely Downhills folk, with the odd fur lined leather clothes that stood out among many of them, there was also a large group of what Max thought were tourists. There must indeed have been a more popular way into the Downhills for there to be some many of them. Possibly they were not actually tourists but just more Downhills people dressed in more contemporary attire. But they moved like tourists and they shopped and took pictures. Plus their ages ranged from young to old. The Downhills folk that Max could clearly identify did not seem to mingle with the others beyond the tourist trading. As he walked onto the street he felt the same disinterested attention come briefly his way.

He had walked to the end of the row and found nothing that looked similar to anything on the map. Three prominent buildings sat in the neatest formation that Max had yet seen here, forming a rough triangle at the end of the street. The closest, on his left, looked to be an old horse stable, horseless now, but with quite a few people moving in and out of it. To the right was the tallest of the three, a building with so many windows that Max knew it had to be or had to have been an inn. There was, however, no signage and the only inn listed on his map could not have been this close to where he had been dropped off. The building in the center was the most nondescript as it had only two small ground level windows. There was a small worn path which led to a thick weather beaten oak door. It was also the busiest of the three buildings, with people either going in and out or just milling about outside the door. Could be a good place to get some directions and since Max had not caught the unforgettable scents of either of his attackers from King Day, he thought it might be okay.

It was just before he would have started for the building, Max noticed that the people who had been making their way along the shops that he had already passed had suddenly become very quiet. When he looked back over his shoulder, his breath caught in his throat. Everyone on the row was looking at him fixedly.

The weirdest thing was that there was not much hostility in their stares. Just a very careful curiosity, which every one of them had. Everyone with the exception of those who were souvenir shopping. But all the others, even the small children were watching him. What the hell had happened in the time it took him to walk the length of the street? Something about him was certainly peculiar to them. A few looked away after a moment of checking him out. Some, when he returned their stares, turned away and went about what they were doing. The younger ones seemed the most curious and continued to watch him unabashedly.

The people in front of the building were watching him as well. He was really unnerved, but he could not turn and leave now. What was worse was that he had clearly been going toward the center building. If he turned aside now it would be obvious why. What was he so worried about? Hell, he was a good foot taller than most of the people here!

So Max continued on, up the street, and onto the small worn path. The small gathering of folk standing outside the building gave him no challenge as he walked up. A few even stood aside, muttered a quick 'Mornin'' and let him pass. The door opened as he approached and another mother with a set of children emerged from the building. Max caught hold of the door as the woman struggled with some large packages. The strong sweet scent of fresh baked bread poured out of doorway and up out of the mother's bags.

A bakery.

"Oh thank you…" the woman started then looked up at him a bit startled. She turned to look at those gathered outside and then back at him. "Thank you."

"No problem." But her oldest kid, who had to be all of five years old, had grabbed a hold of Max's coat and was… sniffing it!

"Come Carr." The boy's mother quickly jerked him away and up the path. Max did not look to see if anyone had watched this exchange. He just walked inside.

Fake lanterns posted on the walls lighted the room warmly. Fake, Max knew, because even with the overwhelming aroma of baked bread, he could smell no burning wax nor oil as he walked passed them. It was weird, taking notice of things specifically because of their smell or lack thereof. More and more it was also increasingly easier to do.

The room was crowded with patrons providing the other overwhelming scent of the Downhills folk. Some were seated on one of the benches that which had been set at either side of the room; while others sat at one of the small tables near the entrance. Most stood in winding line in front of the bakery counter. There was a little bit of a line now too, and all Max wanted were directions.

There were two women behind the counter. One was dealing with those customers in line as the other, an older woman, was staring at Max.

"Can I help you?" she asked warily. Her voice was hard and sharp. The entire room turned when she spoke. Again Max saw the stares, but there were far fewer people in here than were outside. He walked up to the far side of the counter that she stood behind.

"Yes ma'am. I'm looking for Dr. Henry Forrest's carpenter shop. I'm a little lost here."

"What do you want with Henry?" that question came from the woman who had been working the counter. Her manner was plainly hostile.

"Shush Brina." said the older woman. "Henry is a busy man."
She then stated flatly. It was a much nicer way of asking what Max
wanted with the man.

"I'm sure that he is." He said as diplomatically as he could. "I
work at Haley Museum. He recently visited us and asked for a school
faculty package. I'm just here to drop it off…" and Max saw that the
woman was about to hold her hand out. So he quickly added "…and to
answer any questions he might have."

She saw through that one, obviously, but did not ask for the
package. For a moment she just regarded him. The rest of the room was
unnaturally quiet.

"Henry's is on the far end of the fountain… around the bend
here and about four warrens down." She said finally.

"Thank you." He said as if she had just made any sense to him
what so ever. As casually as he could he turned and walked back toward
the door when he noticed a small child, peeking out from behind his
mother's long leather coat, eyeing him fearfully. He tried a little smile
as he walked by and the little boy smiled back, with a mouth full of
fangs!

His eyes went wide and Max stopped mid stride with his hand
on the door handle. He looked to the mother who immediately picked
the child up and walked to the far end of the room. Now everyone was
looking at him. None of the eyes were kindly.

"Past the Fountain, Mr. Madigan." The woman who had given
the directions said.

"If he gets that far" said… Brina? The younger one working the
counter.

This was getting bad, fast. Screw it! He was just going to head
back out the way he came and let the Museum deliver the damn thing.
This was a very bad idea.

Max pulled the door open and walked outside, expecting to see
the group of people that had been there before, but they were gone. The
street was much quieter now. Even the tourists seemed to have moved
on.

Despite his decision to leave Max peeked to his right and eyed
the street. He could barely see around the bend. Maybe he could just go
and take a quick look around the corner? If he saw the shop then he
would stay, if not, he would leave. Simple.

But that kid… Max looked back at the still quite bakery.
Something was coming together in his mind. The one kid sniffing at
him… the other had oversized canine teeth… the claw marks that were
still etched on his neck…

The Fountain came into view before he realized he had started
walking. It was called Lakefolk Fountain, a pre-quake monument just

about as old as Mountairy Rock. It was carved by and named for the Lakefolk family, who had founded the Downhills community. Like a hazy dream, white with a pearl-like sheen, the fountain sat in the center of a circle of prominent buildings. It was flanked by one queen Rockwood, and other less striking edifices. A small number of tourists were here as well, taking pictures and shopping. One small group was being led by a tour guide. Was this that big of a tourist attraction? Big enough for a guided tour? He had barely been able to find the place yet here they were; a tour group, if the overweight guy, with the huge digital camera and ridiculously large Gortex winter jacket, was any indication. He was straying from his guided tour as were some others. Some of the strays simply lagged behind. A few others sat along the edge of the small pool surrounding the fountain, their jackets and scarves discarded near the water.

That was because the water was scalding hot and throwing up a thick cloud of steam. The source of the Fountain was an underground spring, part of a series of waterways that ran beneath parts of Mountairy Rock. It was another one of the great mysteries of Mountairy Rock because the source of such geothermal power had not yet been discovered. The unnamed Lakefolk artist who had carved the beautiful piece had placed it over the spring, harnessing its heat for this display. There were other springs in the city, most of which were far better known than the one here. Still the Lakefolk Fountain still drew a little attention. The tourists here were showing particular interest in it, and the shops surrounding it benefited from the extra traffic. Funny that he had never really heard much of this as a popular spot. What had gotten these people interested enough in it to visit it in the off season?

The shops surrounding the fountain were various craft shops. There was another bakery, an electronics shop, a tannery and something that probably was a flower shop. They all sat along the far side of the little court that held the fountain and Rockwood. There were other shops that were hidden behind the tree's huge girth and low canopy. The Carpenter's shop must be on the other side Max thought and so he walked across the court. There were stone posts placed around the court, the kind usually used to keep someone from driving a car into a protected area. But these were spaced too far apart for that. A closer look revealed that each post bore a sculpted top with an inscription below. He stopped to read the first that he neared.

It was some kind of bird; a falcon, or an eagle. The inscription below read:

FOR HAWK

FIRST TO FALL

There were ten more posts that he could see on this side of the court. They were varied in age and wear. Max guessed that while some seemed to have been made in the last ten to twenty years others had been carved well over a century ago. This kind of display takes time, skill, and money to keep up. Very elaborate for a bunch of gypsies. He wished that he knew more about the Downhills people. There was obviously more to them than a small camp of displaced refugees. Perhaps he should have realized that before. Their community had been here as long as any other.

The next post held a sculpted symbol, similar to the symbol for music. The inscription below was printed in some kind of Slavic writing. There was no translation here, so the post could not have been meant for anyone outside of the community to read. But what of those inside the community?

The Downhills consisted of more than just European descendants, if just looking around told him anything. Several of the store fronts Max had seen bore Native American "sounding" names. The tannery was named "Hunters Moon" Leathers for example. The Native American influence in the Downhills was just as strong as any other, though Max could not identify which specific tribe it was. One of the eastern woodland tribes he suspected. The Mohawk, Seneca, Honique, and Susquehannock all had, at one time lived within a stone's throw of what would be Mountairy Rock, but he saw nothing to identify any of those historic tribes.

The next post was sculpted far more elaborately than the others. The entire top had been carved into a clenched fist holding a broken ring or circle. A smaller feminine hand, sculpted out of a much lighter colored stone, caressed the fist. Sculpted on the wrist of each arm was a broken manacle; Slave chains. The inscription below it was written in another language:

MAHABA NI TONGO

It was African… yet another of the founding cultures of the Downhills. Their influence was just as easily seen in the many dark faces that walked these streets wearing the distinctive fur lined coats. The electronics shop was named "The John Henry Repair Shop".

So… were these posts set up independently or by the group as a whole? Whoever erected the posts had no interest in anyone else reading or understanding it save for those who knew the languages. That meant more than half of the Downhills would not know the meaning of quite a few sculptures. Could that be right? As he looked around Max thought he saw the answer… had in fact, been seeing it all along.

Perhaps the divisions between the cultures had come down long ago. As he looked around at the Downhill's people milling about the Fountain he certainly could not tell the social divisions, if there were any. The small groups of people were themselves diverse, cutting across racial lines at least, and without any obvious cliques.

Maybe they could all read the posts.

As he rounded the plaza, a new shop came into view bearing a large, carved wooden cup above its front porch. Next to the cup was a sign, also made of wood, which read:

FORREST'S CARPENTERS SHOP

It was the closest building to the Rockwood, its front porch sat in the shade of the lower tree branches. There were all manner of carved wooden objects, presumably for sale, displayed on the porch. Bowls, chairs, canes, little wooden boxes, bird cages, plaques and a number of other items which Max could not identify at first glance all shone with a well polished gleam. On many of the carvings the symbol of the cup was prominently etched. Looking more closely, he could clearly see the symbol was on the steps and on the porch railing as well.

The door to the shop opened, and out walked the short bearded man in glasses who Max had seen at the Museum. His shirt was flannel, which, along with the blue jeans and boots, gave him a lumberjack look. In his hands was a wooden object that Max could not make out because of the large chamois cloth the man was polishing it with.

"Well, hello." His smile was warm but something told Max that he had been expecting him.

"Dr. Forrest?"

"Yes. I remember you from the Museum. What brings you… to my little shop?" he finished polishing the object and placed it on top of a table among other pieces. It was a wooden obelisk, about a foot and a half long.

"You expressed interest in joining the M.R.U. faculty at the Museum? Dr. Carey put together a packet for you sir, and asked me to deliver it." Max held up the envelope.

"Ahh! The information I requested." His voice was light and kind; but he paid no attention to the envelope, he was looking directly at Max. "So you brought it down here yourself?"

"Well," Max explained. "… the address was very vague. The postman wouldn't take it. Besides we figured you might have a few questions that I could answer."

"Well thank you. But you're not a member of the faculty are you?"

Crap! He remembered that Max had told him that he was just a researcher.

"Uh, I work as a teaching assistant," don't fidget. "…in addition to my other duties." He explained but now Forrest was looking past him.

"Then why don't you come in?" he said with some of the lightness in his voice gone.

"Sure." And when the old man turned to go into the shop Max snuck a look over his shoulder. The court had gone empty. If there was anyone still in the area then they were on the other side of the

Rockwood. Even the tourists had gone. When he turned back Forrest was looking at him expectantly, still waiting for him to join him on the porch. Despite that Max turned and looked back at the court again. Where had they all gone?

Then he glanced toward the shops that he could see from the porch. There in the window of the Tannery, two faces were watching. In the windows above the first floor of the flower shop were more curious faces, all looking in his direction. When had they left? He had not noticed the silence then… but it was quite apparent now.

…even the tourists?

"Come in," Forrest repeated, "We've got coffee on." He was holding the door open. Max took a step up onto the porch when he heard the voices.

Somewhere back behind the Rockwood, their voices rose; angry, arguing, and excited. The voices cut around the wide trunk and through the low branches of the big Queen. They were speaking in a language Max could not identify. A woman shouted, and the voices yelled back with even more anger and fervor.

They were Men's deep voices that shouted down the woman's softer one. So no matter what had started the exchange the men clearly were not to be interfered with.

"Please come inside Mr. Madigan." Max looked back and saw that the kindly and cheerful look was gone. It had been replaced by a graver look and Forrest had one fist clenched tight, choking the chamois.

"I think…" but now he could hear the footsteps, more than a few of them stomping through snow. The faces peering out of the shop windows were turned, no longer focused on him, they were watching something or someone who was on the other side of the Rockwood.

"Mr. Madigan…" Forrest was more insistent now, but Max stepped off of the porch and down to the street. The footsteps left the deep snow and now were clacking and smacking against stone; the cobblestone of the street surrounding the court. Close now, he could discern their voices but still not the language. Eight… no, nine of them; one was not speaking.

He probably should have just run right then but he had been running a lot since New Years. He was taller than everyone here in the Downhills. He started toward the tree.

"Mr. Madigan!" Whatever it was Forrest had planned it was just going to have to go down here in the middle of the street.

"No! This way!"

Now THAT was a familiar voice.

…Somewhere to his left, down past the tree, in between the buildings closing off the end of the square…

He looked back to Forrest, who snapped his head back from that same direction to look at Max. He had heard it too.

"FORREST!" Now that came from one of the men on the other side of the tree.

"Mr. Madigan it would be best if you came inside." Forrest had come to the steps of the porch. His eyes were hard and held a dangerous edge. The men came around the right side of the tree.

There were ten of them, none too much younger than him. They stopped as soon as they saw him standing in front of Forrest's shop. The moment of hesitation only lasted a few seconds. After a second of looking back and forth from one to another, and then specifically to the tallest one in the center, the decision was made. They slowly advanced.

"You shouldn't have come here." Their scents drifted to him even as the leader spoke. He was a wild haired, thick muscled Downhills fighter. He had on worn blue jeans, tucked into calf high strapped up leather boots. Despite the weather, he was bare-chested, wearing nothing above the waist save for a lone blue stone, hanging from a thin braided string around his neck. The wild hair was thick, dark brown and blowing in the winter wind. He was one of the few of this gang of men without some kind of facial hair having just barely the hint of shadow. Though a thick coat of it covered his bare chest and arms. His shape was familiar. The scent of the man he had fought with in Wolf's Den tree was in the air. Perhaps this was him?

"I came here to visit Mr. Forrest." Max said. The rest of the Downhills men all bore enough of a resemblance to the leader that they could all have been brothers.

"You don't know Forrest." One of the others said.

"Lotarre." Forrest greeted them.

"Forrest." The leader answered through clenched teeth.

"We can handle this, Forrest." Said the guy to the leader's right. This one wore black leather pants which flared open at the bottoms to accommodate his boots. He was wearing a tight red tee-shirt with a symbol printed on it that was similar to the music-like symbol he had seen in the court. His hair was just as wild as the leaders though it was jet black. It slid down the sides of his face sticking out like a serrated blade cutting around his mouth forming into a wicked goatee. A black leather vest was clutched in one hand; a sheathed hunting knife was in the other. Those two were going to be the main problem. If it came to a fight, he would have to hit them first and hard. The rest would fold and back down if he could do that.

"His coat is mine."

...the rest except for that guy. We all know how this goes.

"I don't want any trouble." Keep the conversation going. "Mr. Forrest asked for a school packet and I'm just delivering it." Max began to edge to his left. There was a slight path there, and an alley beyond, from where that voice had come. But should he trust her? She was the reason…

The door to the Forrest's shop closed behind Max. Forrest himself had obviously gone inside. Yea, this was a great idea.

"I want his hat" said a fourth one.

"Shut up." snapped the leader. "You're not here to see Forrest."

None of them were wearing hats and only two of the… nine? Ten? Only two of them were wearing coats. Then they had not been outside and just happened to see him. Someone had to have run and told them he was here and then they all rushed right out. The adrenalin was pumping into their veins and many of them seemed eager for this to escalate. The one standing next to the leader was smirking. Max started backing up to the porch.

"Yea I am. 'Was' that is." The two on the far ends were trying to creep around him, to surround him. Max's own heart began pounding against his ribs. Where was that cat with the freakin' warning now?

"Well," said the second. "…your business with Forrest is done. You can see us now." as he walked right up to Max.

The number two man was going to swing, Max knew, as soon as he came in range and thought he could get away with it. That was how it always started, with somebody "sneaking" in the first punch.

Not today.

The snarl was instinctive, as was the baring of his teeth. It felt natural, and good until…

"Oooo!" said the second. "Kitty's got teeth!" and he smiled, as did the rest. Nine fang filled mouths. Only their leader did not smile.

"Oh shit." And he dipped as the one creeping up on his left tried to sucker punch him from behind. The blow glanced off his shoulder and Max bolted to his right.

But these guys were used to ganging up on someone. The creeper was just flushing him into three others who had already positioned themselves to cut him off. This made him stop dead in his tracks, which was what they wanted. The second attack came from behind, just when he was stopped by the three man blockade. The leader, Lotarre, came at him with a viscous punch.

Max fell against the rail of the porch; he had not known that he was so close to it. They closed in to put him down. They were whooping and laughing.

"Here… Kitty, kitty, kitty!"

"Shouldn'a come down here!"

"Watch the coat! I want the coat!"

"Just get him!" said Lotarre.

"Lot is still hurting" came the feminine voice from between the alley to his far left. It was far quieter now.

Max grabbed the rail to the shop and in one bound jumped over it and onto the porch. Forrest's carvings were all over the porch though and Max came down unable to find a clear space to land and fell in a loud crash.

There was more whooping and shouting as the gang leapt after. The three who had cornered him all jumped onto the rail simultaneously. They all looked particularly alike, triplets, their hair tied back in pony tails with similar bindings.

"Grab him!" that Lotarre guy was shouting to them. "Hold him." He was running the long way around to the porch, instead of leaping over the railing. The triplets responded by leaping at him as a group.

They were organized and had clearly done this before. The Maniacs had just been amateurs, Max knew that now. These people weren't like them. What they were was incredibly strong!

The three slammed into Max with an amazing force knocking him to the ground. All four slid across the porch, knocking over everything that had been set up. Wooden boxes and plaques, tables and chairs, toys and knick knacks all came tumbling down like a giant block play set. One of the triplets fell into the front wall of the shop and just slumped there against it. The other two grabbed him around his waist and his legs, immobilizing him from the waist down. The third must have been the guy who grabbed the arms. As it was he couldn't move his legs, so strong was that guy, and the other was trying to switch from his waist to his arms. Something hard rolled into Max's hand.

POW! The wooden obelisk cracked when it met the skull of the man wrapped around his legs. He fell back against the railing, cradling his head. The other tried to grab the little wooden pyramid while Max was just trying to get up.

CRACK! The triplet lost a tooth when Max swung his knee up.

Finally free, he jumped to his feet in time to see two more men hop up onto the railing. The whooping had come to a stop when they saw that he had taken out three of their own. More of their gang ran to either end of the porch, cutting off his only possible escape routes. Lotarre ran up onto the porch eyes blazing.

Was there a slight limp in his gate?

"I don't want this!" Max yelled at him.

"I know what you want!" shouted Lotarre rushing at him.

There was no time for anything else; Max met him with his shoulder.

"OOF!" and the Downhills gang leader fell back down the porch steps and Max fell backwards into the Shops door.

"GGRRRR!" The Second ran past his fallen leader; that hunting knife drawn and the sheath discarded.

The shop door did not feel very thick when Max fell against it. Four small windows were carved into the door but it was too dark inside to see anything. It did not matter, Max was sure Forrest was watching.

"Watch this!" The door splintered open and glass flew. The floor inside was lower than the porch landing. Max tripped down a small set of steps but managed to stay on his feet.

It was dark inside; although, a tiny fire burned in the pit of a hearth in the center of the room. The light from the outside poured in from the doorway, lighting the… the light was blocked by shadow!

"GRRR!" the Second charged through the doorway after him, knife raised high. His friends were right behind him, and the whooping was starting up again.

Forrest was nowhere to be seen in the dark shop; Max's eyes had yet to adjust to the darkness. The far end was pitch black but Max sprinted in that direction anyway, mostly because it was in the exact opposite direction of that doorway full of Downhills.

Their boots smacked loudly on the hardwood floor as they raced across the room. As cluttered as the porch was, the inside of the shop was amazingly Spartan. A hearth fire pit was situated by itself, dead center of the room so there were no obstacles. The rest of the room was still too dark to see. The way that they had flown through it, anything else would not have been much more than a blur anyway.

The dark end of the room came up quickly and Max saw the door. There was the tiniest crack of light at the bottom, a possible way out.

…Closer and he could see that there was a cloth draped down over it.

…Closer and there was a sink and covered window to the right of the door. Almost there!

…Closer and… where was the doorknob? Hell with it!

BAM!

The sunlight, reflecting off the bright white snow, blinded him for a second, making him slow down instinctively as he squinted his eyes. That there was a wall in front of him was all he could tell and so he immediately cut to his right.

The first of his pursuers, the knife wielding Second, whether from knowing the layout or not being caught off guard by the light, jumped from the back door directly at Max's back.

But the glare must have had some effect because instead sinking the huge hunting knife between Max's shoulders; he missed and brought the blade down past his right cheek. The resulting collision sent them both rolling to the ground.

Knowing that he could not afford to be caught on the ground by the gang Max used the momentum to get some distance and quickly rolled to his feet before the next pursuer that came out of the backdoor could get at him.

In the twisted and backwards layout of the Downhills, they were in neither alley nor backyard but in the middle of yet another street, narrow as it was. There was no choice in which direction to take, the Downhills gang was pouring out of the carpenters shop blocking one end and Max was already moving toward the other. So he ran.

The snow slowed him as did his dress boots and long coat; additionally, he was uncertain of which way to run to. Half clothed as most of them were the Downhills boys did not seem to mind running in the snow. Plus he was sure they knew the terrain. But Max had a head start and his legs were significantly longer than theirs. If he could just avoid a dead end, he might just make it out of the Downhills in one piece.

At the end of the narrow street he made a right turn, hoping to circle back around to the Fountain where he would be able to trace his way back to where the cab had dropped him off. That had to be the closest exit out of the Downhills.

The turn brought him to another long narrow street that again, looked more like an alley. He could tell that the street was running at an angle which was taking him away from the Fountain. Damn! He would have to take yet another right at the end of this street.

The Downhills gang was howling threats as they chased after, but Max never looked back. From the sound of their boots mashing through the snow falling away he knew he was outrunning them. Bless his long legs!

Apparently they realized it too. The big hunting blade that the Second had been carrying whipped past Max's leg and disappeared into the deep snow only to burst forth almost a meter away as it ricocheted off the cobblestone beneath.

"JEEZ!" From the way it bounced that knife might have broken through bone had it hit him. Were they going to throw anything else at him? He chanced a quick glance over his shoulder to see the gang still chasing after; one of them stumbling for some reason… he had just thrown something! There was a loud clatter and Max spun back around to see another blade bouncing off the alley wall.

The alley ended in a "T" intersection at one of the biggest buildings Max had seen here in the Downhills. It was built a little differently, more modern. Max had not seen this huge building towering over the smaller ones when he was in the Fountain court. How far had they been running?

He cut right at the intersection onto an even narrower street that would never have been able to accommodate vehicles. The Downhills gang roared triumphantly behind him. Why?

The alley was tight and came to an end along another street that cut out to his left… then ended in a dead end.

"SHIT!" Max spun about. There was no way out, save for going back against the Downhills gang and he was pretty sure that he would not win that fight. They were too well organized, and seemed to be as strong as he was. Their footsteps in the snow sounded closer… their howls got louder.

The street seemed to really be a back alley. The buildings had few windows and the only doors were thick service doors. Was he strong enough to bust one open?

He was going to have to be.

Backing up as far as he dared Max charged at the door, unfortunately his dress boots could not get enough traction in the loose snow so he could not get enough momentum.

Bam! With no force behind him the door did not give. The howls were right around the corner.

"That was sad."

Who? Max stepped away from the door and looked around. That voice again… Where was she?

"Better hurry." Above! The building blocking the end of the street was not as tall as the goliath next to it. It looked to be the back of a tenement or a brownstone. Maybe… three stories tall?

There was a balcony on the top floor. A drying rug was draped over its banister. Was she up there? It was not that high. Could he…

The howls rounded the corner and the Downhills gang slid into view. Lotarre and company slowed as they spied him. The Second had his hunting knife back in his hand. They grinned those toothy grins when they saw he was cornered. Except Lotarre, he looked up at the surrounding buildings that blocked Max in. Those hard eyes narrowed then he lifted his head and breathed in the cold air.

The rest of the Downhills gang waited behind him, sensing his hesitation. Several of them sniffed and snorted in imitation, curious as to why they were not closing on Max. Lotarre was not even looking at the man that they had been chasing. Instead his eyes were cast up at the rooftops. Some of them scanned them too but there was nothing there save for a rug blowing in the winter air.

Their leader's eyes narrowed even further, and drew down from the rooftops until they pointed back at the tall well dressed Museum researcher. Something Lotarre alone caught, either in the air or on the rooftops, had drawn even more anger from him. His lips drew back in a snarl and he bared his teeth. Only the knife wielding Second seemed to understand what was going on in their leaders mind because he gave a slow, almost dismissive headshake. The rest just got more excited as they sensed that whatever had forced them to stall their attack had now passed.

But Max had noticed very little of this. In fact his back was turned to the small knot of Downhills muscle waiting at the end of the street. Instead of watching them he was examining his boxed in enclosure…

…at the windows, each in succession, all the way up the building.

"GET HIM!" and they rushed up the street.

Without a hint of hurry, or worry, Max leapt to lowest window landing one boot toe on the narrow windowsill. Then with just that foot hold he jumped to another, again landing just one foot on the sill.

The first of the Downhills gang to reach the end of the alley jumped at him, trying unsuccessfully to grab a leg. Max was moving too fast now, and his leaps were gathering momentum and height. He bounded up the wall, from window to window and from one side of the alley to the other. The Downhills gang hesitated for only a moment. Some attempted to mimic Max jumping onto the window ledges only to find themselves promptly crashing through those windows into the buildings.

The Second grabbed two of the others and together they broke down the door that Max could not. The sounds of them smashing through the inside of the building were easy to hear. Without much delay they must have found a staircase because their stomping boots soon were heard climbing them in cadence. Lotarre was unwilling to let Max get out of his site and followed him up the walls, managing to land and climb without falling into the windows or back down to the ground.

It took quite a powerful final leap to grab hold of the balcony's railing but Max got it and pulled himself up. The door to the balcony was wood, old and warped but set well into the door frame. He did not think he could get this one open either not that it would do him much good, the sounds of the Downhills gang who had ran inside were getting closer. So he looked up and saw that the roof of the building was not too much higher. The jump should be easy.

The sounds of his pursuers climbing the walls made him look down. The leader had climbed past the others and was nearing the balcony. Max might not be able to make the jump and climb up before Lotarre got there. Damn!

Clawed hands scratched at the brick face and Lotarre set himself against the window. His next jump would bring him directly onto the balcony. But he was too eager; he leapt never noticing what Max was doing.

The rug hit him mid leap and, like an anchor, dragged away his impetus and dropped him back down the building. One of his men sprang from where he had been purchased on the building and caught him, slowing his fall enough that both might survive the landing.

Max hopped onto the roof not bothering to see Lotarre hit the ground. The Downhills men inside the building were too close for him to wait another second.

"Ung!" Snow on the ledge made him slip and stumble. From this height the Downhills was laid out before him. This was not the tallest building by far but it still provided a good view. As much of a maze as Max had found it to be when he was on the ground, it was even more confounding from up there. The buildings varied as they got taller although not many of them topped three stories. There was still no common direction or any order that he could discern. The Downhills was northeast of Ivy Hills, but Max was not sure now which direction that was. Let's see, if the sun was…

"Better move" her voice again, a soft whisper. Funny, Max instinctively inhaled searching for her scent but caught none. Where was she?

A loud crash as the Downhills gang burst onto the balcony and Max took off. He raced across the rooftop and sited its nearest neighbor; one story lower and to his left.

Not too far.

Worried about his footing in the snow Max now took broader steps and after a quick run he jumped to the next rooftop.

CRASH! His foot punched right through the roofing and he fell in all the way to his crotch.

"JEEZ!" His voice was joined by the now very unhappy inhabitants of that home. Quickly he looked over his shoulder to see where the Downhills gang was. Still on the other roof but they had a clear view of him.

"UNG!" he pulled his leg free. Luckily he was not hurt; his pants were not even torn. An angry Downhills face peered up at him through the ragged hole.

"Sorry." And he got up and ran across the rest of the rooftop as lightly as he could, afraid to fall through again.

CRASH! Behind him the Downhills gang landed with even worse results. Two of them fell completely through the roof. Two others and the Second landed along the roofs edge but slipped on the snowy surface. The Second slid off and over but managed to catch hold without falling off the roof completely. That knife was still in his hand.

The next nearest rooftop that Max could see was angled at a hard incline and was covered with snow. If he could make the jump all the way to the top maybe he could then slide down the other side…

A few steps back to get a running start…

There was howling and barking behind him as more of the Downhills gang leapt through the air.

…and he took off.

Again the snow killed a lot of his speed and he fell far short of the top and landed right in the middle of the slanted rooftop. A cloud of loose snow exploded around him then his boots slid out from under him and he could not see anything as he fell.

The roof fell away from him, too fast for his outstretched hand to grab, and he tumbled.

God bless the Stone! His legs curled up on instinct, shifting his center of gravity and turning his body fast enough that he landed on his feet. He stood up, long black coat settling back into place around him, on a second level roof.

"Impressive."

His head snapped around. There perched in shadow on an outcropping inside of an alley just a few buildings away, was the woman he had seen at the Museum. The shadow was dark and he could barely make her out, save for the gleam of her eyes, and a flash of a sharp toothed grin.

FWUMP! The rest of the snow that he had loosened from the roof above landed on him rudely. For half a second he thought the Downhills gang had caught up with him again. No, they were just getting to the edge of the other rooftop and were peering down at him. They could not risk the jump straight down; too far. He could see them pointing and planning to make the same jump he had.

When he turned back to the woman she was pointing over his shoulder, back the other way. There was another rooftop, set in between two larger buildings, leading off onto another street. She wanted him to go that way? Why should he trust her? But she was gone when he turned back around.

More howls as the Downhills gang were making the jump far above him.

No time.

Just run.

The path across the rooftop between the two taller buildings led to a very narrow street which was made even tighter by the awnings and covered booths that ran along its length. It was crowded with people. Apparently this was what happened to all the tourists who had disappeared earlier. They were shopping and moving about as casually as they had earlier.

He looked back and saw the falling Downhills gang, who had been unable to land as gracefully as he had. All save one, the Second. He landed on the opposite side of the pile of his buddies and was now in a crouch with his blade hand outstretched away from his body. Their eyes met, the Seconds were dark and even with his intent to capture Max.

Time to go.

The rooftop led around to a street long balcony which overlooked the people below. He jumped the small decorative railing that separated rooftop from balcony landing. There were huge picture windows revealing dark lit rooms filled with people, a few of whom looked up as Max ran past. There was another craft shop, another tailor and then in the last a group of old Downhills folk were seated around a table. One in particular caught his attention. Forrest's eyes were locked onto his before Max realized who it was that he was looking at.

Snow flew as he skid to a halt. It had felt like he had been running all day. So how the Hell had Forrest beat him here? Unless he had just run in one big circle? The first turn was… north right?

"Run fool!" the hushed whisper again. Across the street and down an alley… or was it just another tight street? Max saw the flash of garnet hair duck back out of sight around yet another alley or street corner. A burst of snow to his right from back at the beginning of the balcony reminded Max that she was right; the Second appeared and ran at him.

Max glanced at the window before moving. Forrest's eyes were hard but not nasty or angry. If he was going to say anything, Max did not have time to hear it. He took a quick hop up onto the railing and soared across the avenue to the top of a snow covered awning.

Half expecting the whole thing to collapse under his weight, Max braced himself for the fall but the awning held without swaying or giving much at all. He did manage to dump a good hundred pounds of snow onto the shopkeepers and shoppers alike, who cried out in surprise. By the time any of them managed to look upward it was the Second who they saw sitting on top of the awning, sliding awkwardly, trying to get down to continue his chase.

Max passed by the street where he had seen the girl duck and raced along farther up the avenue hoping to cut across at the next block. Too late he remembered that the Downhills' streets were not laid out like that. There was no cross street after a good minute of running up this strange avenue.

Strange because the street was way too long to be as narrow as it was without another crossing street. Unless he had missed one? The vendor carts were jammed sporadically all over the street. Some were sitting right in the middle of the road, others were leaning up against the line of buildings and some were even built into the building entrances themselves. He could not afford to back track, the Downhills gang were weaving through the vendors not too far behind him. So he tried instead to keep an eye out for an opening, which had to be coming up soon.

It did, but only as the street itself began to turn. It ended in a cul-de-sac but there was an alley tucked in tight next to the smallest building there. The cul-de-sac was a bit of a plaza, much like the court he had seen earlier. Max spared very little attention to see if there was anything of interest here. His focus was on the alley and getting there.

There was howling behind him. The Downhills gang was signaling to each other and that was not good. They lived here, so they had to know the Downhills like the backs of their hairy little hands. It was possible that they were coordinating an ambush if they knew where the alley led.

But he had little choice. From the first attack on the porch Max knew he could not take them in a fight. Nothing in their manner made him feel that they would hold back if there was a crowd of witnesses either. Lastly Lotarre and the Second seemed to be intent on taking this incident beyond the "mess him up" point and far into the "dump the body" area. He made it to the alley.

It curved around evenly. There were no side doors or windows along the long stretch of brick wall. The two buildings must have been built simultaneously; they bent and twisted at the same points making a path so tight that his elbows would rub the walls every few running steps. Also the snow that had covered most of the Downhills never made it to the ground here, as it had been trapped on outcroppings overhead. When the alley banked sharply to his left he finally heard the sounds of his pursuers entering the alley behind him.

Hard to his left the alley opened up into the back of two buildings. Steel doors on either side looked way too thick for him to bust open. A six foot brick wall blocked the other end of the alley, above which snaked another wider alley. His legs were beginning to burn with exhaustion but Max continued on and made the leap in a single bound landing atop the brick wall in a crouch.

The wall was actually a part of the buildings forming this new alley. It created a landing in between the two and was another rooftop in effect. This alley twisted upward as well as to the left. Max pushed on, it had to open out onto the street somewhere.

It turned into another brick wall to another landing going up and veering to the right. This time that Max almost did not make it. The cold air was starting to burn his lungs raw. Even the sounds of the Downhills gang behind him could not stir anymore adrenalin.

Another brick wall landing and Max had to pull himself onto the top of the wall to find… yet another brick wall.

But now the buildings opened up, spaces between them leading to alleys that led back out onto the street, a good six stories below! Where in the Downhills was he now?

Six stories? It was a jump he could never make, especially now, but he would only get higher if he kept following the landings. The walls of the alleys were bare, nothing he could use to slow his fall at all if he chose to jump.

Keep going.

"Hunh!" he kicked and kicked until he made it atop the next landing. The howling, barking, and pounding footsteps were getting closer. If he kept running until they eventually caught him he would be in no shape to fight back. Even if they had been just as worn out as he was they would take him down by strength of numbers alone. Plus these back alleys were perfect for getting rid of trouble makers. They could just leave his body here. How often did anyone come back here?

"JEEZ!" another landing. Maybe he should just gather his strength and wait for the fight. Or even riskier maybe he should just jump down between the building openings trying to scratch along the wall to slow his fall. Deep breaths… Deep breaths…

"One more." What? Again he inhaled instinctively when he heard her breathy voice and again he could not catch her scent. Could it still be a trap? Was she wearing him out on purpose or leading him to a better ambush sight? Deep breaths…

He could probably make a good stand on top of the wall. It was a good defensible position. Unless the Downhills boys carried guns, not that they had shown any but still…

Max looked at the wall. The alley looked open beyond it; the buildings were too far back to be seen. One more?

The Downhills gang was howling just two landings away.

The brief rest had his legs feeling a little better. One more.

He sprinted but as much of a rest as it had been he still barely made it onto the top of the wall.

But he was glad he did. The buildings opened up onto on wide snow covered rooftop that blinded him for a moment with sun glare. It took a precious second but Max finally got a good look at where he was. The Downhills were laid out before him on either side of the rooftop and to his right, he could see Finley bridge, which connected Ivy Hills to Brookhaven. More over the hilly nature of the Downhills meant that while one side of the building was a good six or seven stories up; the other side was easily a good two floors lower. Surely there was another connecting building that he could find.

Max raced to the other side of the rooftop and saw what he wanted. There it was; a lower building that was very near to yet an even lower one that could get him back down to the ground. The great thing was no more climbing! Going down was going to be a hell of a lot easier than getting up here had been. The first building had a steeple roof so narrow that there was no snow on it. It was crested by a huge cross. If he remembered right this would be Saint Mary's, closed long ago it was another of the Downhills few known historic sites. Max thought he could catch the cone of the steeple easily enough and still make it to the next roof. There had to be an easy way out of the Downhills once he got to the church. The bridge should only be one major street away. Home free!

The howling got closer and Max knew the gang was only a landing away. He only took a few steps back and then launched himself into the air.

PRYA KAYLERA LAKEFOLK

Half way down he saw the shadow leaping at him but being in freefall there was nothing he could do. The collision was powerful, catching him midsection and knocking the wind out of him. The attacker hit him with enough power and momentum to reverse Max's course. At first he was certain they would both fall all the way to the ground which, considering how high he had ascended the Downhills rooftops already, it would be quite a ways down. His body writhed and twisted as his instincts tried to get him turned around and into some kind of landing posture. That was proving to be extremely difficult. Mostly because of the strong arms wrapped tightly about his waist. Max grabbed onto the surprisingly narrow wrists and tried to pry them free so that he could get himself turned around before…

"HUMPH!" The snow covered rooftop of a smaller building he had not been able to see when he first jumped slammed into them. It would have been a worse landing had they not been falling at an angle.

They rolled in the snow both trying to end up as the one on top. Too beaten, too run out, and too surprised by the sudden attack, Max ultimately lost and found himself pinned. One hand was grasping his attacker's bare shoulder, his claws straining against the inside of his leather gloves, the other was being held tight by a hand with claws of its own, over his own head. Strong muscled thighs straddled him and stole the leverage from his legs.

"GRRRR!" was all he could manage but the growl froze in his throat when he saw beautiful lupine auburn eyes staring wickedly into his. A pearly white fanged grin sat in between fire red lips, split down the middle by a lone finger that was shushing him. An explosion of garnet colored hair fell down around her face which was so close to his now that it tickled his cheeks. The scent that he had searched for, that she had hidden before somehow, now flowed through his nose and pooled right behind his eyes. It was heady, warm, and his eyelids almost immediately drew half closed from it. His hand relaxed on her soft shoulder but he did not pull it away.

"…Max…." she said in a low whisper, drawing his name out long and slow, like she was trying it out, seeing what the very sound of it told her about him. That shushing finger slid down to her bottom lip as she said his name, her nail, or claw just as flame red.

Her other hand slowly eased its grip on Max's wrist and then slid down his arm to his chest. She held it there for a moment, letting it rise and fall with his breathing.

"…Maxxxxxx…" she breathed again and leaned into him, arching her back. Sweet breath brushed his lips, she was so close. Then she took the finger from her lip and placed it on his.

Soft, warm.

Her thighs slid up through the snow on either side of him and gripped him tightly. They were bare. She was wearing some kind of thick leather fur lined skirt that was slit up on both sides so her legs slipped out easily enough.

How could she stand this cold?

On her feet were calf high fur boots, bound by thin leather straps. They looked warm enough, but with only the skirt…

The top she wore was more sports bra than shirt, it was so tight. The rest of her was bare from the shoulders. But she was so warm!

Through his own coat, and two shirts Max could feel her heat. He was lying in a good six inches of rooftop snow but she was so hot on top of him. Or was it him? She was so close, those lips, eyes, her husky, warm whisper…

"…shall I keep you this time?" She pressed into him, and he could feel her full chest slide over his. Her face came even closer.

"Wha…?"

"…shhhhh…" she quieted him and Max knew why. From far above there came a series of shouts and howls. Their voices rose as they drew near and then Max and the girl watched as the Downhills gang leapt off of the rooftop a few floors above them and landed onto the steeple rooftop of the church. Some fell but most made it to the very next landing which Max had planned to use himself. Snow flew and the howls continued but none of them looked back. If they had then they would have easily seen the two of them hiding almost in plain sight.

"You planned this. You led me this way." She only smiled back at him her own eyes becoming half closed as she inhaled his scent.

"Why did you help me?" he asked but she just lowered her head, blinding him with her deep red hair. A hot breath touched his throat and Max knew she was taking in his scent even deeper. His blood pumped hot behind his ears.

"…again…" she answered and brought her head back up and met his eyes.

"Again?"

Her smile parted her lips and Max saw the canines gleam. A very red tongue flicked out and slid along the sharp point. She pressed even closer and despite his own layers of clothes he could have sworn he felt her nipples pushing into him.

"When I was here before?" The night of the second break in. He been thrown into the river, came ashore near the Downhills, but… he could never remember how he had gotten home.

"I was…" he had been near to death that night he was sure. "…was cold…"

"…I warmed you…" the heat between them was making him loopy. His body was beginning to respond. He tried to focus.

"Why did they attack me?"

She pursed those lips. "…Lotarre…"

"The guy with you at the Museum? On King Day?"

"… wants what you have…" she had unbuttoned his coat and slid her hands up under his shirt. How could her hands be so warm?

"'What I have'? The Stone?" and for the first time she seemed surprised. That still did not wipe the smile from her face, so closed to his.

"…stone?…"

"Yes. The Stone from the museum break-in. The Stone that makes me like you." And that broadened her smile. She leaned back exposing her neck to him in what would have been a good laugh had she dared to break the quiet.

"…you think you are clan?" she asked looking down at him almost amused.

"Clan?"

"…yes…" she lowered her face, once again just a breath away from his and she smiled at him, this time deliberately flashing her fangs at him. "…clan…"

What did she mean? Downhills clan? Not by showing him her fangs she did not.

"I mean…" he showed his own teeth, canines top and bottom. "… like you."

But she just smiled and twisted her mouth. She looked away from him briefly, and upward. Her eyes searched the rooftops for any sign of the Downhills gang. When her probing fingers found the Stone he wore on a string around his neck she turned back to him and pressed close, again grinding herself into him, her smiled wicked.

In spite of the danger, cold and strangeness, Max's body responded to her ferociously. Her thick strong thighs were warm enough to feel through the leather of his gloves.

"…you are not like me…" she breathed into his ear.

"I mean…" then she snatched the Stone hard and the string popped. In a cloud of flying snow and a playful laugh she bounded off of him and leapt from the building.

He tried to grab her before she took off but she was too quick. When he got to his feet he saw her standing on another rooftop a good fifty feet away and ten feet higher than where he was. The Stone swung back and forth as she dangled it tauntingly from her hand.

"… no majiks…" he heard her say under her breath, like she expected him not to be able to hear. "… let's see you claim the house now…"

The last time Max had lost the Stone; the effects had taken seconds to wear off and left him nearly comatose. Now, however, he still felt strong, still felt his canines with his tongue but for how long? Without that rock he might not make it out of the Downhills. Lotarre and his pack would tear him to pieces. He had to catch her. But he was still tired after the earlier chase, so he supposed she could outrun him. Plus she obviously knew the Downhills even better than those others. If he lost sight of her it was over.

But how long until his body broke back down and he lay bleeding on this snowy rooftop? He had to hold out for just a moment… catch her unaware.

The Stone spun easily on the string and swayed back and forth. Still Max did not move even as she wiggled it, teasing. Her smile was both excited and condescending at the same time. The message clear: You aren't much without this.

Still Max just stood and held his ground. Even as the howls of the Downhills gang rose from below again. They must have circled back. But he did not look around at their rising cries nor did he stare at the stone. With every bit of nerve he had left he kept their eyes locked and tried his best to look as though he was only curious as to why she had leapt away instead of dying to get back the Stone. A nasty ache began to creep its way up his spine.

The girl was impressed by his lack of panic. She folded her arms and impatiently tapped her foot in the powder. But still the man from the Museum just looked at her, no sign of worry on his face. His scent was pulled away in the wind so she could get no sense of him. She held the Stone up on the string and looked at it. Perhaps this was not…

By the time she looked back Max was gone; having jumped a good thirty feet into the air leaving only a faint trail of snow. The Downhills woman snapped her head up, following that trail to see him coming down on her fast. It took all the heart that he had not to go for the Stone first, he had to get her.

It was a good strategy because her first reaction when she caught sight of him was to dodge hard to her right; but she then feinted left with the Stone that was in her left hand. She would have gotten away and taken it with her. Instead Max landed hard into her slamming her down into the snow and pinning her. He snatched the string out of her hand and once again held the Stone. Thank God!

The girl was smiling. In fact when he landed on her she had squealed with delight and offered no resistance to his taking away the prize. She also did not try and get away; she just writhed in the snow beneath him.

"… I'm cold…" she pouted through her smile. Her hands went to his neck. Something in her smile, her eyes, and her voice would not let Max think that she meant him harm. He knew that he should not trust her but he could not help himself. Her affection for him was too apparent, and displayed so unashamedly.

The sharp points of her nails, or claws, slid across his neck gently. Her fingers found their way beneath his scarf and she pulled, sliding it away and then wrapping it about her own neck. It was then Max realized that he had her pressed into the snow.

Somewhere he managed to find some feelings of guilt so he stood up off of her and then pulled her to her feet. Too naturally she leaned into him when she stood.

"… come…"

It was so warm. The hot, smoky air hit Max's face when she opened the door. It was a hatch really, set into the old thatched roof and hidden in the pattern. The girl made a show of opening it, almost prideful, and then she dropped into the darkness inside. The roof felt pliant under his feet so Max walked as gingerly as he could to the edge of the open hatch, crouched down and looked inside. The snow covered landscape all around reflected way too much sunlight even as twilight approached and his eyes could not adjust. Whatever was down there was hidden in the blackness.

He stood. Yet another rooftop in the Downhills and it was getting late. The girl, Prya, had guided him here, traveling from rooftop to rooftop, back street to backstreet. She had done this without further conversation and Max had not been too eager to open his mouth either; because the howls of the Downhills pack would break out every so often. The course she had lead them on steered them clear of anyone.

Anyone Max could see.

But he had assumed that she was showing him the way out, not leading him back to her place. Looking around Max saw that he had lost his sense of direction again. The Downhills was supposed to be a very small neighborhood in Mountairy Rock but from where he was standing he might as well have been in a foreign country. The skyline was Downhills as far as he could see although there was the faintest outline of a King Rockwood just on the western horizon. Not that it helped, Max could not guess which one it was. Honestly it should not take him that long to find his way out. If he simply picked a direction and walked until he hit either the river, the park, or found himself in North Hills then he should alright. Only problem was that the Downhills gang would most certainly be on top of him before he could even get close to one of those goals. They were undoubtedly still out there searching.

So he leaned forward and jumped into the darkness inside the hatch pulling it closed behind him.

There was a fire burning inside the warm room. It was the only light source, casting a soft, flickering gold glow. Because he had been running across the snow white top of the Downhills all day his vision was now a bit sunburned. There was a soft white haze hanging over everything that he looked at and it kept his irises from opening fully. It might take a while for his eyes to adjust.

The room was not that big, but it was large enough that the fires light could not reach the corners. The floor was wood and much of it was covered with a huge, unevenly shaped fur rug. The walls were fixed with shelves filled with a disarray of items; clothes, jars, books… more clothes. As he looked farther along the wall he saw an array of stranger items. The most glaring of which was an animal skull. It was big, about two feet wide and its mouth held two impressive saber like canines. Couldn't be real… and what was this girl doing with it anyway? There was a tribal mask, large and ornate. It was Native American he guessed, possibly one of the Downhills tribes and it looked old.

Where the shelves ended began a wall covered in a huge intricately stitched cloth. The beautiful design embroidered on the wall-hanging was hard to see because tacked into the wall through the cloth and displayed before it… were several weapons.

Not guns, these were bladed weapons. Two spears, a twin set, crossed each other and divided the wall into four triangles. In each triangle hung a different set of weapons. On the left hung a large traditional wood bow with a matching quiver filled halfway with arrows. There was significant wear on the quiver and Max saw that there was a thin hairline crack along the length of the bow. In the bottom triangle hung a large shield bearing similar designs to that of the mask on the shelf. This too, showed signs of wear as nearly the entire bottom half appeared to have been ripped off which left its edges jagged. In the same triangle with the shield hung an axe and this too had the same design and markings. There were torn leather-straps dangling from the handle that looked as though it too had been through some extreme wear and tear. In the triangle on the right hung a more modern compound bow, painted similarly to the carved designs of the traditional bow. The arrows for the bow were attached to the bow itself. There was space for seven arrows but there were only three displayed. It was an odd high tech contrast to the older bow. In the upper triangle was another shield, as new and modern in comparison to the battered shield below it as was the compound bow to its traditional counterpart. It was hard and had a bit of sheen to it but Max could tell it was not metal but doubted it was plastic. Now that he saw the differences Max looked to the twin spears dividing the wall. They were not identical. Just as with the bows and the shields one of the spears was old and the other new. The older one's spear tip was chipped to boot. It was such an

144

odd display for a young woman to have that Max wondered if this was her place or someone else's. A few deep breaths told him different. The room was filled with her scent which sat heavy in the room by itself. He may have been the first visitor she had brought here for a very long time.

"This is where you live?" he asked to the darkness; the girl was nowhere to be seen but Max could smell her fresh scent clearly and could hear her soft breathing. She was doing something in the shadows; he could hear cloth being drawn against cloth. But he could not see her, his eyes were still a bit snow blinded.

Though it was quite warm Max had not taken off his coat. Part of him was eager to get back to civilization; part of him was unsure what this girl had in mind. Maybe the exits out of the Downhills were being watched, so she brought him here until it was safe to get out. Did she mean for him to stay the night?

"… where I…" she answered from somewhere beyond the firelight. Max looked hard until he could see the fires glow reflecting off her eyes. "… I am the center of a lot of unwanted attention…" she continued. "…No one knows of this place…" such an odd way of speaking Max thought, like she was just giving brief bits of thought.

"I know what you mean." He said. His eyes were finally adjusting to the dim light. The rest of the room emerged from the shadows that faded away like a receding fog. The outline of her body stood out from the archway she was leaning against. Relaxed and yet watchful, she was peering at him just as hard as he was looking at her.

"… not yet you don't…" and she walked into the light. She had removed her fur boots and now strode barefoot onto the rug. The skirt was different too, a darker brown. Had she changed in front of him in the darkness?

Her eyes held his for a second, and then she sat on the rug, legs sliding out of the slits on both sides of her skirt. It was hard not to notice the smooth curves of her bare legs as she folded them underneath her. She held out her hand expectantly, eyeing the Stone dangling from his clenched fist, and smiled.

He hesitated but there was nowhere for her to run really. The fire was not very bright but his eyes finally adjusted and with the exception of one other opening which looked to be a bathroom, there was no other way out save for the hatch. And after he caught her without having the Stone she had to be thinking that he really did not need it.

Max opened his coat and then sat down at the edge of the rug. The Stone was wrapped tightly about his hand and it took him a second to unwind it. Before he held it out he looked into her eyes. If she was playing him he could not tell. Yet she had helped him. The Downhills gang surely would have caught him if it had not been for her. When she had taken the Stone earlier, it had seemed more test than theft. Maybe she had really been insulted when he suggested that he was like her.

She took the Stone by the string and held it up for inspection, letting it spin slowly in front of her face. Her expression rotated from curiosity, to doubt, to disappointment and then back to curiosity. Soft red tipped fingers traced the engraved symbol on the Stone's face.

The clawed tips were not like his own claws Max saw. They were more like ordinary finger nails, albeit thicker. She had painted them that fire red color and the paint was now chipped from the day's activities. The claws remained extended from her finger tips even now, whereas Max's own claws had only appeared the few times he had been cornered and fighting.

"You said that I'm not like you." He began as diplomatically as possible in case she had been insulted. "What are you then?"

She held out the Stone to him then. With her inspection of it over she turned her attention to him. The rug did not move when she slid forward on it and closer to him. First she inspected his coat. Her hands swept along its length to the snow soaked edges.

"... didn't think you'd be in a fight..." sounded more like a question. She began pulling at his gloves.

"I wasn't the one who started it" he answered while watching her examine his fingertips. An eyebrow rose when she heard his answer.

"... the tussle at the museum..."

"Yea. You two were the ones trespassing. You boyfriend attacked me."

"HE'S NOT..." and she caught herself. "... not chasing you because of that fight." Her nonchalant speech pattern had dropped. Max remembered some of what she had said during their run.

"You said something about my having something he wants. I thought you might have meant the Stone."

Sharp teeth flashed in her smile. "...not the Monument..." and she held his eyes and arched her neck making her meaning obvious. Soft lupine eyes...

"Monument?"

"...don't know much..." she laughed a little. "...should see the witch..."

"Who?"

She placed her hand over his mouth quieting his questions. "... You are not Clan. Lot will beat you into the street if you come here again. He may even break Rule again and try for you at the museum. He's afraid..." and she placed her arms around his neck and pulled him intimately close. Her sweet, heady scent filled his head.

"Afraid of what?"

"... you..." and she kissed him, fully, like a lover. His own hands moved naturally around her pulling her body into his. Their eyelids fluttered against each other… her breath caressed his cheek….

This was insane.

He pulled away from her; she laughed and smiled that wicked grin.

"… should get you home…" and she stood and pulled him to his feet. "… again…"

Prya Kaylera Lakefolk got Max safely out of the Downhills, "again" she had told him. He believed her. That was all she was going to tell him it turned out, that and her name of course.

Lakefolk was one of the biggest families in the Downhills, Max had gathered. He had heard the name before, sparingly whenever the history of Mountairy Rock came up in conversation or study.

It was a surprise to find that many of the Downhills people were of African descent, though obviously of a broader and more diverse ancestry than most African Americans. That particular fact had never come up. There were few African American families of means in Mountairy Rock, and here was an almost legendary family that he had not even known.

Prya left Max at Cobbs Bridge and he stood there for a moment, staring back at the Downhills.

So the Stone had nothing to do with them, whatever they were. Oddly, it was only now that Max could tell the difference. From their collective smell, to the different shape of their claws, it became very apparent. But then what were they?

And how long had they been that way? It would explain the self enforced isolation and their hostile xenophobia throughout their entire history in this city. Had they been this way when they first settled here? Could it go back that far? Why had there never been any signs? How could they have kept it secret for so long?

Lakefolk, Sylvain, and Forrest, there were more names but these were among the oldest. Could they really have nothing to do with the Stone? Or the Maniacs?

It was possible that they really were unrelated, but Max was sure of one thing; they certainly did not want to keep it that way. It was no coincidence that Lotarre and Prya visited the Museum after Max had gotten hold of the Stone and right after the Maniacs had attacked. Damn! Why had he not thought to ask her about them?

He still had yet to decipher the etching, or come close to discovering the origin of the Stone itself. There was so little that he did know and he wasn't making much progress other than to get himself into one running scrap after another. With King gone there were not going to be very many opportunities for him to catch a break at the Museum.

Max took a deep cold breath and started the long march back to his apartment. There was still most of the North Hills to walk through.

THE LINE-UP, THE WITCH and THE WARRIOR

Coffee had never been Max's preferred source of caffeine, soda was. Unfortunately after a week of Pepsi fueled fourteen hour days his stomach felt like the lining was being eaten away by the acid. So the morning after getting chased out of the Downhills Max sat himself in line at the small café in Rebel's Keep, hoping that plenty of cream would ease the burning in his gut.

There was always a bit of a line early in the morning, most of the staff who worked in the various towers of the Inner Bailey stopped here on their way in to their officers. The unwritten rule was that you could not be considered late if you were waiting for coffee. This morning, like most, no one was in a rush after having received their cup o' Joe. The seats of the café were filled and there was standing room only by the newsstand. The dichotomy between those who casually drank and conversed and those who stoically stood in line struck Max as a bit amusing. At least until he caught sight of his own gaunt face in the reflection of the counter top.

With a handful of creams in his free hand he started to make his way out of the café when he heard his name called. Standing among the group of drinkers by the magazines was Dr. Pini, Historian, and several of either his staff or students, or both. The cheerful smile was back, the last time Max had seen the man was the night of the Maniacs break-in. Pini waved him over.

"Good to see you Max! I didn't think you drank coffee? Slave to the caffeine demon eh?" Waaay too energetic for this time of the morning.

"Had to make an exception today, been a rough week."

"Hmmm… How are things in the South Tower?" the smile seemed a bit forced. Max never paid attention to the inner Museum politics but he had gotten the sense that there were several members of the staff who ranked in the "Out of the Loop" group. Dr. Pini may have been kept in the dark as to everything that had been going on since the break-in and was looking for Max to give him some info.

"Fine. Dr. Collins has got everything running well and Dr. King calls back here regularly." With no interest in becoming a player in the inner politics of the Museum Max tried to wrap it up quickly hoping to avoid giving Dr. Pini the impression that he was an ally.

"When is Dr. King due back?" There may have been a slight hint of worry behind that smile. Did he want King back sooner or later? Max told himself it did not matter to him.

"… uh… we're not sure, but it's unlikely that he'll… uh… return before the end of the month. Could be longer if they meet bad weather."

"Oh? They're not still searching? Hasn't He found Robert?"

Damn. Apparently Doc Collins had not gotten around to telling everyone about Bazillions' death yet. Well Max certainly did not want to be the one to drop the news. Especially not this way. If he told Dr. Pini about Bazillion right here and right now, he would end up having to tell everyone here at the café. Then everyone that they told would come running to him to hear it for themselves.

"I'll check with Dr. Collins and try to get the latest news. You'll be in the East Tower?"

Dr. Pini seemed mollified by his promise to update him. Max had found him to be a nice enough teacher when he had taken his classes some years back. So he did not like putting him off like that, mostly because he had no intention of seeking him out later to explain.

The rest of Dr. Pini's group did not appear as satisfied so Max high-tailed it out of the café before any of them got the nerve up to question him further. It was going to be another long day as it was.

"This is him now." Another disembodied voice whispered in his ear as he approached the South Tower lobby. It was Sheriff Lynne's voice. But where…

"Hmn… Big boy. He's got 'the look' to him." A second voice, a gravely, level, man's voice answered hers. Instinctively Max sniffed the air, and found Lynne's scent almost immediately, the jasmine very familiar to him by now. Then among the other more familiar scents of the lounge, South Tower and the Museum itself, wafted a new one.

A strong masculine scent that reminded Max of rawhide.

"What look?" Lynne asked. He still did not see them, which meant that they had to be in the back of the lounge.

"Player" Rawhide answered.

Mrs. Dana sat in her usual position behind her desk, waiting on three lines of students, faculty, and vendors, where she looked much like a spider at the center of a web. The room was a little crowded because of that throng of people and Max could not see to the back of the lounge where the Sheriff must have been. If he could not see back there then how could Sheriff Lynne have seen him coming when he had still been out in the South Hall?

"Let's get to it" said the man. Now Max could tell the voices were actually coming from behind him.

They had been sitting on one of the sofas set to the right of the entrance. It was a position, Max noted, that effectively hid them from the view of anyone entering the room. It took some effort but he stayed on his course to walk past Mrs. Dana's desk even as he listened to their footsteps approach him from behind.

"Hey, Mrs. Dana" he said and prepared to slip past knowing they would stop him before he got to the stairwell, but, hopefully, too late for them to avoid Mrs. Dana's wrath. Or so he thought. Instead of hearing Sheriff Lynne call his name, or having she and her friend walk in front of him to cut him off, a hand came down on his shoulder, the man's hand and it was heavy with a firm and forceful grip.

"Hold on Madigan" came the gravelly voice.

He was actually a few inches taller than Max, which surprised him. At six foot, three inches he seldom met people as tall as he. This man's shoulders were wider as well so this was also the first person he had seen in a long time who was actually bigger than him. King had been the last.

The man's frame was large and filled out the worn ankle length brown leather coat he wore. Large, stained leather boots gave him an outdoorsy look which he topped off with that "unshaven yet trimmed" look on his beard and mussed dirty brown hair.

It may have all been an effect he put on for that "Marlboro Man" look, but Max did not think so. The stranger had turned him around and their eyes met. His were level and certain, his mouth was firm and set in a tight line, whatever he wanted with Max he was determined to get it. The rawhide scent filled Max's nostrils, reminding him of strength earned through wear and tear. The calloused hand on Max's shoulder was some evidence of that. Like the slight twist in this man's nose where it once had been broken. And like the faint jagged scar just beneath his Adam's apple.

His other hand was set on his hip which, coincidentally was holding open his coat and exposing the shiny gold Sheriff's badge. Max was not going to be first to break the gaze so he never looked down to read it, settling for the shiny peripheral view.

"We have to talk to you" the man said.

Max held his look for another moment and then slowly, noticeably glared at the calloused hand holding his shoulder. When the man did not move it, Max looked back and saw another challenge.

Anger broiled behind his eyes…

What was with these cops?

…His whole body tensed…

What? Did she bring this guy down here to try and scare him?

…The coffee cup began to crease in his grip…

These people don't know!

…The inside of his lips felt his teeth press against them as his canines grew. The Styrofoam of the cup squeaked slightly as his claws scraped along it.

Oh shit!

Quickly he closed his eyes and took a long a deliberate deep breath. The canines slid back, the claws retracted.

"Are we bothering you?" The man said. They had not noticed.

"Take you hand off of me." Max said meeting his eyes. The Marlboro man looked him up and down and then snorted as he removed his hand.

"Don't put your hands on me again." The old angers were still there. He had never liked being treated like a hoodlum, thug, or child. Not back when he was a kid running around the streets and not now that he was a college graduate working on a Professorship.

"Or what?" Marlboro spat back.

"Alright, alright." Lynne cut in. "Mr. Madigan we would like to talk to you. We tried to reach you at your apartment but must have missed you."

When he turned to her he did not see what he had been expecting. He assumed she had brought the cowboy with her to intimidate him; however she did not look satisfied. In fact she seemed to be irritated with both of them now.

Quickly Max tried to think of the best way to tell them to go to hell.

"We would like you to look at some pictures and see if you can pick out the men who attacked you at the museum." She then pointed to the Marlboro Man. "This is Sheriff Rogan. His district has been having problems with this gang as well" She began reaching into that portfolio where she kept the sketches of him and the snake maniac.

Sheriff Rogan looked Max up and down. "You're the hard ass who works for King right?"

Again Max met his eyes and while the two stared hard at one another, Sheriff Lynne pulled out a small photo album.

"What? You're not gonna answer me?"

Max turned from him dismissively and faced Sheriff Lynne as she handed him the open book.

"Don't think…" Rogan was trying to lean into his field of vision. Lynne quickly pushed him off.

"Stop it, Ford! I didn't let you come up here for this."

Max watched the exchange out of the corner of his eye. He had read that the Sheriffs of Mountairy Rock worked alone, one per predetermined section of the city. It was a twenty-four hour a day job. No days off… no vacation… no second or third shift… no back up. There must have been rules or procedures for them to work together, and apparently Rogan needed her permission to be here. But WHY did he want to be here?

Sheriff Lynne handed him a small photo album. It was spread open with photos on both pages. Two rows, of three pictures apiece; mug shots.

"See if you recognize any of these men."

The maniacs were easy to pick out. There was an odd symmetry in the way their unkempt hair fell about their faces and the strange worried look in their eyes. The night of the second break-in, while hanging on the leaning scaffolding, Max had seen that same look in the eyes of a Maniac who was clutching the swaying metal with everything he had. It had been a lost, fearful look, almost like a child looking for its parent.

"You recognized one of them?" Lynne pushed.

"He's one." On the first page; middle picture on the bottom row. The hair was shorter than most but Max had seen him definitely. Then his finger trailed over to the next page and the first picture was… whoa! Jean?

Jean… Max could not remember his last name, was really beaten up in the photo. Probably from the fall his took off of the East Hall.

"And him. Definitely."

"This one? Good." Lynne took the book back.

"Hey! I didn't see the rest." Hell, he could identify them all probably.

"There were only two that attacked you" she argued.

"Two? What are you…" … AH SHIT! The night he got jumped outside the student center, there had been only two! And Max had not even seen those two on that page. No one knew that he had been there the night of the second break-in. That was where he had seen Jean and the other guy. Not that it mattered, a Maniac was a Maniac. But he supposed it could mess up their investigation. Not to mention that he would now have to cover for his slip up.

"I wanna see the ones that broke into the museum." And she would want to know why. "So if they… come back I can… I'll know who they are."

"No. In case we need you to identify them for court, I want to keep your memory uncompromised. Besides most of these guys are either in lock up or in way too bad a shape to give anybody any trouble. We have the first guy you picked, soon we'll find the other." She placed the photo album back into that portfolio carry all.

"But you have his picture?" Max asked.

"That was from a previous incident."

"Still, they could be hanging around the Museum" he argued.

"We've got the Museum covered now. You'll be fine." …Sure.

"Unless you know these boys from somewhere else?' said the cowboy. He was quick, or maybe just more suspicious of Max than

Sheriff Lynne. How could THAT be?

"What?" Max could not keep the snap out of his tone… and as the anger built again he found that he did not want to.

"I understand that this may just be about some bad imports you and King have been bringing in." His voice was full of sarcasm and challenge, but his eyes were watchful, looking to see Max's reaction. What had he said earlier? Something about Max having the 'Look'?

It was hard but Max kept himself from battling with Rogan. Instead he turned to Sheriff Lynne. "Are we done?"

"I'll be in contact with you Mr. Madigan." She placed her hand on Rogan's arm and turned him to leave.

"I'm not finished." Rogan stated.

"Yes you are. Let's go." Lynne pulled him out behind her.

Max watched them go and then turned to see everyone in the lounge watching him. Upset, he forgot protocol.

"Uh, Mr. Madigan? DID I SLEEP WITH YOU LAST NIGHT?"

There was a new pile of paperwork waiting for him on his desk when Max finally made it up to the office that he shared with Fatima but he hardly noticed it. She gave him a look when he walked in but he took no notice of her as well. He walked in and sat down while wondering to himself just how badly he had messed up.

At the very least, he had just helped to hinder the police investigation. The Maniacs who had attacked him at the Museum might get away because he pointed out a couple of guys that they probably already had locked up. Those two Maniacs who attacked him outside the student center knew what he looked like and where he worked. It would only be a matter of time before they ambushed him again.

The Sheriff suspected him of being involved, which was right of course, just not in the way that she suspected. If those Maniacs he pointed out had alibis then she and her Cowboy buddy would be back. And what was his deal?

He finally saw the pile of work on his desk. Flipping through the top couple of folders told him that most of the work was what it had been for the past couple of weeks; administration work. More requests for; forms, approvals, access to labs, and notices of firings, hiring's, transfers, and new exhibit packages, invoices, and legal documents. Depressing.

"I know." Fatima said knowingly from her desk. She was staring at her own pile of accumulated work. "I didn't know Dr. King did so much."

Max frowned at this. "He didn't. He couldn't have. His own research took up most of his time." A nasty thought occurred to him. "I guess we're catching a lot of work that Collins and the other

Department heads used to deal with themselves. With King in Africa, they've been dumping it all on us."

"No…." Fatima was always ready to believe somebody was getting away with something at her expense. "They better not be!"

But they probably were. "Even if I'm right, you know King will expect it all to be done when he gets back. Who's it going to fall on anyway?" he asked. Fatima huffed, folded her arms and frowned her face up in deep thought about how to turn the tables on her enemies. Max looked at the pile of work on his table and wondered how much of his future would be spent in filing and red tape instead of his own pursuits. It was like walking through… mud, uphill. He would never get anywhere with…

His head snapped up. A shadow moved out of the room just as his eyes focused on the door.

"What the hell was that?"

"What?" Fatima was suddenly standing up at her desk, ridged, with a fearful look on her face. "Don't play, Max!"

He realized that he had stood up at his desk as well, which was probably what triggered her to do the same. Now he could see the fear in her eyes, fear that something was about to happen again.

So he sat back down. "Sorry, just jumpy."

"Well calm down. You're making me crazy!" She laughed nervously and sat back down too, but she kept her eyes flicking from Max to the door.

Something had been there. Max inhaled, sifting scents in the room. Someone… a woman. Someone… new and that person had been in the room, not just passing by. How could she have been in the room with them? It was a small room really. There was nowhere that someone could have hid and not be seen. Could the shadow have been someone just passing by the door from out in the hallway? His eyes fell on a chair set against the wall. A fragrant scent reached his nose and Max pulled it in. A perfume it was, the toxic chemical taste of it was a poor imitation of a true floral scent. The smell… the taste of it, was too strong for it to have come from outside.

Okay, he wanted to check it out but he did not want to alarm Fatima any more than he already had. It took some restraint but he managed to actually look through five more folders indifferently before moving.

He grabbed some of the folders and nonchalantly got up, walked around his desk then dumped them in the trash by the chair. Fatima was watching him until he dropped the folders.

"You'd better get those done" and then she looked back down to her own work.

Deliberately he missed the trash can with the last few pieces of paper. So he knelt to pick them up. This covered his placing his hand on the seat as he stood.

The chair was warm, like someone had been sitting in it for a while. The feminine scent was stronger here but still faint. He looked to the door but nothing was there.

So as casually as he could he walked out into the hallway. It was empty, but the scent was there. He drew a deep breath. Did he really want to do this again? Another chase? Another… beating?

The elevator sounded at the end of the corridor. As he heard the doors opening he found himself racing down the hall. The scent grew stronger and Max prepared himself for another fight. He got there just as they were closing and stuck his hand in…

…but the elevator was empty. What the hell?

The scent led him right here and was strongest right here but the elevator was empty. So he turned and looked at the stairwell that was a few feet away. If that door had been opened he would have heard it… right? He walked to the door sniffing and noticing that the scent got weaker.

He looked back to the elevator as the doors began to close again. She was in there…

The doors clanged against his arm once again and shimmied back open. Max peered upwards toward the ceiling and the infamous elevator trap door. But there was no trapdoor, just a lot of ceiling lighting. Empty.

But the scent was getting stronger… definitely a woman's scent. Max drew the elevator air deep into his lungs, letting the various scents scrape along the inside of his nose. The woman's perfumed fragrance came in strong, like she was standing right next to him. He could smell her perfume, the stretched leather of a briefcase, the coffee and croissant she had for breakfast and even the relaxer in her hair. Where was she?

Max closed his eyes and inhaled again and the scent got no stronger but neither did it get any weaker. She was here somewhere.

Closing his eyes allowed Max to focus on the scent but it also forced him to pay attention to his other senses as well. Like the soft whisper of… Max could hear her breathing now… he could feel the heat her body was giving off on his skin.

He opened his eyes but the elevator still sat empty. No way, she was right there.

Then slowly, he realized that he was looking right at her. It was, like waking very slowly from a dream, in that space of time between dreaming and being awake where you come to realize that you had in fact been dreaming and that you are now awake. He was looking right at her, had been looking at her the entire time.

She was what Max's father would have called "Essence Fine". Tall, dark brown skin, long black braided hair, and dressed sharp. She was probably close to forty years of age and was still strikingly beautiful. She wore a brown calf length skirt that snuggly hugged legs covered with opaque black stockings visible only for a second above the black leather calf high boots. An animal print shawl lay across her chest and over her shoulders, partially hiding her form fitting sweater. Max could see that there was something around her neck, a locket possibly, because he could see the multi-colored string peeking out just beneath the braided locks but the item itself was hidden beneath the shawl. Her briefcase was held out before her defensively and her manicured nails dug into the leather. She eyed Max with a look of fearful wonder for a second when their eyes met but then she quickly composed herself.

"Going down?" she said with an almost annoyed expression. She lowered the briefcase and then stood there plaintively, waiting, coolly brushing a loose braid off of her face and pushing it behind an ear. The acrid tinge to her scent told Max that it was just a cover. She was scared.

"Who are you?" he demanded. Even as he was looking at her now he began to imagine her sitting in that chair, watching him the whole time. Or was it more than just imagination? Did he actually see her and just not realize it? Was he now remembering the "dream"? How the hell had she done that?

Her hand went up under the shawl and balled into a fist as she grabbed whatever it was. Looking him directly in the eye she mouthed something, hardly even breathing, then stated firmly; "Let go of the door."

It was like someone tapped a tuning fork against the bottom of his spine. His resolve to confront her evaporated and his arm weakened. The doors own strength became too much for him to keep open and Max watched the woman slide out of sight as the door almost closed.

Almost.

When their eyes lost contact that grating vibration that weakened him down to his bones stopped. Anger flared and Max growled violently. Quickly he jammed his hand into the door frame again and slammed the elevator door back open.

The woman jumped back against the elevator wall in fright, gasping out her fear. Max stepped into the elevator not noticing the ivory claws topping each of his fingers that were then pressing deep into the wood paneling on the inside of the door.

"WHO ARE YOU?" he growled. The woman did not answer though she shook with obvious fear. The one hand was still balled in a fist under her shawl; the other was frantically digging into her briefcase. What was tied around her neck?

…A Stone?

"…Not going to ask you ag…" without any warning that she had found whatever she had been frantically digging for, the woman whipped her hand out at him as he closed in on her. A bright red and yellow powder exploded right into his face.

"Ung!" Max fell back throwing his hands up defensively and releasing the door as he did so. Every opening on his face suddenly felt as if it was on fire. The burning intensified with every second and he spat and coughed and then screamed and yelled in pain. Somehow over his screaming, Max heard the elevator doors close.

He tried rubbing the powder off but that only made it worse and managed to spread the burning fire from his face to his hands as well. The insides of his nostrils blazed when he inhaled and the fire shot to the back of his skull. Ragged gasps for air through his mouth immediately drew the hot burning fire across his tongue, down his throat and into his lungs. He spit and rolled away from the elevator but each breath burned hotter. It was as if the cloud of red and yellow powder clung to him. Tears burned out of his eyes but the blaze was not going to be put out that easily.

Effectively blind Max stumbled further down the hall. There was a bathroom down here somewhere he knew. Papers and thumbtacks popped off a bulletin board as he felt his way along. Finally he found the door. His hands were so hot he could barely feel the door knob to turn it but somehow he managed and banged his way inside. The sink was to his immediate right he remembered and he staggered that way only bang his shins into the rim of a toilet bowl.

Max fell against the wall behind the bowl and nearly lost his footing. WHO THE HELL MOVED THE DAMNED STALLS? The pain got worse; making him wonder if the powder was not in fact an acid. His face could be melting off right then! It felt so terrible that Max thought to dunk his head in the toilet.

Fuck that.

"ARRGH!" He pushed off from the back wall and ran smack into the now closed stall door.

"GAA!" would have been 'God Dammit!' but his tongue was inflamed and searing. Though his hand was numb he hooked it over the top of the door at his wrist and jerked it open, right into his face. The pain lanced and he heard the latch on the stall door click.

Another "Gaa" and Max turned and dropped to his knees. The bowl was a lot closer than he had thought it would be and his elbows hit the rim with a jolt.

He felt for the lid and flipped open only to hear it slap back down. The burning was getting worse and his hands were now on fire. Despite the burning inside of his mouth Max clamped his lips shut, flipped the lid up again and jammed his head into the bowl as far as he could.

The powder had dug into his skin deeply and relief was not immediate. It took almost ten minutes and several "Are you Ok?"'s from a few passersby who before Max could stand to take his head out of the bowl. Quickly he left the stall and moved to the sinks where he a turned the faucet on full blast and continued trying to remove the last of the powder. His eyes were red and still stinging but he could see again. Well enough to see that he was in the women's bathroom.

"Da!" Max stood and looked into the mirror above the sink but he could barely make himself out. His eyes could not focus and they still streamed tears. Once, as a teenager, he had been hit with pepper spray but this was far more debilitating. Leaning closer to the mirror he thought that his skin looked a little red but was otherwise unmarred.

What the hell was that? Who the hell was she? Max blinked as those questions raced through his mind.

"What the hell happened to you?" Fatima voice sounded behind him. When he turned to look at her Max found that he could barely recognize her.

"What happened to your face?" Her voice was full of concern, and a little fearful. He could hear her breathing start to increase and go a little ragged as she pushed it in and out of her nose while probably clamping her lips shut. It was the one remaining sense that Max had left and Fatima's fear filled it.

"How bad is it?" he asked her.

"Your eyes are swollen, and your face is all red. What happened?" Blurry as she was Max could see that she had her arms wrapped around herself. In spite of his pain, her fear hurt him more and he knew that this incident was only going to make working at the Museum harder for her.

"I…" was just attacked by some crazy bitch in the elevator! "…I'm having a bad reaction…" No way would she buy this. "Shell fish I think."

"You're allergic to shell fish?" Her voice was high and tight. She did not believe him. "Max I watched you wolf down whole trays of shrimp at Museum functions." Oh yeah.

"I know. I haven't broken out like this in a while. I thought I was over it. It's been awhile but this is what happens."

"What's that red stuff on you?" Fatima demanded.

White hot DEATH! "I don't know."

"Let me…" she was reaching to wipe it off, he thought.

"I'm fine! Don't touch… it's too painful." Max stormed out of the ladies rest room, jamming his shoulder into the door frame as he did so. Why the hell hadn't he just stayed in the office?

"It's a picture of Mayor Rhoades smoking a Rockwood tree", Amanda explained. It was almost ten o'clock at night and Max's vision had only gotten marginally better. It was bad enough that he probably should have stayed home but he did not want to miss an opportunity to see Amanda again, even if that meant he would bump into things all night.

The date was her idea and she had brought him to the "Proposition 615" protest rally at the city council meeting in New City. The crowd was so large that very few of the protesters got into the actual meeting. The demonstrators were made up mostly of students and representatives from a few interest groups, the largest being the Rockwood preservation Society. They had been very organized and imaginative if what Amanda was describing to him was accurate.

"And there's one where the tree has been cut and keeps falling over and over. That's the biggest" she continued. They walked arm in arm with her guiding him most of the way. Maybe Max played up the blind man bit a little much but he found that the more she had to explain to him, the closer she held him.

"That big blur next to the light?", he knew he was wrong.

"No, that's prop of a Queen Rockwood on fire." She turned and looked into his eyes. "Did you see a doctor?"

"Does Fatima and a bottle of eye wash count?" He probably should have gone to see a doctor but that last thing he wanted was to bring more attention to himself. Besides, he really was feeling a lot better. "I'll be fine."

"This is terrible." Amanda was shaking her head.

"No really, it's getting better."

"No I mean this demonstration. There's no news coverage. There isn't a single news van out here. And I don't see any photographers taking pictures either."

Max looked about himself but he doubted that right now he could pick out anything that she could not.

"Maybe they're inside the council chambers?" he offered.

"Then where are the vans? No. The Mayor got them to back off" she accused.

"He can't do that." Max blinked back a few stray tears. "He's not popular enough."

"Then where are they?" came a deep masculine voice. Max turned as he saw Amanda turn. The blur walking toward them was not much taller than Amanda's blur, maybe even a little shorter.

"Craig! Are you seeing what I'm seeing?" Amanda greeted the blur. There was new car smell in the air.

"They're trying to bury us Amanda." it said. Max could not be sure but he thought that the blur was standing a little too close to Amanda.

"Hi" he said stepping up.

"I'm sorry", Amanda quickly said. "Craig this is Max, Max – Craig. Craig works for the R.P.S.. Max here is a researcher at the Museum."

"Hello Max." The blur reached out a shadowy maw. "You work at the Museum?"

Max reached and shook the hand which gripped his a little too hard. Craig was a knuckle grinder.

"Yea. I'm in King's Research group." The grip tightened.

"King?" Craig responded. "He should be here! His voice carries a lot of weight. I've been requesting to meet with him for weeks. But I've been getting no response. Isn't he concerned about Prop 615?"

"Well," Max pulled his hand free. "...a lot's been happening at the Museum. He's not even in the country right now."

"Not in Country? Well what could we expect, Amanda? He's in the Mayor's pocket." Max could not be sure since the man's eyes were hidden in the dark blurry shadow of his brow but Craig seemed to be directing that remark at him. Did he have his hand on her arm?

"Dr. King really doesn't get involved with the politicians that much. Mayors come and go, but King's been head curator and a Dean at M.R.U. going back almost twenty years. Knowing him... I doubt he even knows who the Mayor is now." The truth was that King and Rhoades played golf occasionally but he probably did not know what Prop 615 was about.

"Well where do you stand Maxwell?" Craig asked. Something in this man's manner made Max think that he was putting on a show... for Amanda?

"Well... Craig, how did the R.P.S. let the media block out this protest? Rockwoods are a NATIONAL treasure. The NATIONAL media should have been called. Mayor can't stop them."

Craig just regarded Max for a moment.

"...Maxxxx..." came a strong, low, resonant voice, soft but clear through the din of the shouting, singing protestors.

Prya's voice...

...somewhere in the crowd.

"Well?" Craig asked with smugness in his voice that Max had no doubt was matched by an equally self-righteous look on his still blurry face. What had he missed?

"Uh..." he stammered. Same as in the Downhills; only he could hear Prya.

"Never mind all that" Amanda cut in. "Is there anyway King might make a statement about Prop 615, Max?"

"I'm sure he'll address it. Problem is; when? He went to Africa to find out who murdered one of our researchers. No way to know when he'll get back."

"Seems like his priorities are straight" Craig said sarcastically.

"What? A man is dead." Max felt a flare of defensive anger. It had been a while since he had to vie for a woman's attention against some other guy. Craig was trying to attack Max through King and trying to link Max's character to those opposed to Prop 61… 4? 5? Whatever the hell it was anyway. He was starting to push too far and Max was tired of being pushed, attacked, chased…

"A man whom I heard was smuggling drugs into the country. If King…" Craig was going on.

"Robert wasn't a smuggler! He was a Doctor of Anthropology and a good man. King went to Africa to find out why one of his researchers, a former student, was murdered. Jackass." Great, now he was defending Bazillion!

"Ok, Ok." Amanda stepped in between them. "Craig, we'll see you later."

"…aw… let them fight…" Prya's voice again. Max couldn't help but look around. Most of the rest of the crowd was just a blur.

"Aren't you coming with us?" Craig asked. "…to the Student center? We're going to regroup there after the council meeting is over."

He sniffed instinctively trying to catch her scent. Unfortunately his nasal passages were still inflamed from that yellow and red powder. Just breathing still burned and he could not smell a damn thing.

"ow."

"No I'm sorry, Craig." Amanda was telling her friend. "Tell me about it later." Max could see the subtle slumping of the Craig's blurry shoulders. The ass had bated him into nearly hitting him on purpose and it had almost worked. Amanda pulled Max and they walked away from Craig and the crowd.

"Before you ask; yes, I went out with him", She admitted. Max truly had not thought that. Craig wasn't just jealous or lovelorn; he was trying to impress Amanda by making Max look bad. Why would he be that pressed if he had already gone out with her? Of course if Craig had any real sense he had probably seen all the good things in Amanda that Max had.

"Really? Why'd you break up with him?"

"We weren't really going together. Just a few dates…" she took a deep breath. "…a few weeks ago."

"Right before you and I went out? How LONG before?" Max stopped their escape run and looked at her. Her eyes were coming into focus.

"My last date with him was the night before 'Our' first." Amanda smiled tightly at him. "It wasn't going anywhere", She offered.

"That explains why he attacked King like that. He thinks you all are still dating.", Unless… "Are you?"

Amanda smiled and looked away as she started walking again.

"Where's my scarf?" she dodged coyly. Max grimaced.

"…scarf? This scarf?" Came the low voice once more.

Crap.

They walked through the crowd of protestors, making their

way away from City Hall. Amanda continued to describe the various protest signs to him but Max was preoccupied. His focus was divided between wondering if Amanda was still dating other people and trying to find Prya in the thinning group of protestors. Why she was even here tonight. Was she stalking him? Or was she actually here for the protest? With his vision blurry and his nose out of commission he could not tell if there were other Downhills folk in the crowd.

She wasn't wearing Amanda's scarf was she? God help him if she decided to walk up to them.

"Catching a cold?" Amanda asked. He had been sniffing more and more frequently as they walked through the crowd trying to catch a trace of Prya. It was not getting him anywhere and it pained him terribly but he could not help it.

"Uh... I don't think so... could be allergies."

A young woman stepped out of the crowd and for a moment Max's breath caught in his throat. Then the feminine form called Amanda's name. The distance was too great for Max to see her properly but as she drew closer he thought she might be one of the protesters.

"That's Tara." Amanda told him as the girl emerged from the background haze of crowd goers. "Craig probably sent her to get me to go to the 'After Protest Party'." She introduced Max to her friend who only acknowledged him briefly before launching into a list of things that had gone wrong that night. From the way she was talking it seemed like Amanda was a lot more involved than she had let on. Her inviting him down here might have meant a lot more than he had initially thought. While the two women conversed Max diverted his attention away and toward the crowd. His hearing was the only thing unaffected by the powder and right then he was using it to try and hear Prya's voice again. Even though they had begun to escape the crowd the volume of their voices still enveloped them as it resounded off the tall buildings in New City Square. Still, very much like before, he seemed only to catch her voice when she wanted. She was keeping quiet now.

"Ok, ok." Amanda was saying to her friend. Something important had been said and he had missed it. Amanda was looking at a piece of paper that Tara had handed her, she then turned to Max.

"I swear this'll only take a second. Don't move."

"Uh 'Don't move'?"

"You'll be fine!" she laughed.

"Sure. I'll be right here." He tried not to sound too distracted. Briefly he wondered if this really was some game the guy Craig had come up with, to get Amanda to stay. If only he could concentrate on his date then...

"...Max..." this came from right behind him.

Prya stood there with that slight smile on her face, watchful yet calm. It was her companion who jumped a little at how fast Max had turned. It took a second for him to draw in the details. Her eyes were wide with fear and she stood a little taller because she was rigid. Almost as if she was ready to run. It was the woman from the elevator.

"HEY!" Max jumped himself a little when he realized who she was, throwing his hands up protectively in front of his face.

"... so young…" Prya was laughing but more importantly, the woman she was standing beside was not attacking. Her fearful demeanor was fading as she watched Max backpedal.

"Sorry about using the Bane. I think we both scared each other a little." She said. Prya was still laughing. Max looked from one to the other.

Prya was dressed a little more conservatively than when he last saw her. The fur skirt remained but she now wore a rather expensive looking black leather jacket, matched with calf high black leather boots. It was a good look to mix in with the crowd, or a least not to stand out as someone from the Downhills. And… oh crap! She wore Amanda's scarf loosely about her neck.

The woman who had burned his face off was still carrying the briefcase which Max was certain still contained the red and yellow powder. She was dressed just as sharply as before and her braided hair was swept over one shoulder. Again Max found her strikingly beautiful, but the burning of his nose and mouth reminded him how dangerous she was; something else his father had once said about women who were "Essence Fine".

"Bane?" he asked.

She took a breath before answering. "Yes. It's like… mace. I hope you're feeling better?" Maybe she was sincere, but Prya was still laughing and that made Max grind his teeth.

"Who are you?" he demanded.

The woman looked to Prya quickly before answering him. Her hand made a slight movement toward her chest but then quickly went back down to her side. He remembered that she wore something around her neck. It was still there, again concealed beneath her clothing. A Stone?

"My name is Rasheeda Landry. Ms. Lakefolk spoke to me about you."

Max looked to Prya again. The laughter had stopped but she still had a playful smile. Out of habit he sniffed again only to receive more of the residual burning. Even though he had discovered that the Downhills people varied greatly in ethnicity this woman did not match what he would have expected. She was too tall, her skin too dark, and she was not wearing any of the fur or leather clothing he had seen on almost all the rest. Plus Landry did not sound like a Downhill's name.

"She told you to come mace me?"

"No. I was protecting myself." She said with an air of authority.

"You had trapped me in the elevator and would not let me go."

"You were spying on me in my office, Lady! And then you…" he did not know quite how to say it. "… I almost didn't see you…"

Prya snickered and looked to Rasheeda. "…good eyes…"

Ms. Landry smiled a little. "Yes… well… I heard about your problems at the museum and in the Downhills. I didn't want to disturb you but I still wanted to see you."

"Why?"

"Ms. Lakefolk told me of your visit to the Downhills. You've stirred things up quite a bit but not just there. There's been talk about you all over the city."

"About me?" Max could not help but to feel she was playing him, at least just a bit. She was composed and a little fearful, but he could sense she wanted something. Still, if there were others out there who knew about the Downhills or worse; that he had been at the Museum during the second break in, then he would be better off knowing who they were.

"Who's talking about me?"

"Well," she hesitated. "… not 'you' per se. No one knows who it is really."

"Who 'what' is?"

"… new power…" Prya offered. She was playing with Amanda's scarf. Max looked over his shoulder to see if she was on her way back, but his sight had not gotten any better. A coy laugh let Max know that Prya found the situation amusing.

"The incident at the Museum…" Ms. Landry began softly, cautiously.

"I didn't have anything to do with that." If she thought he had killed the guards and those Maniacs that would explain why she "maced" him.

Prya was no longer smiling but watching him thoughtfully. Had she believed that he had killed those guards? Had she been thinking that all along?

Ms. Landry seemed to consider his denial, but not like she believed him, more like she did not want to challenge him directly.

"There are… those who think you did" she said.

Again "Who?" he wanted to know. Was she talking about the Maniacs?

"… the girlfriend…" Prya warned.

Max looked over his shoulder; if Amanda was coming he could not see her. When he turned back Prya was gone and Ms. Landry was digging in her briefcase. He took a few steps back.

She laughed a little when she saw this, paused, and seemed to reconsider him. Then she pulled a card from her briefcase and held it out to him.

"Call me and we'll talk" she said. Max was hesitant to take the card. She saw this and then cleared her throat before quietly adding, "...about the Serpent Cult."

The card was blank save for her name: Rasheeda Revan Landry, and her phone number printed on the card. He only nodded to her before she walked off, not really willing to commit himself to calling her, or believing that she really knew anything.

The Serpent Cult? Max thought of the Maniac with those eyes, fangs, and claws.

Damn. Prya still had Amanda's scarf.

WEST OAKS

"Not exactly where I thought Marc would end up." Steve stated with a grimace on his face that matched Max's own. The two of them had gotten off the bus a few streets back having mistaken a huge upscale brownstone for the building for which they were searching. An easy mistake, Marc Gray was a Criminal Defense Attorney who maintained his own practice in a similar brownstone. The one that they had confused for his happened to be on the affluent side of West Oaks. The Rock City Arms, however, was an apartment complex on the "other" side. Neither one of them really knew this section that well but they both recognized a ghetto when they saw it. This was not what they thought they would find when they came looking up their old friend. The building was poorly maintained, just enough Max supposed, to keep it up to code. The lower level apartment doors and the windows were barred. There was a huge sign announcing vacancies in front of the building. The amount of rent they were seeking was clearly printed on the front sign and he saw that it was just about what he was paying in Ivy Hills. If he had not been working for the Museum and gotten a discount then this was the kind of place he would have had to turn. It made him wonder how good Marc's practice could be if this is where he was living.

"Watch it", Steve murmured a warning but Max had heard and scented them long before his friend had seen them. A small group of men stood or sat outside the front steps of the entrance. Some were drinking, Max could smell the dark liquor, and some smoking and it reminded him of a club in Jamaica he once went to. Always a risk, these little encounters, but having been seen in turn they were now committed. Steve was dressed casually, as usual, but Max was dressed for work which could either cause some problems or eliminate them. Growing up he had always seen this group in one form or another, in one place or another. What happened next always depended on variables that could not be calculated. Perhaps these guys were harmless, ranging from an innocent group of guys, to drunks and potheads too high do anything. Or maybe they were drunks and potheads who were just aware enough to play the "Stick-up" game. Could be that they saw Max and figured him for a lawyer or a cop and thus would decide that it would be too much trouble to try something. Or maybe they looked at his nice overcoat and figured that he was an easy mark. Maybe his height would scare them off, or it could challenge them and incite them. Funny how Max used to run this game in his head whenever similar situations had arisen in the past. Now with the Stone beneath his shirt, pressing against his chest, the only thing that he was considering was how fast Steve could get down and out of his way.

But nothing happened. Max and Steve simply nodded to them as they walked past and up into the building's vestibule. Inside Steve let out a nervous breath as casually as he could, that almost made Max laugh out loud. Instead he held it in as he searched for Marc's name on the building's bell system. It was a directory, with each tenant having a code for their apartment. His gloved finger slid down the directory looking for his friend's name.

He found it listed as his Practice; Gray Law office. When he punched the code in there was no discernable beep or buzzing to let him know that the code had worked. Steve nudged him impatiently.

"Hit it again." And he did, twice more before…

"Yo! Off the damn bell! What?" came the irritated response. It had been awhile since either one of them had seen the man. Max looked to Steve who looked back at him and then leaned forward.

"Marc?" Steve asked.

"Who's that?" still upset.

"It's Steve and Max. From M.R.U.? Uh… Gentlemen's Hall?"

"Steve and Max?"

Max grimaced, and then mumbled, "Goat-Boy and Pickle."

"OH SHIT! Come on up, Man! 602!"

Steve frowned at Max as the door buzzed and they walked inside. "I hate that name."

The inside of Marc's dimly lit apartment certainly did not have the ambience of a law office. There was a huge dining table set up in his living room as what Max guessed was supposed to be a conference table. A couple of file cabinets sat in the corner but apparently they were not up to containing the massive amount of paperwork that Marc had accumulated. Piles of papers sat stacked next to the cabinets and on the dining table. There was a T.V. set up in a corner with a Playstation, running, but unattended.

Marc himself was in the middle of getting dressed, the disarray of the "Conference" room was reflected in his own appearance.

"Damn it's been awhile! Goat-boy what y'all doin' up this early?"

"Alright with the 'Goat-Boy'." Steve snapped.

"We heard you had your own practice man." Max jumped in. "How'd you pull that off?"

"Aw I had to leave the firm I was with man, you know, a lot of political bullshit. They weren't trying to give a brother a real chance at partner. At one point I was bringing in more money than some of the senior partners but not being recognized for it, you know? They made two other cats partner ahead of me who were full of shit… just because they were friends of somebody or played golf with somebody, or was somebody's daughter. So I said might as well do this thing on my own."

"You were with Simons, Tragan and Lancaster?" Max asked. He was just filling conversation until he could get around to asking about their mutual friend Jean. Marc and he had been roommates.

"Yea," he continued. "For three years man. Been on my own now for a year. Business is good. I'll be out of here and into a real office as soon as some things come through." Then as if that thought reminded him, "Uh, so what's up? You need a lawyer?" he actually stopped getting dressed.

Max could tell that Marc was hoping for some more work, but he certainly was not thinking of retaining him… not that he could afford a lawyer anyway. He had seen enough to know that Marc hadn't really changed much since Freshman year at M.R.U.. Still, the man had made it through Law school and into a fairly big firm… although Max was fairly sure that Marc had a "friend" himself who helped him to achieve that. Better to get down to business.

"Actually I saw Jean a little while ago." he stated.

"Where?" Marc demanded a little too harshly.

"Uh… around the Museum."

"That mutha' Fucka' stole my God damned car! Where around the Museum?"

"We had a break-in a little while ago. I think he was one of the people involved. The Police showed me a picture of him. He didn't look too good."

"He's on that shit! He stole my car and sold it to a chop shop. Fuckin' cops found it too late. Then the mutha' fucka' tried to break in here last week."

"Really? Jean's that bad?" Steve had been watching the Playstation run but now he was paying close attention.

"That shit gets the best of us man." Marc went back to dressing. "And Jean was always close to that edge."

"He never graduated right?" Having been suspended Max had not been there during the years where they all might have graduated together but as it turned out very few of his friends actually got their diploma on time.

"Naw," Marc told him. "But he got a good job. He used to rent the apartment across the hall until he hooked up with those guys."

"What guys?"

"The mutha' Fucka's who put him on that shit. Some kind of

punk rockers and shit."

"Black leather? Wild hair?" Max was already sure.

"Yea." Marc was surprised. "How you know?"

"That's who they caught breaking into the Museum."

"That's where you work huh? Nice. Yea that sounds like them. Probably looking for something to sell." Marc put on the finishing touches to his wardrobe. Max was impressed; he finally looked the part of a lawyer and a sharp one at that.

"Probably..." Max thought of something else. "He used to live here?"

"Yea man. Next door. It's still up for rent, but you'll have to clean out all his shit." He produced a briefcase from beneath the table, then grabbed a bunch of papers from one of the many stacks and tossed them inside. "I gotta early court appointment Fellas."

"Cool. Maybe I'll take a look at his old apartment."

"What do you want with Jean anyway?"

"Like I said He might be involved with the break-ins at Haley."

"The Super is never gonna let you into that apartment." Marc said as he grabbed his jacket. "He put a big pad lock on the door so Jean couldn't come back and get his shit."

"I'll ask him if I can take a look. Where's the super?"

Marc looked at him oddly. "What? You work security for the Museum?" he asked. Behind him, Max could hear Steve shuffle his feet. He had insisted on going along when Max decided to visit Marc, figuring that it had something to do with the Museum break-ins. But now he had to be wondering why Max did not just let the police do their job. Marc had just asked the one question that Steve had wanted to ask all morning.

"Something like that." Max answered. They walked to the elevators together. Marc explained that the Super lived in the penthouse.

"And I'm in kind'a a rush." he said as the doors opened.

"No sweat. We'll take the next one." Max and Steve stood back.

"Cool. Hey, what ever happened with you and the Phi Gamma boys?"

"That was a long time ago." Max said.

"Yea," he nodded at Max knowingly. "Shit's in the past." Marc said as the doors closed. For a moment the two stood there waiting for another elevator to take them up to the Super.

"Wasn't he in that frat?" Steve asked.

Max just turned and started back the way they came.

"Hey? Where you going?"

"Stay here." It came out a bit as an order. Seeing Marc again had brought up some bad memories and some hard feelings. While he was just getting around to getting his degree Marc had already begun his own practice. When he thought about how many years he had lost...

"Hey! Wait up! What about the Super?" Steve fell into step beside him as Max walked back toward Marc's apartment. When they got there he stopped and looked across the hall. There were two apartments on the other side of the hall. Only one had a pad lock on the door.

"Well? We can't get in." Steve shook his head at the door.

Trying not to be obvious, Max walked up and inhaled deeply through his nose.

Nothing. When he awoke that morning he felt fine. The effects of the bane were pretty much gone. His vision was fine and his skin was no longer tender where the powder had burned him. There had been no real opportunity to test his sense of smell so he guessed it was possible that his nose still was not up to... snuff.

Max pressed his ear to the door and made a show of listening while he sniffed again.

"Somebody in there?" Steve asked in a whisper. "You hear something?" No he did not, but he did finally catch Jean's scent. And he was sure it was Jeans because it was accompanied by the tangy, body odor and cheap leather scent of the clothing the Maniacs had been wearing. It was very faint, but that could have been due either to the door being closed or to Jean not having been there in a while. The pad lock was on a latch which was nailed to the door. He reached up and grabbed the lock. It would be nothing to pull it off.

"Wait, Max." Steve reached into his pocket and produced his key ring. In addition to the fistful of keys there was a set of metal dog tags on the ring. He nudged Max aside and placed one of the tags against the door and forced it under the latch. Then he carefully, with a "Cheshire" cat grin on his face, pulled the latch plate, nails and all, out of the door.

"This way we can put it back." he snorted. Max's lips went tight but he nodded his thanks. This was probably going to go down as an endorsement of Steve's constant bad judgment and his ever lowering set of morals and standards. Max wanted to get in that apartment and... well he would just have to remember to chastise Steve extra hard about something else later.

The smell that Max had picked up from the door was an old scent, possibly from when Jean had first come back to his apartment only to find it padlocked. He knew this immediately because as the door opened he and Steve were hit with a stench so bad that they both blinked in unison.

There was not a word Max could think of that could describe the condition of the apartment. The first impression it gave was that it had been vandalized. A vast sea of "junk" stretched from the door to the backrooms and likely beyond. The old frayed furniture was covered in dirty laundry and empty fast food containers.

"Man there better not be a body in here." Steve had his nose scrunched up and his deviled eyebrows drawn together. The wicked grin he had sported while breaking in had been replaced by a sad, tight lipped grimace and again Max's face bore its twin. The place stank of rotting food but at least the distinctive scent of blood or decay was not in the very still air.

Carefully he stepped over the debris on the floor to the only bare spot that he could see. With only that one step the smell got ten times worse.

…Magazines, milk crates, pizza boxes,

He kicked a lump of clothes to the side to find another spot of floor. Steve took a step in behind him and something crunched under his clumsy heel.

…Old shoes, plastic shopping bags, and the remains of an old coffee table,

Max was far enough in that he could see into the kitchen. The refrigerator door was open but the light was not on. The smell was getting worse as he took another step.

…Old CDs, empty soda bottles, a broken vacuum cleaner…

"What are you looking for?" Steve asked. Max heard him moving something around and turned to see him sorting through a scattered pile of DVDs. He already had a few tucked up under one arm.

"What are you doing?"

"What?"

"Put that shit down! What are you? A looter?" Max shouted in a whisper.

"He's not coming back!" Steve argued back heedless of his carrying voice.

"Yo!" he whisper/shouted. "Keep your voice down!" Steve complied by continuing to dig through the pile of DVDs.

There was nothing there in the living room that Max could see that looked important. Nothing that said: "Here's the key to finding out where the Stone came from and proof that you and King had nothing to do with the break-ins."

"Huh?" Steve asked still rooting through movies. Max had not realized that he had said that out loud.

"I'm going to check his bedroom." He covered. Then Max picked his way through the clutter on his way to the backrooms. The smell as he passed the kitchen was so bad he thought he might gag. It was almost as if he could feel the grit in the air sliding down his lungs. The dim morning light was more than enough for him to see yet even more take out containers sitting in the open frig. Not that it was going to do them any good but Max closed the refrigerator door. Why hadn't the Super?

"So when did you start working security for the Museum?" Steve called from the front room in a mocking tone.

"Keep your voice down." Damn it!

There were papers and notes sticking to the refrigerator door. Sticking, Max noticed, by tape and not magnets. He stopped to examine a few of the tattered papers. They were nothing but women's phone numbers, final notices, and party flyers. The most recent were dated August of last summer. August of last summer was the last time Jean had cared enough about his bills to post them on his fridge.

Only five months ago that was.

"Did King tell you to do this? Can't the Museum afford to hire their own investigators?" Steve yelled the question from the living room.

"Quiet!" Jean's life had fallen apart in only five months?

The bedroom was even more cluttered than the living room. The floor was covered in discarded and filthy clothing. Jean's funky body odor still hung heavy in the air of the room. Max switched to breathing through his mouth only to find that he could actually taste the smell of the room and quickly clamped his lips together. Across the mess, Max spied the curtained window. Anything for some clean air.

As he traversed the floor his foot came down awkwardly on a lump too hard to be just a roll of socks. He kicked aside a crusty tee shirt to find an old wallet, which was full of Jean's scent as well. There was no money in it of course but it was jammed full of other bits of paper. Mostly receipts from fast food joints and plain receipts with only the dollar transaction imprinted on them. Several business cards sat wilting in his wallet as well, including an old school ID, Jean's original pledge card, Marc's business card… and a picture of Jean's family. Three brothers, four sisters, and both parents were still alive, it made Max wonder how he could be in such dire straits right now.

Something crashed in the living room and Max hopped through the mess to get back. He found Steve standing by the couch tossing clothes aside and pulling a green jacket free of the pile.

"You do know we're NOT supposed to be in here? Stop stealing his stuff!"

"This is mine!" Steve held up the green jacket triumphantly. "He borrowed it freshman year and never gave it back. I love this jacket!"

"Fine. Let's go." Max could not hide his disappointment. Somehow Jean had fallen in with the Maniacs but there was nothing here that showed him how. As bad as the place smelled he could tell that no one had been in there in a long time.

Max replaced the latch on the door as best he could; Steve had bent it a little.

"What was up with Jean's? That apartment smelled like the inside of a trash truck!" Steve said. He had turned his favorite jacket into

a makeshift bag to hold his looted items. They walked back to the
elevator and Max pulled one of the DVDs free and read its title.

"What's this? 'Chunky Asses'… '23'? You're stealing porn,
Steve?"

"I'm gonna sell it!" The elevator doors opened and Steve
stepped on after snatching the DVD back. "He owes me money too! He
was always borrowing my stuff. There's a pawn shop a few blocks away.
I bet Jean sold a bunch of stuff there already. You should check it out,
Mr. Investigator."

Damn; a good idea from Steve.

Max stepped in behind him, looking at the assortment of loot
cradled in the jacket Steve held onto protectively. Just as the elevator
doors started to close he suddenly reached and snatched the jacket
away, spilling everything onto the floor.

"Hey!" Steve screamed. Max held the jacket up before him.
"This is MY jacket! You borrowed it from ME!"

The Maniacs had been decapitated in King's
first office, Max and Fatima used his second so this was King's third
office, the one Bazillion used, or used to anyway. Unlike the other staff
members Bazillion had the balls to redecorate, well at least a little. He
was smart enough not to throw any of King's things out, however he
did move them all, neatly, to one corner of the room. Then he replaced
them with a few pieces of modern art, his framed degrees, and a rather
expensive looking leather couch, upon which Max was sure Bazillion
had spent most of his time asleep. Though King preferred his main
office this was by far the best of all three. The huge picture window
gave a wonderful view of the courtyard and of Wolf's Den Tree. It was
also a little remote, being in the South Hall instead of the East. It meant
that Bazillion was not likely to be disturbed for trivial reasons.

So it seemed to Max that this was the best place to make the
call. The card Rasheeda Landry had given him sat in his free palm, the
edges starting to crinkle from his sweat and his tense grip. "The
Serpent Cult" she had said evocatively. His mind played back the
memory of his encounter on the docks and he recalled the long, thin,
claws and the slit snake-like eyes of the Maniac he had fought. Then he
thought of Jean, his onetime friend, and the lost, listless look in his eyes
in the police photo.

A "cult" she had said. What did she know?

The phone rang three times. Max checked the time on his cell
phone. It was nearly six o'clock now; he had been late to work after
stopping off at Marc's apartment. That had forced him to play catch up
all day. He might have called her earlier in the week but between his
work and Fatima not leaving him alone in the office he had found no
time. He certainly did not want to call her from his cell phone or his

home.

A shadow walked past the office door. The scent told him it was one of the janitors. He half expected Fatima as she had also been tailing him all over the Museum. At first he suspected that she was up to her old games but quickly realized that she was still too nervous to walk around the castle by herself. She even stayed in the office through her lunch break which again gave him no opportunity to call Landry. So he walked her out at five-thirty and watched her go. Still, there were a great number of students, faculty and staff there who had been running in and out of their office all day so Max decided to use Bazillion's.

The phone rang three more times. Maybe she had expected him to call earlier. Looking at the card again showed him nothing new; it remained just as blank as when she gave it to him, with just her name and phone number printed on it. The area code matched Mountairy Rock, and the first three numbers, 5-4-8, matched the northern part of the West Oak's section of the city. It was a residence, a land line and not a cell number. Most likely a home number he thought, due to the lack of a business name printed on the card.

Another three rings. No answering machine then.

Max hung the phone up and grabbed the few things he had brought with him to Bazillion's office. His thoughts returned to the Maniacs.

There had to be a way to track them. The police had arrested more than a few and he doubted he could get access to their information without arousing suspicion. The only one that he had recognized was Jean but that seemed to be a dead end. Since his apartment had been padlocked he would have no reason to go back there. Still, if they really wanted the Stone then the Maniacs were likely to come after him again, probably when his guard was down. It would be better to find them first and…

…let the police know where they were… right?

A very familiar feeling passed through him when he thought about facing the Maniacs again. Almost like an urge it was, filling him with a little bit of excitement. Better to squash that before he did something reckless and ended up getting eaten by that Snake-Maniac.

The small digital clock on Bazillion's desk flashed Six O'clock dead even and it was now dark outside. Tomorrow was going to bring a lot more work and stress so he should head home, get some rest and maybe work on his own research just a little more. Staying out any later would also give the Maniacs another shot at him.

Where the hell was the damn Pawn shop Steve was talking about? This was Max's sixth trip up the strip of shops at 52nd and Ogontz Avenue in West Oaks. He had already past the Liquor store three times, the gun shop twice and the other Liquor store three times as well. The take-out joint had been closed when he had arrived here, as many of the strips stores closed when it got dark apparently, but the hot delicious scent remained in the air right by the doors. It was a smell he had not experienced in a few years, since his last extended stay with his parents back home; Cheese steaks. As long as he had been in Mountairy Rock he had never been to a steak-shop that had gotten it right but the smell that was lingering at this particular doorway was almost perfect. He had never had reason to come to West Oaks before. Most of his time was spent in the Museum or on the College campus in Ivy Hills. Every once in a while he might hit New City for a night out and he had grown up in Brookhaven before his family moved to Philly. So the rest of Mountairy Rock was not so familiar. It would have been if he had known there was a good steak shop down here.

There was still no sign of any Pawn shop. It was possible, Max thought, that one of the little junk stores could be mistaken for a pawn shop. It just was not likely that Steve would have made that mistake. As often as relying on Steve's judgment had burned Max in the past, there was precedent for his accuracy in regards to money making schemes. Not that he ever made any money or that his ventures ever turned out to be anything other than utter failures, it was just that he knew all the places to go to get involved in illicit opportunities. So Max was sure that if Steve thought he saw a pawn shop, then there probably was one somewhere on this strip.

So with tremendous effort he pulled himself away from the steak shop and began to walk the shops again. Since he was passing storefronts that he had already inspected, he could not help but to let his mind drift. There was so much in front of him now; his research project, the extra duties for which he was now responsible since King had left, the Maniacs, Jean, the Downhills people, Sheriff Lynne, Prya, the Landry woman, the Stone, Amanda…

She planned on cooking dinner for him this Friday, at his apartment since that would not fly too well at her place with Rosette. There was a chicken dish, Amanda had told him, that she was dying to try. It seemed as though she fancied herself something of a cook and was hoping to show off a little. That was just fine because Max was looking forward to eating a home cooked meal for the first time in a long time. The Museum had been so busy at the end of the previous year that he had not been able to make the trip home for the holidays.

No Thanksgiving turkey.

None of Mom's sweet potato pie.

Whenever a woman made the "I can cook" claim Max usually took it with a grain of salt. He had found that many women make the claim as a matter of course, not really ever expecting to have to prove it. Kind of like when they make the obligatory "reach" for the check at dinner even though they have no intention of paying. Even those that were serious about their culinary skills still managed to disappoint on delivery. During quite a few dinners Max had to remind himself to smile with his eyes as well as his lips when he swallowed different chunks of unrecognizable and tasteless debris just so that his date would not have her feelings hurt.

Still though, missing the holiday had turned out to be just the beginning of a series of stressful events. So Max could not help but be a little optimistic and he was actually looking forward to the dinner. Plus Amanda had been so very genuine and open with him that he just naturally trusted her.

Too bad she could not say the same about him.

He rounded the corner at the end of one block of stores and turned onto the next street. A stiff west wind raked across his face and Max drew in the scents that it brought with it. Nothing familiar.

How safe was it for Amanda to be dating him right now? If the Maniacs attacked them while they were out…

He was pretty sure the Maniacs did not know who he was or they would have turned up at his apartment a long time ago. They did seem to recognize him on campus and that could be trouble. If Amanda were with him when they attacked, he was not sure he could protect her, especially if that Snake-Maniac came after him. Worse if they saw her with him and went after her later…

She would not be able to protect herself he realized. If they wanted the Stone badly enough they could go after it through her and she was not even aware of the danger.

He should stop seeing her for her own sake.

Why had he not thought about this before? Despite the viciousness of their attack and his almost dying at the hands of the Snake-Maniac, Max, for some reason, did not take them seriously. That could get him killed… it could get HER killed he told himself but the still very real danger did not manage to worry him much.

One hand reached up and pressed through his jacket pushing the Stone against his skin. It was doing more than changing his body. Was it taking away his fear? Amanda was in danger he told himself again. She was in danger.

What was he going to do? Stop seeing her? Any woman he became involved with would be in the same danger.

Except Prya.

The Maniacs would have a tough time dealing with the Downhills woman. She had fought him at the Museum with a lot of skill; surely she could take on a few Maniacs. He doubted that they would or could venture into the Downhills unchallenged. Even that Snake Maniac would be in trouble trying that. Plus she could get around, the way she led him through the Downhills proved that.

The memory of the Downhills rooftop grew strong just then;

her hair, her smell, and the warmth of her body as it pressed him into the snow. Her lips were so red… her hand so warm when she slid it under his shirt and grabbed the Stone. Her laugh was almost childlike when she leapt away from him and then squealed when he captured her.

That was when she pulled Amanda's scarf off of his neck.

Absorbed in thought Max sped up and had walked block after block without really noticing the change in scenery. West Oaks, like each of the four major sections of the city, divided by the park, had a few blocks of abandoned buildings. Just as he reached the border between currently opened shops and derelict buildings his nose picked up a familiar scent.

"Landry", he gasped almost before he knew he had caught that faux floral scent. The street was empty and Max stopped right in the middle of the cross walk and inhaled deeply.

Yes it was her alright. Somewhere… nearby…

Slowly he turned in what was becoming his pattern for tracking a scent. First he rotated his head, trying to figure where the scent was coming from and which breeze was carrying it. He found it quickly and looked up the street in that direction.

He wondered how far the breeze was cutting it; that is, shifting it away from the direction of its source. This could have had him walking in circles but tonight it seemed as though the night wind was bringing the scent directly from the woman. The scent came down the border street with the still occupied buildings on one side and the abandoned store fronts on the other. These shops had not been open for quite some time, Max could tell. Their signs were faded, sun-bleached, and printed in vintage styles that he had only seen in old movies. They all seemed to be derelict.

The scent grew stronger as Max approached an alley on the abandoned side. It was wider than most alleys but too small to be a proper street, he thought. There was room enough that someone had bothered to lay small strips of sidewalk down each side of the alley. In between lay a narrow cobblestone street. It reminded him of some of the old world streets he had seen in the Downhills.

Or was it the new scent that he was just now picking up?

Deep inhale… Prya?

Her scent was stronger than the Landry woman's, strong enough that he knew she was somewhere ahead of him down that dark street. The sharpness of it told him that the Landry woman's scent by comparison, was an old one. The narrow street was lined with old abandoned shops as well that seemed even older than the others. Max was passing by a small shop that had suffered a fire ages ago when something changed.

Not the scent, that remained strong, but something did change… or rather something stopped. Max came to a halt in the middle of the street. It seemed quieter. Some noise in the background of the night that he had not noticed before had suddenly stopped as he had drawn closer. He stood perfectly still and listened, focusing intently. His ears became hot and began to itch as the sounds in the alley became clearer. Then he heard it... he heard HER;

She sniffed.

Prya. She had heard him coming and had grown quiet, probably unsure of who he was. What was she doing in West Oaks? Her heady scent was hot in the air. Was she was following him?

No. She had sniffed to catch his scent, to figure out who it was that was coming up the alley. He had surprised her.

The wind outside the alley howled with a sudden gust and pulled a cold breeze out of the alley, flushed it and then brought new scents out from deep in the alley. Prya's scent came first, heady and warm, then among a batch of new scents was the very familiar mix of leather and sick body odors; Maniacs.

Without thinking Max rushed forward, passing the burnt out shop and then two more until he came out of the alley onto a new cross street. Coming to a stop, he had to inhale again because he had lost the scents in his rush to get down the alley. Prya's scent was still there, as were the scents of the Landry and the Maniacs. Again he followed his nose and it turned him back around. The building at the corner of the alley was neither boarded up nor hollowed out. This corner office had been restored and was being used. Still, the front door had been kicked open. The scents were all coming from inside.

As quietly as he could, Max crept to the open doorway and peeked inside. After a moment his eyes adjusted to the darkness. The building was definitely being used. The outside was not all that different from the rest of the old store fronts in this neighborhood but the inside was plush. The floor was covered with thick wine-red carpeting and the walls had a fresh coat of paint the same color. There was equally plush furniture, huge potted plants and vibrantly colored paintings in what looked to be a reception area. It would have been very nice except that the furniture was overturned, the paintings knocked off the wall, and the plants lay strewn across the floor. Max recognized the Maniacs style easily enough.

The scents lay heavy in the room, Prya's above all. She was still here, he was sure, although Max could hear nothing. Landry's scent was old and Max was beginning to understand how much he could learn from his nose. He was certain that the woman had last been in the room that same day and the Maniac's scent was even older. They probably had been here the previous night.

There was a back room.

The Maniacs must have had a ball in here, he thought. It had been an office until it had been torn apart in a frenzy of vandalism. So much like the night of the first Museum break in… except thankfully for the lack of bodies.

In the center of the frenzy, Prya stood with her back to him.

The Downhills girl was perfectly motionless, but still appeared to be relaxed. She was wearing the black outfit she had worn the night she and her boyfriend had jumped him at the Museum. Dark as it was he could nevertheless see the silhouette of a black skirt that she wore over the body suit and that she was carrying the spear he had seen on the wall of her room.

"Prya?"

And just like that she took a breath, shifted her weight and Max could "hear" her again. Careful of the wreckage on the floor, Prya stepped and turned around on the balls of her feet to face him.

"… so loud… heard you three blocks away…" she still spoke in that careful, dreamy… seductive speech pattern.

"I doubt that", Max parried. "But I could smell you all the way back in the alley. What's going on?" Despite himself, the condition of the room and the lingering smell of the Maniacs Max could not help but to search out her dark shape, straining his eyes to see her as she moved against an equally dark background.

Prya looked back down at the mess that was the room. "… she's gone…" she whispered. "… the Sick ones…"

"Who?"

"… took her…"

"You mean the Maniacs?"

She looked at him curiously. "… who?"

That was when he realized that "Maniacs" was what he had been calling them in his own head since he first ran into them. What had she just said?

"The 'Sick ones'?", he asked.

"… scented me… should be able to scent them…" She cocked her head to peer at him. Her eyes were partially hidden by her wild garnet hair.

"Yes." Max answered, and then inhaled deeply through his nose to be sure that he had been right about when they were there. "But I don't think they were here when she was."

Prya snapped her head up at this and gave him a sharp, doubtful look that contained a little surprise as well. Then she closed her eyes and inhaled deeply herself. Max caught sight of the silhouette of her rising bosom. With a sensual grace she turned in place still breathing in the room's air. Her head swiveled side to side in rhythm with her carefully placed steps. The black skirt she was wearing opened a bit as she spun, briefly showing her leg, bare above the calf high leather boots. The body suit was just a top.

When she had turned 360 degrees, Prya drew her eyes tight,

looked at Max and drew her pursed lips up to one corner of her mouth. She did not believe him.

"She left here not too long ago but Maniacs' haven't been here for a least a day... I think." Max had not had these new skills for very long and her unconvinced expression was making him doubt himself. Maybe her nose was better than his.

He watched her turn back around and begin kicking the debris and papers around on the floor with her toe. At first he thought she was just expressing her frustration but as she continued Max thought he saw a bit of a pattern forming.

Suddenly she dropped low to one knee and began sniffing in earnest. Even as she did so Max caught the newly exposed day old scent of the Maniac in the air. Just as abruptly she stood, whipped her head around and glanced over her shoulder at him. Her hair flew around and covered half her face again. Was she smiling?

"... good nose..." was all she said. Then slowly, without taking her eyes off of him she began to circle him. Yes, she was definitely smiling... and switching the hell out of her hips. With his eyes now adjusted to the dark her black body suit and hip hugging skirt made her very feminine form to stand out against the maroon carpet and walls. It was a wonder how she was able to walk so sensually and with such apparent natural ease. Max let himself look her up and down... and then up again, meeting her eyes to see that she clearly enjoyed being watched as much as he liked watching her. With a flash of those canines Prya spun away from him and he realized that she had walked past him to the front door.

He was about to call after her when he saw her stop at the doorway. The loose relaxed pose she had then stiffened as she inhaled the night air. Carefully but not sneakily, Max walked up behind her. He searched for something to say, anything to get his mind off the way her thin waist opened into those full hips.

"Um... why do you call them the 'Sick Ones'."

"... filled with sickness...", she breathed in deeply again. "... lost..."

"What kind of sickness?" He leaned past her out of the doorway and breathed in the night air himself. Maybe he could track them... but it was her scent that filled his head.

"... burning from the inside out..." She stepped out of the doorway and down onto the street. "... the weak ones..."

"Who are they?"

She let out a frustrated huff. Again her hair whipped as she looked first one way up the street and then quickly up the other. Finally her eyes looked up the side of the building and seemed to be considering something. Max followed her gaze but could see nothing of interest. When he looked back at Prya she was staring at him.

"Come on", she said, breaking her dreamy speech pattern for only the second time. "Let's see how good that nose is." She then crouched low, gathering herself and then sprang straight up, leaping up to the second story of the building. Red clawed hands dug into the brick and she scraped and kicked her way upward. The building had three floors and when she reached the top Prya did not bother to look back down.

Max quickly did his own survey of the street and wondered if they were being watched. Probably not, in this section of West Oaks there were too many abandoned buildings. Funny though; he had not seen any bums.

A low grunt and Max launched himself up onto the building, beating her initial jump by making it almost to the third floor before having to grab hold of a windowsill. His boots found easy purchases and in seconds he was up on the roof. To his surprise Prya was there waiting for him. Half of him expected this to be yet another chase but instead of running she was looking at him expectantly.

"Where is she?" she asked.

For a second he did not know what she meant. Then the night air rippled and a strong breeze blew across the rooftop and brought with it faint scents.

He inhaled deeply, closing his eyes in concentration, looking for that one specific scent. There were Maniac scents, the stale scent of rotting wood, rust, roof tar, the thick foliage of the Park... one breath, two... nothing... no Landry. He shook his head.

"I'm sorry I can't..."

"... this way..." she said abruptly then ran and jumped across the gap between buildings. She did not stop there. With athletic grace Prya sprinted over that rooftop and leapt to yet another.

Max saw that she was not stopping, so he took off after her, remembering having chased the big gray cat much like this. The cold night air pulled the heat right out of his thighs as he soared across the top of the alley way. But his heart was pumping hard now, sending hot blood through his limbs so he barely noticed the cold. There were still remnants of snow left over from earlier that month and he almost lost his footing when he landed.

Prya did not stop so neither did Max. He kept up the chase never losing sight of her against the gray night sky. It was a good thing he could see her, because he soon noticed that she barely made a sound as she ran. Her footfalls came down without the loud thumps and rough scraping sounds that his did, and if she was breathing hard Max could not hear over his increasingly ragged gasps for air. Those gasps became wheezes as he tried to follow as she leapt and climbed to higher roof tops, which she seemed to do whenever possible.

The run was not so long in distance as his cross city chase of the big gray cat but it made up for it with a hell of a lot of climbing. It seemed like he would run out of gas and lose her for sure when at last he clambered onto a rooftop to find her waiting for him. He nearly fell out he was so out of breath; huffing and puffing with his hands resting on his knees. Her laughter echoed into the night air.

"… 'Heir apparent'…"

"Hey… fuck you…" he would have said it to her face but he was bent over and could only lift his head high enough to see her hands on her hips which were shaking as she belly laughed.

"… soon as you're ready…" and she laughed again.

"… you… just… wait…" The cold night air was tearing his lungs up, making them feel raw and tender. But he desperately needed air so he kept drawing it in through his mouth, which did not warm it as much as if his breathed through his nose but…

"… fuck…" he HATED running!

At last he could stand. With a grunt he clamped his mouth shut and tried to gain control of his breathing. In seconds his nostrils went raw but he was able to calm his heaving chest. Then he noticed something in the air.

"Where… are we?" he asked Prya. She watched him closely and then tilted her head back and took in the scents that the air was bringing them. From the way she turned her head back and forth, Max guessed that she could not smell it. He turned his own head in the direction of the wind and walked over the roof towards the side from which they had just run. The wind was filled with a multitude of very faint scents, including one familiar one. Somewhere between where they had been and this roof top, was the Landry woman. It was something about the wind, he realized. She had moved them across West Oaks to where they could catch the southward moving wind.

Prya walked next to him, folded her arms and tilted her head back again. Once more Max could tell that she could not smell Landry's scent. A small look of frustration crossed her face and then she looked to him expectantly. Max smirked at her.

"Soon as you're ready…" he said. Her hands tensed just a little and her lips drew tight but she said nothing. He was sure of it now; her nose was not as sensitive as his. As fast as she was Max probably could have beaten her to this roof-top given a little more practice. The fight at the Museum told him that he was also far stronger than her. In the Downhills she had told him that he was not "Clan". Now he wondered what exactly she was.

"Lead the way", she said impatiently.

The smirk grew into a grin and without taking his eyes off of her, Max leapt from the roof top. He did not leap for the building from which they had just climbed; instead he jumped for another building nearly four stories down. It was as far of a fall as the fall from the South

Tower on the night of the second Museum break-in but Max felt sure that he was ready for it now.

He landed with a loud thump and a spray of loose gravel, dropping to one knee and one hand to shed the momentum of the fall. Without delay he sprang up and began running for the far end of that roof. Just as he was getting there he heard a thump, skid and a muffled grunt behind him and could not help smiling as he leapt again across the wide gap of a one lane street to another roof top. Hearing a muttered curse behind him only made him smile even harder.

The scent grew stronger and Max pumped his legs as he realized they were close. So close that Prya had to be able to smell it on her own, but a quick glance over his shoulder showed Max that she had not been able to stay on the roof tops as he had. Her dark shape leapt over a dumpster in an alley a block behind him. So he kept moving, leaping and climbing another taller building until he found himself right on top of the scent.

Now he could hear Prya as she climbed the fire escape behind him on the far side of the roof on which he was now perched. Her breath came in tiny little puffs and soon those puffs were right behind him. She coughed a little and he laughed.

"Fuck you…" and then she took in a deep breath through her nose and then went stiff. She pushed past him to the roof's edge and looked down into the alleyway below. Between the two apartment buildings there hung several clothes lines tethered to fire escapes on either side. Clothes pinned to the line whipped in the night breeze.

"… foolish…" she shook her head. Then she stood up again and took in another couple of breaths, deeply snorting the air. After a second she cocked her head and gave Max a sidelong look. For a moment she looked as though she might ask him something, but she just turned away looking a bit frustrated.

Understanding Max stood himself and inhaled the air again. All the way here from the rooftop, he had been concentrating on tracking the faux flower scent that belonged to Landry. It had not occurred to him that he should have been checking for the Maniacs as well. Luckily there still was no hint of them on the wind.

"Can't smell them", he said. For another few moments they stood there. Prya made no move to acknowledge that she had heard him. Another cold gust hit them both. After cooling off a bit after their run his body temperature had returned to normal and he could now feel the cold night air. Max hunched his shoulders and grimaced at the Winter-itch beginning to attack his thighs. His jeans were not cutting it in this weather.

Prya made no move. The wind pulled the hair from her face and Max saw that she had her eyes closed.

So he looked back down into the alley and stared at the clothes swinging in the breeze. There were several lines and it took some time but Max thought he saw the shawl that Landry had been wearing when he first met her on the elevator. His eyes trailed the line on which it hung to the fire escape it was tied to. The window closest was filled with empty plant pots. They were easy to see as they were silhouetted against the drawn shade by the light inside. Shadows moved over the shade intermittently so… somebody was there. Max had a strong feeling that the window was not where Landry was. It was the only window where there was a light on though. There was another window a floor up that seemed more promising. Another strong gust of cold wind…

"Any time you're ready…." He said.

Prya snapped her head up finally and looked at him with anger in her eyes but she said nothing. Instead she stepped up onto the edge of the roof top and leapt for the fire escape. Her landing was pretty impressive. She had grabbed the bottom of one landing with her free hand while the other still held the spear. She then dropped herself down onto the next landing without making a sound. Next she crept up to the window and peeked inside through a rip in the shade.

There was no way Max could match the grace he had just seen but he wanted to get there before she smashed in the window to some innocent person's home. The distance was not a problem; he managed it without much of a jump, but he cleared the railing of the fire escape only to land hard with a loud rattle and stumbled into the brick wall. Prya was looking at him over her shoulder; her eyes gleamed like a cat's as it reflected gold light from the window at him. He was again reminded of the big gray cat. The rest of her face was in shadow but he could tell she was upset with his noisy landing.

"SHH!" Max shushed her jokingly. She simply shook her head and turned her attention back to the window. Carefully he crept up beside her and peeked over her to the window.

"I don't think she's here. There's a window one floor up that…"

"… haven't learned…" she whispered harshly.

"Excuse me?"

Again she tossed him a look and then pointed to the window.

"… witch trickery… for the weak minded…"

He looked again still sure that this was the wrong window. "Witch trickery?" Landry had done something to him before; he recalled the disappearing act in the elevator. Now when he thought back on it he was certain that he had seen her sitting in the office with him and Fatima. He just had not reacted to her at all. Then she had done something to him to shake him up in the elevator when he had finally caught up to her. So there was some kind of trick here?

The harder he examined the "real" window the more anxious he grew to have a look at the one above.

Prya snorted when she saw him looking up. Then she grabbed the bottom of the window, jamming her sharp nails into the wood and pulled it open. Max reached to grab her but she was too quick and just like that she slipped past the shade and into the apartment.

"Jeez, Prya!" He waited outside, no point in going in. It would only cause more of a ruckus. In a second she would see that this was the wrong window he was sure.

In a second she would come crawling out embarrassed.

Anytime now.

Okay she was being hard-headed. Carefully Max pulled the tattered shade aside. The potted plant shapes in the window were simply printed designs on the shade. Max looked inside. It was a kitchen. Prya stood off to one side of the window giving him a good view of Rasheeda Landry, standing bent over at the refrigerator door, with plate in one hand, glass of wine in the other, and a drumstick in her mouth.

"Pwya? Hohw bid yohu fihgne me?" Evidently she had not anticipated having visitors calling on her through her window. She was wearing a bath robe that was way too small for her, not that Max minded…

…she must work out.

Prya frowned a little and then tilted her head to Max as he climbed through the window. It was hard to tell what she was feeling at the moment. The look on her face could have been alarm, anger, or even amazement. In a very unladylike fashion Landry spit the drumstick out onto the plate.

"You?" she crossed the kitchen and put down the plate. "You knew where I was?"

"… good nose too…" Prya snickered. "… just not too bright…" and she tapped a bright red nail against the window glass.

"You scent tracked me here? That's not possible." Landry said sharply. Max frowned at this.

"It's not possible to track you 'here'?" he was pointing at the floor. "because only a month ago I wouldn't have thought it was something a person could do at all."

"I… yes of course. But…" she self-consciously tugged down on the bottom of her robe. Max was sure he had not been looking at her long legs… her smooth thighs.

"It's just that I made sure to cover my tracks when I left my office", she tried to explain.

"… then hung a sweater full of your perfume out the window…" Prya chastised.

"I… well yes. But we're halfway across West Oaks!" She shot a look past Max out the window. She was worried about being found by someone else.

"… the Sick ones?", Prya asked. Did she talk like that ALL the time?

"Yes. After I spoke with you I wanted to find out more about what they've been doing. I…" she paused still looking out the window. "Just a second." Bravely she stepped in between the two of them and climbed out the window. Max could hear the turning of a metal wheel and the flutter of cloth on the wind. Then Landry stepped back inside clutching a ball of clothes.

"You can still smell my perfume on this? It's been washed!"

"… hardly…" Prya wrinkled her nose at scarf.

"It's a bit…" Max searched for the words. "… it's like it's just… fake… very distinctive. And I couldn't track you from your office. Prya took me all the way to the other side of West Oaks where I caught this scent on the wind." Funny though, that the scent was fading now, almost gone. Max sniffed again perplexed. What was happening?

"I never noticed how strong it was." She walked back to the table. "If you could track me, then they can."

They?

"Who? The Mani… um the 'Sick ones'?" Max asked.

"… no… they can't track…" Prya shook her head.

"I think they can." Landry stated plainly.

"… they're nothing. Just sick fools… lost… no will but their masters." Prya almost spat it out.

"If they could track…" Max said. "… then why have they never followed me to my apartment?" They had three nights after his dip in the water to track him down and get him in his sleep, and several nights and opportunities after that.

"… they can't get past… they are nothing…" Prya said shaking her head. Clearly they upset her. Max thought that maybe she was just relieved to see her friend okay but still angry that Landry had been attacked in the first place.

"Not all of them I think." Landry sat at the table and ran her hands up through her braids stopping to pat the top of her head. "Some have been given the status of Lieutenants in their Master's army." One hand again tugged down on the bottom of her robe.

Master? Max remembered several of the Maniacs using that title including the one on the scaffolding and the ones outside the Student Center… then there was that green flash of light…and that thing on Jeans back…

"I believe one of those killed your guards on New Year's Eve", Landry said.

"What do you mean?" Max asked.

"The 'animal' attacks?" she said unsure. "… and the claw marks on the victims at the Museum?" Landry was looking at him without the hesitant fear he had seen in her eyes before. "They were done by one of the 'Sick ones' who has been given power. A power that has transformed him much like you have been… are BEING transformed."

He could tell that Prya was watching him so Max kept his eyes on Landry. He ran his tongue over his teeth feeling for the unnaturally long canines but his mouth was normal. "Being transformed" she had said. He was afraid to ask; into what?

Landry seemed to be waiting for him to say something but Max could not find words. Even the questions he had were stuck in his mouth. He sniffed constantly. The flower scent of Landry's perfume was gone. Actually the air was very clear; he could not smell anything.

"You encountered one of these changed 'Sick ones' on the Museums dock didn't you?" she asked drawing him back. Now there seemed to be a little worry in her eyes. Not wanting to scare her Max looked down and away.

"He was… different." he said. Landry had gotten her information from some pretty good sources. When Max had not seen either of the drawings Sheriff Lynne had shown him of himself or the Snake-Maniac on T.V. or in the newspaper then he knew that the police were trying to keep everything quiet. But it was clear now that Landry knew about the fight at the dock and the first break in at the Museum, or at least some parts of them.

"Yes I suppose he was", she said.

"You think he could track you? He really didn't have much of a nose." Max remembered to the flattened slits clearly.

"I don't think they scent and track with their nose, but they were able to track me to my office well enough."

"So what are they? Why do you call them the 'Sick Ones'? Who is their master? What are they…"

Landry stood and shook her head. "Wait. This is too much tonight. This isn't even my place. You'll wake the baby." She then quietly walked out of the room. Max and Prya then looked at each other with questions on both their faces. Then each sniffed the air several times and then looked back at each other. Neither one of them smelled anything. Perhaps he would have been worried but Prya just smiled.

"… witch tricks…" she said pointing to the stove. There was a small pot of what looked like water sitting over a very low flame. It then made sense to Max. Landry's surprise at being found by her scent, and the fact that Max had not smelled the perfume inside the apartment until she had brought in the stinking shirt were because she had taken precautions. Now that he thought about it, he could not smell anything in the apartment at the moment.

Landry walked back into the room.

"Come back tomorrow… at a decent hour. We'll talk then."

"… he'll be alone…" said Prya and she turned and exited the window. For a few seconds Max stood there alone with Landry.

"Apartment 410", she said.

"I'm sorry?"

"Apartment 410. Ring the buzzer next time." Her smile was nervous but warm.

Max turned and hopped out the window. After the shade settled into place, he closed it, then stopped to examine at it. What was the trick?

Then he saw it. Someone had written on the window, probably just ran a finger over the dirt on the outside of it. Whatever it was had been wiped away. Either Prya or Landry had done it when they had gone out the window. Some kind of Spell? Magic writing?

On the roof he found Prya waiting. The winter winds had picked up and her hair whipped about her face. Even so she looked at him evenly. She seemed to be waiting for something.

"Guess your friend is ok", he said.

"… witches…", she faltered a bit and clenched her jaw. Then she turned her back to him and began walking away.

"Witches what?" he called after her.

At the roofs edge she paused and looked back. "She is my friend", she said over the night's wind. "But witches lie."

LOCKED UP

There was very little noise when his sneakers came down hard on the sidewalk. He shed all the momentum easily, letting himself drop into a crouch. His fingertips barely touched the cold ground though his hands were ready to catch him in case he had misjudged the force of the impact. Moving around with the Stone tied around his neck was getting easier and easier. In fact he would have preferred to get home by jumping from rooftop to rooftop; the way Prya had led him to this side of West Oaks. However since he would be coming back tomorrow the "regular", way he needed to see the path from ground level. Plus… well he just was not sure he could find his way home by rooftop.

Prya had ducked quickly out of sight when she took off and although Max thought he had a good chance of keeping up with her this time, he doubted that he would be able to keep track of her. It was obvious to him that she knew tricks and techniques about tracking that came with experience. It probably would not be that hard for her to lose him if she wanted and she did seem to want to be alone.

"Witches lie" What had she meant by that? That Landry was lying? That she HAD already lied? Or that she was going to lie? Or maybe just that she MIGHT lie? They were friends, that much was evident. Max thought he saw relief in her eyes when Prya caught Landry's scent from the clothes line. She only referred to her as "the Witch" though, not by name, or at least not in front of him. With the strange pattern of her speech maybe she was really talking about Landry's witch trickery. Like the way Max had not been able to see the "witch" in his office, or the way he had been so sure that her window was not the right window… Could those have been the lies she was talking about?

No, Max did not think so. For a second Prya had broken out of that dreamy way of talking and that was when she told him that witches lie. So what was Landry lying about? Or going to lie about?

Winter itch began to attack his legs in earnest and Max had to stop to scratch. He had not seen a bus stop since coming back down to street level and doubted that he would find one running on a route that he was familiar with. If the buses were still running that was; because he

190

did not even know how late it had become. He pulled his cell phone out and saw that it was nearly two a.m. and that he had a couple of messages.

One text message was from Steve asking him where he was. That had been at Ten O'clock. He probably had stopped by Max's apartment, without calling as usual, to bum some food.

Voice mail flashed two message icons. The first was from his Uncle reminding him to come by and see the apartment to be sure he wanted it. Max had already seen the apartment with its view of the Museum, the reservoir, the Great Lake and the city skyline. His heart leapt a little and for the first time in a month he thought of something other than Maniacs, claws, stones, or blood.

The second was from Amanda and his heart made a different kind of leap.

"Hey Max… This is Amanda… just wanted to see what's up… just getting in from study group at the library… give me a call if you get a chance…"

He looked at the time on his cell phone's display again… much too late to call her back.

Damn.

If he could just get past all this… just make it out to the other end… there was Amanda, his great new apartment, and the letters D and R in front of his name.

…so much in front of him…

Damn… he forgot to get that scarf back. He would be seeing Amanda on Friday too. But should he? The Maniacs went after Landry at her home although Prya had hinted that they could not track him the same way. Max was not so sure he could trust that. Amanda did not have any witch tricks to protect her.

The crazy itching had subsided while he had been standing there but he knew that as soon as he started walking it would just flare back up again. Making things worse was the fact that this section of West Oaks was clearly not as desolate as where Landry's office was. Though it was still very late there were more than enough people out that he did not want to walk down the street scratching his legs like some nut. And the itching could get just that bad. Maybe he should call a cab?

When he got to the end of the street he was on Max checked the street sign; Washington and Overbrook, a notoriously bad place to be. A month ago Max might have been a little concerned about being here but then a month ago he would never have had any reason to be here at two in the morning.

Maybe he was too cavalier. He hardly paid any attention to the scant groups of travelers, never even looked to see if any of them took notice of him. Only when one group crossed the street behind him did he even bother to turn an ear their way.

"Yea, yea, that's him", said a familiar voice. Immediately Max stopped walking and turned around.

There were seven of them now. The Phi Gamma emblems almost glowed in the night light. They stopped as a group when he turned to face them.

With only about ten feet of sidewalk between them the Phi Gammas and Max stared at each other. Seconds passed, he could hear their breathing increase, could see them shift their weights to the balls of their feet. They thought he would run.

Right.

"What's up, bitch? Snitch-ass bitch!" It was the same leader from the group that tried to ambush him on King Day. It was the same voice from the Student Center; Yasir. "You should'a stayed your ass in Ivy Hills, mutha' fucka'!"

Max tried not to smile. "Why?"

"Cause this is West Oaks an' where snitches get stitches" said another Gamma.

Max curled his fingers to make tight fists. Clawed tips stabbed into his palms. He could not let it go too far. "You all do know that was about a decade ago... along with that 'Snitches get stitches' line."

"Phi G's don't forget, Snitch! Now catch this hurt."

The latest generation of his old fraternity might have talked tough but they obviously did not have much practice in walking the walk. Unlike the Downhills gang they were not coordinated nor practiced. They made no attempt to surround him or to cut off his escape route and they actually came at him from one direction.

Yasir caught the first blow and fell back into the rest of the Rho Phi Gammas; for some reason, they all had remained in a group on the sidewalk instead of fanning out. Max watched Yasir and his buddy, who had tried to catch his leader, both hit the ground. The rest of the Gammas hesitated but just like the Downhills Pack and the Maniacs, they seemed dedicated to the fight and started to rush him.

Almost on queue Max heard the sirens. So did the Gammas who froze in their tracks. Somewhere the police were driving with their flashing lights through West Oaks. The wailing sirens got louder very quickly and soon Max could hear the hard driving engines. They were on Washington and coming closer; he could see the red and blue light's glow reflecting off the high building walls. There was always something going on in West Oaks, he would never be able to get a cab to come get him.

The first two cars that shot by the corner they were standing on were the black and white Mountairy Rock police cars that he saw every day. They were old Chargers that were so beat up that Max could clearly see the dents and crumpled metal even in the second that they passed by him in the weak street lamps light.

Following them was another car, a pretty new looking black car, sleek and plush. It's make was too hard to figure out in the dark night as it too jetted by him. Tires screeched in a sudden and violent cry as it skid to a halt abruptly and slid sideways down the street a ways.

The car then completed the turn and came about back down the one way street toward him and the Phi Gammas with its engine roaring. What the hell?

It turned ever so slightly and passed him again but the driver hit the brakes again and the car skid to a stop just a few feet away. Both doors opened at the same time but the driver got out first,

and the gun came up fast.

"FREEZE MADIGAN!" Sheriff Lynne pointed her gun right at Max's head. Its barrel looked huge and he thought he could feel the spot in between his eyebrows where the bullet wanted to go.

"Hands where I can see them! All of you!", she shouted at them. His hands had already gone up as soon as he saw the gun. She was enraged, disheveled and… she looked like she had been in a fight.

There was a flash of light and then the next thing Max knew was that he was seeing the dirty graffiti filled stone wall of the building he had been standing next to racing to meet his face. His jaw collided with the mortar and there came another flash of light. Someone had hit him… hard.

"Told you, boy…" A rough gloved hand smashed his head into the wall again and another grabbed his wrist and twisted. "I wasn't finished with you." A sour rawhide and tobacco smell filled his nostrils.

"Down." Sheriff Lynne grabbed Max by the collar and easily pushed him to the ground, face down. Rogan had not let go of his wrist and Max screamed as it twisted.

"Shut up!" The two Sheriffs shouted together. Something hard was pressing deep into his neck. At first he thought it was the gun until it shifted and ground in a bit more.

Lynne was standing on his neck. His head was turned so that he could see her other foot shifting as it fought to keep its balance. The rough hands found his other wrist and brought that behind his back to join his other. A click, a rattle and then his wrists were handcuffed and started to go numb immediately. Finally he got his bearings.

"What the fuck!?!"

"Shut up, boy!" Rogan then stood and placed his foot down hard into the small of Max's back. "'for I get rough. On the ground the rest of you!"

"Think you're slick Madigan?" Lynne was yelling. She took her foot off him to walk back to her car. "You're not getting' away with this bullshit tonight!"

There was a click followed by a static hiss and then she said,

"Got the ring leader here on…" she paused and Max could tell she was reading the street sign. "… on Overbrook. I'm gonna take him in directly." And a click ended the static hiss.

"Whoa now!" Rogan thankfully took his boot off of Max's back and stepped in front of Lynne. "YOU are taking him in?"

"What? Do you want the credit or…", she started.

"Credit? Lynne I want MY prisoner." Max could see Rogan pointing over his shoulder at Max.

"You're prisoner? What the hell do you mean? This is my case!" she stepped past him and walked back over to Max. Then she reached down and grabbed him by his collar. "Get up, Madigan!" She tugged him up a bit and he got an even better look at her. Her face was dirty and bruised. The cream colored silk blouse was torn where he could see it poking out around the bulletproof vest she had strapped on. Max chanced a glance and saw that Rogan's vest could also be seen just beneath his jacket.

"This thing tonight went down in my ward. We're standing in it right now." He said calmly but firmly. The big Sheriff's face showed evidence of his being in a fight as well.

"YO!" Max yelled. "What the fuck are you arresting me for?" he could get up and toss both of them halfway down the street. He could…

"Shut up, Madigan!" Lynne shouted back. "You know why." Then she looked back to Rogan. "You can't be serious!"

"I respected your ward…"

"Only because you had to!"

"And now so do you." Rogan walked over to them and reached down and grabbed a fistful of Max's jacket and hauled him to his feet. "You can have the rest of them." He waved a hand at the prostrate Gammas. "Now should I drive us to my station or would you like to?"

Lynne maintained her grip on Max's collar. "I've got seven dead bodies at the Museum he's got to answer for! And after tonight…"

"I had nothing to do with that!" Max yelled. The Gammas began to complain in earnest as well. Yasir had recovered from the punch to his solar plexus and was coughing up weak accusations at Max but the two Sheriffs seemed to be ignoring the students for the most part.

"Shut up, Madigan! Lynne, these boys have been doing whatever it is they do here in MY ward. We caught Madigan HERE! He's mine." And he yanked Max hard away from Lynne.

For his own part Max had finally gotten past the shock of having the gun stuck right in his face. When Rogan pulled him, he allowed himself to be pulled and then went with it, hard. He dipped his shoulder into Rogan and shoved him away making the man fall against Sheriff Lynne's car.

"Sonova…" Rogan pulled his own gun and leveled it at Max's

194

head. "That's a good way to die, boy!"

"Down!" Just as she was saying it, Lynne kicked Max in the back of his leg right behind his knee. It made him drop again to the ground and again she stepped on his neck. "Try it again!" she challenged him.

Now she was stepping on his neck so hard that Max could not look up. The Gammas were out of sight behind him but he could still see the Sheriffs from the ankles on down. He watched Rogan's boot walk back over to them both.

"Ought'a stomp his ass right here."

"No. Let me take him back. You've still got to get to High street." she countered.

"What do I need with High street if I've got him? I'll get all his buddies once he flips."

Max heard another car coming up the street from the same direction that the two sheriffs had come. Red and blue flashing lights grew brighter and brighter. A car door opened and there were more black booted feet joining Rogan's.

"Take this guy to the station. Put the others in the wagon", ordered Rogan in his gravelly voice.

"Rogan I'm serious" Lynne's heeled shoes stepped between them. "Mann was from the 'One'."

"What do you think I did?" Max asked, but it came out like a barked order. It was ignored.

"Lynne, think for a second. You really don't want to bring this guy back up to 'One' with everybody watching. You know what's likely to happen?" The rough hands forced him up again. Now there were six uniformed cops there, all standing with their hands on their gun hips. Sheriff Lynne was in front of them, blocking their path to Max. Her eyes were locked with Rogan's, who was smiling.

"I'll even let you question him", he said.

Lynne looked quickly at Max and then turned sharply heading for her car. "Let's go."

"Hey! WHAT am I being arrested for?" Max screamed at her back but she just hopped in her car followed by Rogan. Two of the uniformed officers grabbed him by either arm and slammed him up against their car. There they patted him down and pulled out his cell phone and wallet. One of them read him his rights. He could hear the other cops cuffing the Gammas behind him.

"No I don't understand these rights! What I am being arrested for? What's the charge?"

"You and your friends killed a cop tonight."

"What's this?" the older cop pulled on the string around Max's neck. The Stone came up out of his shirt and was held before his eyes by two cheese-doodle encrusted fingers.

For the most part Max had taken the quick ride to the 27th precinct without further argument. He only spoke when one of the two officers in the front of the car tried to cajole him or to interrogate him and then he only asked what he was charged with and stated that he wanted a lawyer.

"Lawyer up all you want, motherfucker. It ain't gonna help you." the driver had said. The other officer had seemed more reluctant to attack Max. He had even said that he was unsure how Max could have been involved that night giving the distance from the incident.

That had given Max a little hope because while he was certain he had killed no one; he did not want to have to rely on Prya or the Landry woman for his alibi.

"Good luck charm." He said to an older cop. They were now in what Max thought was booking. Everything he had on his person was turned over to them and that looked like the Stone as well.

"My good luck now." The string burned his neck when the Stone was pulled over his head. Was it just his imagination or did he feel just a little bit smaller now?

"Anything else?" the cop looked at Max as though he thought Max was indeed hiding something. The same old angers came boiling up so fast Max did not realize he was speaking in time to stop himself from saying it.

"Nope. Been ditched the murder weapon."

The older cop moved suddenly, raising his fist as if he were going to hit Max. It looked like defiance but really it was the shock of having said what he had indeed just said that froze Max in place as the Cop's fist stopped just short of his face.

"Gonna take care of you. You'll see.", said the cop, obviously disappointed that he had not shaken Max. "No luck in the Tank."

The "Tank": A huge caged pit, filled with drunks, gang bangers, and drug dealers. The place stank of body odor that rose up as Max descended the small set of steps to the front of the tall bars.

Inside the Gammas were spread throughout the ten plus other detainees. They sat confidently on the benches whereas the assortment of bums, drunks, and others gave them a wide berth. At least they were doing well for themselves here. One of them noticed him and quickly spoke up.

"Snitch is back."

"Don't drop the soap, bitch!"

"Gonna be a long night for somebody."

The old cop snickered and opened the door. "Looks like your crew missed you." He shoved Max inside. There was another step he had not seen and he stumbled and fell unable to catch himself with his wrists still handcuffed. The floor was filthy and covered with something Max did not want to identify. He tried to push himself to his feet but a wave of dizziness dropped him onto his face.

The Gammas erupted in laughter, all save Yasir who was not at all satisfied. He hopped up and walked up to stand over Max. He did it so fast and suddenly that Max flinched away which brought more laughter from the Gammas.

"Nowhere to run now…" he started but took a step back himself when Max stood suddenly.

"I didn't run before", he said boldly but another wave of dizziness washed over him. He had been without the Stone for less than two minutes but he felt it none the less. Still he took a breath and then clenched his jaw, there had to be some power left.

The rest of the Gammas were on their feet and standing behind their leader. There was fear and hesitation in a few of the eyes watching him. Perhaps they were remembering how fast he put Yasir on his ass. One of the Gammas, the guy standing in the back, even looked reserved and regretful, maybe some hope there? But the rest…

Max turned and looked over his shoulder at the old cop who was watching with a grim smile. He looked back at Max for a moment with a little surprise on his face. The realization that Madigan and his new roomies were not friends, bloomed on his face with the raising of his eyebrows and a sneer that showed a missing bicuspid. Then the old cop looked past him to the Rho Phi Gamma leader and lowered his eyes as if to say: "I don't see anything."

"Yea, yea." The Gammas got the message clearly. Gone were the uncertain and fearful eyes. Yasir was smiling confidently but Max saw that he allowed the rest of the Gammas to move around him instead of stepping forward with them. They closed in on him and he clenched his cuffed fists behind him. They were no good to him behind his back but it was the fact that he could not feel clawed fingertips digging into his palms that really worried him.

"Take him to room 3." Rogan's rough gravelly voice came from behind him. Max turned and inhaled. He had not caught the now familiar smell of rough worn leather yet there he was; all six feet five or six inches of angry cop standing by the door. Next to him, not so small herself was Sheriff Lynne.

Another inhale, then another… her scent was… barely… there! The power was fading fast.

"You're ready for him already?" The older cop asked obviously disappointed.

"Will be by the time you get him where he needs to be." Rogan then tipped out of the room. Paper crinkled behind him and Max turned again to see the old cop sealing a large manila envelope.

"Won't be seeing these again for a while." He said with a mean smirk.

His body went tense all over. It had been a mistake to let them take him in, a mistake to let this cop take the damn Stone!

The Gammas shuffled back away as the cage door was again opened. There were a few taunts tossed his way but he hardly paid them any mind as he was focused on the envelope holding the Stone. When the officer took his arm to lead him out Max jerked away.

"Please!" said the old cop while brandishing a battered and discolored Billie club. "Please give me a reason Jackass! This has been up more ass than Chamberlain and yours is next." His old hands grabbed Max hard by the arm, more pinching than holding and he roughly lead him out of that room and down a hall to another. At least the old guy had brought the envelope with him.

For the second time Max found himself in a police interrogation room. This one was far worse than the one in the 1st district. The table was old, wooden and had been wrapped heavily in duct tape in several places. Here was the unmistakable scent of blood. It was older, perhaps years, but Max could still smell it. There were dark stains on the broken table and on the floor… and in the corner… and against the wall just under the big picture mirror.

Someone was whispering but he could not make out what they were saying. Something about… the 1st district… they were arguing… one voice was a woman's… Sheriff Lynne's?

"Sit your ass down."

The old cop closed the door in Max's face. There was a small window in the door and Max peeked out to see him leaning against the far wall, envelope still in his hand.

"I said SIT DOWN!" he yelled when he saw Max peeking at him.

There was only on chair in the room, a very fragile looking stool. He doubted that it could bear his weight and he did not want to risk falling with his hands still handcuffed behind his back. So instead he leaned against the table which felt a hell of a lot sturdier than it looked.

The whispering in the other room had quieted and soon Max was not sure he could really hear anything at all. Also he could not smell the blood, which had been so evident to him before. Slowly aches began to creep into his muscles, tender spots bloomed onto his skin, and he began to notice how exhausted he was.

God… he needed that Stone!

After what had to have been a couple of hours the door opened without warning making Max jump and nearly fall. Rogan walked in followed by Lynne who was carrying the envelope.

"Sit down, Madigan." Rogan ordered but he did not wait. The big man walked right up to Max, grabbed him by his shoulders and shoved him onto the stool, which swayed, but held.

Rogan then stood on the other side of the table and placed his rough scarred hands palms down on the duct taped surface. He glared hard at Max for a few moments.

This might have been menacing or even intimidating but Max was too busy dealing with the growing cramps in his thighs. The aches in his knees were getting worse and his spine felt like it was starting to fuse into one long solid bone. The mounting exhaustion was making him breath heavily and he squeezed his eyes shut every few minutes just to rest his eyes.

"You wanna tell me about tonight?" Rogan made it sound more like a threat.

The terrible pain his body was in only made the anger bubbling inside him all the easier to let out. He balled his hands into fists to keep from going completely crazy.

"Wanna tell me what I'm charged with?" he met Rogan's glare with his own.

"Son, you don't know…" Rogan began but Max had had enough.

"I'm not you're fucking son! Tell why you picked me up! Charge me with something! Or take these God damned cuffs off me and let me go!"

Rogan was around the table in a flash. One hand grabbed a fistful of Max's jacket and lifted him easily off the stool. The other hand cupped Max's face and drove his head back into the wall behind him. The impact was jarring, his legs went numb and his feet stumbled. The only reason he did not fall was because Rogan had not let him go.

"Who the fuck do you think you're yellin' at, SON? You ain't on the top ridge no more. This is West Oaks, and a cop is dead!"

The hand crushing his head against the wall felt even stronger than the Snake Maniac's had. Of course if that was true; Max's head would probably be so much mush right now.

"What were you and your friends doing in West Oaks?" the rough hand pushed harder. Max could feel the vein on the side of his face strain to force blood to his head. He could even hear its quiet little pulses in matching rhythm just a beat behind his pounding heart. It was too much.

He could not take anymore.

"Lawyer", he barely croaked out. Head against the wall he could now smell the blood stained deep into the crevices.

"Ain't no Lawyer gonna touch you after what yall pulled tonight." A little spit hit Max's face but he hardly noticed as the pain in his body was in became overwhelming. Now his stomach was cramping. It felt like someone was trying to pull out one of his ribs.

"Fuck you…" Max was not even sure what Rogan had just said to him. "… Lawyer!"

A door opened and slammed shut but Max could not see it beyond Rogan's wide shoulders. Keys and something else hit the table behind him but Rogan never turned to look.

"Ain't done yet." he said while glaring into Max's eyes but he was not talking to him.

"Sit him down." Sheriff Lynne's voice cut hard through the room. There was the slightest faltering in Rogan's eye Max thought, or was that just him getting angrier?

"We had a deal." he said finally turning to the woman who had brought a chair in with her and was sitting on the other side of the table.

"Yes we did, but now he's asking for a lawyer."

"Don't hand me that crap Nikki! This ain't the 'One'. Ain't nobody here but MY people." Rogan's hand had dropped to Max's throat and promptly cut off his air.

This was bad. Max thought that all the rough treatment had been a scare tactic, a bluff to get him to confess to whatever it was that had happened. If Rogan had not even been worried about Max demanding a lawyer then how far was the man willing to go?

"I'm here." Lynne said quietly but firmly. THANK GOD! Now if she could just get him to let go before Max passed out.

Even more roughly Max was forced back onto the stool but at least he could breathe again. His fused spine cracked and his left knee popped when his butt hit the seat. Rogan was behind him, pacing. Max could tell because the ankle length leather coat kept brushing against his back with each pass. Sheriff Lynne sat in front of him her hands folded on the table. The room went silent and Max realized that she had asked him a question. Whatever it was had passed his ears unnoticed because his focus had suddenly turned to the beige envelope lying on the table.

There were four bulges in it. The first one was his keys, the second… his wallet, and a third matched the shape of his cell phone. The last was the Stone. It was the smallest bump in the envelope but Max thought he could see the concave outline. If he could just…

A sharp smack to the back of his head woke him up.

"She asked you a question?" Rogan spat.

"Rogan please!" Lynne shouted.

The cramp in his side spread over his whole rib cage. It was getting harder to breathe.

How long had he been in here?

"One more time…" Sheriff Lynne leaned to catch Max's eye. "What were you all trying to do tonight?"

"I…" Max fought down a ball of bile trying to climb out of his throat. "… who all?"

Rogan's fist slammed down onto the table. It gave a little at the duct taped middle. "You wanna play this game?"

"Please Professor, we're not stupid. What were you doing in West Oaks tonight?" Lynne's eyes were soft; her eyebrows were raised almost understandingly. Maybe she would let him have the Stone.

It was just under a little bit of paper.

It was getting harder to breathe.

"Answer her!" Rogan was yelling right into his ear.

"Look at you, Professor," Lynne's voice was so soft by comparison. "You're sick aren't you?"

"Sick?" he was freaking dying. Was it all catching up to him? Every bit of damage he had done to himself since this year had started? At least it was not as bad as it had been in the bathroom. Not yet anyway.

"We can get you to a hospital. They can fix you up." She said.

"Wha?"

"The Doctors can give you something to get by. You'll feel better." She said it so sympathetically, but what the hell was she talking about?

"We know you're hurting son." Rogan scoffed. Then Max knew.

"I'm fine." He mumbled unconvincingly.

"Fine?" Now Lynne snorted a little. "Professor it's obvious you've been using your own product. I know the shakes when I see them. Come on. Talk to us so we can get you to a hospital."

"Just let him stew in the tank all night with his buddies. I'm sure he'll talk... eventually." Rogan voice had a smirk in it but Max could not take his eyes off of the envelope.

He did not have to touch the Stone; he could just grab the envelope... then smash Rogan into the wall, kick Lynne through the mirror/window and break, in half, any cop in the station who tried to stop him. There was at least one cop outside the door, undoubtedly more on the other side of the mirror. They would have guns but Max was fast... would BE fast if he just...

"What is it?" Lynne asked. She then picked up the envelope and held it up. "What's in here that's so important?"

Slowly she unwound the little string and opened the flap. Then carefully she let the contents slide out onto the table. The Stone came out last bumping into his cell phone before coming to a stop. The string was trailing up into the envelope which Lynne then placed down on the table.

She then picked through his belongings using her pointer finger like an examine tool. With a flick she turned his cell over face up.

"Are you looking to call somebody? Your dealer?"

Max tried to look away. His neck was so stiff.

"No that's right; you're the dealer." Lynne pushed his cell to the side.

His lungs seemed smaller… tighter. He was getting dizzy.

Her finger came down on his keys; she slid her finger through the key ring and picked them up.

"Lot of keys…" she said. Max heard Rogan shuffle his feet behind him. He could just reach out… grab the Stone… then…

The keys came down by the cell phone in a loud harsh crash. The noise rang through his ears and alerted him to the headache that was just brewing behind his left eye. He pinched his eyes closed trying to squeeze out some of the dizziness but it did not help. When he opened them Lynne was looking through his wallet.

"You… haven't told me why… you arrested me."

"We're not complete idiots, Professor. You just happened to be in West Oaks tonight?" Lynne's voice had caught an edge and Max finally picked up that she was emphasizing calling him Professor; mocking him. Though now she was not even looking at him; she was flipping through the cards and receipts he had in his wallet.

"Ain't got all night Lynne." Rogan muttered behind Max. If she heard him she showed no sign. Instead she pulled a card out of the small stack she had been looking through.

"'Rasheeda Revan Landry'" She read out loud. With a flick she turned the card over and showed it to Rogan. "It's a West Oaks number." She said.

Rogan took the card and read it, looked at Max with even more suspicion then exchanged a shrug with Lynne. Without saying anything he walked out of the room and slammed the door shut behind him.

"Who is Rasheeda Landry?" Lynne asked.

"…she…" Max was staring at the Stone again. He needed to get it. Lynne finally noticed this.

"What's this?" she picked up the Stone by its string and let it spin. "You were wearing this?"

"… good luck charm…"

"Not working tonight." She dropped it back onto the table and would have been done with it but Max was still staring. "Is it religious?"

Max had not thought of that. Some kind of spiritual talisman? Landry had called the Maniacs a "cult".

"… Landry…" he said. He had to get that Stone; just make contact with it for a moment. His vision was tunneling.

"Yes? Who is she?"

"She's…" but he was hand cuffed. He could grab it with his teeth.

"Professor?"

But if he lunged for it and failed then she would never let him have it. He had to be casual. There were more cops probably watching from the other room.

"She's... my lawyer."

Lynne's face went white and she got up and ran to the door. "Rogan!" She grabbed the shoulder of the old cop who was still out in the hall. "Take him to the tank!" and she took off.

The old cop walked in frowning, snagged Max by his collar as he was leaning halfway across the table and hauled him up.

"Let's go." He shoved Max out into the hall and down another corridor. Then after stumbling down a small flight of steps Max was walked back into the West Oaks holding tank.

The Gammas all stood when Max was brought back up to the Tank. A look passed from the leader to the old cop and they both nodded to each other.

"Turn around." The old cop ordered. Max complied and felt the tight hand cuffs relax and fall off of his wrists. The iron barred door was opened in front of him. "In ya go, Professor. Have a good night."

Max stepped in rubbing his wrists and looked around. The Gammas now spread out and began to converge on him.

Without urgency he ran his hands over his face, specifically his mouth. Despite the smell of the room he then took a deep breath. With the Stone now palmed in his right hand he looked over his shoulder and flashed the old cop a smile.

"I'm not a Professor. Not yet."

They kept him in the tank overnight. If Max had not been so relieved to have the Stone back it would have been the worst night of his life. After the Maniacs and the Downhills Pack had fought him so fanatically, Max was surprised to find that it only took having to put three of the Gammas down to keep the rest of them from giving him anymore trouble. They sat huddled on the other side of the tank along with the other assorted guests. The Gamma leader glared at him. He had not attempted to join in on the brief fight, a fact that had not gone unnoticed by his frat brothers. While he glared at Max the other Gammas glared right at him. It was clear that he was the focus of their anger now. Even so Max did not dare go to sleep, not that he could, so he had plenty of time to think.

They had nothing on him, the police. Now that he passed the shock of the initial arrest and the Stone's withdrawal, Max could see that. Something big had gone down in West Oaks tonight. A police officer had been killed. The Maniacs were involved. Sheriff Lynne had seen him on Overbrook Street and had freaked, assuming he had been involved somehow. But she knew that she did not really have a legal reason to pick him up. That was why she went after Rogan; she thought he was about to unknowingly call Max's lawyer.

They couldn't have that.

So they left him here to stew, expecting that a night in this place with no "fix" would make him even more pliable. With the Stone now hanging around his neck and hidden under his shirt he could not help but to smile a little. He was a 100% and ready.

The thought that they might have noticed that he had taken it back and would try to relieve him of it was only a minor concern to him right now. He had no intention of letting them or anything separate him from the Stone again.

The sun had risen and filled the cell with light filtered through a scum covered window. The clock on the far wall outside their cell told Max that it was half past eight when he heard the arguing. There was a group walking up the hall and their discussion was not too polite.

Rogan was the loudest. He was belting out accusations and talking about not letting them get away with "that freak shit" in West Oaks. Lynne was shouting as well though instead she was demanding answers for… something. Max recognized the voice of the guy arguing back. He had seen him before in a place very much like this.

The door to the floor opened and they walked in. Max had chosen a seat far back in the cell so at first he could not see them.

Rogan's rawhide scent cut through the B/O smell and Max felt a little anger swell inside him.

"Let it go, Max" he told himself. There was nothing to be gained by smashing Rogan's head against the bars of the tank until Lynne begged him to stop.

Then Lynne's jasmine scent with a little citrus cut through the dank air. The memory of looking down the barrel of her gun played in his mind. He should have… whatever.

"Let it go Max." he whispered to himself.

"Mr. Madigan?"

They were standing outside the cell now. Max could see them in his peripheral vision but had not yet bothered to look up.

"What the hell?" Lynne whispered at the sight of Max sitting on one side of the room while everyone else in the tank was jammed together against the far wall.

"Time to get up Madigan!" Rogan punctuated this by banging something on the bars. "Sleep it off… at home." He noticed the peculiar separation too.

So Max stood and turned to face them. Lynne was staring open mouthed at the scene, Rogan was smacking a binder against his leg, and Tragan, King's lawyer, was looking at him like Max was the ugliest mutt in the pound.

"He's coming out." Tragan said into a cell phone. Though Max could hear the background noise coming out of it he did not hear anyone respond on the other end. He walked to the door and inhaled deeply, taking in Tragan's cigar smoke scent. Mixed with it, faintly was the smell of cedar.

He regarded the two Sheriffs. They were looking at him as well. Rogan just glowered but Max could see that Sheriff Lynne was surprised at his condition.

"Good morning." he said. Her eyes narrowed and Max smiled inside.

"Don't say anything Mr. Madigan." Tragan ordered. He snapped the cell phone closed and turned and walked out.

Max stepped by them slowly, wanting some excuse to confront the two Sheriffs. Some excuse to…

He followed Tragan out but when he reached the door he turned back and looked at Rogan, and smirked.

His reaction was instant. Rogan dropped the binder and rushed across the room cursing. Lynne grabbed his arm and struggled to keep him from getting to Max. One punch… Max would let him get in one punch and then…

"What's this?" Tragan had returned probably because Max had not been right behind him.

"Rip your fool head off, junky!" Rogan was shouting. Lynne had gotten in front of him and was trying force him back. She was much stronger than she looked. "Nikki let me go!"

"Let's go Mr. Madigan." Tragan grabbed his arm and pulled. Max in turn grabbed Tragan's wrist and yanked it off of him. But he never took his eyes off of Rogan, who was gaining ground. Just a little closer.

"Mr. Madigan," Tragan was rubbing his aching wrist. "I'm sure you don't want to keep Dr. King waiting," Rogan was almost in arms reach. "… in the car."

What? King was outside? Tragan had walked off again, not bothering to see if Max was following, which of course he was.

The limo was not a stretch; that would have been too gaudy for King. Yes it was big but it was also elegant. It was also a foreign car. Not foreign as in Porsche, Ferrari or Honda, but foreign as in he had never heard the name before. It was black, that deep black in which your reflection looked back at you in shadow.

Max had passed Tragan in the station and was the first to reach the car. The door opened just as he got there and he was surprised to see a shapely pair of feminine legs seated next to the door. Nice legs, the kind you only see on T.V. too. Who was the Doctor messing around with? King's thick cedar scent poured out just as his deep canon like voice sounded.

"Today Mr. Madigan."

"Yea," came Fatima's voice and she leaned forward with a wicked smile on her face. "We haven't got all day." Those were HER legs? When did Fatima get girl legs?

Oh God he had dirty thoughts about Fatima!

He got in and sat on the opposite side, facing Fatima until Tragan cleared his throat. So Max slid over and was then facing his mentor.

Dr. Odom King looked no worse for wear from his trip to Africa. In fact he looked a little sharper in his black suit. Lying beside him was his ornate walking cane. King only pulled that out for big events. What was going on?

Max saw that Fatima was dressed up as well. Her usual dress attire was nothing he ever found noticeable but this morning he had to admit, if only to himself, that she looked impressive.

Straight to the point; "What's going on?" he asked. King wrinkled his nose a bit. The stench from the tank still hung in Max's clothes.

"That is the same question I had prepared for you. Why were you being held by the police?"

"I don't know. Something happened in West Oaks last night. I think it must have been the same guys who broke into the Museum because Sheriff Lynne saw me and broke off a police chase to arrest me."

"You were not arrested. You were never charged. You volunteered to go with them for questioning." Tragan said almost dismissively. Max got hot.

"I didn't 'VOLUNTEER'! Okay! Then why'd they put me in cuffs? You think I want…"

"Mr. Tragan…" King's voice could stop a train. " … was just telling you what the official line will be should you seek to press charges."

"Press charges? Of course I'm going to…"

"This is the West Oaks 27th Precinct. It's your word against those of Two Mountairy Rock Sheriffs. No one will believe your version of events." Tragan was not even looking at him.

"Except," King said, directing his gaze at Tragan who immediately sat a little straighter. "… for those in this car."

"Of course. I merely meant that pressing charges would be a waste of time."

"Difficult perhaps. It is up to Mr. Madigan." And King looked to Max.

Pressing charges felt very hollow to him now. What he really wanted was to deal with it himself, especially now that he had the Stone back. But that would only start more trouble and really give them something to lock him up for. Maybe later when he had cooled down a bit, he could make a better choice.

"I don't know. They were rough but…" had they gone too far? Or was it just the withdrawal that had made everything so unbelievably painful?

"Rogan wanted to rough me up… and Sheriff Lynne was right there with him." He said.

"You should see the gang members they caught. All six of them in the hospital. I think two are dead." Tragan almost scoffed. "What were they thinking killing a Sheriff?"

"They did say a cop was killed. A Sheriff?" Max asked.

King looked up. "Former Sheriff. You met him; Derrick Mann, the Sheriff that Nicole Lynne replaced."

The image of the older man came back to him easily. He had introduced himself as a … "he said he was a detective."

"As of midnight New Years eve he was. The start of the year was the beginning of Lynne's tour as Sheriff of District 1." King told him.

"I would have thought her to be ambivalent at best about Mann's death. The Mayor really embarrassed her by having him chaperone her around on her first case." Tragan said haughtily.

She might have been irritated that night but Max could only remember the cloth covered bodies and the smell of blood.

"She was pissed last night." He said quietly.

"Are you considering pressing charges then?" Tragan asked.

"I don't know." Max snapped.

"Decide soon." King stated evenly. "In the mean time we will drop you off at your apartment. I had hoped to get you released in time to attend the memorial service but you don't look to be in any condition."

"Memorial?" Max asked. There had already been a service for the guards who had been killed.

"Robert's service. Dr. King brought his body back." Fatima said in a very tiny voice.

Now Max realized why they were all dressed in black; Robert Bazillion's service. The very realness of his death now hit Max.

He should be there… rivals or not.

"Where is it?" he asked. Fatima looked to answer him but King spoke first.

"It's in fifteen minutes. You won't make it. Get cleaned up, get some sleep. I have work that I need you to start on as soon as possible."

"I should be there." was all Max said. Then there was a silence as he and King stared at one another. It was true that he had never liked Bazillion but it was never a venomous dislike. They had been rivals, not enemies. Maybe King understood that, maybe he did not, but he should not be trying to keep a staff member away.

"You won't get there in time. Though it was short notice to most I expect no late comers entering the hall while the Reverend is speaking. If you can get cleaned up in time then come to the burial."

Max nodded dumbly. The effects of last nights run was starting to catch up to him Stone or no Stone. How was he going to make it through a service?

The limo pulled onto the street where Max lived and slowed to a stop in front of his building. Before he got out he remembered something else King had said.

"You need me tonight?"

"Yes. Despite the political climate I was able to bring home several artifacts that Dr. Bazillion had not been able to send. I would like you to check them in, and enter them into the data base so that we can get some feedback from other researchers. I imagine you were unable to get very much sleep last night, so you can work at the Museum after hours."

"Tonight?"

King did not bother to look in Max's direction. "Tonight. At the latest."

Before the door closed Fatima leaned forward again and said to Max quickly, "Church Falls."; the place where Bazillion would be buried.

He watched the black limo leave for a moment and then rubbed his eyes. Depending on how many artifacts King had brought back it could take hours or even days to get that done. He could run to the Museum now but then he would be wiped out later tonight.

That was no good because he needed to see Landry tonight and he did not want to go back to West Oaks bleary eyed. And he still had the funeral to attend.

Damn. It was probably a little callous but Max could not help to think of how Bazillion had stuck him again.

THE SERPENT CULT

In his time as a student and then as a researcher Max had gone days without sleep before and he had always managed to do it with very little discomfort. But those overnight marathons had always ended with him at a desk, sitting down and reading not leaping from rooftop to rooftop and getting his ass kicked by surly cops. Could be that he was getting older.

The funeral was solemn enough, he thought and mercifully quick. It would have been a disaster if he had started nodding off during the Rites. Bazillion's family seemed an odd contrast to what Max had expected. He had three younger brothers and two older as well as two sisters; one older, one younger. His parents were both alive though very advanced in age. They were all warm and friendly, even humble he thought. His older sister was especially nice and seemed to be the unofficial head of the family. She thanked him for coming and told him that Bazillion had often talked of him. Whatever he had actually said she acted as though Max and he had been the best of buds. Go figure.

He watched as King gave his condolences. Bazillion had been recruited, groomed, and mentored by King as had Max. No doubt the family knew him well. King had come to meet Max's own parents before hiring him as an assistant.

There was a gathering afterward but even the lure of a free meal could not get Max to head anywhere other than his bed. So as everyone rallied around the buffet table, Max walked to the bus stop. Church Falls was not far from campus or his apartment but he still managed to drift off in his seat.

It was twilight when Max woke, half dressed in his only good suit. He woke to a pungent musky scent, a heavy weight on his chest and a freezing wind washing over his bare legs.

"mmrow?" came the quiet interrogative.

Ugh! "Get off!" and Max shoved the smelly cat to the floor and stood from his bed. Little good it did, his chest now stank of whatever cat had been to crawling through all day. "Where've you been anyway?"

The cat simply looked up at Max with the same plaintiff and unreadable expression. It uttered another whine that sounded like a question

"I don't know what that means."

"mmrow?"

"That either." The thing had communicated with him before. It had said something and he had heard it in his head. He looked down at the cat and made eye contact. For long seconds the cat stared back into his eyes... then licked itself.

Max shook his head and walked into the bathroom where he took off the rest of his suit. Too tired to hang it up he simply draped it over the shower curtain rod. He would take care of it later. He looked into the mirror at his bare chest.

The scabs from his wounds were gone but the scars remained. They had not seemed to heal any more than they had from the first weeks after the Snake Maniac had given them to him. They were pink but faint, the skin raised a little and they were sensitive to the touch. At least they had not grown into keloids.

"Where were you when I was thrown in the lock up huh?" he shouted out to the bedroom. He fingered the Stone, now always hanging on his neck, and wondered briefly if he would ever be able to take it off safely. As bad as it was when he got arrested it was nowhere as bad as when he had first taken it off.

Another mewl from the cat and Max looked down to see it as it entered the bathroom.

"What?" Why was it here now?

The dirty face and musky smelling cat offered no answer but seemed content to study him once again, to give him that questioning tilt of its head. He had wanted to understand what exactly Big Gray had to do with all this but it was late. The clock on his dresser flashed half past Seven. King expected work done on the artifacts he had brought back and Max wanted to get enough done that he might leave with enough time left to visit Landry at a decent hour.

A quick shower, then shave and Big Gray was still there. At least there did not seem to be any urgency in his manner. Or was it HER manner? Not that it mattered; he was not going to pick the stinky thing up to see.

Still there had to be something going on. Big Gray had first appeared when Max had gotten the Stone. Then he appeared when the Maniacs had shown up at the Museum. He did suspect that the cat had come into his apartment when he was recovering from his dip in Cobbs River. Maybe it sensed that he had lost the Stone for a little while last night. What else was there?

He finished dressing and was halfway to the door when he realized;

"The Artifacts?" he turned and asked the cat. Again it simply looked at him. King had brought back more artifacts from the research site in Africa. The Stone had come in the first shipment Bazillion had sent back. There was probably an entire crate of Stones sitting in the Museum right now!

Damn it! He had been so obsessed with sleep that he had completely ignored what was going on. What if the Maniacs knew that there were Stones there now?

The phone rang just as he was walking out the door. He tried to ignore it and closed the door behind him but he could still hear it. The answering machine picked up and the caller's voice came through clear to his ears.

The door cracked a little he was in such a hurry to pick up the phone.

"I'm here! I'm here!"

"…I thought you wanted this apartment?" his uncle's voice was strained and irritated.

"Of course! Yea! Hey Uncle Dave."

"Well where have you been? I checked with your landlord and you still haven't told him you want out of the lease." His voice was still strained.

"I'm sorry." Max worried for a second. He really did not know his Uncle that well and suddenly his chance at living in that amazing apartment did not seem too sure.

"There's been a lot going on at the Museum."

"I've read something about that. A couple of men were killed in a break-in?" His Uncle's voice seemed to be losing its edge.

"A couple of break-ins actually." Max said. He did not want his Uncle to think he had been half-assing and ungrateful about the loft… even though he had been half-assing. "I was… actually attacked on campus by a couple of them."

"What?" Now his Uncle's tone changed completely.

"The police are handling it but it's made work a little bit of a nightmare."

"I know some people in the department. Maybe I could talk to someone…."

Max wondered what Sheriff Lynne's face would look like if his Uncle did that. It brought a smile to his face. That smile disappear when he realized that would actually happen is that the police would tell his Uncle that he was suspected of smuggling and drug dealing. The apartment would disappear but more importantly his Uncle would tell his parents and he did not want to have that phone conversation!

"No, no. The police are taking care of it just fine. It's just been hectic at work that's all."

"You're sure? Your father'll kill me if something happens to you."

"Yea I'm good." Max looked at his watch. It was getting late. "But anyway don't worry; my lease is actually up the first of March so

I'm ready."

"All right fine. But you come see this apartment!"

"Right."

"I mean it Max."

"Ok. I'm there." But his thoughts were already drifting to what lay ahead of him at the Museum.

He ignored the elevator and practically leapt off the building by jumping down every flight of steps in the stairwell. Likewise he ignored the buses and hauled ass all the way to Haley's.

Whew! He had not run this regularly since grade school but he was barely winded by the time he ran across the docks. Almost, he missed noticing the guards.

Two new guards, dressed in black and gold uniforms as opposed to the light blue ones he was used to. The uniforms were impressive, the guards... not so much. The tall male looked to be pushing sixty and Max could not be sure that the old man could even see his approach while wearing glasses that were thicker than a deck of cards. His partner noticed him though and pulled the tight uniform top she wore even tighter, tying it on the side. It was obvious that she had never worn any kind of a uniform before. Her pants were way too tight, especially for a woman of her... fullness. Max did like the matching black sneakers though. They stopped him at the dock side entrance.

"I.D.?" the woman asked him with a smile.

"I.D.?" Max echoed unsure.

"Yes sir. Anyone looking to gain entry to the Museum after hours or through the employee entrance must now provide identification." said the older man.

"Sure." Max pulled out his work I.D. and was going to hand it to the man who was holding a clipboard at the ready but the female guard reached and took it from him.

"Thank you... Maximillion?" she started and then smiled a broad smile that made Max think she was proud of her pink gums. "Your parents must wanted you to make some money givin' you a name like that."

"Yea. I've been a big disappointment to them." The old guy was reaching, trying to get the I.D. from the woman who was now laughing some kind of rapid fire staccato giggle.

"You're funny, Maximillion. I'm Tracey."

"Hi." he said. "You guys don't work for the Museum?" the arm patches they were wearing were not the Museums patch and that meant they were from an independent firm.

"No Maximillion we're from City-Guard." She looked him up and down making sure he saw her doing it. "You are tall."

"When did the Museum hire you guys?"

"I don't know, honey. My supervisor called me last night and told me to be here today."

"Your people set this up earlier this week." The older guy said and finally got Max's I.D. away from his partner. He looked over his glasses to read from his clipboard and begin flipping through the pages to the "M"s.

"So you work overnight here?" asked Tracey.

"I will tonight." King must have added the extra security. He must be just as worried as Max was that the artifacts would attract the attention of the Maniacs.

"Your wife must not like that." Tracey stated the obvious question. The old guy read his name aloud from the clipboard and then handed him back his I.D.

"She's not thrilled. Nice to meet you." Max answered. He walked in between them and entered the Museum. There were more of the City-Guard security people all over the place. The Museums regular security staff was still there as well. That made for a lot of uniforms walking about the Castle doing nothing. Would it be enough to deter the Maniacs?

There was another checkpoint in the South Tower lobby but this one was run by the regular security staff and so mercifully quicker. It was all very impressive, but if the Maniacs had more of the Snake Maniacs it would not matter.

Did THEY know the Stones were here?

Big Gray did.

There were a few students left in the South Tower Labs. Late as it was they would probably be here long into the night while they tried to catch up on their Maniac-stalled research projects. None of them came up to him or bombarded him with questions when he entered the lab. Max guessed that King had already been over all the backed up projects and given his own direction and advice.

It was a relief. He would no longer have to hide out in the other offices or take the East Tower stairs to get in. As a matter of fact none of them gave him more than a nod as he passed through.

There was one project that seemed to be up and running that was of interest to him. Joel Williams had his virtual map running. Max walked quietly behind him so as not to disturb him. He was furiously typing code into his laptop which was connected to the now repaired server. The main terminal screen displayed a steadily revolving tiny virtual Castle. As it spun on the screen Max could see the cityscape behind it. There was Cobbs River, the Great Ridge Wall, the reservoir, and the line of buildings where his apartment was although he could not see it. From what he could see there was a lot of detail.

"Goes all the way to St. Raymond's Cathedral." Joel said over his shoulder, never bothering to stop typing.

"The Cathedral? You've mapped the Park?" he could not have, no one had yet.

"Nope. Just a topographical estimate. Don't even have Old City in the map yet." he said.

It looked impressive. From the initial project proposal the map could be converted to display Mountairy Rock from different eras. Pretty daunting task but Joel was moving with a passion now. It was in the opposite direction from the Cathedral but Max wondered if the map included the Downhills.

"Wanna walk through?" Joel offered. Max asked for a rain check and headed out of the lab to Kings Office. That was where the new artifacts he brought back from Africa would be.

The Office was a neat as ever and the scent of blood was barely a whisper now. Three crates were stacked right in front of the desk. King was nowhere to be seen and his scent was faint. He had brought the crates in but he had left a while ago.

The manifests were sitting on the top crate. They stated that there were twelve new pieces, six in one crate, four in the next, and two in the bottom. The other shipment sent from Bazillion had a weight discrepancy. He checked the weights and circled them on the sheet. If he did not find any more Stones he would weigh the crates himself to see if there was anything missing.

He popped the seal on the top crate and pulled the top off. There were three oddly shaped packages, wrapped in newspaper and poking out of straw bedding. He grabbed the largest and pulled it out of the straw. It was light but solid. The newspaper came off easily enough and Max saw that it was a mask. It was colored green on black and those colors were vibrant despite the obvious age of the artifact. There were very intricate carvings on the inside of it that would have required not only skill but precise tools. It was nothing like what he had seen before but then African art of that region was outside of his field of study.

Still, it was terribly odd. It was unusual because it would have exposed the wearer's mouth and nose. Most of the detail carvings of the mask lay in the crowns around the eyeholes, which lead up and part way around the wearer's head like feathered ears. Was it supposed to symbolize some type of bird?

There were, however no Stones. So he placed the mask down and reached for the next package. This one contained a bracelet and it was quite strange. The mystery was not the lions head stamped on it nor the one broken ring welded to the outside of it but that it had been made of metal: steel… Damascus steel.

An artifact made from forged steel, from a dig site that was supposed to have been undisturbed for more than a thousand years before steel was first invented was a major contradiction. Somebody screwed up.

The bracelet was roughly carved about its edges so that its original casting was completely changed. Could it have come from another part of the world? That would certainly change a lot of what King had been projecting they would find.

The lost tribe's existence was doubted by most of Kings peers and any contradictory evidence would undermine his theory's standing. Although the discovered sites were not thought to be places where the tribe actually lived, they were more like way stations, stopping points for a tribe that had been nomadic during the Diaspora. Still what were items of this variety doing at the site?

King himself had loaded these crates so he must have already thought of this. A lot of work was going into this project... a lot of work for nothing if Dr. King was wrong about the tribe.

This was big but Max's concern now was finding the Stones. He placed the bracelet next to the mask and grabbed the next package.

A broken piece of masonry, it was indistinctive otherwise. Nothing about it stood out to Max and it did not "feel" like magic either. Why had this had any importance?

The next three pieces were buried deep in that crate but none of them impressed Max much. They were not Stones so he just kept on, moving on and sorting through the second crate.

A headdress.

A piece of pottery.

A spear head.

A staff.

Again no Stones. What the hell? Maybe Bazillion had not found any more Stones. Or maybe King had not packed them, thinking they were not important or a part of the find. He pulled open the last crate.

The first object was small, a little shocking since the crate was so large and the manifest said there were only two artifacts in it. It was heavy too, at least five pounds. He pulled back the wrapping to reveal a warped and mummified face.

It was a human head, and not that old. There were still strands of hair dangling from the leathery scalp and teeth in the twisted mouth. The eyes had been removed and replace with two glittering green gems. The base of the head was wrapped in some kind of cloth and attached to a wooden base. It was designed to sit on a flat surface.

Max placed it on King's desk and it looked up at him, it's wide open green eyes and twisted, gaping mouth seemed to scream at him. In their search for the Lost tribe there had never been a find that included any actual bodies: no graves, no body parts, nothing. Could this have been an actual member of the Lost Tribe? Keeping heads was a practice that spanned the history of the world but nothing they had found on the Lost tribe had indicated the practice of this particular ritual.

The last piece was the largest. It was broad, flat and hard. Max had to feel through the straw around the edges of the crate to find where it stopped. It took a second but he got his hands under it and pulled it free, spilling a lot of the straw onto the floor.

It was a shield, wooden and wrapped in leather bindings. The face of it bore an insigne that was so deteriorated he could not determine what it was.

A face maybe?

The shield itself was three feet long and two feet wide, broad and flat at the top and narrow and pointed at the bottom. The most striking feature was the broken piece of Ivory, an elephant's tusk, which framed the outside of one side of the shield. The tip was still pointed and extended about half a foot out from the bottom of the shield.

He turned it over. There was an arm strap affixed to the center of the concave underside and set at an odd angle. The handle was bolted toward the bottom of the shield. If he slid his hand through the arm strap and took hold of the handle then he would have to keep his arm pointed down to have the shield sitting straight. Who could fight that way? Most traditional shield bearers held their arms up. If he held his arm up…

The tip of the tusk rotated up as he raised the shield up pointing forward. It must have made a wicked weapon when it was used.

He had never seen anything like this. The craftsmanship used to make all the new pieces was amazing but none it matched. No one item from any of the crates seemed to be related to another. They could not all be of the Lost Tribe if even anyone of them was.

He sighed. Again there was no sign of even a single Stone. A few months ago he would have been terribly excited about examining these artifacts. Now, however, he was worried that there might be an army of hissing, fang-faced Maniacs just outside the walls of the Museum.

The clock on his cell phone told him it was nearly Nine O'clock. The process of logging in the artifacts was a lengthy one. Hopefully he could get out of there at a decent hour.

It got cold fast. Mountairy Rock was just like that. The "Hawk" came swooping in from the Lake and swept away whatever tiny bit of warmth the streets had managed to collect during the clear and sunny day. Max took a cab to West Oaks, the second he had taken this year and so his entire "cab fare" budget was gone until next New Years.

It was well worth it not to have to brave the cold, winter itch, and any Maniacs still lurking about in West Oaks. He rode with the window down partway, much to the delight of the cabbie, who cursed him under his breath in Creole. Max ignored him, and concentrated on sifting the faint, fleeting and numerous scents that came in through the window.

Not a whiff of the Maniacs. Either they were not about or he had missed the scent. He had come to West Oaks directly from the Museum, easy to trail if they had wanted to, but again there was no sign of them. To avoid leading them directly to Landry's Max had the cabbie stop about a few blocks away.

He tested the winds again when he got out of the cab. The freezing air burned his nostrils. When the cab pulled away he listened to the sounds of the deserted West Oaks streets. It was half past Eleven O'clock, not late according to the usual West Oaks night scene but the "Hawk" had driven everyone inside. Maybe that meant the Maniacs as well. Snakes WERE cold blooded.

But Max was warm. He told himself that he had done it just to stay keep winter itch at bay. He told himself that it was just like wearing long johns. The hood of his sweatshirt stuck out of his collar and his legs had the added protection of his sweatpants beneath his jeans. He told himself it was just for the cold.

Despite the freezing wind Max continued to drag in deep breaths through his nose with every breath. If there were Maniacs here, he wanted to know well in advance. He rounded the corner of the street where Landry's building was and checked for scents.

Again nothing but the cold wind, but he was still nervous.

Quicker steps now, he wanted to get into the building before Maniacs or head cracking Sheriffs showed up. It was at least a seven story apartment, maybe eight, and it was one of the older buildings in this section of the city. Whoever owned it did a mediocre job of maintaining it, so Max guessed that the rent must not be too bad. How much could they charge in this part of West Oaks anyway?

Max walked into the vestibule and looked to the intercom. A small touch screen display asked for the room number. What was it again?

410.

"Yes?" asked an unfamiliar female voice. He checked the touch screen and saw the number "410" blinking back at him. For a moment Max wondered if Landry had given him the wrong room number on purpose. Maybe she was still scared of him and had run? No, it made no sense for her to have given him a number at all then.

"This is Max…" No doubt Landry already knew his name but this new person may not have. "… uh, and I'm looking for Mrs. Landry?"

The only answer was the buzzing and click of the door release. "Thanks." he muttered unsure of whether or not the intercom was still on and stepped through into the small lobby where there was a double set of elevators. There was no wait, not at this late an hour and soon

Max hopped off onto the fourth floor.

He did not have to look for the apartment though. At the far end of the hallway facing the elevator stood Landry. She was dressed now, though casually and barefoot. She stood waiting for him with her hands folded in front of her holding Amanda's scarf.

"Hello Max. I thought you might have tried the window again anyway." She smiled and that made him feel a little at ease.

"No", he said as he walked up to her. "I was afraid I would pick the wrong one again."

"No", she laughed. "It's only effective when you aren't expecting it. I believe this is yours… or your girlfriend's?"

"Thanks. Prya?"

"Yes. She was here earlier and asked me to return it to you. Come on."

She led him to apartment 410 and they walked inside. Immediately Max noticed the strange "covering" scent as he entered the room. Landry, he then realized, had given off no scent when he met her in the hall. He sniffed again.

"Can't smell anything?" she was smiling at him knowingly.

"You had something simmering on the stove the last time… it had no smell, but it…"

"Hides all smells? Yes. You aren't the only thing in this city that tracks by scent." Her tone was a little graver now. "If you stay in this apartment long enough it will get into your clothes and onto your skin and eventually your personal smell will be covered to. It lasts a few hours. Sit down."

The apartment was not hers, she had said that when he was here last. It was sparsely furnished with mismatched, previously owned furniture. There were no pictures, paintings nor plants here. Having seen her office, he figured that her living space would be even more refined but this looked worse than his apartment. Maybe she lived at her office. So who lived here?

There was a couch and a love seat, each from a different set, surrounding a small wooden coffee table. Max took the loveseat and sat down. Briefly a gust of old scents rose from the cushions as he sank into it; young, feminine… then slowly… gone.

"You were worried about me tracking you?" he asked.

"No. Well… yes, but not only you." she said as she sat down on the couch and picked a dark red folder off of the coffee table.

"The Mani… um the Serpent Cult?"

"Yes. There may be some of them who can track by smell as well. And they've been to my home. Fortunately their noses aren't as good as yours."

"Who are they? Why did they come after you?" he had a ton of questions spilling all over each other in his head. "Where did they come from?"

"I'll try and tell you."

Metal clanged loudly from the other room and Max was on his feet in a flash. Landry jumped to and quickly held her hands out to him as if to hold him back.

"No! It's alright! That's Alana!" She dropped the folder and papers spilled out onto the table and floor.

Right; it had to be the woman whom had answered the intercom, whose smell hid in the couch cushions. The covering scent had made him feel that it was only Landry and himself in the apartment. But there was more…

"I…" then he realized why it had been such a start. "I can barely hear her." he said. Now that he was listening he could tell she was in the other room but it was still difficult to hear her footsteps, or movements of any kind.

"Right. I'm sorry it's… more Witch trickery as Prya says. Drives her crazy." she laughed a little nervously. "Alana please come out here and say hello."

Out from a doorway that had to lead to the kitchen, where Max and Prya had confronted Landry the previous night, stepped a very young woman. She was baby faced, but solemn and sad. In her arms was a small bundle… that quietly yawned.

"Alana this is Max. Max, Alana, and her daughter; Kai."

Kai was wrapped in a dark green swaddling cloth and her little caramel colored face peeked out from the folds about her head. Her eyes were open briefly then her mouth stretched into another yawn and just like that the child slept. Her mother held her protectively and regarded Max with those very solemn eyes.

"Alana is my apprentice." Landry told him. "Some tea, Alana please." And the young mother drifted back into the kitchen.

"She's fifteen." Landry said. He had not asked but he sure was wondering. Why would she pick a fifteen year old mother to be her apprentice?

But he did not ask that. Instead he sat back down while Landry gathered her papers back up.

"Anyway, where was I?" she asked.

"You hadn't even started. The 'Serpent Cult'?"

"Yes. The Serpent Cult. They've become a plague in West Oaks. They have been here for maybe a year now, probably more." She evened out the bunched papers by tapping them on the table.

"I've done a little tracking through a network of other…" She looked up at him. "… well witches." He nodded to her seriously and she continued. "… but I haven't found any other trace of this group anywhere, at least not yet. But that could mean that Mountairy Rock is the first place it's sprung up." She then flipped through the papers quickly, pulled one out and passed it to him. "Have you seen this?"

The paper had a symbol hand drawn on it. Two curved lines meeting at a point inside of a circle. Max turned the page on its side and the two curved lines looked like two halves of a heart symbol just broken at the top.

"No. What is it?"

"It's their symbol. Many of them have it branded into their skin. I've seen it on one their chests."

"What's it mean?"

"It's a snakes head." She explained. He looked at the paper again. Sure, he could see that. Landry went on. "It's the mark of the one they call their master."

"Who is he?"

"What are you?" she asked.

"Excuse me?" He was hoping that she was not going to get all cryptic.

"Max, you are different now that you've been touched by power. Surely you know that. What you are now is far different than what you were. There are many in the world that have been touched by power. Although few have come across anything with as much power as the thing that these lost boys call their master… or as much power as you've touched."

Alana entered bearing a tray with a steaming tea pot and a set of cups on it. She set it down on the table silently, regarding Max with caution in her eyes. She still had not uttered a word since he had come into the apartment and still remaining silent, she walked back into the kitchen. Max shook his head "no" when Landry offered to pour him a cup. She continued on as she filled her own.

"Their Master is not a 'he'. It's an 'it'. Well, an 'it' at best. At worse it may be a demon." She carefully watched his reaction as she sipped her tea.

"A what?"

"A demon and though that term is used to describe many types of entities and creatures… in this case I believe it is accurate."

"And what exactly is a demon?" Max asked. He wondered if this was the part when the lying would start.

"This demon is part natural and part unnatural; a hybrid born of some person of power, perhaps a witch like myself, but fathered by something entirely unnatural."

"Fathered by something unnatural?"

"Yes, and it was done long ago. This demon is old… probably as old as, if not older than, the city itself. It had to have been dormant and asleep for quite a while. Sometime in the past year it became active. At that point it was probably very weak, yet still strong enough to influence those who were vulnerable. Since then it's been growing

220

stronger and gaining access to all aspects of its power."

"How do you know that?" Perhaps it was Prya's warning that had him on edge and suspicious.

"I don't. But if the Sick Ones had been taken by something less powerful, then I believe they would not be as elusive to the police. There are some people in this part of the city with a measure of… power… that have been able to deal with matters similar to this. However they have met with very little success when it comes to this Cult. The Demon must be strong or the Sick Ones would not be able to evade capture by both the men with power and the police. They would not move as freely as they do, or kill and take victims at will."

"Take victims?"

"People have been disappearing in West Oaks in larger numbers over the past year. I believe the Demon is a physical being… and is feeding."

"Oh come on!"

"The Demon is old and wise. The Sick Ones hide their numbers to appear smaller. But if the Demon were weak then none of Sick Ones would have become this." She pulled another sheet from her little stack. It was a photocopy of the police sketch Sheriff Lynne had shown him after the second break-in. It was the drawing of Snake Maniac.

"What is it?"

"You encountered this at the Museum. Didn't you?"

"Yea. It's a bad drawing."

"Yes. He wasn't wearing a mask for one." she said knowingly.

"Ok. But what is it?"

"It WAS a person, changed by the demon, one of its lieutenants. But you dealt with it, you and the Sheriff." She was giving him too much credit.

"Not really." He admitted. The last he saw of the Snake Maniac it was hissing just fine as it tossed him off of the Dock. Sheriff Lynne had been the one to finish it. If she had that was. "It could still be out there. I survived Cobbs River… though I hadn't been shot."

"No, Max, it's dead."

"I… what? They said it leapt into the river."

"Yes. But it never survived. Its body was found a day or two later.

Max almost stood up. "What? Wait then that means the police know that…"

Landry placed her hand on his arm and stopped him. "I'm afraid it wasn't the police that found his body Max. Those that did find it are not likely to turn it over to the authorities. They care very little about your legal situation."

She did know a lot. "Why would they keep it?" he asked.

"Max," she began and took a moment for a deep breath. "This

city is old and far more complex than you know. There are many... factions, old families, individuals who hold power that compete with one another. For the most part things have been quiet for some time. Then the pot got stirred up at the end of last year. The murders at the Museum and your running around Mountairy Rock fighting the Sick Ones has thrown everyone into a tizzy."

"Factions? Like who?" They were getting off the subject but then everything that came out of her mouth seemed to bring up more pressing questions.

"Like the Downhills for one. You really made a mess going down there." She took another sip.

"The Downhills are a Faction?"

"The head families of the Downhills are. The Forrest's and the Lakefolk both hold... they each have a strong voice among those with power in this city. The Sylvain's are influential too."

"They came to the Museum first. They attacked me. That's why I went down there." He defended himself.

"No. You went there first. Sick and near to death, you may not have survived the cold either if not for Prya."

Oh. That was right. He remembered what Prya had said earlier. That she had "warmed" him. The fuzzy memory of running through the Downhills, frozen near to death played back in his mind briefly. What had happened to him after seeing... Pryas eyes? Something had happened... but it was too elusive for him to remember now.

"Ok. So that caused me enough trouble that someone would keep evidence from the police just to get me locked up?"

Landry hesitated, looking at him as though she was gauging his state of mind. "It wasn't your visit that caused that as much as what Prya did because of your visit."

"'What Prya did'? What did Prya do?"

Landry almost smiled at him. "She called off her wedding."

The memory of the Downhills pack leaping across thatched rooftops after him filled his mind's eye. Their anger had definitely seemed more personal than just xenophobic, especially for one of them in particular.

"Lotarre?", he asked even though he was sure.

"Yes."

"But I NEVER..."

"No?" she asked with her lips pursed to smile. Then, as he gave her a sharp look, "Of course not." She was smirking now. "But then you didn't have to. You provided her with a great opportunity; an excuse to get out of a marriage she has never wanted."

"What did she tell him? That I..."

Again she cut him off by placing her hand on his arm. It was strange but that little touch calmed him.

"She's a lot smarter than that. No, all she had to do was cancel the wedding when you arrived. It wasn't necessary for her to say that you had laid any claim on her. But of course that's what she has them believing; that you have her… attention. It is enough to buy her time."

"Attention." He remembered Prya had said that herself. It seemed she had used him to get herself out of a jam and had simultaneously gotten him into one. "So THEY found the body?"

"No. It's complicated. There are many things at play here. There are those outside of the Downhills that do not want Prya to marry Lot either."

"Why? And what has that got to do with me?" he was getting frustrated. How big was this city? Was she just running him in circles?

Was she lying?

"Well," she sat back and thought for a second. "Lot's family; the Sylvain's almost run the Downhills, but they have no vote… no voice among those holding power in the city. The Forrest's though, have a voice, as do the Lakefolk. Other factions in the city don't like the Sylvain's… temperament. If Lotarre married Prya then the Sylvain's would have their voice heard. It's political." She finished with a bit of a shrug.

Now Max did stand. He hated politics.

"And if I'm in jail for a murder I didn't commit, then she would have to marry Lotarre?"

"I don't know. It's possible that's what they're thinking but it's also possible that Prya could hold off the marriage until she has helped you get out of this bit of trouble. She saved your life after you crawled out of the river and that has bound you to her in some of their eyes."

"So who has the body? I could just take it from them." He did not realize that his hands were balled into fists.

"Even with as much power as I sense in you I doubt you could do that. Not that it matters now anyway, they've most certainly already destroyed the body."

GREAT! He plopped back down into the love seat and rubbed his eyes. It was a lot to take in. Still there were things he needed to know.

"Did the person who recovered the body find the Stone as well?"

"The Stone?"

"Prya called it the Monument."

"Surely you still have it?" Her eyes were wide.

"I have the one I found." He reached for the string around his neck then stopped himself. Exactly how much should he trust her? He had gotten the Stone back from Prya with a lot of luck on his side. But she had not really shown as much interest in it as Landry was right now. Still he needed answers and he was sure he would have to give a little to get what he wanted. Slowly he pulled the Stone out over his collar and let it hang from the string. Her already wide eyes got even wider. "But the uh… demon, must have given one to that guy to change him." He said.

"No." she answered quietly still staring the Stone.

"No?"

"Their master, with the same substance that it uses to seduce them, to bend them to its will, also slowly transforms them. The Sick one you fought on the Dock has probably been under its influence long enough… and been strong enough to survive being changed."

"Christ! Then if they don't need the Stones what did they break into the Museum for?"

"They want its power." She was still staring at the Stone. Her voice became very quiet. "All things are drawn to power."

"And this thing is changing all of them into Snake people?" They all had that smell, every one of them. How many Maniacs were already like that now? Only one of the damn things had almost killed him.

"Not all. It doesn't want an army. It wants power. Few people can be transformed as the one you encountered on the Dock had been. Most die. Fewer still, is it willingly to give that kind of power to. And I believe it fears you more than it craves this Stone."

"Me?"

"Because of what you are or will become. You and this demon are ancient adversaries."

"Come again?"

"What I mean is… well… not YOU exactly, but what you are being transformed into. I think that you are supposed to destroy this creature. I think those who carried the Stone before you did just that." Her eyes finally came off the Stone and rose to meet his. "Can't you feel it?"

Max was not sure he was buying everything she was telling him. He did have to admit that every time he had encountered the Maniacs there had always been that strange familiar feeling. It was like it was something he had done before, had been doing all his life. He spun the Stone around and looked closely at it hoping it could tell him something more. How long had he been planning to examine the thing? How long had he put off researching the symbol? It was strange how easily he had taken to it. It had changed his body; of course it could have affected his mind as well.

"So what does it want?" he asked. He meant the Stone, but knew she would think he was asking about the demon.

"Power… and revenge I believe."

"Revenge? For what?"

"May I see the Monument?" she asked him.

"See it?" Max wondered what would happen if he gave the Stone to her. How long before he started going through withdrawal again? He felt good and was sure he had fully recovered from his wounds but... Could she use it herself? He needed answers but he could not risk losing the Stone.

"Why do you call it that?" he stalled.

Landry smiled. "You don't know anything do you? That is what it is. A monument to those that created it and who they were long ago. How did you get it? Was it passed down in your family?"

"I found it the night of the break in.", he told her. Her face went hard for a moment. He ignored the look and asked, "Who created it?"

"You 'found' it?" she asked him in return.

"An overseas shipment was broken into by the Maniacs... er the Sick ones. They must have left it by accident."

Suddenly she seemed to consider him in the same manner she had when Prya first introduced them. Maybe she did not believe him. The violence and fear of their initial encounter seemed to drift back in between them. He wondered if she had been watching him in his office with the same expression she was wearing now.

"It's not possible that you just found the Monument, Max. With so much power it must have always been tied to you."

"I just found it." He reiterated.

"Only dark and sick magiks could change you the way the Monument has without being part of that which you are. If it was dark magik you would be seeing very adverse side effects, like the Sick Ones. May I see it?"

"There have been side effects." Was he telling her too much?

"There have?" Her eyebrows rose and her hands tensed.

"After the attack at the Museum, after my swim in the river I took off the Stone for only a second. I nearly died of the wounds from the fight and could barely get the thing back on."

"But Prya told me she got it away from you in the Downhills and that you didn't lose your power."

"I don't think I was hurt then... maybe. But when I handed over the Stone at the police department I went through some serious pain and withdrawal. I don't know why."

"Withdrawal? That would be an effect of using dark magiks." She seemed to believe him.

Reluctantly Max lifted the Stone for her to examine but he did not take the string from around his neck. She settled for this, stood, walked over to him and looked at the Stone closely.

"It doesn't feel dark. I don't sense any wrongness and I do have a sense for such things. You say it you just found it?"

"On the floor of the Museum on New Years."

Landry held her hands up and passed them over the Stone and

then over Max as though feeling for heat. "It's old. I can sense its power. Yes… it IS tied to you."

"There may be more."

"More?" She got a little taller as she rocked to the balls of her feet.

"Something else was taken from those shipping crates. Could be as many as twenty other… um… Monuments out there."

Her eyes went wide. "Twenty?"

"The crates were used to smuggle something in. If every Stone is approximately the same weight as this one then there are at least twenty unaccounted for." This could be a mistake he thought. If the Stone really was as powerful as she had been saying then maybe it was not a good idea to tell her that there were so many in play. She could make a run for them herself or tell one of these 'Factions'.

Her wide eyes stared unseeing. "Twenty?"

"Can this demon use the Stones like I have?" he asked her. She blinked and looked at him like she had not been listening. Before he could repeat the question she said;

"No… but it can feed off of their power, for a long time. Or it can twist its power, ruin it… make it dark. That would make the Stone less powerful but if there are so many… they can't be allowed to have them. You must get them back."

"Huh?" he stood up.

"You already know how powerful just one of the Monuments can be." She was insistent and Max could see real fear in her eyes. "I can't imagine what the Demon could do with the power of twenty of them. You must get them back." she repeated.

"If it can use the Stones for its own power and not to turn the Maniacs into Snake-men, then why does it want mine?" he tried not to notice that he had said; "mine". "Why did it send them back to the Museum for just one?"

Landry shook her head blinking. "I don't know. Maybe it needs all of them. Maybe…" then she seemed to calm down a bit. "Are you sure there are more?"

"No!" he took a breath and tried to calm down himself. "SOMETHING else was missing from the crates they ransacked though."

She nodded and then turned from him in thought. He already knew what she was going to say;

They needed to be sure. Whatever it was the Maniacs took they needed to find and if possible, take back.

She was patting her head through her braids while pacing now. Every time she turned her eyes glanced at him quickly. Whatever she was going to say, Max thought, she already knew what it was. Now she was just worried about how to say it to him.

Before she opened her mouth he spoke. "What about the factions?" While he was certain it was probably a mistake to tell any of the mysterious factions about the Stones it certainly seemed better than what he was sure she was going to try and get him to do.

"What do you mean?" She stopped pacing.

"Earlier you said there were some people of power who had failed to get rid of the Cult."

"Failed." She repeated firmly.

"But if they knew that the Demon had the Monuments…"

"No Max." she shook her head resolutely.

"It might make a difference…"

"NO!" She turned away so fast that her braids whipped all the way around her head and popped her in the face. "Their failure had little to do with their power and more to do with their resolve." She walked back to her couch and sat down placing her finger to her temples.

Max remained standing. She looked up at him. "What is the worst neighborhood in all of Mountairy Rock?" she asked.

Easy. "North Hills."

She exhaled. "After that."

"Oh… West Oaks. But it's a distant second."

"And third?" she asked.

He had to think. Ivy Hills… Brookhaven… South Hills… the Downhills… if there was a third worst neighborhood…

"None as bad right?" she cocked an eye at him. "That's because each of the neighborhoods in Mountairy Rock are pretty much governed by one of the groups or individuals of power that I was talking about. Each… except for the North Hills which, as you said, is the worst neighborhood."

"And West Oaks?"

"West Oaks is blessed with a group of very powerful men… who do nothing. When the Cult first arrived here they were warned and did nothing. Even as people, homeless and indigent mind you, began to disappear they did nothing. Now the Cult has grown beyond their capability to stop it."

"Whose capability?" he asked. Landry just shook her head and looked down into her hands. Max began to feel the same horrid feeling he felt whenever King asked him to take charge at the Museum. If there was a chance that someone else could take care of this then he wanted them to take it. Hell… he did not even live in West Oaks.

But the Maniacs had still come to the Museum… and they would be back. They would be back as soon as they felt they were strong enough. As soon as this "Demon" had taken enough power from the Stones that it already had in its possession. They would attack the Museum again and more people would get hurt. Max could hear Fatima screaming, could feel her breath, ragged and uneven as she had bucked on his shoulder.

Max had held this question back. A part of him had hidden it in the back of his mind. It really had first formed the night he was attacked outside the student center but he just dismissed it then. It came back when he saw the Maniac lurking just outside the Museum after his run with Big Gray but the disaster that night had become just forced it to the back again. Now, with the thought of twenty something Stones sitting in the hands of the Maniacs the question screamed and wanted an answer.

"Where can I find them?"

WILD, WILD WEST

Landry did not know exactly where to find the Maniacs but she knew they were very close to where her office/home was; the abandoned section of West Oaks.

He stood in front of her office, just at the corner. The door was now closed. Perhaps she had braved a visit during the day and closed it up. With her ability to hide her scent he would not be able to tell if she had been here recently.

It was freezing. Max had abandoned his jacket and jeans back at Landry's. The wind cut through his sweats easily, numbing his thighs, but he barely noticed. As cold as the night had grown his body had grown tense and jittery. Every sound made his head turn and every gust of frigid wind flared his nostrils. He had made a zigzag line across West Oaks searching for signs of the Maniacs but finding none he had come here. And here he finally caught their scent.

The hot, sick, body odor scent was fresh. Two of the Maniacs had come past Landry's door sometime in the past few hours. Max looked down the dark empty street in the direction the scent lead and took an even deeper breath. Tracking them would be easy,

...for both of them.

Her scent had slipped past his nose on an aberrant breeze and was gone in an instant. That had been enough for him to be certain she was following him. He looked over his shoulder and back up the alley next to Landry's office. She had probably been in the alley at some point then moved...

He looked up to the rooftops. She was up there. How long had she been trailing him? From back at Landry's? Or had she been out looking for Maniacs as well?

He took a breath and prepared to leap. It would be nice to catch her off guard. Max could already see the look of surprise on her...

WHUMP!

"YOW!" Max did leap a good five feet in the air. He twisted and turned about mid-leap, teeth bared and claws extended from his fingertips. Prya was standing up from a crouch wearing a wicked grin.

His feet came down on a thick patch of ice and Max slid into the side of the building and fell onto his ass.

"…nice…" Prya muttered, she walked over and held her hand out to him.

"I'm fine." But he took her hand and she pulled him to his feet easily. Again he could feel how strong she was.

" 'Yow'?" she mocked.

"Shut up." But he could not help smiling himself.

She was dressed in the tight, form fitting, all black outfit again, still with the flowing black skirt as well; although tonight her legs were not bare. She was carrying the spear again too. The end was capped with some kind of cover, like a sheath he guessed, that made it look more like a club.

She looked up at the clear night sky. The moon shone high and bright bathing everything with a pale blue tint.

"…good night to hunt…" and she looked back at him and raised one questioning eyebrow. For a moment Max was unsure of what she was really inviting him to do.

"Really? With me?" he asked innocently.

She pursed her lips. "… still have that nose…"

He gazed upward at the moon and said, "You sure your fiancé won't mind?"

"I… Landry." She shook her head sharply, in irritation. "…witch…" she muttered.

"Whatever game you're playing…" Max started but Prya snapped her head at him.

"Game?"

"Prya somebody's keeping evidence that could clear me and my boss in the Museum murders because of what you did."

"…saved your life…" She let her irritation show.

"And I'm grateful. Really, but telling your people that you and I…"

"I didn't… they assumed!"

"Yea! Cause you let them! Is that why your fiancé and his brothers came at me so God damned hard? They were gunning to kill me Prya!"

She looked away and folded her arms defensively. "… held your own…"

"No I didn't!" He glared at her. Despite how cool she was trying to seem Max could see she was bothered. Maybe she did feel bad about what she had done. "Do you know who fished the body out of Cobb's River? It can clear me."

She shook her head with regret. "That's gone."

Great. "What about your boyfriend? You gonna clear that up?"

She looked back at him with hard eyes. "I'm hunting." And she turned and walked down the street in the direction of the Maniacs scent.

Great.

Six blocks. They walked together silently save for the occasional sniffing of the air to make sure they stayed on the right trail. In between watching for Maniacs Max would watch Prya. She made sure to stay just a bit ahead of him, keeping her face hidden behind her hair. A few times she lost the trail and Max had to mutter "Left." or "Straight ahead."

The city had not bothered to plow the snow in this area and several blocks had streets covered with ice. It made the going slow but the tracking even easier. Maniac boot prints showed up every once in a while where the snow was softer.

They followed the two Maniac scents and the prints for six blocks before they mixed with two more sets of trails. Max picked them up clearly but Prya had to crouch and kick through snow to detect them. The group had met in the open doorway of a burnt out gas station then continued on together. The doorway was filled with their stink so the group of them had been there very recently.

They were catching up.

Max scanned the area. Very few street lamps were working here but with the moon so bright this night his wide pupils did not need much more light to see well. There was an old warehouse just across the street here behind a fence that marked its lot. That lot stretched on for a while before the gate ended at what appeared to be more abandon buildings, storefronts. Behind this strip Max could see the tops of trees. That would be the edge of the park; he could smell thick pine on the breeze.

There was very little cover between the remains of the gas station and the warehouse. If there was anyone in there, he would not be able to get close without being seen. He looked hard but there was no sign of movement. With frustration he noticed that there were no footprints leading to the warehouse. Where the hell had they gone?

Prya looked about as well and snorted in frustration. Before when they had been tracking Landry, she had looked to him and his "good nose" whenever she lost the trail, but tonight she kept her eyes forward… and her mouth closed. There were no more smart remarks or weird speech patterns. Maybe she was actually sorry about bringing her personal problems down on him. Of course that meant that he was dead on about what she had done.

She stopped looking about and almost turned to him then. It was a quick twitch; he almost missed it. Was she about to say something? Or simply demand that he find the trail again? He watched her take a deep breath and begin a slow turn back toward him. Her lupine eyes gleamed in the moonlight out of the shadow of her mane of hair. Her look was pensive. He wondered how he looked to her.

Then the wind died down for a second.

Someone shouted. Max barely heard it but it definitely been a shout. Then another, a different voice this time and he turned around and looked at the abandoned streets behind him. Whoever it was they had to be a couple of blocks away. The wind picked up again,

and Max smelled rawhide…

…and Maniacs.

Before he could think of what to do, Prya took off at a run chasing the faint scent. She bolted across the first street and down one alley to get to the next block.

Was it because she had heard the voices or caught the scent? Was she just after Maniacs or did she catch Rogan's scent too? Max figured she would have bolted at any excuse she could just to get away from him.

So he leapt after her; though he was not in too much of a hurry to catch her. Instead he just kept her in view and marveled at how hard and fast she ran. Her strong thighs pumped like pistons driving her through the alley and around the corner…

… where he lost sight of her.

As he emerged from the alley and realized that he had also lost the scent of both rawhide and Maniacs. He was unsure of when exactly; probably while he was admiring Prya running instead of paying attention.

Maybe the wind shifted, it was practically howling now at the alley's opening. He looked down one end of the block first, then the other. There was another break in the buildings on the other side. The Maniacs had to be more than a block away he had figured. Prya must have run that way.

Again he ran. In the next alley he saw a fire escape and leapt for it, managing to bounce to the first landing easily. Unable to leap while on the fire escape frustrated him but he made it to the roof finally. Silhouetted against the far edge crouched Prya. She was looking down onto the street with a lot of interest. The cold air rushed over him and brought the scents of the Maniacs and of Sheriff Rogan but he no longer needed them. The shouts, jeers, and wicked laughter of the Maniacs were more than loud enough. Likewise the grunts and curses of Rogan let him know how close he was.

Max crept to the edge of the rooftop next to Prya and peered down.

They were there. Rogan was lying face down, trying to get up, while surrounded by three… four … and one more on top of the mailbox, five Maniacs. He was coughing, spitting up blood, and cursing them in between. The Maniacs were laughing at him, walking about him in circles only stopping in order to kick him back down every time he came close to getting to his feet. Their laughter cut through the wind which was picking up. It scraped against the buildings walls, cleared their scents out of the air and whipped their wild hair about their faces.

All of them had weapons. Max saw a baseball bat in one Maniac's hand but the others were carrying weapons that he recognized from the Museum.

He looked closely but he did not see Jean.

Another kick and Rogan went down prone, unmoving. The Maniac, who had kicked him in the head, raised his hands in triumph and the others whooped and hollered. Then another walked up…

…make that SIX Maniacs…

…carrying a fireman's axe. There was more cheering as he placed the axe against the base of Rogan's skull, getting the angle he needed to swing correctly. Then he raised it above his head, eyes wide and eager, looking to get Rogan's head off in one chop. The cheering got even louder and the laughter rang out like a chorus.

With a howl that echoed above the wind, the Maniac swung hard with so much force that his empty hands pulled him off balance and he tumbled over Rogan's prone body.

Empty hands.

At the precise moment that he began to swing the axe, two loud cracks rang out, sounding almost like gunfire. The bottom of Max's feet stung with his flatfooted landing, but it had been necessary to for him to concentrate on getting the axe instead. The street was covered in a large, rough sheet of ice which broke into chunks and shards around his feet. His hand stung too, and a bruise was beginning to form on the ball of his palm where it had hit the handle as the Maniac was starting to swing. At least now he had a weapon.

The howls and laughter stopped suddenly as the Maniacs stared at him. Max had wrapped Amanda's scarf tightly around his nose and mouth before he jumped but if any of the Maniacs here were also in on the Museum break in then they would recognize him immediately.

And they did. Several pointed and a few screamed, "It's him!" The wind grew even more violent. The street ended at a tall boarded up brownstone. The wind slammed against it and was redirected, causing it to swirl randomly. Loose snow and debris began to get picked up in the maelstrom.

The Maniac, from whom Max had taken the axe, climbed to his feet and walked up to Max…

… hissing.

There were no visible fangs and his skin had only the slightest stippling to it but his eyes held wide oval slits.

"YOU!" the Maniac hissed.

Max turned the axe over in his hand and with the blunt end he backhanded the Maniac's jaw.

Another screamed as the "Near Snake" Maniac went down flat on his back. Then the group of them charged him at once.

He leapt again, a huge arcing backward flip, to get out of the circle of Maniacs. The swirling wind pushed at him, even lifting him a bit. At a good sixteen feet in the air he looked down on them and saw how quickly they adjusted and all turned on the rough ice. They would be on top of him before he could recover from his landing. So he tried to bring the axe around his body hoping to swing it as he landed. But the weight of the axe blade pulled at him and combined with the rough wind was enough to turn him awkwardly.

Damn! He landed on the side of his face and luckily not the blade end of the axe. Despite the pain in his head Max tried to roll and braced himself for the Maniac's steel toed boots.

It was muted by the wind but a long throaty howl echoed down to the street. The Maniacs stopped in their tracks. Still dazed a bit, Max only heard the collision of bodies, the pained grunt of a Maniac and a satisfied feminine growl.

"Wha…" Max looked up to see Prya standing over a leveled Maniac. The spear she had been carrying was unsheathed and the point end had been rammed right through the thigh of the lead Maniac, pinning him to the ground. She was smiling a broad, mean grin that told him that she had not missed. She had pierced the Maniac in the leg because she wanted to see him scream in pain.

Again some of the Maniacs were surprised but many recovered quickly and shifted their attack from him to Prya.

With a spray of blood she pulled the spear free and in the same motion clubbed the closest attacker with the blunt end.

There was both grace and strategy in the way she moved. She shifted her weight using the blow she had just delivered as a momentum builder. With her feet now set a little more than a shoulder's width apart she swung the spear again.

Two more Maniacs caught the blunt end again and dropped with their hands clutching their broken bones. One Maniac managed to get behind her and rushed with a short sword raised high.

Unable to swing the axe unless he wanted to hit him with the blade end,

…although he was not sure why he was having a problem with that…

… Max leapt up and caught the short man by the throat. The Maniac went bugged eye, choked and his legs went slack. He released him and let him drop in a heap and turned again in time to see the bat swinging at his head.

Duck, drop, roll, stand, swing…

The blunt end of the axe came across a set of knees and another Maniac fell.

Leap, kick, duck, punch…

Just two left.

The last two were both trying to backpedal away from Prya, taking blows each in turn from the now sheathed spear end. They stumbled actually, while she almost danced after them seeming to be playing with them instead of finishing them off.

He could not help but marvel at her. The Downhill's woman was in full control of her body even on the windy, icy street. Max watched as she shifted her hips back and forth. The skirt whirled about her, giving him clear view of the shape of her legs in the black body suit. The power in her thighs was apparent as she managed to hop from one side of the street to the other while still delivering blows. She was even more of a problem for the Maniacs than he had been.

Tired of covering the distance between the last two who were now separated, Prya swung the spear in a frighteningly fast arc over her head and brought it down sharply between the eyes of the closest one. The Maniac collapsed like a deck of cards, the small knife and club he had been carrying clattered away on the ice. She then turned on the last one and began to stalk after him casually, twirling her spear all the while. She did all this while at the same time managing to turn them completely around. Now the Maniac, while backing away from her, was backing directly into Max.

Prya looked over the poor kids shoulder and into Max's eyes. Her smile might be terrifying to the Maniac but it was not meant for him and Max's breath caught in his throat.

He could not ignore his ever growing attraction to her anymore. Especially with the display she just put on. As if reading his mind she spun the spear again and dropped the last Maniac right at Max's feet. Her smile broadened.

"Can SHE do that?" she asked, her blood red hair whirling from the blustery weather.

Prya would never have a problem defending herself against the Maniacs. She was a better fighter than he was. They sure as hell would not be able to get to her in the Downhills, not with a whole neighborhood of…

"Clan?" he asked her. Her answer was a cryptic and wicked smile. Her round full thighs rolled over each other as she walked right up to him and planted her foot on the Maniacs throat. She brought that smile right up to his face and leaned into his body. Flame red finger nails popped up over the scarf covering half of his face and pulled it down. Those fingers hooked into the collar of his sweatshirt and pulled at him until he gave in and dipped a little, bringing his face to within a half inch of hers.

"…Clan…" she answered him. Her eyes reflected the light of the one good street lamp. They were a soft brown, open and wide as he peered into them. Her hand then found its way into one of his.

Then the Maniac who she was stepping on gurgled.

Suddenly, save for the pained breathing or gurgling of any still conscious Maniacs, the street became very quiet. Even the wind stopped for the briefest of seconds. He cocked and eyebrow and ear toward one end of the street.

Nothing. Not sound. No hint of any more Maniacs.

And then the other; no movement, no… Wait!

Footsteps… running… Maniac boots… and they were headed away. Someone had seen the fight and ran… possibly to bring reinforcements?

Their feet scrabbled on the ice ready to pursue but then there was a moan. Behind them Rogan was groggily climbing to his knees, cursing.

"Kick… yo ass… boy…"

Max smirked at him and then took off after the retreating footsteps. A strong wind rose again from the far end of the street and howled down at him; shifted and pushed at him. It also brought with it the sweaty foul scent of the fleeing Maniac. He had run almost twenty feet when he noticed Prya had not charged after.

The rough ice almost cost him his footing when he stopped and looked back. She was standing over Rogan and looking back at him with her head cocked to the side. Then she nodded to the semiconscious figure.

"…a Sheriff…"

"What?" he started to turn and chase the footsteps again but Prya inclined her head to the wounded Maniacs.

"So?" he demanded but she just looked at him. Anxious as he was to catch that last Maniac, he looked again at the crumpled forms of his buddies scattered across the street. It was possible, he supposed, that they were recovering at least as fast as Rogan was.

"He'll be fine!" and he started to turn again.

"… more are coming…" she said evenly, making no attempt to raise her voice over the wind.

"Then he'd better get his ass up and run!"

"… won't make it…"

"Too bad!"

She looked at him puzzled and with a little disappointment in her eyes. Rogan dropped back onto the ice with a moan.

"…a very tough position… the Sheriffs…" she said so quietly that Max almost did not hear her. "…Rangers…"

Why was she telling him this? "Your friend there spent the better part of yesterday violating my civil rights!"

She snorted. "… man's law…"

"You want to help him? Go ahead!" and he started off again but he made sure to keep an ear focused behind him.

"… my way…"

Still running, he glanced over his shoulder. Prya walked deliberately over to the nearest Maniac…

…and then took the sheath off of the spear.

He stopped too abruptly and slipped on the ice falling hard onto his back. "OOF! What…" Damn that hurt! "What are you doing?"

She drew the spear back ready to drive it through the Maniacs chest.

"Stop!" Max was to his feet and racing back down the street. Prya looked up at him with her eyebrows furrowed in frustration. "You're not going to…"

"… you would leave this man to that end?" Her voice was sharp and clear. Max could see she was angry.

"I would leave them to each other! Not murder a bunch of…" he almost said; "kids".

"Max," She, at least, was no longer pointing the spear at the Maniac. "We cannot just walk away now. Either we take the Sheriff to safety or we make this place safe for him to recover."

The idea of leaving Rogan here to deal with the Maniacs felt really, really good. From up on the roof, he had looked like a victim but down here on the ground the man looked more like the cop who had rammed his head up against the wall. It would serve him right if Max left him here on the street with the Maniacs.

But if they recovered before he did or if there were more coming… well he would deserve it. Prya seemed to have other thoughts.

"Fine. Then YOU take him to safety."

"… your way…"

"What?"

Then she repositioned the spear tip on the nearby Maniacs chest, about right at the boy's heart. "…my way…"

"You can't be serious." he said but the look in her eye was strong, steady and intent. "You would kill these… guys?"

"… murderers…" She had a point. Max looked back at the Maniacs still on the ground. The "Near Snake" Maniac lay motionless, though still breathing. Two more lay; face down; one's leg was twitching. Another crazed looking Maniac was holding his broken leg and rocking himself while staring straight up into the night sky like there was something important up there…

… Nope, nothing there.

Another Maniac whose legs Max had got good with the blunt end of that axe was dragging himself up the street over the ice and snow.

The last one lay there on the street, just looking at Max.

But this Maniac lacked the overwhelming crazy look the rest had. He was younger; maybe still a teenager, with little facial hair. His hair was just as wild but not as dirty as the rest. His scent was also not as bad as the others, though he still stank, it did not smell quite so foul.

The look on his face did not match the rest of the Maniacs either. It was twisted with pain, something that the other Maniacs surely acted as though they never felt, and fear. He began to shake as Max continued to stare at him. Then…

Oh Jesus he was crying! He definitely was not like the other Maniacs. No stink, no filth, fear and… regret in his eyes; …this one was new.

"… lost… little hope for them…" Prya said to his back. "… my way is better for all."

"Even him?" he pointed to the crying Maniac. Prya looked down her nose at the boy.

"… no… but the others…this one… still dangerous…" and she drew her spear back again ready to thrust it into the Maniac she had already targeted.

"Wait! Wait Goddammit!"

"… little time… they're coming…" and she drove the spear hard.

But Max was beside her and managed to grab the shaft and divert it enough to spare the Maniac.

"GRRR!" Prya turned on him. Lightning fast her hand whipped at his throat with her bright red nails extended like claws. He could barely duck back in time to keep them from ripping out his larynx.

"Stop!" he yelled but Prya was moving again. She jerked the spear from his hand and spun it about. The move was one he had just seen her perform and Max was ready leaping forward and grabbing the shaft before she could start to thrust it into his gut. "STOP!"

For a brief second Prya's face was twisted into a snarl, her teeth were bared, and a low growl rumbled from her throat. Then her narrowed eyes opened, her mouth closed and her eyebrows rose in a sympathetic expression.

"…so new…" she whispered then closed her eyes before speaking again. "… you must decide Max. But do not leave this… like this…"

She let go of her spear with one hand and reached up and touched his face. "… it would be beneath you."

"You would kill these kids?" he asked her again.

An inpatient breath hissed between her teeth, but her voice was calm as she answered. "… you claimed responsibility for all their lives when you stopped the Sick One from taking the Rangers head. To walk away now… invites the consequences of everyone's actions here this night to be your burden… whether or not you choose it."

Her eyes never wavered.

"… I would choose the consequences of taking their lives… not of leaving this man to die…" she pulled the spear away from him and waited. He thought that he understood what she meant, at least partially, and she had made a good point. It was not a point he wanted to be concerned with himself but the strength of her eyes forced him to consider it.

Killing the Maniacs was not an option for him. He would not do it himself and he could not stand by and let Prya do it either. She and Landry had been calling the Maniacs "Sick Ones" and now he could see why. Whatever was happening to them might not be their choice nor under their control. They could be…

"Victims…" he finished the thought.

"… they chose…" she corrected him. "…over loneliness…" Prya was looking at the youngest of their attackers. Then she gestured to the "Near Snake" Maniac.

"… and are now gone… forever."

"Fine." Max said finally and Prya turned to see him reaching for Rogan who was still just trying desperately to climb to his knees.

"HUFF!" Rogan was a hell of a lot heavier than Fatima and bigger. The man lay awkwardly over his shoulder and Max found it hard to carry him not only because of the weight but because of his size. If he got into another fight, he would have to put him down.

So they ran a light jog in the opposite direction that the Maniacs had run. Max wanted to question the young Maniac but there was hardly any more time for that. Prya offered to stay and watch the boy but he was not sure he trusted her to leave the rest of them alive without him there. Besides reinforcements were likely on the way and he did not think she would be able to handle however many they might bring. And Max knew from experience that could be a lot.

He asked her to carry the Maniac, figuring she was strong enough to tote the boy but she flat out refused and offered to dispatch him once again. So that was that.

Of course she snickered and laughed as Max struggled to keep Rogan on his shoulder. She was practically skipping up the street as he plodded along slowly. The going got worse as the Sheriff regained his senses.

"What the hell?" Rogan began to buck and kick. He drove his knees into Max's chest.

"COOL IT!" Max growled but that only made the man fight even harder.

"Let me go!" Rogan yelled and Max gripped him tighter, giving him a mighty squeeze. The Sheriff grunted in pain, cursed and fought even harder to get away.

They were running out of time. The Maniac who had gotten

away probably had already alerted the others. There could be another group of twenty-some odd Maniacs on their way at that moment. The Sheriff was fighting him but he was hardly in any condition to defend himself against a real attack. They were still too close to where he had been attacked. So Max had continued on.

But that younger Maniac had looked like he was still lucid. There was a chance that he could give information to the police and answers to Max.

The Stones, he might be able to lead Max to the Stones.

"Let go!" moaned Rogan. Damn. Max was certain that either that kid would be gone by the time he got back or the Maniacs would be there in force.

He looked up the street they were traveling on and tried to gauge how far from a busier street they were.

At least eight long city blocks.

Damn.

He ran as hard and as fast as he could.

He only fell twice.

And made sure he fell right on top of Rogan both times.

West Oaks was bigger than he had been imagining in his head. Of course he should have known better. West Oaks was nearly a quarter of the entire city. The Park separated it from Ivy Hills to the north and City Lake was the boundary on the eastern side. So there was plenty of room on the ridge for the rest of West Oaks to sit.

It turned out to be more than eight blocks which would not have been so bad if he had not been hauling two hundred and fifty pounds of funky leather and tobacco smelling dead weight! About a block from a brightly lit intersection where cars were stopped at the light Rogan regained full consciousness. The sheriff was pissed.

"OOF!" Rogan kneed him in his gut and Max dropped him to the sidewalk.

"Mutha…" The curse trailed off out of Max's mouth because after the Sheriff scrambled to his feet he reached into his coat. The movement was easily recognizable and Max snatched the man's arm quickly before he could draw his weapon. With his other hand he pulled the scarf down and bared his teeth fully meeting Rogan's eyes with his own.

"God Almighty!" The Sheriff's hand came out of his coat empty. He must have lost the gun earlier which was why Max had not seen any dead or wounded Maniacs. "I don't F'in believe it." Rogan said.

The two stood about ten feet apart, eyeing each other. Max was watching to make sure Rogan did not pull an as yet unrevealed backup gun. The Sheriff seemed to be trying to fathom Max, looking him up and down.

"… the fuck are you supposed to be?" he said his eyes resting on

Max's head. Again he wondered how much he was changed because of the Stone. Rogan had been in his face not less than twenty-four hours ago but he saw no recognition in the man's face. Then Rogan saw Prya.

"You..." he looked her up and down. "What are you doing in West Oaks?"

"… sloppy Rangers…" she answered. She was standing a little farther back and facing a little away from Rogan. The wind blew steady at the intersection and Max noticed that her hair was hiding her face.

"What Clan are you from?" he demanded from her. Prya turned and sprinted away. Max was curious about how much Rogan knew about the Downhills people but he figured it was better to get while the getting was good.

So he threw the Sheriff a full and throaty growl that felt as good to Max as it must have been scary to Rogan. Then he sprinted for the closest alleyway, where Prya had just run to herself, and put Sheriff Rogan far behind him.

They were gone. Max peered around the corner of a red bricked building at the end of the block where they had last left the Maniacs. There was no sign of any of them. There was blood, a studded strap, and a few teeth, but no Maniacs. Their reinforcements must have gotten here already. The wind had died down again and he drew in the cold night air in search of their scents but the stench of old leather and stale tobacco was sunk deep into his clothes now and overwhelmed his nose. Unless he took off the hooded sweat top he would never be able to track them tonight. But it was way too cold to do that.

He turned to Prya, who had been quiet the whole way back, and she lifted her head and took a halfhearted sniff. A minute headshake told him she could not scent them either.

But she seemed to be distracted and that was all she offered and. Max watched her a moment. She was worried about Rogan, or more likely what Rogan would do after seeing her here tonight.

"Downhills people aren't allowed in West Oaks?" he asked jokingly.

Her head gave the slightest movement at his question. He thought maybe she would not answer then,

"… carrying weapons…"

"Are you going to get in trouble?"

She tilted her head back a bit and he saw her mouth open in a silent laugh. "… not a child…"

"But still…" Max offered.

"…don't worry…"

"What's Clan?" he asked. She looked up at this. In the alley her eyes were two shiny sparkles peeking out of the shadow her hair cast over her face.

"…not you…"

"I know that. But you're… you took those Maniacs apart with no problem."

"…so did you…"

"Prya, you know what I mean."

She retreated from him a bit but did not look away. "…the witch never told you?"

"Told me what?" he asked. There had been a little worry in her voice.

"…soon Maxxxx…" and she walked past him and out onto the street without another word.

So they followed the street in the direction Max thought the Maniacs must have gone, all the while listening and trying to catch their scent.

The night was very silent now and it was on its way to morning. The far eastern sky was just beginning to lighten, although Max thought he could just have been registering the growing glowing haze because of his more sensitive eyes. It was hard to figure, with all the activity, but it could not be more than four in the morning. The fight seemed to have taken only a minute or two and it only took them a few minutes to get Rogan away… maybe.

He stopped dead in his tracks. There was the slightest sound, a click or a snap, somewhere. His ears itched and he turned his head searching the dim alleyways for movement. He listened for more of the sound. It could have come from behind him.

Prya had stopped too and was holding her spear low and tight.

But the next sounds they heard, voices, footsteps, came from ahead.

A block or two, and maybe one over it was.

After a quick look, one to the other, they each bolted off of the street and into the breezeway between the nearest two buildings. It ended in a dead-end but Max jumped as high as he could onto the brick faced wall where his clawed hands found easy purchases. Using the corner where the two buildings met, he clamored to the top and hauled himself onto the roof.

Prya was right behind him and arrived at the top a few seconds later. He threw her a smirk and she rolled her eyes at him, but he thought he could see her trying to hide a smile.

The wind was stronger here and colder but Max barely noticed as they raced along the roof top toward the voices. Twice they leapt across breezeways together as they moved from roof top to roof top. The voices were growing louder, until finally, at the end of the street, they saw them.

Maniacs.

There were fifteen of them now. The five he had beaten up were each being carried by two of the new ones. Most of them were quiet but the "Near Snake" Maniac was cussing, spitting about going back and finding "him". There was little doubt that he meant Max.

The only other Maniac making any noise was the new one. He was not at all pleased to be going back to wherever they were going. The two Maniacs carrying him laughed as he struggled and cried. His legs seemed to be useless, Max remembered that he gotten both his kneecaps with one swing of the back of that axe. They were dragging him by those legs, allowing him to scratch and grab at the ice covered ground feebly… enjoying his pain.

The street opened up onto the warehouse district at the old storefronts. The group of Maniacs made a bee line for the tallest building, a four story factory. There was an old beaten up sign hanging by a thread sideways across the front of the building. The first part of the sign must have already fallen but the rest read; "GEAR co." The building sat off of the street quite a ways so that the back half of it was right on top of the scrub and brush that had grown over the parking lot. It looked like it was sitting halfway in the park itself.

"With all that cover, it's not going to be hard to get to that building without being seen… but we're going to have to take the long way around the…"

"Rusia Vywal!"

What?

BAM!

The blow caught him right under his eye just as he had turned. It was so hard that it turned him back around and his feet caught the edge of the roof. He fell.

His hands reached out desperate to grab a hold of the ledge but found nothing.

CRASH!

The old heap had no windows to break out but his body did a nice job of caving it's roof in. Whether it was the Stone or the give in the roof of the abandoned car that spared his body, Max found he was able to move and tried to get up. Almost too late he saw the dark figure descending on him.

He rolled quickly and the boots narrowly missed his head by a second. The car bucked and the crates holding it up cracked and gave way. The junker fell in a crash dumping Max onto the ground.

With an effort he rolled when he hit the ground and looked up just in time to see the dark shadow of his attacker coming down on him again. He was sitting on a big patch of ice and Max could get no traction to move out of the way. Another blow caught him in his shoulder and flipped him over onto his back. At once he saw the long black hair, the leather pants and animal skin jacket. His attacker moved against him again.

"Wait, Lotarre!" he yelled but the second kick came anyway. Unable to get up he tried to block it with his arms but missed, catching the blow in the ribs. Where the hell was Prya?

There was a flash of light and Max saw the blade.

Lotarre growled and drew the blade back to jab at Max's midsection. Desperate, Max growled in return and kicked out but his foot only glanced off of Lotarre's thigh. It was enough to stop his momentum and force him to adjust. And it was enough to push Max onto a patch of dry ground.

He scrambled to his feet in time to dodge another attack. The blade flashed, slicing through empty air, whistling as it did. Max back pedaled, ducked and dodged. God help him if he walked back onto another patch of ice.

"Lotarre! Stop! Wait a minute!" He had to stop this fight but that whistling blade did not stop singing. "I DON'T WANT PRYA!" but the words came out hollow and Max felt a pang as he said them. He could almost smell her scent right now.

Where the hell was she!?!

Lotarre kept coming. The blade flashed, whistled and was getting closer. "Rusia Vywal!" he screamed again.

Max's back came up against something solid that did not give. With no other option he made a desperate lunge and grabbed Lotarre's arm just above the elbow. The whistling stopped and the blade hovered, quivering just a few inches from Max's left eye.

Lotarre growled and grabbed Max's collar with his free hand and pulled. The blade dipped closer.

He snarled in return and his claws dug deep into Lotarre's arm.

"Listen to me. I'm not gonna fight you over some girl!" The blade began to move away as Max had finally gained leverage. He was stronger than Lotarre. A lot stronger. He squeezed his hand and blood sprouted out of Lotarre's arm making him scream and pull away.

Max let him take a few steps back but watched him carefully. Lotarre glared at him with hard eyes while he clutched his bleeding arm. Max was not intimidated.

"Don't make me have to beat your ass."

"You are strong, but I am stronger." Lotarre said with such assurance that it gave Max a little hesitation.

"Really?" he asked.

"Really." And Lotarre looked up.

Max followed his gaze. Their fight had taken them back up the street away from where the Maniacs warehouse was located. He stood against a broad garage door of what had been another storage warehouse. Lotarre was looking at the rooftops above and there, Max saw, several dark figures.

Lotarre had brought the Downhills pack with him.

"Prya is mine." he said.

It was the same gang that had chased him through the Downhills, Max recognized most of them. They were stronger than the Maniacs but not as strong as the Snake Maniac. These guys fought as a group and if Prya had not hid him they would have had caught him easily. But that had been in the Downhills, he doubted they knew West Oaks that well.

Not that he did. The two nights that he had been running down here was mostly a blur. They might catch him if he ran.

They would kill him if he stayed to fight.

"Mine." Lotarre repeated. The wind shifted again. The rawhide stench was blown away from Max's face. Lotarre's eyes lit up suddenly and a half second later Max knew why.

Prya was still here... somewhere. She must be watching. Her heady scent charged Max. He drew it in... then got reckless.

"Funny", he said with a slight smile sliding up his face. "She doesn't seem to think so."

Lotarre lunged again but he was slower now. Max dodged easily and slammed his fist into the man's face, knocking him to the ground.

Howls rang out. Max looked up to see the Downhills pack leaping off the building. They jumped as a group and Max saw that it was not random because they landed all around him, blocking the exits from the street. Each drew a wicked and gleaming blade, each a bit longer and more curved than hunting knives.

He should have run.

Lotarre's second ran at him first, throwing his blade ahead of him, straight at Max's throat.

It was a good throw but with his blood pumping, Max was already in mid-fight form and he ducked it with only a second to spare. It made a "thunk" sound when it hit the garage door which shook hard and rattled loudly from the impact. The Second kept running at him, barehanded. There were Downhills brawlers to his left and to his right in larger numbers. He figured that one group would jump him from behind when he ran for the other. Even though he wanted to get away from the garage door so that he would have some room to maneuver he knew that it was the only thing guarding his back right now.

So he let the Second come to him. He thought he was ready but the Second lead with a feint hard to his left and Max fell for it. The right fist caught him in his gut and punched the wind out of his lungs. The next was aimed for his head but Max's arms were up and blocked that one.

Another to his midsection and he doubled over falling to one knee.

245

Downhills boots slammed on the ground as the rest of them rushed up to help beat him down. It sounded like a lot more boots than he remembered.

All of a sudden there was shouting and cries of warning. Bodies slammed together and more bladed weapons flashed. Max heard maniacal cries joining the Downhills howls. The street became a melee of dark dressed fighters.

A Maniac slammed into the Second and pulled him off of Max. They rolled away and he scrambled backward until the garage door came up against his back. For a brief moment he was left alone as crazed men grappled around him. The Maniacs flooded the street and heavily outnumbered the Downhills pack. Never-the-less Lotarre's gang did not back down, they stood their ground and fought back; each one seeming to be able to hold his own against multiple opponents. Soon it looked like the fight was a standoff with people squaring off.

He took a deep breath getting his wind back and then stood with his fists clenched.

"Ok Max… everyone here is an enemy." He waded in swinging.

Not really caring what he hit; he interrupted more fights than he started or ended. But he drew very little attention of his own and did not come under attack himself. Then he saw a break in the crowd, a lane toward an open street. Max had had enough; he was going home.

He broke hard for the hole in the mob when bright lights suddenly filled the gap and a siren wailed. Blindingly bright light bathed him from the headlights of a police squad car and a gravelly voice boomed over a megaphone.

"Mountairy Rock Police! Put your weapons down and your damned hands up!"

He could barely see past the high beams but he was sure there were guns pointed in his direction. A hand clamped down on his shoulder and he was pulled around to see a furious Lotarre.

"MINE!" he screamed yet again. His eyes were wild and Max was sure the man was totally out of control. He probably had not even noticed the police…

…or the large shape moving up behind him.

It happened fast. The thing grabbed Lotarre from behind, by his animal skin hood and simply whipped him up over its shoulder into the air. It was dressed like a Maniac, though it was busting out of its black leather clothing. The skin was shiny, scaled and there was not a patch of regular flesh left. Not on its claw tipped hands, or its fang filled face. Its head undulated back and forth like a snakes and it whipped out a long forked tongue at Max.

"HSSS!"

He backed up and the headlights lit its face up. The pupils drew to slits and it actually looked past him at the police. Then it hissed again. It hesitated, its eyes flicked back and forth from the headlights to Max and back again. This thing was a lot farther along the "Snake" Maniac path than the other ones he had encountered. He did not want to fight it.

Pick the cops! Pick the cops! Pick the cops!

"Shoot it!" someone behind those lights screamed.

Good idea!

"Hold your fire" ordered the rough voice of Rogan.

Dick.

The thing reached out in a flash, Max had no time to react. One huge clawed hand wrapped itself around his throat and he was pulled into the air. The claws tore through his hood and found their way to his flesh beneath. The scale covered hands squeezed hard enough that his vision went blurry instantly and a loud buzzing rose quickly in his ears drowning out the sounds of the fight, the hissing of the Snake Maniac, the yelling of the police, Prya screaming his name and Rogan giving the order to fire.

The ground slammed into the back of his head and Max felt a hot sticky substance covering his face. The smell of foul Maniac blood filled his nose and the acrid taste of it his mouth. The figure of the Snake Maniac towering above him emerged from the gray haze that had been his vision. It was swaying, hissing at the police and glaring at them with its one remaining eye.

It stepped by him, ramming one huge and very hard knee into his head as it passed him on its way to the police. Max tumbled hard and ducked behind the big things legs. So big around was it that he found himself in its shadow, shielded from the police lights.

"Put 'em down!" Rogan's voice was loud and clear.

Max broke.

Gun fire erupted behind him.

He made his way back into the crowd of Maniacs. Sometime, while he was being throttled by the "Mega" Snake Maniac, the Downhills pack had decided to take off. There were no more of them in the crowd now. Maniacs tried grabbing him as he cut through them but most of the attempts were halfhearted. As the police lights grew brighter the Maniacs began to scatter and run as well.

They ran in all directions to escape, that is all save one. Not a one of the Maniacs ran toward the warehouse district even if it meant running by default into the police. Groups of them stormed the police line and finally as Max made his own getaway into the dark alleys, more shots rang out.

DINNER

Something cracked when Max collapsed onto the bed. He hoped it was not the frame; he could not afford a new one. The old mattress pushed up against his body in a hundred different uncomfortable places and still smelled of Cobbs River water even though he had flipped it over. It was the end of a long brutal day and Max felt relief surge through his body as he finally was getting some rest. The day's sun was fading to twilight outside his window. The neighboring building was fading into the growing darkness. Slowly the windows winked their lights on one at a time and seemed to hang by themselves against the graying backdrop.

There was a couple arguing in the window almost directly across from his. He watched as the woman slammed a pot onto their stove and turned on a burner.

He was never there. He hardly cared. They were supposed to be a family.

Because he had to work. Because she always nagged. They weren't his kids.

Max arched his back and stretched his muscles trying to get rid of the day's aches. King had not been satisfied with his work on logging in the artifacts and had let him know it. So with very little rest after last night's fight, Max had endured a tedious and exhausting day at the Museum. That had been a blessing for the most part; the work drew his focus rather than let him stew on about everything he had learned the previous night.

Sheriff Lynne had come by, but only to speak with Dr. King. She had not even spared him a look. There had been no visit from Rogan, so Max supposed that the Sheriff had not recognized him the other night... or perhaps he had spent the day in the Downhills.

It had been that thought that had led Max back to his apartment rather than risking a return visit to the little valley himself. All day long he wondered what had happened to Prya just before Lotarre ambushed him. She must have scented him and somehow Max had missed it. She realized they were being tailed and then split...

... without giving him any warning.

That should have bothered him more but he found it easy to

come up with reasons that she had not warned him:

There was no time.

She thought he had caught the scent first.

They had captured her without his having noticed...

That was not right. Lotarre had not scented her until they were both down on the street. He was not exactly surprised that she was there but still he had not known.

Why had she run?

No way was she afraid to fight them. He had seen her in action against the Maniacs and had even fought her a bit himself. Together he thought that they would have been able to hold their own against the Downhills pack. Unless there were other consequences to her turning on them that he had not figured on. After all, when she had helped him before, she made sure to do it secretly, though Lotarre must have suspected.

That guy was going to be a problem. Max had hoped it was Prya they had tracked that night. Surely if Lotarre wanted to find him he would have come back to the Museum, not ambush him in West Oaks. So it had to be Prya that they were trying to find. It was Lotarre's reaction to catching Prya's scent that bothered him the most. It had not seemed as though he had been expecting it yet he was not really surprised when it happened either.

Either way he had been infuriated and Max was sure Lotarre had been ready to kill him. He would come for him again and again until this was resolved. How long before his apartment was no longer safe?

The News had reported on the previous night's melee in West Oaks. A gang war, they thought, between two previously unknown gangs. Twenty-something Maniacs had been caught. "Most of the gang", the T.V. said, although Max knew there were plenty more. There was no mention of the Mega Snake Maniac but he doubted that the police would have released that information to the Press even if they had caught it or killed it. Caught it? Killed it? He doubted they could have done one without the doing the other.

The Downhills pack was not mentioned either. It was possible that they could have blended into the group of Maniacs but Max did not think any of them had been arrested.

Too bad.

Prya had certainly gotten away. She was amazing. The way she moved... her confidence as she fought through the Maniacs with more skill than he would ever have... he would never have to worry about her.

As a matter of fact he felt more confident when they were together. If they had not been interrupted by Lotarre and his brothers, Max was pretty sure they would have tried to crash the Maniacs layer that night.

It could all have been over.

Well, he would still have to deal with the Downhills pack. Convince Lotarre that he was not a threat…

… not really.

Even then, lying on his bed, Max could see Prya's hips swaying as they fought together in West Oaks. He could almost feel the heat of her body again from when she had tackled him in the Downhills…

He lay bare-chested on his bed, his skin was still damp from his shower but he had thrown the jeans on anyway. It was warm in his apartment but the air was stale and a bit ripe. It had been a while since he had cleaned up in but that could wait.

Tired fingers traced the engraved symbol on the Stone still hanging around his neck. His wounds from last night were now peeling scabs leaving pink tender flesh beneath. No doubt if he took the Stone off the wounds would reopen and he would find himself bleeding all over his bed. So yet another excuse to keep it on… to delay researching it, because that was what he had been doing all along…

… just keeping it.

What kind of "researcher" was he anyway?

The Stone had yet to be dated. The symbol had yet to be deciphered. Jagged lines that could be lightning, water, or maybe four mountains, inside of a broken oval, slid under his fingertips. He had let it remain a mystery for too long, had let the growing number of questions about it pile up.

Why? Mostly because, as crazy as everything had been and as much danger as he had found himself in… he had felt strangely comfortable while going through it all. The Stone…

A dark shape blocked what little light was coming in through the window. Big Gray sat staring at Max on his window sill. Wow, maybe now he was going to see how the cat had been getting in.

Not this time. It simply placed its paw against the glass and seemed content to wait. Almost, it seemed to be saying; "you're up now, don't be rude, get up and open the window."

His buzzer rang out. Funny, Steve had always found a way into his building and into his apartment as well without having to ring the buzzer or knock. Max hoped up with a groan and walked into the living room and hit the intercom.

"Yo?"

"Ready for dinner Max?" Amanda's warm raspy voice answered.

The dinner, she had promised to make him dinner. For a second he hesitated.

Prya's excited smile flashed in his mind.

This could be a mistake. Going any further with Amanda might only endanger her. It would be hard to beg off now though as she was right downstairs. This would have to be the last dinner. A quick meal and then he would make some excuse… see her home… then go out looking for…

…Maniacs, NOT Prya.

The thought of a regular meal seemed very dull to him now. Amanda was great… but the image of Prya standing perched on a Downhills rooftop in that slit skirt with her spear in her hand was overwhelming.

Two hours… that's all it would take and then he could take her home.

Then his stomach growled. Decision made.

He looked over his shoulder at the mess his apartment had become in the past week. Dirty clothes thrown on the couch, pizza boxes on the coffee table, mail and those damn flyers people kept sliding under his door, were piled up on top of the T.V., and Max did not think Amanda would need his heightened senses to pick up that smell.

"Max?" came Amanda's uncertain voice from the intercom.

"Sure." he answered with a smile in his voice. "Come on up!" he held the buzzer for five seconds. Five seconds were now gone.

He ran to the living room window and opened it wide. The hot stale apartment air rushed out.

Then he grabbed every discarded piece of laundry off the floor and off the couch… including his funky sweats… ran them into the bedroom and threw them into the back of the closet. Big Gray was gone from the window which was good because he had to open this window as well.

The bed was a mess so he just pulled the quilt over it evenly and smoothed it out quickly.

Not like he was going to get any anyway.

Back into the living room he grabbed; the empty fast food containers, mail and bits of paper, receipts, and other trash, up and carried it all into the kitchen and dumped it into the already overflowing trashcan.

He pulled the trash bag out, only spilling a little and rushed out of his apartment and down the hall to the trash chute. The elevator was in between the chute and his apartment and it told him that it was in the lobby now.

MOVE IT MAX!

"'Ut the hell is all this runnin' fo'?" Old Man Alt was standing in the doorway to his apartment. Max had not heard him open the door so that meant he had just been standing there the whole time.

"Sorry Mr. Alt!" he apologized but did not stop moving. Mr. Alt shouted to his back.

"Heard your lease ran out Madigan! Guess that means…"

Back to his apartment, he left the door open to help air it out and ran to his thermostat. He pushed it up to ninety-nine. Hopefully by the time Amanda got here he would have closed the windows and the room would have warmed back up.

He ran to his bathroom…

…wiped out the sink…

Ugh! …flushed the toilet…

…grabbed his toothpaste and squirted too much into his mouth. The tub was a mess. He just pulled the shower curtain closed…

…spit.

Max cupped his hands under the faucet and sucked in a mouthful of water…

…gargle.

He picked up about five empty toilet paper rolls and dumped them into the wastebasket which was now full so he picked it up…

…spit.

He ran back down the hall to dump the trash. A quick look at the elevator;

…fourth floor.

"Guess they finally got tired of your foolishness!" Alt screamed at him.

"No Mr. Alt. I've found another place." Max said as he dashed back to his apartment. "In Chestnut Circle!" he could not help himself.

Back into his apartment he bolted for his bedroom and dove under his bed where he retrieved a scented candle. Cucumber, his mother always sent cucumber. It would have to do.

He snatched the only clean shirt he had left out of his closet. Good thing everything went with jeans.

On his way out he closed the window and then rushed to the kitchen where he lit the candle. Where to put it?

The papers on top of the T.V. had to go. He placed the candle there and ran to the kitchen to dump the papers into the now empty trash can.

Her scent preceded her into the room by a full minute before she appeared at the open door. Fresh, feminine, almost flowery… it awakened something just behind his eyes… and there was something else; hot, spicy… she had already cooked the chicken.

"Hey Stranger." Her smile was so warm under her big knit hat. In her arms sat a big brown bag. The top of a loaf of garlic bread and stalk of celery poked out of the bag. Max smiled.

"I think I've seen this bag on T.V.!" he joked as he took the bag from her. "You just put a good ending on a bad week." And he meant it. The fatigue, aches, pains, and worry were all fading with just her scent coming through the door.

"Whatever! Thanks." and she placed her hands on his shoulders and pulled him down for a kiss. Her flower scent invaded his head when he kissed her. There had been a lingering tenseness in his shoulders

252

Howard Night

that eased just then. "I hope you're hungry." she said.

"Of course." He patted his stomach. "The pit is bottomless." He stepped aside to allow her into the room.

"Wow. You're a neat freak huh?"

"I chose not to live in squalor." He said haughtily as he walked past her to the kitchen and put the bag down on the counter. She gave him a twisted smirk.

"I see you missed a pair of drawers when you were cleaning." She kicked them out from under the coffee table.

Crap.

She took off her winter coat and looked for a place to put it down. It was winter and Max had only seen her in thick sweaters. Now she was wearing a sleeveless form fitting black top. Max had thought that she would have had much more 'Flesh' to her considering the roundness in her thighs but she was in fact very lean. The top was a crew neck so no cleavage though. She laid the jacket across the top of his couch and then removed the big knit hat. The round braid had been rolled up inside the hat and now slid down over her right shoulder. She caught him looking at her and twisted her lips in that knowing smirk again. He loved it.

It had not been that cold this morning when he had gone to work but he was sure the temperature had dropped. Still Amanda had worn a skirt and some pretty nice heels which she kicked off after she inspected his carpet.

Pretty toes.

She walked into the kitchen and looked around. Then after glancing at him first as if for permission, she opened his cabinets.

"I hope you have some clean dishes." She reached and pulled out two plates and then laughed as she blew about a quarter of an inch of dust off of them. "Good Lord!"

"Hey, I never need them!"

"What do you eat on?"

"My food always comes with plastic utensils and very convenient Styrofoam containers."

"Oh no! I should have known you couldn't cook." She placed the dishes into the sink and rinsed them off. "You've got dust all over that stove too."

"I can so cook." Max began to empty out the bag she had brought. "There's no dust in that microwave."

"That's NOT cooking!"

"It's MICROWAVE cooking." He corrected. "And I can make a variety of dishes."

"Please. Like what? What can YOU cook?"

"Uh… ravioli." He pulled one hot plastic container from the bag and popped it open. Steam rose past his face and the delicious smell of cooked chicken hit his nose. Maybe she could cook.

"From scratch?" She had her hands on her hips.

"Yes from scratch. I open the can myself."

"You are terrible." She pulled open a drawer. "Where's your silverware?"

"On top of the fridge." He pointed and she found the box still packaged in plastic. He liked the way the muscles in her calves flexed when she leaned on her tip toes.

"Oh we get to use the new ones?" She smiled and ripped open the box.

"The only ones. Just never used them."

"What do you... never mind. What else can you cook Master Chef?"

"You know I can make a really good omelet."

"Really?"

"Yea. I'll show you tomorrow morning."

"Ha!"

The chicken was terrific. It was a first, he had to admit. Here was a woman in Mountairy Rock who could actually cook. It must have been the one and only dish that she could make. Good cooks or beautiful; women were either one or the other.

"No. I haven't been back in a while. I've been spending my summers here trying to finish up." Amanda was telling him. They were sitting on the floor by the coffee table, the meal done. She was playing with the end of her braid which was tied with a thin leather strap.

"You don't go home for the holidays?" he asked. He sensed the sadness she felt about home emanating from her again.

"I've been spending the holidays at my grandparents." She looked down as she said it, almost hiding her face in shadow. The only light that was on glowed dimly from the kitchen. Neither had noticed that they had not bothered to turn on any other which was just fine with Max. He could see her just fine.

"Still not getting along with your Uncle?"

"My cousin is thinking about coming to M.R.U. in the fall. My uncle never liked her following me around when I was home and he definitely doesn't want her way out of state and hanging with me. She's been talking about going to M.R.U. ever since I first came here but she was little then and nobody thought anything about it. Now though, my Uncle has said he's not paying for her to go out of state but we all know that he just doesn't want her here with me."

"Your Uncle has that much of a problem with you? Why? Broke curfew? Bad grades? Ran a brothel out of the house while your Aunt and Uncle went away for the weekend?"

"It's not that." She laughed. "When my Aunt and Uncle first took me in they were really young." She pulled the strap from her hair

254

and began to pull apart the long thick braid. "My Uncle was not ready to take on a child. I think it cost him a lot; his time, his money, and the things he was hoping to do.

"And he always let me know it. I was always too much trouble or in the way, or just not good enough. As I got older I started to resent him as well. I became a smart mouth and every little mistake he made, I would have to comment on. So we never got along."

Max could see it clearly in his mind. "And when your cousins, his daughters, were born…"

"They got the royal treatment and I was cast aside. But not by my Aunt." She turned and looked into Max eyes. "My Aunt Adi is the best. If it weren't for her I would have turned on my cousins. But I love them so much."

"And of course they worship you the way little sisters always do." Max guessed. Amanda looked at him suddenly. Her braid was undone and her long hair fell almost to her butt.

"You have a little sister?"

Not anymore, but that was a long time ago.

"I'm an only child." He answered then hopped up and gathered the remnants of the meal. "How the hell are you still single if you can cook chicken like this?"

"Easy. Have you seen the pool of eligible men? Ex-cons, multiple baby-mamas, gay…" She got up right after he did and helped him move the dishes into the kitchen.

"… and the rest of you just don't get it."

"Get what?"

"See?"

"Ha ha." He also saw evidence of her smart mouth. But it was not mean, or condescending. She talked to him in a way that made him feel trusted as if she was sure that he would understand that she was being playful.

"Did you hear what happened in West Oaks last night?" She went back into the living room and curled up on his couch.

"What happened?" He glanced to his window. He had been checking all night to see if Big Gray was had returned. So far it was all clear.

"Those guys who broke into the Museum had a riot last night. The police caught almost the whole gang." she said. Max sat down next to her and she casually leaned into him. "Guess you guys can stop worrying huh?"

"Hardly." Max figured that there were probably twice as many Maniacs free as were in lock up, but he did not mean to tell her that. It came out naturally. Her trust in him was contagious and made him want to confide in her as well.

"Why?"

So what to say? A lie felt distasteful, yet he could not tell her what was going on no matter how much he had the urge to. So keep with the truth. "There were so many of them the night of the second break-in that I'm not sure we can count on the police having them caught them all. Plus they're not really a gang; they're more like a religious cult. Fanatical you know? We're not sure what they were after. So we don't really know how to guard the Museum or protect the staff. If… if they were after a specific person then just sitting all the guards in the world in Rebel's Keep won't help. It'll only take one of those crazies to hurt someone away from the Museum." Or, he thought, anyone who was with them.

Her eyes were filled with concern for him, so much so that he could almost feel it. How had this happened? Just a few hours ago he had been intent on no longer seeing her.

"Oh my God. Are you worried?" When had her hand fallen on his leg?

"Uh… no. I don't think they've been back to the Museum since that night and the police don't think the gang really knows the staff well enough to follow them to their homes." He hoped. "Plus after the thing last night… well maybe they'll be able to get them all."

Amanda noticed her hand on his leg and seemed to be as surprised as he was. She removed it gracefully, examining her nails nonchalantly. "I saw you the other day." she said. "You were dressed up and looking so tired I decided not to bother you."

"Where?"

"You were getting off the bus near the Admin building. I liked the coat you had on. You looked good." She flirted. "But your face was so drawn."

"I was coming from the service they held for one of the members of the staff."

"Someone who died at the Museum?"

"No. A researcher who… died in Africa."

"A friend? I'm sorry."

"Thanks but he wasn't really my friend. Although… turns out he told his family about me. His sister thought we were friends. Actually we hated each other." He almost laughed.

Amanda beamed that warm smile again. "Sometimes friendship starts out that way. Maybe you guys just never got the chance to get past that part of it?"

"Maybe. And then maybe he was just an ass." And he did laugh this time. "But I pushed myself harder because of him. He beat me in everything. I always had to work extra just to keep up; he set the bar so high. And he did everything before me; finished projects, turned in research, got his Doctorate, even stole a couple of girlfriends." He wondered if it had been Bazillion who had discovered the Stone would

256

he have already found the meaning of the symbol.

"I know the type. But he made you better. It's good to have a rival. What was his name?"

"Dr. Bazillion."

"Robert Bazillion?"

Please no.

Hours later Max stared up at his living room ceiling listening to Amanda's quiet breathing. Sometime after conversation and when he would have tried to kiss her she had fallen asleep on his couch and he had not minded. She lay curled against him her head cradled on his neck. Her slight breaths brushed his collar bone. Every once in a while she would shift a little and her bare foot would brush his leg or she would snuggle closer to him. Warm and content, why did he not fall asleep?

The police had not found the Maniacs warehouse. If they had they would have raided the abandoned building immediately and it would have been on the news earlier that day. Max should have told them himself, anonymously of course. This whole thing could have been over.

But he had not. Instead he kept imagining himself creeping through the underbrush to get into the warehouse. Almost as if he had to finish it himself. But why? For what good reason? What would he find inside?

The Stones. They had to have the rest of them and he had to get them back before anyone else. Landry had to be wrong; the Snake Maniac must have had a Stone. It was altering them the way that his had been changing him. That one Maniac last night was hardly even human. He wondered how long the Maniac had been using his Stone.

How much more would Max change?

He glanced at his hands. Normal... for now.

Again he wondered what he looked like when the Stone changed him. Rogan had not recognized him at all but Prya had never said anything. Of course she was so different that maybe it was not a big deal to her.

His thoughts turned to the Downhills woman. The heat and excitement he had felt for her just last night barely flickered now. Max had never been finicky when it came to women, nor had he ever been much of a playboy. And it usually took more than just being out of sight for him to lose interest. It had been a good while since he had seen anyone though. That could explain his shifting attraction or even the fact that he was thinking about women at all while all this was going on.

Amanda shifted again and drew herself closer to him. He leaned, kissed on her forehead then leaned back and watched her continue to sleep. Her lips were parted slightly and her breath was a quiet whisper against his skin.

The heat that Prya could make burn in him was amazing but the feeling that he got just from being with Amanda seemed to ripple over his skin, fill his muscles… make him lighter.

He should stop this now… before something happened…

… it would be his fault.

It had been an amazingly normal day. Not just because of the lack of telepathic street cats or Snake-like cult members but also as it was the first that Saturday Max had not worked in quite a while. The exception, of course, being when he was unconscious for five days following his dip in Cobbs. Also it was the first day he had spent with a woman in long time as well. Too long.

It was strange but fun. The next morning he woke on his couch to find her gone. At first he worried but her scent was still strong in the air. So he checked the kitchen but it was empty. Then when he went to his bedroom he found the door both closed and locked. Amanda opened the door and was already dressed with her hair tied back into the braid. She was smiling innocently at him.

"Uh… excuse me?" he said then walked in and pretended to check the room as if something might have been going on. "Why is MY bedroom door locked in MY apartment?"

"To keep you honest!" and she slipped past him into the bathroom.

First they went shopping; his refrigerator held very little edible food and he had promised Amanda an omelet for breakfast. So they went to the Mom and Pop corner market. As comfortable as they had become last night Max found that he was even more relaxed with her now. She even offered to pay with a very believable face.

Max cooked while she watched and made smart remarks about his technique. She had brought jelly at the market; she liked to put it on top of her omelets. He frowned his nose up at the purple mess she made. His father did the same thing with scrambled eggs and he had never liked it.

"It's good!" she defended it, popping another bit of the purple mess into her mouth.

"Whatever. You don't mix your foods that way. Jelly is like a desert. You wouldn't put icing on top of a steak."

She just took another bit and smiled at him as happy as she could be. They did not leave his apartment after that until late in the afternoon. Another food run but this time they elected to eat at a small restaurant just off campus. It was Saturday; so it was crowded but neither minded waiting to be seated.

"How are you gonna be able to pay for an apartment in Chestnut Circle?" she was asking him about his Uncle's loft.

"He still owns it." He explained. "I'll only have to pay the utilities and a small rent."

"Oh you're gettin' over."

"Hey, it's in Chestnut Circle with an unbelievable view of the Lake."

Then a hushed feminine voice cut across the restaurant to his ear. "That's them right there."

What was that?

"So your Uncle's got money huh?" Amanda was teasing. "I thought you had to work for a living." The hostess waved them over. Amanda grabbed his hand when he hesitated, pulled him along after and they followed the hostess through the restaurant.

"Him and your girl? I told you she warned him." This second voice, was deep and very familiar. Max scanned the room with narrow eyes.

"That bitch!" It took a second but he quickly found some familiar faces. Just ahead of them, seated around a large table, was a group of six or seven people all looking their way. The Gammas, many of the same ones he had spent time with in the "Tank". There were angry yet cautious looks being thrown his way now, however he did not see the faces he was expecting; the ones that went with the voices he just heard. A couple of the Gammas looked away from him and toward the other side of the restaurant. Max followed the brief glances until he finally saw them. On the far side, seated by the window sat the Gamma's leader, Yasir. He was sullen and eyed Max beneath the brim of his baseball cap. On the other side of the table for two sat Rosette.

"Your uncle on your Mom or your Dad's side?" Amanda asked.

"Uh… it's my Dad's half-brother." The restaurant was filled the smell of cooked food and that blocked out many of the human scents. Still Max was sure that there were no more Gammas seated in the restaurant. As crowded as it was at their table there was still room for Rosette and her boyfriend to sit with their friends. That meant they had segregated themselves for some reason.

"Never really knew him that well." He told himself to calm down but the sight of the group of them with hostile stares made him tense and ready to fight. The hostess was leading them to a table right past the pair.

Yasir glanced up as they approached. Max saw the anger flash on his face as soon as their eyes locked.

Amanda's head turned in their direction when Rosette stood up suddenly. Max began calculating fighting odds. He could take the Gammas, all seven of them easy, but Amanda could get caught up in the fight and there were several women with the group on the other side.

"What the fuck do you think you're doing?" Rosette burst out without heeding the rest of the restaurant. Heads turned and conversations died quickly as they became the center of attention.

"Going to dinner." Amanda did not even seem fazed. Instead of being surprised or getting as loud as Rosette she remained calm and balanced. He was impressed.

"How the fuck you going out with him when you know I was seeing him?" She walked around her table and stood in Amanda's path. Rosette was smaller, more flesh and less muscle, plus she moved so sloppy. Amanda had a grace to her, very supple but strong.

"I told you she warned his ass. Back stabbing…" said Yasir who was leaning forward hard in his chair with his cap pulled down low on his head and his eyes now hidden.

"You weren't seeing him." she said, still calm, but she had stopped and was now standing a few inches from Rosette. "You don't even like him so what's the problem?"

"The problem is you should've minded your own damn business." Yasir said from where he sat.

"Warned me about what?" Max said calmly but as strongly as he could manage. He stared Rosette right in the eye and she actually took a step backwards. Then he turned to the Gammas leader who was still keeping his eyes down. "What did she have to warn me about?"

"You know what it is. Watch your back." Yasir threw Max a biting look.

"I thought we were done with this?" Max met the man's gaze. Just then he heard the scraping sound of several chairs sliding on the restaurant floor. The Gammas on the other side had gotten up and were moving fast. Amanda was still holding one of his hands so Max drew the other into a tight fist. He could feel the points of his claws digging deep into his palms.

Not here… he could not let this happen here.

Then the footsteps began to recede. Max looked over his shoulder to see that the larger group of Gammas were walking out, all of them.

"What the fuck it this?" Rosette was furious and turned to her boyfriend wanting an explanation. Yasir just lowered his head even more.

"Right." Max said. Then to Rosette; "See you." He and Amanda walked around her then continued to their table.

As they continued to follow the hostess Amanda peeked over her shoulder amazed. "Why are they leaving?"

"Guess they got tired of his shit."

"Wow." She was trying to keep from smirking at Rosette who was looking back and forth from the exiting Gammas to her boyfriend. Max took Amanda's hand and pulled her to their waiting booth.

"I never did thank you." he said.

"You don't have to." she replied softly.

"Why though?" he had wanted to ask her earlier. "Most people believe their version of what happened. And they're your friends…"

"They aren't my friends." she snapped. "They're Rosette's boyfriends. Plus everything that comes out of their mouths is a lie."

She sat down and folded her arms. "I turn a couple of them down and they run around telling people I'm a dyke."

"Thank you Amanda."

She smiled at him. "You're welcome Max." Then she glanced over her shoulder at them one last time. "This is ridiculous. None of them were even old enough to be in high school when that went down."

"The fraternity is still under probation though. They're still paying the price." he explained it again. It was something he used to think about a lot.

"Yea well why did they rush then? They knew before they signed up that they wouldn't be able to do any on campus activities."

"Because it's easier to get in now. What they are is the bottom of the barrel when it comes to pledge candidates. Probably couldn't get into any other Frat."

"Now that makes sense." She nodded. Over Amanda's shoulder he saw Rosette stomp out of the restaurant and Yasir dragging behind her.

Dinner was a little tense at first. They made small talk; mostly ripping Rosette and the Frat boys apart until their dinner arrived. Then the conversation flowed more naturally.

"Chestnut Circle is nice but I like Ivy Hills." she was telling him.

"I grew up in Brookhaven, I miss it."

"They've got the most Rockwoods right? It is pretty over there. I never really thought of Mountairy Rock as being big but just when you think you've seen it all, a whole other neighborhood pops up that I never heard about."

"Tell me about it." he said thoughtfully. "The Museum sent me to the Downhills a few weeks ago."

"Where's that?"

"On the other side of Cobbs River."

"You mean North Hills?"

"Just east of North Hills actually, in the valley. Kind of hard to get to."

Amanda finally looked over her shoulder. Max realized that she might have a hard time at home tonight.

"Worried about Rosette and her friends?"

"No." she said twisting her lips in the way Max was starting to love.

"You should stay the night again, just to give her time to cool off."

"... sounds like you have a little plan there." She said sliding her smirk from one side of her face to the other.

"Just offering you a safe place to rest your head." Max shrugged innocently.

"Riiiight. Well thank you very much Max but 'Zetta is going home today anyway. She'll be gone all week. So I'll be fine. Plus I have an all-day study group tomorrow."

"Oh... that's good."

"Ha! Don't look so sad. I'm definitely going to be coming back over to your apartment soon."

"Really?"

"Yes; I forgot to pick up my scarf."

10,000 MANIACS

Though it was the day of rest, Sunday brought with it the foreboding reality of work and school to both of them so he walked her back to her apartment. The scents of the Frat boys hung in the air but were more than a day old he guessed. They were long gone but Rosette was waiting for her inside. So after a long kiss goodbye Max waited to see if either stormed out. Sure enough Rosette left after about ten minutes and passed by without even noticing him.

He resisted the urge to go up and knock on her door. He really did have to get some sleep if he wanted to be ready for the ton of work that had to be waiting for him at the Museum. King had not instructed him to work this weekend which was probably because Max had been working so many weekends that his mentor probably just assumed he would be there. It was odd though, that King had not called him when he had not shown up. Maybe he was giving him some slack because of everything that had been happening. Maybe King also thought that he and Bazillion had been friends and that Max had been overwhelmed by his death. The big man had never shown that kind of compassion before but there was always a first time.

As soon as he opened the door to his apartment he could smell Amanda. Her fresh scent lay heavy on his couch, his rug, and his bed. He needed a shower but the fatigue he had been carrying with him all week was pressing hard on him now. Off went his jacket, his shoes and his shirt and he plopped down onto his bed.

He would only sleep a little while, and then he would get up, shower, and make sure he had something to wear to work tomorrow… He heard the thump and sat up quickly. Then the cold wind rushed across his chest. The window was open again.

The spicy, musky scent rose to his nose, and the bed shook as Big Gray jumped up onto his bed. "mmrow?"

"What?" Max yelled. "What do you want?"

The cat sat back on its hind legs and their eyes met. Max went stiff all over, bracing himself but nothing happened. But the cat continued to look at him.

"Get out!" he yelled. The cat did not move from the bed. He

slammed his hand down on the mattress and Big Gray never even flinched. Max yelled some more but the cat not only was not intimidated but hardly seemed to notice his yelling. Finally Max got up and walked to the window.

"Time to go! Come on!" and now the cat began to move. It jumped off of the bed and leapt onto the window sill, half way in, half way out.

"Go!" Max waved his hands at the cat but it was still useless. Once again their eyes met and once again there was nothing.

He moved to actually push the cat out but stopped himself. It had already proven itself more than capable of climbing down to the ground from the seventh floor but that did not mean it would survive being pushed out.

"MOVE!" and finally it seemed to get the message. It grudgingly spared him one last glance and then leapt. Max looked out after it and saw the gray shape moving swiftly down the building.

So he shut the window and locked it. Afterwards he could not remember falling asleep but he had lain awake for a long time.

The wail of his alarm clock woke him much too soon. Still he felt as if he was way behind the ball on sleep. And there would be very little time to catch up this week if he knew King. The bed was warm and Amanda's scent still lingered. It was hard to get up but somehow he managed it.

He ran the shower hot and stood under the spray too long. Compared to steamy heat in the bathroom the rest of the apartment was cold when he got out. At least it helped him wake up. Last night he had forgotten to make sure that he had clothes for the day so when he opened his closet door he was hit by the pungent smell of his still damp sweats.

"Ugh!" The whole closet reeked. Maybe it was just his sensitive nose but every clean shirt in there now smelled like his sweats. The clock read Seven O'clock. King expected him to be in by Eight. He would never make it if he tried to wash something, and he had already missed the weekend.

So he grabbed the shirt he had worn on Friday. It was still filled with the smell of Amanda's hair and just the memory made him smile. He had to see her tonight, even though he was sure that he would be putting in another late night at the Museum.

He was right. King piled it on him. It was a huge workload that once again did not take into account his own, now again delayed, research. Fatima grumbled and sniped all day long. The rest of the staff came after him again as if King had left the country once more. Despite the amount of work Max was feeling pretty good. It was another return to normality that, until this moment, he had been unaware he was in desperate need of. There was very little time to think of Maniacs, Downhill fighters, or witches. At least until twilight.

He had run down to the café trying to get a muffin and soda before they closed. The day's newspaper had not been there when he had arrived that morning but now he could see that there were a few copies left. The headline read in bold print: WILD WEST OAKS.

The riot was still getting press. More so now because a couple of the Maniacs had died from wounds suffered during the fight. That brought the tally of homicides this year to fifty-one and there had only been forty-something days. Most of the deaths had been related to the growing gang problems both in West Oaks and the southern section of Ivy Hills. There were a number of deaths being blamed on a potential serial killer, some crazy attacking prostitutes in the southern section of Ivy Hills. Then there were the deaths at the Museum. Mountairy Rock had its problems just like any other large city but this was happening at a rate of more than one homicide a death a day.

Three more happened on Friday. How many more before this was all over? The Stone, the Maniacs, Prya and the Downhills… there was so much in front of him.

But did it have to be?

He could take off the Stone and just weather through the withdrawal. Maybe he could just give it to Landry or turn it in to the police as if he had only just found it. Then all he would have to worry about would be work, moving and being with Amanda. He could still smell her fresh scent in his shirt and it had buoyed him all day. It was flowery…

Flowery, but fake… Landry. He whipped his head around and saw them walking through the main doors of Rebel's Keep. Landry and Alana, looking very pedestrian in this setting, saw him as well and headed directly towards him. Max looked around quickly; he was not sure he wanted to be seen with either one of them.

"Where have you been?" Landry demanded.

"Excuse me?" he snapped back.

"We've been looking for you all weekend. We thought you might be hurt." Landry stated.

"I've been home all weekend."

"I went to your apartment. You weren't there." Landry had that wary look again. She had been having as hard a time trusting Max as he did her.

"How do you know where… Prya." He answered himself. "Anyway yes I was. All this weekend. I don't remember having visitors." He said and walked away from the café hoping to lead them to a low traffic area of the Museum. There were few visitors today but one could never tell who would walk through.

"I went there three times. You weren't there." Landry said. Max noticed that she was keeping her distance.

"Maybe Prya gave you the wrong apartment number. I spent the weekend in my apartment, with…" What was he doing? "Hey! I was home! What did you want?"

"You never came back after you went to look for the Sick Ones…"

"That was a bad idea. Your girl, Prya brought her boyfriend and his gang to come jump me. For once I was lucky the Maniacs were as crazy as they are."

"They're just a little xenophobic." Landry shook her head trying to defend the Downhills clans.

"The… the Sick Ones, I meant the Sick Ones. It turned into one big street fight and cops broke it up. See?" He waved the paper at her.

"I've seen the news. I know about the fight. That's not why I've been looking for you." She was still carrying her leather case. Quickly she reached inside it and pulled out a thin white object. Max stepped closer to see what it was.

A fang, most likely one from "… the Mega Snake Maniac." he said.

"I… the what?"

"Why do you have that?" Max asked her insistently. He could explain his terminology later.

"I dug it out of… Prya. Whatever this came from… bit her. She's dying Max."

"Wait? She got bit? How?" Max dropped his soda and snatched the fang out of Landry's hand. It was long enough and it had that same sick smell. "What do you mean 'she's dying'?"

Landry took a deep breath and looked around. They were relatively alone for the moment but she was clearly uncomfortable. "Where can we talk?"

Bazillion's office would work. There were still students working in the lab and Max did not want to walk Landry past any of them. Neither did he want to walk them through the South Tower lobby; so instead, he led them through the service stairwell.

The only people who use the service corridors were the regular security staff so it was clear. Thinking he was lucky for a change Max was halfway up the first flight of steps before he noticed that he had lost his little group.

Landry and Alana stood at the service corridor entrance. Landry was holding Alana's hand and her apprentice had a look of horror on her face. Her body was rigid and she was leaning backwards out of the corridor.

"What's wrong?" Max asked looking out into the Keep to see if anyone was watching them. "Let's go."

"She can't Max. What happened in there?" Landry looked

apprehensively into the service way.

"What do you mean? Nothing… oh." The guards had been killed in here on New Year's. Max then turned and looked back down the corridor himself. He could almost see the cloth covered bodies again. "Three of the guards' bodies were found here on New Year's."

"She won't be able to walk through that. Is there another way?" Landry was still staring beyond him and into the corridor as if she was trying to see evidence of the murders. Alana, however, appeared as if she was seeing something far worse. Tiny little movements in her face made Max think that the girl was seeing something that was happening right then.

"Sure. This way." He stepped out of the corridor and walked them around through the South Tower lobby. Here there remained some staff and a few students but none of them seemed to pay them any mind. Max probably need not have been worried.

Alana seemed to be fine by the time Max seated them on the huge leather couch in Bazillion's office. Landry looked about curiously. She probably had been expecting Max to take them to the office he where she spied on him and Fatima.

"This is very nice." she complimented.

"It's not my office. It belongs… belonged to another researcher who recently passed away." Landry nodded but Alana made a fleeting distressed expression that Max almost missed. Was she seeing something here? "So what was that all about?"

"Alana has talent. It's raw and intermittent, so it can be overwhelming to her at times." She was still holding the young girl's hand.

"Talent? Like psychic talent?" it came out as if he did not believe her… which considering the fact that he had recently engaged in a telepathic conversation with a cat, was just a bit hypocritical.

"Yes Max." Landry looked to be about to go into a long spiel about Alana's talent but Max did not want to get off track this time.

"Okay. Whatever. What happened to Prya?"

"She came back to Alana's apartment after you left. I told her where you were going and I guess she followed you. Lot must have been tracking her because after she left he and his brothers showed up."

Brothers? Max had guessed right.

She continued, "Later I find out that she got hurt in the fight you all were in."

"She wasn't in that fight." She had run, he had thought.

"She… must have been involved someway because she was bitten. The Sick One, that bit her, must have had venom sacks. She seemed fine at first but then she passed out and now they can't wake her."

Now Max went rigid. He looked again at the fang in his hand. It was a bit translucent and he could see that it was hollow. She had been there in West Oaks of course but he had been sure that she had never come close to the fight. Why had she? Did she try and help him?

"What hospital is she in?" he asked. He had to… she had saved his life…

"She's being cared for in the Downhills. They'll never let you see her." Landry began digging into her leather case again.

"There's no hospital in the Downhills! She should be brought here to Ivy Hills, to Mountairy Rock Hospital."

"That's not the way they do things in the Downhills." she said. Even as Max opened his mouth to argue she was shaking her head. "It's no use arguing! Even if you could convince them to shed a couple hundred years of self imposed segregation you wouldn't be able to do it in time to save… Prya."

"Save her? How?" and Max watched as Landry finally found what she was looking for in her case. She pulled out a small glass vial topped with a thick latex cover. Max had seen something like this before, he knew what she wanted.

"You want a venom sample." He took the glass vial and held it up; imagining what it would take to get what was needed. Bazillion's desk seemed to sneak up on him and he realized that he had taken steps backward, and was leaning against it. He suddenly felt very tired.

"And from the exact one that bit her." Landry said. "I know it might be impossible but… she's dying."

Prya probably saved him more times in the past month than he had needed saving in his entire life. "I warmed you" she had told him.

Max stood up and looked hard at Landry. "I'll need some of that scent cover stuff you've got… and the Bane."

The cell phone vibrated against his thigh. It was cumbersome and in an awkward position. If he fell, which he seemed to be doing a lot of lately, he would probably break it. So he should not have brought it but in case he had problems he would need to be able to contact Landry. He reached down into his sweat pants and pulled the phone out of the little knit pouch.

"Hey Max." It was Amanda.

"Hey, Amanda." It was impossible to keep the tension out of his voice and she sensed it.

"Everything okay?" she asked. He surveyed the huge expanse of weeds and shrubbery that lay in between him and the Maniac's little base. He could smell the sentries they posted there and could hear them shivering in the cold. It had taken him a good while to make his way around the abandoned section of West Oaks without being seen by the police or the one patrol of Maniacs. Never-the-less he managed to get close enough to see the huge building from the edge of the overgrown field. Max stood in the shadow of the last set of condemned buildings that were in front of the park. He could not see the edge of the ridge for all the trees but the park itself had a distinctive scent and it lay heavy in the air.

"Just been a long day... still have some work to clear up."

"Oh. I know we've only been dating for a little while but I thought it would be nice to go out on Valentine's. We could go back to the Emerald Forest?"

She had been so beautiful on that balcony. "That was great. Are you sure? There's a really nice restaurant in New Madrid." The wind shifted and brought with it not only a variety of smells but a barrage of sounds as well. There was a rustling and the sound of cloth being scraped by thorns...

...someone was trying to sneak through the underbrush. They did not have a Maniac's scent and... they were not headed directly for him.

"Okay! Are you sure you want to go? You don't sound very excited." The soft thrum of her voice threatened to distract him. He was here to save Prya. He needed to focus.

"No. I'm excited. It' just..." The person creeping was circling around the Maniacs. They did not know Max was hiding in the shadows by the brush.

Not yet.

"You know when you were a kid and Christmas break was coming up but you knew that you still had weeks of school and Report Card Day to get through before you got to it?"

She laughed, "Yea. You have a lot of work huh?"

"Yea... and there are still problems from the break-ins that we have to deal with." He smelled the sharp biting cordite scent that he now knew was gunpowder.

"I heard that the police were questioning staff. They think it was an inside job." He could hear the worry in her voice.

"I don't think anyone at the Museum had anything to do with what happened. But the police have more than enough Mani... of the gang that broke in, in custody. I think we'll find out soon enough." The rustling drew closer. Soon whoever it was would be able to hear him talking. Unless they had ears as good as his, in which case they were already aware of him.

"I hope everything turns out okay." Amanda's voice, the quiet vibrating rasp, lowered. She was worried.

"Thanks. It'll be fine. And you and me on Valentines right?"

"Right! And bring my scarf!"

"Okay, let me jump back on this work. I'll call you tomorrow." Max pulled the scarf up over his mouth.

"Okay bye."

"Bye."

Max hurled himself into the air at a slight angle gaining almost twenty feet of altitude. Ten yards of foliage past beneath him and he gazed downward as he reached the zenith. The dark shadow still crept through the high weeds, unaware of Max's sudden flight.

Twisting in an instinctive rhythm, he changed the direction of his fall dramatically. He dropped down into the brush right on top of the dark shape.

"OOF!" Quickly Max covered the man's mouth with one hand and pinned both his hands to his chest with the other. As soon as he had the stranger secure, he craned his head and listened to see if any of the Sentry Maniacs had heard the disturbance.

It was all quiet.

He studied the man who surprisingly was not struggling. He was an older man, with a smattering of gray peppering his thick mustache and balding head. He wore all black, way too much black for someone not planning on doing something sneaky. Probably a cop.

"Hiya." said Max.

"mmm!"

"Gonna take my hand off of your mouth. Your buddies hiding in the bushes have not heard us yet. Please don't change that." The man glanced about futilely, then nodded and Max slid his hand from the man's face.

"Who are you?" Max whispered.

"Not your enemy." Max had been expecting him to say he was a cop, he really, really had been.

"What's that mean?"

"It means that I recognize that you are here to deal with the Cult." The old guy whispered. Max looked at him man again. He had seen him somewhere before.

"But who are you?"

The man took a breath and tried to look around but from his vantage point he could only see bushes, Max and black sky.

"I represent the Men of the Order of Solomon. We have been watching this infestation for some time now." he said.

Oh crap! This guy was a Mason. Now he remembered seeing him at the Museum during several functions the Men of Solomon had run there. The Masons knew about the Maniacs? Their headquarters, the Temple of Solomon, was a huge tower that over looked the park not too far from here. It made sense. If Landry was on the money about the way this city worked then the Masons had to be one of the "factions" of which she had been talking.

"You've been watching?" Max asked.

"Of course. We are aware of everything that goes on in West Oaks."

"Right. Then how did you let them set up camp right under your nose?" He asked harshly. It was occurring to him that maybe it was the Men of Solomon who had found the Snake-Maniacs body and destroyed it.

The man squirmed a little on the ground. "Even with all that we can do, we lack the means to combat that which lies at the center of the nest. I could ask the same question of you. Why have you allowed them to gather in such numbers?"

"Why have 'I'?" Max released the man's hands. After rubbing them and issuing a grateful nod the man said;

"Yes. You are here to deal with them aren't you?"

Max wondered what exactly this man knew about him but there was so little time. The glass vial pressed against his chest next to the Stone. Prya was somewhere in the Downhills dying.

"I don't have time for this. I'm going in." and he crept past the man who did not follow; however he did whisper to Max's back.

"It's in the basement. There's an entrance in the back but it is heavily guarded."

The Maniacs hiding in the brush were easy to avoid. Most of them were asleep and those that were awake did not seem to be actively watchful. They were just sitting on the ground hugging themselves and staring off into space.

Even so, Max moved slowly and carefully. Despite his night vision he could barely see into the dark recesses beyond the broken out windows of the warehouse, which was looking more and more like an apartment building. Anyone watching the grounds might have been able to see his dark shape slipping through the weeds just as he had seen the Mason from the air.

The closer he got to the building the more active the sentries were. These Maniacs were actually walking a circuit, probably just around the building but they were at least looking. Someone around here was organized, because there were at least three of them, maybe four walking the perimeter and there was no point where one of them was not in plain sight of another.

He crept around towards the back of the warehouse where the number of Maniacs was double. None of them had the oily smell of a Snake Maniac. It was too much to hope that the one Maniac he needed would be conveniently sitting right outside.

Again these Maniacs were far more alert than the others. They were watching the bushes and moving about with energy. He could take them, he was sure, but not without them alerting the whole building and he had learned the hard way that the Maniacs were dangerous in numbers. From the smell coming from the building, the sick oily scent so thick it choked him a little, there were far more of them than he had yet encountered.

So he crept back around to the side of the building and watched as two sentries pass by. Always two in sight; one just leaving this side of the building and one just coming around the bend. Maybe he was wrong; he figured there had to be more than four walking the circuit. There were several broken out windows in view but none were on the ground level. Soon enough he spotted one on the third floor. The window was completely open without any broken glass.

He could make that one.

First he had to wait. The Maniac sentries kept walking their circuit always with one about to leave and the other just coming around the corner. He hunkered down among the bushes and watched. Two passed and nothing…

… the next two were just as vigilant…

…then finally one who walked with his head down.

"There's my bitch."

But he missed his chance. By the time he was sure that the Maniac was not going to look up he had already passed by and another more alert Maniac was rounding the corner.

So again he waited. This time it took almost eight Maniacs passes before he saw the one he wanted.

He coiled his legs. The previous Maniac passed and soon had his back to him and then finally, the other dropped his head and studied the ground as he was walking.

The bushes rustled and he was airborne. It was three stories and he cleared it easy. His foot came down on the window ledge without more than a quiet "thunk". He dug his claws into the frame and glanced back down to see his "not so alert" Maniac scanning the bushes. So far so good.

He hopped in through the window and his feet came down on something lumpy, soft… and breathing. It thrashed when he stepped on it making him trip and fall.

It was darker inside and Max could not see the floor moving up so fast. His face hit carpet before his hands could catch him.

"Find your own place!" said a muffled voice. Max rolled until he got his feet under him. From the stink he could tell that he had stumbled into someone's idea of a bedroom.

Bedroom/Bathroom. Whew!

The Maniac grumbled and rolled over. He was wrapped in a heap of old clothes. With the window busted out it had to be just about freezing in the small room. That did not seem to bother the Maniac too much. He just curled, under his mound of stinking clothes a little harder and lay still again.

Except for the sleeping Maniac the room was empty. Dim amber light glowed under the one door the room had. There was a slight click when Max turned the knob and the door opened with a bit of a creek. The Maniac complained behind him with a quiet moan but did nothing else.

The hallway beyond the door was murky. The faint light was coming from the far end of the corridor and was low to the floor. Max guessed because of the way it played on the walls, that the source lay down a set of steps. There were doorways along the hall, that were dark even to Max's eyes. A pair of legs… no… two pair stuck out of one doorway. As his eyes began to adjust to the darkness he could see that the legs belonged to two Maniacs lying on the floor, curled up together.

Nothing stirred as he exited the room and closed the door behind him to keep the Maniac quiet. The doorways along the hallway led to rooms filled with sleeping Maniacs who were all huddled together for warmth. There were piles and piles of darkly dressed and stinking human beings all wheezing and coughing together. How many? Maybe twenty or thirty a room?

Just in this hall?

Just on this floor?

How could the Maniacs have drawn in this many people without the police knowing about it? Why was no one doing anything?

The oily smell of the Snake Maniacs was in the air but not close by. It was extremely hard to track the scent; He kept losing it. The sick funk from the Maniacs threatened to make him gag with every inhale. So as soon as he decided there were no Snake Maniacs on this floor, he stopped breathing through his nose.

The light was indeed coming from the floor below and it cast itself up a set of stairs. He ducked low at the top of the steps and peeked down.

More sleeping Maniacs. This group was sitting around a kerosene heater, the source of the light. There was a couch where a few were huddled. They seemed to be awake but were extremely listless. He took a few steps down and tried to see around the entire floor.

It was some kind of walkway, or terrace inside of the building, that branched off into several other corridors and over looked a dark open area. There was movement and flickering lights from those open doorways. Max hazarded another sniff; Snake Maniacs.

No one stirred as he crept down the steps, even the two Maniacs asleep at the bottom. The terrace looked out onto a very dark warehouse interior. Again Max was amazed with the number of Maniacs here. Landry had said that the thing, the Demon, did not want an army. So what the hell was this?

Quietly he stepped past the heater and the couch on his way to the nearest open doorway. The oily sick Snake Maniac scent was coming from ahead somewhere. A Maniac on the couch swiveled his head in Max's direction. Their eyes met. He wore an exhausted look, like someone who had just run a marathon. His jaw hung open and slid to the side when he turned his head; slack.

Max found himself on his toes ready to bolt, fight or some kind of combination of the two. Should he run back up the stairs and hope to get past the sleeping bears before they became a mass of crazed fighters? Or should he randomly run about until he lucked into an exit?

Or...

The Maniac just turned his head back away and went about staring at nothing. Max checked around the room again. What was wrong with them? Where were the Maniacs that were running riot through Mountairy Rock? The ones just outside seemed the same but...

Max was beginning to think that he need not be as careful and quiet as he was being.

It took three steps to get behind the couch. He ducked down just out of sight and reached his hand over and gently tapped one if the Maniacs.

Nothing.

He shook the Maniac again.

Nothing.

He tapped him on the face, ducked hard behind the couch and waited. After a second the Maniac finally moved.

He rolled over.

So Max left the protective cover of the couch and stood, truth be told, a little disappointed. He walked around it and the heater while stepping over bodies. One of the Maniacs on the floor shifted onto Max's foot. At first he stopped and stood stock still. Then, after looking around first, he kicked the Maniac off of his foot. With a low moan the wild haired man rolled again, found another Maniac and curled up next to him.

"Hey." Max said. No one moved nor paid him any mind.

"Woo hoo!" A few eyes popped open only to then promptly close. Max thought he knew what this was. Whatever the demon was doing to them to control them must have a side effect that was putting them in this altered state.

There were now three visible doorways on this side of the terrace. Max peeked into the first one.

Piles of clothes, book-bags, and shoes filled the room. Unlike the rest of the warehouse these items seemed mostly clean. He checked behind him to make sure no one had gotten up and then he walked into the room. The items in the room were clean in the respect that they did not carry the nauseating sick Maniac smell; however a lot of it was covered by dust. "The Maniacs clothes?" he wondered. "Maybe from before they became Maniacs."

The sneakers, shirts, and kakis were all very un-Maniac-like. There was a small pile of empty wallets, the IDs had been removed and dropped onto a pile right next to them. Max knelt down and picked up the pile of IDs, fanning shuffling through them. The ages ranged from mid-teens to mid-thirties and the races ran the spectrum. That much he had expected but his breath caught when he came to the first female ID in the pile.

COLLINDA STACK

She was 29.

Max shuffled through the handful of IDs in his hand again and found two more female IDs. He had never seen a girl Maniac. A shudder went down his spine.

He peered out of the room to see if anyone had moved. It was still quiet. The Maniacs stayed huddled exactly where they had been before.

The next room held a small flickering fire. There was a set of blankets set around the fire it sat in the middle of the room that was otherwise empty. The oily Snake Maniac scent sat thick in the air. It had just been there.

Max reached into his sweatshirt and pulled out the milking vial. He had to be ready.

One more door here on this side and then he would walk across the terrace to the other side.

A hot blast of air washed over him when he opened the door. It was a staircase that led down into amber light. The Snake Maniac's scent led down here. It was stronger and he knew that it was close.

"HSSS!" It was right behind him.

Max ducked all the way to his knees and felt the rush of air pass by the back of his head as the Mega Snake Maniac swiped at him. He spun while still low to the ground and saw tight black leather jeans bulging with muscle. Max threw a punch at the right knee cap and regretted it as soon as his knuckles met the granite-like bone.

"Ah!" He tried to roll away but the Mega Snake Maniac kicked him back into the door frame. Because his right hand was holding the venom vial Max hesitated to swing another punch. The Maniac hissed then kicked him again. This time Max fell through the doorway and down two of the steps before he was able to catch himself by jamming his clawed finger tips into the wall. Behind him he listened to the vial clinking down the staircase.

The Mega Snake Maniac could care less about a simple flight of steps. It just dove at him; hands outstretched to dig into his flesh. It's fang filled mouth was spread wide, ready to bite.

Max saw the claws, the teeth and could not help himself; he pulled his own claws out of the wall and grabbed the huge forearms of the Maniac before those huge hands could reach his throat. The Maniac had come at him with a ton of weight and with such momentum that the two off them began to tumble down the steps.

With each jarring turn as they rolled down Max watched the

Snake Maniac's teeth get closer and closer. The steps slammed into his back mercilessly with each rotation but somehow he managed to avoid hitting his head. The Snake Maniac, however, was not as fortunate. Max saw its eyes close every time the back of its head slammed into a step. Finally the stairs ended and the two came down hard onto a granite floor.

The impact separated them. They spilled out onto a wide walkway only a few feet from each other. They landed on some kind of raised walkway in a big basement or lounge.

Max recovered first and was on his feet, rushing to get to the Maniac before it could get to up.

It almost did. The Maniac rolled onto its knees but before it could stand, Max drove his fist right in between its eyes. The Mega Snake Maniac dropped in a twitching heap, spread eagle on the floor.

Breathing hard Max spun to check the steps. Maniacs should be raining down any minute. He spared the Snake Maniac a quick glance to make sure it was really down and then took to the stairs leaping the steps five and six at a time as quietly as he could. At the top the door had closed behind them when they fell. So first he just listened for any sign of movement but there was none. Slowly he opened the door and peered out. The Maniacs were still sleeping.

Tension eased off his shoulders as he released the breath that he had been holding. His legs were shaking slightly so after closing the door again he just sat down at the top of the staircase.

"It's okay... almost home."

Back down the stairs he found the Snake Maniac precisely where he left him. Its arms and legs were still twitching. Max looked around the big room. It almost looked like a theater with the raised walkway as the stage, but the floor was empty where there would normally have been seats save for some trash debris.

After a brief search he found the glass vial on the floor in the corner. Then he walked back to the Maniac and flipped it over. Its eyes were wide open but glassy and unfocused.

"Open wide big guy." The Mega Snake Maniac's skull was no longer shaped exactly like a humans. Everything above the jaw seemed wider and shorter. The eyes were beginning to spread and the nose ridge sloped down to a now protruding jaw. Its skin was mostly covered in scales, some of them had peeled and fallen off, Max guessed during their fight. The scales were hard and resistant when he felt them, almost like armor. He realized that his punch between the things eyes would have had little effect if the scales had fully developed there.

He took another deep breath and grabbed the things mouth. The Snake Maniac twitched which gave Max a start and he let go. Then he got a better grip and pulled open the Maniacs mouth. It was like watching a flower bloom, except the flower was filled with teeth. Its fangs unfolded automatically into striking position. He could see the puffy venom sacks behind each one.

Each one… two long nasty fangs…

Two!

Crap! This was the wrong Maniac! Max reached down into his sock and pulled out the fang he had taken from Landry. It was just as long as the ones in this Maniacs mouth. She had expressly told him she needed venom from that one specific Maniac. This Maniac had both its venom teeth but the one that bit Prya should only have one left. Unless… how long would it take for these things to grow back a fang?

It did not look like this Maniac had ever lost a tooth though. Other than the bent scales between its eyes the Snake Maniac did not look like it had been in much of a fight recently and Max was sure Prya would have left her mark on it from that battle.

It was not the one.

Beating this Snake Maniac had not been easy and he had won mostly on luck and chance. There was no way he could count on that happening again. Things turned out well but he could just as easily have broken his neck coming down those stairs. He needed a plan, some way to catch the Snake Maniac that he needed off guard.

First he needed to find it.

There was a service door to the outside at one end of the room and another on the other side. He would check these before heading back up to the terrace.

The smells of Maniacs and Snake Maniacs floated through the air from every direction here, crisscrossing and running over each other. Even as he approached the door the scents grew stronger and faded at the same time.

The door opened onto yet another door lined corridor. Now, however, Max could clearly hear people moving about. The oily scent of at least two different Snake Maniacs floated to his nose; both Megas. The corridor was dark but there were tiny slivers of amber light at the bottom of each door.

The first door reeked of regular Maniacs, at least five of them. The sounds coming from the room were in a sort of rhythm. Almost, it was, like people working on an assembly line. There were no voices though, and the cadence never broke nor faltered.

The next room was the same; although, the rhythm was different. He resisted the urge to open the door to see what was happening.

The light below the third door was much dimmer and there was no sound coming out. Crouching low Max took in a lung full of air then stood in shock.

No way!

He placed his hands on the knob and the door opened with a

creak. The room was little more than a vestibule that led to an empty elevator shaft but it was filled with all sorts of interesting things. There was straw lying all over the floor in front of the open shaft. There were also two piles of clothes just at the mouth of the shaft. Another pile of some of the bladed weapons that they had stolen from the Museum lie in the corner not too far from three sleeping Maniacs. Finally against the wall, tied hand and foot, lay Prya.

"… took your time…" she whispered.

"What the hell?" he said aloud. The sleeping Maniacs did not stir.

"Keep your voice down!" Prya hissed at him.

"Why? They won't even…"

"SHH!" She then snapped her head in the direction of the elevator shaft, her eyes wide with fear and worry. He had been carefully stepping over the sleeping Maniacs to reach her but the fear in her eyes alarmed him. There was nothing by the elevator shaft but he took a breath anyway.

There was nothing new in the air. What was she worried about? So he stepped across the room and looked down the shaft.

WHAT THE HELL WAS THAT?

He only saw it for a second and not all of it at that. At least seven feet long it was,

…the part that he had seen,

… and three feet wide just where it was disappearing from sight at the bottom of the shaft.

…it was…it was a tail.

"Max!" Prya hissed behind him but he kept his eyes locked down the shaft. Whatever it was it had no scent that he could pick up and it made no sound in the bottom of the shaft. Was this what the Snake Maniacs were turning into? Or something else?

There was flash of green light that danced like glowing powder and lit up the bottom of the shaft. For the briefest second Max saw a floor strewn with bones then it went dark again. A strange scent filled the shaft. It was strong and pungent and made his eyes tear up.

"MAX!" Prya screamed. He turned and saw her biting at the straps that held her drawing her own blood with an insane desperation.

"You sure don't look sick." he said.

"Cut me free! Hur… BEHIND YOU!"

Max turned too late and caught the Maniac's fist in his jaw. He stumbled backward into Prya who screamed for him to cut her free again. The Maniacs who had just been almost comatose a second ago now were running at him with the maniacal fire that had inspired the name… uh…he had given them.

"UNG!" The three of them tackled him back into the door. He threw his knee into the one closest and the Maniac fell back. Then Max drove his elbow down into the back of the one trying to pull him to the ground. The third caught him in the face again with a fairly decent punch. Max returned it faster than the Maniac was expecting and he stumbled backward and fell into the shaft catching the edge at the last second.

Footsteps thundered outside the door as more Maniacs seemed to have been alerted to the fight.

"MAX!" Prya screamed again. Her arms and mouth were bloody in her desperate attempt to get free.

"Stop! Here, I'll do it." He grabbed her arms and pulled them away from her face. Then he popped out his own claws and cut through the nylon straps easily. "There!" The door bust open and framed in the dim light stood a tall "Near Snake" Maniac. It took all of a second to recognize his friend Jean but before he could respond more Maniacs poured in…female Maniacs. They were nearly naked but their scant clothing was in better condition than the other Maniacs. And the looks in theses women's eyes did not match what Max had seen in the men. These women seemed to be more in control of themselves but each cast a nasty, almost evil glare.

"Jean!" Max set his feet and braced himself for their attack but Prya grabbed him by the collar and pulled him toward the shaft.

"Hey!" he said. "I'm not going down there!"

"Not down!" she said over her shoulder. Prya leapt across the shaft to the back wall and grabbed hold of the metal framework. In the next instant she climbed out of sight up the shaft.

Max made the jump from where he was, hitting almost the same spot on the wall that she had. The Maniac who had almost fallen down the shaft was still there, dangling and screaming. His fear made Max hesitate for a second. Something below the Maniac stirred at the bottom of the shaft. Two green glowing eyes pierced the darkness. Then there was a flash of teeth and green scales and then the Maniac was gone, pulled down into the shaft.

"Jesus!" Max hauled himself up after Prya who had climbed at least two floors and was prying open the elevator doors. She had gotten them open as soon as he reached her and they hopped onto the floor.

They were now on the other side of the terrace and there was plenty of activity. So many Maniacs were raining down the stairs that they tripped and fell over one another. They log jammed trying to get into the stairwell that Max and the Snake Maniac had fallen down earlier. For a moment no one noticed them.

"What the fuck was that at the bottom of the shaft? It just ate one of the Maniacs! Took him in one bite!" Max was trying to close the elevator doors behind them but it stuck. "Ung! I think you broke the doors."

She turned back to the shaft and started to climb back in.

"Yo! What the fuck are you doing?" he grabbed her bloody arm.

"We can't get out here. … the roof…"

"Fuck that! That thing might be climbing up the shaft right now." He turned back to the horde of Maniacs, who's numbers were swelling up on the other side of the terrace. The speed of that thing… the size of it… of its mouth…, like a forest of teeth… he would rather fight ten thousand Maniacs than risk those teeth.

"Stay right behind me." he ordered Prya.

He charged them with a roar. Several Maniacs turned, shook by the howl and were too late to defend themselves. He pulled a small clear plastic bag that was filled with a yellow and red powder out of the pouch in his sweatshirt. As hard as he could he threw it into the crowd of them. It exploded on the chest of a thick Maniac at the stairs that led up. The yellow and red dust formed tiny clouds of dust that seemed to cling and hover about any Maniac in the vicinity. They dropped to ground screaming and clawing at their faces.

Showing no mercy Max punched as hard as he could, kicked as hard as he could and Maniacs dropped and flew in all directions. Prya's grunts, gasps, and howls were right behind him so he never slowed. He reached the stairs where the mass of Maniacs raining down the stairs pressed down on them.

Still he did not stop, although he changed tactics. Instead of driving them back he pulled. He pulled them off the staircase; some to the left over the rail, some to the right over the rail or a few even over his head. The Maniacs were screaming all around him and the floor, the stairs, the whole building seemed to vibrate with their footsteps.

"Max!" Prya's scream had enough fear in it to make him turn. He thought the thing from the bottom of the shaft had followed them up. It was such a relief to see just two Mega Snake Maniacs wading through the regular Maniacs to get at them.

"Switch!" and he leapt, somersaulting backwards off the staircase and down into the chest of the first Mega. Prya charged up the steps and took his place pulling Maniacs out of their way.

Max and the Mega fell together knocking a bunch of the other Maniacs to the floor. The other Mega was quicker and more agile than its brother. It hopped out of the way when the first one would have fallen into its legs and it came at Max faster than he was prepared for.

A thick size fifteen sized boot bashed him in the face and momentarily dazed him. The sharp claws on its hand tore into his shoulder like hot fire. It pulled Max toward its gaping, one-fang filled mouth. He heard Prya screaming his name.

Wait… she was screaming; "MAX DUCK!"

He pulled free of the claws and dropped to the ground just as the limp body of a Maniac took his place in the mouth of the Mega. It dropped with a crash but the first one was back on its feet and coming at him, claws extended.

He tucked and rolled across a small bit of open floor, then got to his feet. The Mega tracked him well and was hot on his heels.

There was a loud snapping sound…

Max ducked one arcing flash of claws and came up with a crushing upper cut right into its jaw.

…followed by the sound of metal being torn…

The other Mega came across the terrace followed by more regular Maniacs. Max could only spare them the briefest glance while he threw another punch, trying to put the first Mega down for good. But the damn thing had those armor scales all over its face and head.

…then the whole terrace shook while an ear piercing, staccato cracking…

…Metal bolts popped like gunfire…

…Wood pilings splintered…

The terrace itself tilted almost forty-five degrees and the couch and kerosene heater slid against the rail. Max ran for the staircase heedless of the Maniacs, he knew he had almost no time.

With roar that was almost animal like, the terrace fell.

Max was already in the air when ten thousand screaming Maniacs dropped all around him into the dark warehouse below. The Staircase was ripped away from the floor above and it fell as well. He had not counted on this because his leap would have brought him down right in the middle of the stairs. Part of the railing was still attached to the ceiling. It was warped and did not look strong enough to hold him but he reached out for it out of desperation.

The rail bent and swung on whatever last bit of metal was holding it to the floor above. It felt solid though, when his hand came down on it, as if it could hold his weight. Then a stinging crushing Mega hand came down on his ankle.

The sudden added weight nearly pulled Max off. The rail swayed and ground hard against whatever was mooring it to the ceiling. The extra weight was too much.

His ankle burned as the Mega dug in. It reached up with its other hand and grabbed his thigh.

"Ahh!" Max kicked the thing right in the mouth but it was not deterred. Again he kicked, and again.

"Get off!"

But its grip only tightened and Max's leg went numb. He raised the other once again to kick it but, before he could, a thick wooden handle suddenly sprouted out of the Mega's face right between its eyes.

Those eyes crossed and stared at the hunting knife that was sticking out of its head. Then they went slack, staring at nothing, then the clawed hands let go and the Mega Snake Maniac fell into the darkness, dead.

"Max." Prya was standing at what had been the top of the stairs with a smile on her face. "…whenever you're ready…"

She pulled him up into the hallway where it was obvious that she had been busy. Maniacs lay strewn across the floor like broken rag dolls. Some were moaning, most were motionless.

"… trapped…" she said.

"No." Max answered her. "There's a window… end of the hall." He pointed up the hallway but he turned and looked down into the warehouse below. The darkness was gone, filled with the flickering light of a fire that had been started by the broken kerosene heater. It did not look like it would burn the building down but then again it was only just starting.

"…where…"

Max led her down the hall toward the door where he had entered. Impatient she walked ahead of him and kicked the door down. The lone occupant of the room woke with a start and sat up.

"Get your own… uh!"

Prya stormed in and kicked him in the face. Then she picked him up with the obvious intention of throwing him out the window.

"Wait! Don't!" Max limped in behind her and grabbed her arms before she could push him out. "Something's different with this one."

"…different?" She looked doubtful, however, she let him go and the Maniac dropped to the floor. Max knelt beside him.

"He's not all crazy like the others."

"…so…"

"So? Why not? Every other Maniac in the place lost their mind all of a sudden but he just stayed here. And before all the others slept together for warmth but he stayed in here, under an open window." Small snowflakes were now falling in through that window. Max could smell the storm in the air.

"…so?"

"So if he's lucid enough he could lead the police right here. He could help get them off my ass." Things were looking up.

"I have no time…" She was holding something in her hand. "… I have to go but…" She looked at him and gave him a half smile.

"… I will come back with you…" she said as if she were offering him a gift.

"Come back? Here?"

"…yes…"

Why would he come back here? "Why would I come back?"

Her face changed to irritation. "To kill it."

"Kill what? That thing in the elevator?"

She just looked at him.

"ARE YOU OUT OF YOUR FUCKIN' MIND?" His scream at her was powered by his fear of what he had seen at the bottom of that shaft. He looked back over his shoulder down the hall as though the thing might have climbed past the fallen terrace.

"You must kill it!" she said.

"Did you see what I saw? Did you see how big that thing was?"

"It will continue…"

"Fuck that! The cops can handle it." No way was he coming back.

"It is what YOU are supposed to do!"

"It's what Animal Control is supposed to do! I don't know how y'all do it in the Downhills but the rest of the city calls the cops for shit like this!"

"…you're afraid…"

"Hell yeah! Prya what makes you think I can kill something like… What the hell am I even arguing for? I'm taking this guy to the police!" He reached down and grabbed the Maniac roughly by the collar of his black denim jacket and hauled him to his feet.

"You," he said to him. "… are going to bring the police back here." He glanced over his shoulder again and looked at Prya. She had her back to him. At first he thought she was actually upset but then he saw that she was examining something; a small glass vial. He leaned and looked over her shoulder and saw that there was a small amount of a milky white substance in the bottom of the vial.

"Hey! The venom! You came and got it?"

Prya turned and looked at him with a disgusted look on her face. "Of course."

"Well I thought you were supposed to be comatose."

"… why…"

"Hello? 'Cause you were bitten!"

Prya then smiled at him and shook her head. "…told you…"

"What? Told me what?"

"…witches lie…"

Motherfu… "What the hell?" Son of a… "Then why did she… what are… What?!? Is that venom valuable or something?" His hands were in fists, ripping the Maniac's jacket. He wanted to punch something so bad. Prya's smile faded and there seemed to be actual concern on her face.

"I needed it, Max."

"What for?"

"…a cure…"

"But you haven't been bit!" He was yelling right at her. To her credit she did not bristle or yell back. Her eyes still held that look of concern though. "Wait…" He had a sudden, somber thought. "Who was bit?"

She stepped back to the window and looked down to the field below. She answered him but did not turn back around.

"…Lotarre…" she said.

"I'll kill her."

"Max, there is little time." Now she turned back to him "I think the Sick Ones are moving against your house tonight."

"Uh… the 'Sick Ones' just got dropped down about three stories and their crib is on fire. I don't think they'll be going anywhere tonight. Especially after our friend here tells Cowboy Rogan where to…"

"…always talking… they've already left! Gone before you came. There are so many…"

"Ok! But they don't know where I live?" he hoped.

"Idiot. They could not track you because your guardian…"

"Guardian?"

She shook her head at his interruption. "…your guardian protects your apartment. No one who means you harm can find you there. I meant your 'House'."

She shook her head again at his puzzled look. What was she talking about? Guardian? House? He had heard her say that before… but when?

Prya sucked her teeth. "…the Castle…"

SSSSSSSS!

Haley Museum was bathed in a snow filled aura of red and blue pulsing lights. Not even two months into the New Year and there had already been more incidents at the Museum than in the previous hundred years. 1st district police were not going to let this madness continue as was evident by the sea of cars flashing red and blue lights sitting in the parking lot. Swat teams (teams; that's plural!) were running across the causeway and around the moat towards the reservoir. There were police vehicles of a type that Max had never before seen. Something had gone down here, something bad.

He watched all this from the temporary safety of the Administration building's rooftop. Whatever had taken place at the Museum it had apparently happened on the other side, the west side towards the reservoir. That was where the majorities of the cops were or were running toward and there were plenty. He wondered at that. The 1st District was small and did not call for this much man power. Someone must have called in the 5th and 35th districts to help.

An ambulance tore off with lights and sirens blaring. Even at this distance Max could smell the blood in the air. He was too late.

He would have been here if it were not for Landry's lies. He could have stopped them if it were not for Prya's games. The only ones who would have been hurt would have been Maniacs if…

Who was in the ambulance? It could have been one of the guards. Or it could have been any one of the students or staff. It could have been Fatima. Hell it could have been…

Unable to wait any longer Max stepped off the edge of the roof and dropped the four stories to the ground. He landed on an icy walkway behind a row of neatly trimmed snowcapped bushes, stumbled and then fell. It had been a long run from West Oaks on a bad leg. After the battle with the Maniacs Max was running on empty. He tried not to think about what would happen if he had gotten to the Museum in time to catch them.

There were two police cars parked on this side of the castle in between the Administration building and the Museum Dock. They were parked close together and facing in opposite directions so that the two drivers could talk. Neither had seen Max's landing but he did not think he could slip past them to the Dock. The long way it would have to be.

Taking the route all the way around the Admin building, past the old stables and finally along the edge of Cobbs River took him nearly ten minutes. The forced delay was almost too much. If the river had been flowing in the opposite direction he would have been tempted to take another dip just to get back to the Museum faster. The police were still there but he could have cut past them on the other side, in the shadow of the Dock. Either that or he could jump into the river and try to swim against the current to get to the Dock itself.

That was not going to happen. This was taking long enough as it was. Soon though, the Dock came into sight.

As did several more police officers.

They were shining bright lights all the way along the river's edge. Their voices were drowned out by the rushing water but he could see them gesturing wildly. The Maniacs had escaped again via the Dock, the river.

Good. No way could they have survived that.

But why were the police were still here and why were they still gesturing wildly? He had to know what had happened. He could not just walk up and ask; he was still wearing his black sweats. Too many cops had seen him wearing them the night of the break in for him to risk being recognized. How could he…

Damn! Prya was right. He was an idiot. He pulled his cell out of his sweats and turned it on. Almost immediately the voice message icon flashed and the phone vibrated.

Steve… Steve… then Fatima called him five times. He skipped to the last message and played it.

Nothing. She must have just hung up. Cursing Max went back to her first message and played that one.

"This is Fatima," she was upset. It sounded like she was crying. "Max please call the Museum as soon as you get this message if you're alright. They came again… a lot of people are hurt and some are missing… you were here earlier but… if you're home just lets us know… you were supposed… please call."

The message ended. More ambulance sirens wailed on the other side of the Museum. A lot of people?

The second message: "Max? We see you logged out of the Museum. So we know you weren't here. But still call me… us… back please. Something's happened."

The third message: "Max? You have to… Max they came back and they got… they took… Dr. King is gone! The police think…"

Fatima's fourth and fifth messages were blank.

"King?" they took Dr. King?

Did they kill him?

He looked back up at the police on the dock. The Maniacs had tried to escape that way before but it really made no sense. No one could swim Cobbs River; he had gotten lucky and the Snake Maniac had died trying.

Unless Landry had lied about that too.

Or if the Maniacs had another plan…

Max sniffed the air. Could they have run along the river bank? No. There was no way to get off the Docks on this side without jumping in the river.

Deep inhale. Nothing. The Maniacs had not come past here. Then why were the cops standing on the Docks?

Another deep inhale brought in more scents. The wind had shifted. Max could smell the fleeting scents of the police on the dock, the smell of blood, then the sick scent of Maniacs…

… And finally the cedar-like scent of his Mentor.

So he risked getting closer. He crawled on his stomach as he came around the far side of the Admin building. Slowly, because he could not afford for someone to catch his movement out of the corner of their eye, he crawled across frozen concrete, grass, and then parking lot tar. The twin police cars sat farther away now but he still had to be careful. The ground was turning white as the snow fell harder. After far too long he came against the base of the Docks.

The scent of blood was even heavier in the air here. He wondered if it belonged to Maniac or Cop, security or student.

"Had it tied right up to the cross gate, submerged below the water to hide it. Probably was there since the night of the first break-in." Max did not recognize the man's voice; although he spoke with some measure authority. He crept closer trying to hear what the man was saying.

The scent of Jasmine floated down.

"Camera's not angled right. Tapes show them bringing King down here but not what they did once they got to the water." the Man said.

"They didn't kill him." Sheriff Lynne's voice was sharp and hard.

"You don't know that." he argued.

"They would have done it in the Museum." she said. Someone kicked a piece of wood off of the dock. It clattered down right next to Max.

"They're crazy, Lynne. They been doing things without reason this whole time."

"No. They may be fanatical, but they have moved with a purpose. They wanted King for a reason. He's still alive. We just don't know where." She cursed and another piece of wood came down.

"Why would they kidnap him? You said there was no evidence that he was smuggling anything in."

"This case has had me running all over the city chasing drug dealers. Come to find out it's some kind of religious thing. They think King is hiding some kind of holy artifact." she said. Max felt the Stone pressing against his chest.

"Shit! This is way out of hand, Lynne. You know the Mayor's on his way here? And we got this storm rolling in fast. It'll shut the city down and immobilize us." The man kicked another piece of broken wood off of the dock.

"How long you figure King's got?" he asked.

"From what we've been able to get out of the couple of ones who were lucid enough to say a few words… I think they've been killing people… not like the incidents here but more like… sacrificing them. When King can't produce what they want… We've got to find them now."

Max shuddered. There had been bones in the bottom of that elevator shaft where they had been holding Prya, a lot of bones. The Maniacs had taken King.

"Oh my God." Heedless of the police Max broke into a full out run across the parking lot.

"Hey! We got one!" someone shouted from his right.

"By the Docks! By the Docks!" from his left.

"Shit! That fucker is movin'!"

The police in the two squad cars got the alert before Max reached them. They were quick and smart, their doors were close yet not so close that they could not both open their doors and get out. He saw the smooth gleam of the black metal in their hands. There was blood in the air and Max was not the only one who could smell it.

"GRRR!" He launched himself into the air but had forgotten about his bad leg. Instead of clearing the police cars by ten yards Max came down on the hood of the closest one.

"Freeze!"

"Jeez did you see that?"

Max tumbled over the side of the car and onto his back. The police were right on top of him and one bold cop tackled him as he tried to get up.

"Stay down!" he yelled. The other cop moved to cover him while the first pulled Max's hands behind his back.

"Grrrr!"

"Is this nut growling?"

"I don't care if he…" Strong as he was he did not need leverage to lift the officer off of him. Max tossed him with one hand into his partner.

"Hold it!" Sheriff Lynne's voice was a lot closer than it should have been. The police that had been at the dock must have jumped off the damn thing to be here so quick. It did not matter. Max's leg was not so bad that they would be able to catch him. Leaving their shouts and searching lights behind him he took off again.

West Oaks. He had to get back there before the Maniacs did…
…before they dumped King down that elevator shaft.

Three more steps… two… one and Max collapsed. Winded as he was his outstretched arms could not catch him. The cold snow covered ground rushed up and smashed into his face. For a few moments all went dark.

Just breathing was hard but he needed the air so badly. The air grated in and out of a throat gone dry. The breaths were so ragged that his head shook with every gasp. Everything was shaking; his arms, his legs, his fingers… his fluttering eyelashes. He had never run so hard or for so long in his life. What good had it done? The ground pulled at him like a magnet. His legs no longer answered his commands.

His eyes popped open again. How long had he been out?

Too long, he realized, because he was not shaking as much. Fire shot through his chest when he pushed himself off of the ground and out of a few inches of snow. His ears began to buzz just from the effort. His legs felt like they were made of rubber and he could only stand for a moment.

He had not been out long enough.

But they had King somewhere far ahead of him; that was, if they had not reached their home base yet. How far ahead? How far had he gotten?

"Ung!" he collapsed again. It did not matter. He could not fight in this condition anyway. King was dead. Max should have told him…

"Max?"

The muscles in his neck would not let him lift his head, but he did not need to see Landry in order to recognize her voice.

"Max? Oh, my Lord." Booted feet stomped through snow toward him and pretty soon he was looking up at Landry and Alana. "You have to get up, Max. The police are running all over West Oaks."

The two women each grabbed an arm and pulled him to a sitting position. Max tried to say something but his throat was useless. A coughing fit racked his body and he nearly passed out again.

"Max stop. Just breathe." Landry was reaching in that damn leather case again. When her hand came out she was holding something in the palm of her hand; leaves. She place them under is nose. "Here."

His shaking started to slow and the buzzing in his ears stopped.

"Wha?"

"Just breathe. Take a second."

It felt like his body had opened up a third lung. Oxygen flooded his lungs and ran through his veins to his legs. Standing was still shaky but manageable.

"Max wait! You're not…"

"No… time…" his throat was still raw. "King… they got… King."

"The Sick Ones? Why?"

"They want… Stone. Think… he has it." Standing upright was too hard, Max was doubled over; hands on knees. God, he wanted to lie back down.

"They'll kill him Max. When he doesn't…"

"Ya… (COUGH)… think?"

"What are you going to do?"

"Should've told the police… should've have told King… what was going on… where the Maniacs are… too late now…" The regret that washed over him in waves was far worse than the pain his body was in. And it was likely to be far more permanent.

"Why?" she was digging in that case again.

"Tried to run…" He grimaced. King did not even know why he was going to die.

"But you could still reach him!" she pulled out a liquor flask.

"Not in time… in no shape to fight…" Max dropped his head in fatigue. Snow fell from the top of his skull cap. Landry and Alana had a thick coating of it over their shoulders.

"The hell you aren't. Here." She was jamming something into the flask. Then she shook it up quickly.

"Wha's tha'?"

"Drink." She pulled the scarf down from around his nose and mouth then placed the flask to his lips.

"You put too much in!" Alana warned. Max was sure he had never heard her speak before.

"Shh girl!" Landry hushed her and tilted the flask up.

The warm liquid poured into his mouth. There were bits of something chunky floating in it but it was sweet and Max's mouth seemed to have a mind of its own as it swallowed it and sucked more in.

"Too much!" Alana shouted and Landry pulled the flask away.

There was a rising tide of energy bubbling inside of him. It radiated out from his chest, across his shoulders and surged down his legs. Hungrily he grabbed the flask from Landry and sucked it dry.

"No!" Landry pulled the empty flask back. "Max you took too much!"

Maybe, but his legs felt solid under him again and his hands no longer shook. "What was that?" he asked not sure if he wanted to know.

"It's an herbal energy brew. It's filled with caffeine." she explained.

"That'll do." Max said.

"How do you feel?" Landry was looking him up and down.

"Like I was lied to." He locked eyes with her and bared his teeth.

Landry took a few steps back. "I… Max she really did…"

"Save it! I'll deal with you later." That caffeine was really kicking in now. He looked around. They were in an alley filled with a thick blanket of snow. "Where are we?"

"Uh… West Oaks, a few blocks from my office…"

"How did you find me?"

"Alana found you." she said simply. Max glanced at Alana who was watching him with fear filled eyes. "She…"

He exploded out of the alley in a spray of snow. There was no way for him to know how long this caffeine high was going to last, not that he believed it was caffeine, so there was no time to waste. If it could just last long enough for him to get to King…

The memory of how he had gotten to the warehouse before had somehow become lost in his caffeine charged mind. It had to be somewhere east of where he was so he kept on in that direction. Landry's brew made him hyper alert and several times he saw some shadow in a dark corner he passed he thought it might be a Maniac lying in ambush. The streets began to twist and turn as badly as they had in the Downhills. Just when he nearly decided to take to the roof tops the alley opened up onto the street that bordered the park.

It was quiet and there were no storefronts and no warehouse. A moment for a bit of panic and then a moment for rage passed. Maybe… he was too far north?

So he sprinted to the south. His sneakers were terrible on the remains of the ice that lay beneath the fresh snow. Most of the city had seen it melt already but this street here was not so well traveled. The city could skimp on the cost of salting the roads in town if they left the abandoned sections to fend for themselves.

The storefronts came into sight and beyond that, the Maniacs warehouse. King's scent cut across his path just at the moment that Max saw the warehouse. It was sitting there just as quiet as it had been when he had gone there earlier that night. Apparently the fire did not get out of control as he thought it might.

No fire trucks.

There also were no police, none at all. Actually Max had seriously doubted that the one lucid Maniac who he had managed to find and pull out of the building had the presence of mind to make his way to the police station.

Even though he promised.

So no one knew about the building except him, Prya and now

King of course.

The storefronts fell behind him and he entered the overgrown fields. The Maniacs still had guards posted outside, all easy to see against the white snow topped brush. It was very organized of them to not allow a little fire or minor structural demolition to disrupt their routine.

So Max did not slow down. The brush and scrub had been easy to creep through earlier but now, with the snow and while running, he had to keep his knees pumping high and hard. Branches whipped at him, threw snow in his eyes and grabbed at him with tiny little twig hands.

Still he picked up the speed. The witch had drugged him alright.

"He's here!" one Maniac shouted warning. Max had been running so hard that he had not seen this one before he sprang up from his ambush site. The Maniac was talking, however, and that meant a mouth full of regular teeth.

Regular teeth that flew out of his mouth like nasty bits of broken candy cane as Max punched him without halting his charge on their hideout.

The rest of the Maniacs were just as undaunted as before. They converged on him with speed and aggressiveness; swinging pipes, wooden boards, and whatever else they had found since losing their weapons cache in the terrace collapse.

Dr. King's scent got stronger as he neared the building and that seemed to help Max find even more energy, or maybe just made him more reckless.

Some of the Maniacs were landing blows. Amped up as he was, Max was aware of the coming strikes; he simply did not worry enough to avoid them all. Most of them were glancing hits that just bounced off of his incredibly hard muscle. A few near misses tore at his sweats and some even drew blood. Never the less nothing hit him that slowed him or made him stagger at all. Meanwhile the Maniacs were dropping into the snow in groups of two and three.

Finally he reached the edge of the overgrowth right next to the building. The Maniac between him and the snow covered clearing bravely, or insanely, stood his ground. Max barreled into him in mid-leap and drove the man into the side of the derelict building. With his body, Max pinned the Maniac to the wall, then he stepped back and let him slip to ground where he lay still.

Booted footsteps sounded from both inside the building and around the sides where he could not see. For the moment though, he stood alone with no one else insight.

The wind blew around the house from a different direction than it traveled across the field. Dr. King's scent seemed to come from the bushes Max had just run through. Not likely. It was being swept around the building and coming back on the other side. So that meant the Doctor must have been taken to the back of the building, the part that had been heavily guarded before.

The Maniac, he smashed against the wall, had been carrying a very thick piece of metal pipe. Max snatched the pipe up out of the snow and flipped it to check the balance. Then he was off.

Despite the now calf deep snow, it did not take long for him to get up to full speed and when he rounded the corner the first Maniac to come at him was sent flying off into the deep bushes at the park's edge. There had been eight Maniacs guarding this rear exit the last time he was here. Now there were only three and he had already blasted one. The last two, however, were Mega Snake Maniacs.

They hissed at him when he spun to face them. Prepared for their attack Max stayed on the balls of his feet, ready to dodge.

But it did not happen. The two Megas hissed at him and circled but neither charged him. This change of tactics confused him.

Were they waiting for back up? That was not very maniacal.

"HSSSS!" the one on the right said.

"HSSSS!" went the one on his left. Then Max saw the one tooth.

"Oh! I see. I already kicked your ass once tonight right?" Another deep hiss told Max that they might look like monsters but they still understood like men.

One-Tooth got his nerve up first and threw a quick swipe but was so far off that Max never even had to move. The razor sharp claws just whipped through the air.

A strong night wind whipped Amanda's scarf about his neck and almost casually he pulled it down from his face. Max smiled and flashed his teeth at the Maniacs.

Going low he charged in fast at the one on the right and brought the pipe harshly across both of the Maniac's knees. It dropped to the snow falling hard on its side, wailing in anger.

The second Mega rushed his back. Max somersaulted backwards avoiding the sneak attack and swinging the heavy pipe while upside down in mid-air. The pipe cracked its skull with a popping sound and the Mega dropped right beside the awkwardly bent legs of the first Maniac.

While One-Tooth spat and hissed, Max checked out what they were guarding. There was no entrance into the building itself. The big room that he had been in before must be on the other side of the building. The only doors here were old storm cellar doors so warm that the snow melted before it could accumulate on top of them. Dr. King's scent led right to them.

The sounds of excited breathing and hard soled boots shuffling on dusty concrete reverberated just beyond the thick metal doors. Wood creaked and Catgut was being stretched. So... they still had a couple of the Museum's crossbows left over.

The storm doors shook a little. They were waiting.

The doors were built to open outward. There was no way he could pull them open without exposing himself.

"HSSS!" One-Tooth was crawling through the snow toward him.

"Okay, okay." Max was still smiling. "If you insist."

He grabbed the Mega Snake Maniac by its collar and the back of its pants and lifted him off the ground. With a grunt he began to spin the Maniac around and around, lifting him higher with each rotation. One-Tooth complained with more than hissing; it actually wailed.

Its cry was joined by the distinct sounds of police sirens. As Max spun he could see the flashing lights moving slowly across the strip. They would never be able to get into the building in time to get to Dr. King before the Maniacs got him into that pit.

On the fourth rotation Max had gotten the Mega up over his head and had let go of its pants so he just spinning it by the collar of the thick leather jacket it was wearing. Another rotation then he dipped it low, then brought it up high and over his head…

… then slammed the Mega Snake Maniac down through the metal doors.

The doors folded inward, ruined and bent. A cloud of dust burst up and out of the cellar and was followed by the screams of Maniacs. The twang of the released bowstrings was followed by a few broken shafts popping up out of the hole after they bounced off of the concrete steps. Only then did Max drop down into the hole.

He landed on the unmoving Mega's chest and let his eyes adjust for a second. One smart Maniac had held off firing his crossbow because an arrow whizzed past his face. The rest rushed him.

They were only regular Maniacs and in the tight entrance to the cellar they could not surround him. His fist delivered bone snapping blows and soon he found it difficult to find his footing there were so many of them on the ground. In seconds the crazed screams changed to baleful moans and then only one Maniac was left standing.

The cellar widened out just beyond the steps. It was empty save for the fallen Maniacs. Dr. King's scent was close but still not in the room. The scent drew him towards another set of steps and a doorway guarded by the last Maniac.

The wild haired man was shaking, clutching a small hatchet defensively in front of him. Max looked him up and down pitifully. Obviously this Maniac was not as heavily influenced as the others.

There was shouting beyond the doorway. King's voice rang out among a few Maniacs.

Give the old man some credit; he was not screaming with fear, he was yelling in anger.

Max growled at the Maniac in the doorway. It was a low

sustained rumble and he walked it right up to the cowering man with his scarf pulled down and his teeth bared. The Maniac shook even harder, his breathing became erratic then his eyes rolled up into his head and he fell down across the steps.

Boots chewed through the snow outside. The police were right behind him now. Dozens of car engines roared, they had come in force. He would never be able to get past them. At the end of this night the best he could hope for was a jail cell. He tried to focus on getting to Dr. King. He could hear the scuffling and shouting that had to be just a little ways ahead.

The doorway led to a short hallway, there was an unconscious Maniac lying across the floor. Max smiled; he had often wondered what kind of damage the big guy could do.

Rounding the corner Max found himself in a familiar corridor. There were three sets of doors and the closest was the one where the elevator shaft was. A deep bellowing scream rang out and faded off.

King had been dropped down the shaft.

Max kicked the door open to find another battle. Three Snake Maniacs were all locked in combat with the group of four female Maniacs and the Snake Maniac Max recognized as Jean. They were trying to toss each other into the shaft.

"JEAN!" He had no idea why they were fighting each other but for an instant he thought there might be a chance to help his friend. But King was already at the bottom of the shaft with that thing.

Max was on top of them before they could react. One grappling with Jean dropped down into the shaft unconscious. The Maniac on the right was knocked into the far wall. He would have let the last one go but the Maniac was a little faster than the others. He jumped Max and locked his arms around his neck.

But Max was not trying to really fight any of them; he just wanted to get past him to the shaft. So because the Snake Maniac was only concerned with trying to kill Max he could not keep himself from being pulled over the edge.

King's screams echoed up and now they were screams of terror. Was it down there now? Was King seeing those teeth? For a second it made him hesitate at the edge of the shaft but the pang of fear was quickly dampened by the witches brew. One elbow to the Maniac's gut and Max was able to shift his weight. Both he and the Snake Maniac toppled over the edge.

"Wuff!" The dry bones at the bottom of the shaft snapped and crunched when they hit the bottom. The Maniac managed to land on top of Max and knocked the wind out of him. Disoriented he flailed about with the Snake Maniac clinging to his neck. Panic sunk in and he thrashed trying to look about for the huge tail or the gaping maw of teeth that he had seen swallowing that other Maniac.

Where was it?

He needed air and the Snake Maniac was trying to crush his larynx. So Max grabbed the Maniac by the throat as well and pushed.

The Snake Maniac, whose arms were shorter, could not maintain his arm hold and he fell back. They both rolled and tried getting to their feet but the pile of scattered bones made the footing hard. The Maniac fell again. Max managed to climb to one knee.

Where was it?

The elevator shaft bottomed out onto some kind of service tunnel. The only light came from the shaft above but it provided enough for Max to see. The tunnel went off in two directions both ending in darkness; however, the sound of running footsteps was coming from his left.

"Dr. King!" He called down the tunnel but it came out garbled. His mouth felt funny, the canines felt so large now that they were wearing on the inside of his mouth. He placed his hand to his face. Something was wrong with his jaw line and...

... his arms were covered in fine brown hair.

A nasty bitter scent flowed at him from down the tunnel. It was like really pungent urine mixed with stale sweat. The smell was so strong it made Max spit. Across the tunnel floor the Snake Maniac whipped his head in the same direction. His tongue flicked in and out and his eyes grew wide. Then without giving Max another look, he took off down the tunnel.

Stalled by the bones for a few moments Max kicked and scrambled after him. The entire length of the tunnel was covered in human remains and he found it hard to run. The Snake Maniac did not seem to have this trouble and pulled away. As the tunnel got darker Max had to follow the sounds of his footsteps, King's cedar scent and the horrible pee smell.

The tunnel turned and climbed upwards steeply. The end was hidden by the rise in the tunnel floor but Max could now hear the Snake Maniac and King. They were both grunting as if they were fighting. He pushed himself even harder pumping his legs to the point where he was almost bouncing up the tunnel.

As he hopped over the crest he saw the Snake Maniac standing over his mentor. Dr. King was a strong man yet his arms pushed feebly at the Maniac who had his clawed hands around the man's throat. Screaming, Max leapt into him and the two fell against and, in a burst of dusty red brick and wood, thru the wall behind him.

The storm had broken, sky had cleared and stars shone down brightly filling the small alley with blue light. The police sirens were distant.

He and the Snake Maniac rolled until Max came up on top.

"Hssss!" and POW! Max drove his fist into the Maniacs face

three straight times before he was thrown off. But each successive punch landed with less force than the preceding one. They landed dead center between the Maniacs eyes and should have been enough to keep him down. Instead the Snake Maniac forced his leg in between their grappling bodies and kicked Max into the far wall.

The back of Max's head smacked loudly against the bricked wall and he slumped into the snow. Suddenly it felt so good to be off his feet.

The sugar high was wearing off.

Max watched the Maniac climb to his feet. His serpent's eyes flashed in the dull blue starlight telegraphing a mixture of fear and excitement. It had to be wondering why he was just lying there. Was he hurt? Had the Maniac won? It took a cautious step forward.

Then it jumped at the sudden collapse of a bit of the wall they had just come through. Its head spun around,

(UGH!), without the need to turn its shoulders at all,

… to see a disheveled Dr. King stepping through the ruble. The huge man stumbled a bit but made it past the hole and out into the alley. He had lost his glasses, his clothing was torn and his proud main of hair was filled with dirt. King eyed the Maniac and keeping his back against the unbroken part of that wall, carefully began to slide away.

"HSSS!" The Snake Maniac began to turn the rest of his body toward King. Max took a deep breath.

"GRRR!" the growl was mostly for the effort it took just to get to his feet. When he stood his head swam.

"Come on Max" he said to himself. "One more to go."

The Snake Maniac's head turned back and forth between Max and Dr. King, who was still moving away with his back against the wall. The big man edged on toward the end of the alley. If the Maniac decided to go after Dr. King, Max was not sure he would be able to catch him in time. The boost Landry had given him was wearing off nearly as fast as it had charged him up. He was weak and dizzy and did not to want to have to run.

So he stepped forward and the Maniac hissed at him with rage. Max made sure to circle him, trying to block his path to Dr. King.

More hissing and…

…then there were other noises from the tunnel opening.

They were voices. The police had followed them down the shaft and now were coming up the tunnel. Max could see the wavering light from their flashlights as they got closer. Did he smell a hint of jasmine? It was almost over… thank God.

The air was then filled with a repugnant stench, like rotten eggs and gasoline. The Snake Maniac hissed and began to back away from Max and the tunnel opening with unmistakable fear in its eyes. Its tongue whipped out of its mouth in a fury, tasting the air that was pouring out of the hole in the wall.

The stench made Max gag a bit. He thought he might actually throw up it was so bad. Even the police could be heard coughing far back in the service tunnel. There was the tiniest flash of green light and he looked into the dark recess of the hole in the wall. There were two sinister narrow eyes watching him.

"Christ."

One huge, pale white claw came out of the dark and rested on the cracked wood of the hole. Then two more knobby pale digits, making three in all, came to rest on the ruined wall. The wood cracked and gave way as the paw pushed down on it giving it too much weight. The scale armored arm followed it, almost four feet in length Max saw, and its massive shoulder leaned out into the light.

His heart leapt when something moved up behind him. It was the wall on the other side of the alley. Max had back pedaled without knowing he was even moving. He gripped the red brick face behind him with fear.

Another paw entered the light and joined the first. Its fingers touched down with a controlled power; with an almost casual ease. Even as the lights behind it grew, it still moved fluidly and without hurry. It dipped its massive head into the light.

Max's claws tore into the wall behind him as he saw the head, which was as big as his own body, slide out and taste the air. It was similar to an alligator's head, he thought, though maybe a little more round, like a... a...

It looked directly at him. Terrible, evil, unyielding... beautiful jade eyes fixed onto his. It... she... flicked a long thin, flat forked tongue out, tasting the air. Max could not move. He could not breathe. He could not look away from those eyes.

There were shouts in the tunnel behind the beast. For one precious second those eyes released him and turned to spy Dr. King, who could not see the beast from where he was; his eyes were still riveted on the Snake Maniac as he continued to inch away down the wall.

The colossal head turned back and looked into the tunnel. The dithering light from the police's lanterns made its emerald eyes glow. Then with another freezing look at Max, the demon slid out of the hole and turned. Its claws dug into the wood and brick wall and it pulled its mass up. The long sickly white body moved much like a lizards with its legs splayed wide against the wall. Each paw easily grabbed hold of the building and soon the thing had pulled itself completely out of the hole, seven foot ridged tail and all.

The lithe body snaked its way up to the roof and the monster peeked over. The long gone clouds must have uncovered the moon as well because the monster's face was bathed in the pale light making it

298

Howard Night

luminescent. It peered about, obviously taking in the scene back at the warehouse with all the police.

Max still had not moved nor had he taken his eyes off of it. His fingers squeezed the brick on the wall behind him so hard that bits of it chipped off. The Snake Maniac moved into his peripheral vision but he dare not look away from the demon now clinging to the wall maybe two stories up. It was fast, he knew, and when it struck there would be no time to react. He would have to see it preparing to strike… and then move before it did. Somehow he knew this… there would be… a sign?

"HSSSS!" Narrow serpent eyes and venom dripping fangs blocked his view of the Demon. The Snake Maniac bobbed his head ready to strike.

"POLICE! Don't move!" the command was sharp enough that the Snake Maniac actually turned to look. Bright beams pierced the darkness and lit up the glossy scaling skin of the Maniac. The Police had made it through the tunnel and were standing part way out of the hole in the wall. Leading the way was Sheriff Lynne. Her gun was leveled on the Snake Maniac though it could have been pointed at Max for all he could tell. When the Maniac moved the Demon came back into sight and once again Max locked his eyes on the thing.

It was looking down now, as the police made their way over the rubble at the hole in the wall. The jade eyes and fang lined mouth betrayed no emotion, anger nor fear. There was a glint… and then a flash of green that moved along the creature's body like a ripple on a pond. The sickly albino skin changed color as the ripple of green ran over it. It changed, from pale white, to green with an intricate pattern that showed inside the ripple, to the dark reds and browns that matched the color of the old wood and brick wall to which it clung. In the pale starlight the demon, now camouflaged, almost disappeared. Max would not be able to see it at all save for his night vision, the fact that he had watched it as it changed and that knew where to look. The huge head dipped back below the roof's edge and slowly the serpent turned and began to make its way back down the wall, quietly, eyeing the police officers below.

"HSSSS!" the Snake Maniac had turned to face the police completely, unafraid of the guns pointed at it. Lynne motioned with her head and the police spread out behind her.

"Lay down on the ground!" she ordered.

"That don't look like no fucking mask." One of the uniformed officers said.

"I said; LAY DOWN!" Lynne shouted but the Maniac simply hissed again. Behind and above them the invisible demon stopped crawling down. It rolled its hips smoothly and its tail whipped back and forth. It bobbed its head from side to side with its eyes on the formation of cops. Then it raised its head, keeping those beautiful jade eyes on them by looking down its snout. Finally it dipped its head low. It was judging the distance and Max knew suddenly; this was it.

It happened faster than his eye could register. The demon dropped off of the wall and landed in the snow behind the police and then suddenly all four of them were in the air. The first cop, the one closest to the demon was ripped in half. The second lost and arm and a good portion on his midsection. The third was bent backwards at a horrible angle. He was slammed into Lynne, knocking her into the air as well. All that damage from just one swipe of the demons ridged tail.

Before they hit the ground Max had turned and leapt up the wall. The brick face was easy to climb with his claws. He was nearly to the top when he heard the gun shots.

Two loud bangs rang out. Max turned and looked down to see the hole in the wall light up from a muzzle's flash. One cop had either stayed in the tunnel or had just arrived in time to see his fellow officers' fall.

Again Max saw the demon bob, raise, and then dip its head, faster this time. Then it struck, like a cobra, its head shot into the hole in the wall and drew back just as quickly. No more sound came from whoever had been in the building. After a second the demon turned away from the hole and looked at its handiwork across the floor of the alley. It was so fast…

"Ung…" the Sheriff rolled over and looked up. Max could see that she was hurt, probably broke a few ribs by the way she was laying. She looked up and her face was filled with terror. The Demon stepped smoothly through the snow on the alley floor towards her its jade eyes shining with its obvious intent. Its mouth opened slowly, almost as if it was yawning, exposing a horde of unfolding wicked teeth.

One shaking hand slid out from under Lynne. It still held her side arm and she tried to raise it.

The Serpent's head bobbed, raised and dipped.

Max crashed into the demon's neck right behind its cranium. Clawed hands dug into the sides of its head just behind its jaw line. He had misjudged his attack. He had been going for the creatures head and its eyes.

The demon's mouth smashed into the ground just a foot in front of Sheriff Lynne, slamming it shut. Still its lunge pushed it forward, digging through the snow, and grinding it against the ground until the snout batted her back a few yards.

The demon was up quickly and began whipping its head back and forth. Max clung on for his life squeezing the scales as tightly as he could. The monster howled its frustration. It was a loud, rage filled bellow that sparked as much fear in Max as just seeing the creature for the first time had. It made him grip all the tighter.

Then the creature switched its whipping motion to a hard and violent shaking, like a dog shaking off water after a bath. The hard group of scales Max had been holding onto broke off beneath one hand and then, without the opposing force for leverage, his other hand lost its grip. He was bucked off into the wall just above the hole, dropped hard onto his back atop the rubble and then rolled into the alley.

His cheek came to rest in the snow on the ground and several yards across the alley he saw Sheriff Lynne lying on her stomach and staring at him in turn. She was in pain, he could tell, and was frightened. He could smell her sweet jasmine-like aroma, now tinged with an acrid odor; fear. But she was still holding her gun, still trying to raise it up. She was a fighter, and despite the fear boiling out of her pores she still had the courage act, to keep fighting. It shamed him. Max had been frozen against the wall and he had seen the thing before while this was the first time for her.

Those jade eyes glowed on the outside of his peripheral vision. Staring down on him with clear intent, they bobbed…

Sheriff Lynne had gray eyes; he had not noticed that before. He took a deep breath.

… then raised. Max rolled onto his toes and as the demon dipped, he jumped and lashed out with one clawed hand. The huge serpent's scales, like most lizards, did not cover it completely, and there was clear soft flesh right in the crook of its neck. His claws found skin, then flesh, and then hot, foul blood.

It gushed forth in thick nasty blobs and chunks. Immediately the creature drew back and howled. Or tried to howl. Max's claws must have found its windpipe as well because the Demon gurgled instead. So shocking was the thick, foul smelling blood now covering him that Max did not see the demon begin to whip its head, snapping its jaws. Back and forth it went, as though it still felt Max's claws digging in its throat and was trying to dislodge them.

The whipping action brought the demons head back around. It nearly snagged Max, catching him by his sweatshirt and smacking him off of his feet again. The sweatshirt tore and he hit the ground. He looked up to see the creature ambling off toward the back of the alley leaving a trail of its blood behind. Then it disappeared into a branching alleyway that Max had not seen before. He could still hear it though and the sound of its claws scraping against the ground beneath the snow, the spatter of its stinking blood, the gurgle of its breath… the click of a gun being cocked.

Lynne was on one knee, her gun hand shaking but more or less pointed in his direction. She was breathing hard; those ribs must have been killing her.

"Don't… move…" she grunted the words.

"You gotta be…" Max started when she just pulled the trigger. Three shots and Max fell, trying feebly to dodge. He hit the ground and a second later there was a loud thump behind him. Lynne was still holding her gun up but it was pointed past him now. He looked over his shoulder to see the Snake Maniac lying on its back, two smoking holes in its chest.

"Christ!" he said. The Snake Maniac shook a bit and then went still. Breathing hard Max climbed to one knee while watching it carefully. "Thanks. I…" when he turned back to her she had her gun pointed this time unmistakably at him. Her eyes were hard to read as much pain, fear, and anger played across her face.

Then her eyes looked past him to the end of the alley, but the gun stayed on his chest. He could probably snatch it, he thought, right now before she looked back at him. His legs tensed, ached, and then spasms ran across them. Cramps ran up his legs and across his torso. He grunted at the sudden lancing pains and Lynne's eyes shot back to him. Max had to put one hand down to keep from falling over. Waves of fatigue and dizziness washed over him. The caffeine high was gone and he was crashing but there was other pain as well.

"Ung!" What was happening? He had not felt this kind of pain since… he looked down. The front of his sweatshirt had been ripped away.

His chest was bare.

The Stone was gone.

His eyes ran over the ground all around him but he did not see it. It was getting hard to breath.

He looked over his shoulder back down the alley replaying, in his mind, the sight of the creature dragging itself away. Had it grabbed the Stone? Had Max seen it hanging from monster's mouth with the bits of his sweatshirt?

"… have to make sure it's dead." Lynne said.

He turned back to see her lowering her gun. She was looking at him expectantly. "Hurry." she said.

Max stood and nearly doubled over. The pain was so intense, much worse than before. It did not make sense, he thought as he stumbled down the alley. It should not be worse; he was not as injured as before.

He found the branching alleyway easily and followed the trail of the Demons black blood, easy to see in the snow. It led him out of the alley and into the thick foliage that sat at the edge of the park. The underbrush was matted flat and the snow plowed deep in the creatures wake so Max found it easy to follow. The cramps kept him doubled over and he could barely raise his feet up and over the tangle of broken branches. The stink of the blood was making him gag as well. But he pushed on; he had to get the Stone back.

The park was surrounded by two sets of tall chain link fence. They had been placed there both to keep people out of the park and to keep the larger animals in; even though few large animals ever made the ascent to the city level. When he reached the first of the fences he found it bent and knocked down. As badly as the Demon had been hurt it still had the strength to get through the fence. Max made his way past, cutting his legs on the barbed wire that was now strewn across the ground.

A steady throb located right behind his eyes and halfway down his neck, pounded in time with his heartbeat. It was making him dizzy, and he had to fight to keep his eyes open... he had to fight to stumble in a straight path. The withdrawal was worse this time yet he could still move... barely. Why was it worse?

Could it have had something to do with how he lost the Stone?

He remembered that he had lost it the night he chased the cat across the city. His legs had cramped up then.

Once, voluntarily, he put it down and he nearly bled out.

Once Prya had taken it, and he had noticed practically no pain.

Then he gave it to the police and it had been sheer torture being without it.

But now the creature had taken it...

The second fence was bent far worse than the first and it was covered in a lot more blood. The Demon had taken longer to get across this one. It was dying...

...he hoped.

The smell of the park washed over him. Despite losing the Stone and the stench of the creature's blood, his nose could still pick up other scents. The further into the park he went, the more varied the scents became. Flowers, pine, animal scent markers... water, his nose caught them all. Even the ground here had a different smell, much more... earthy... rich...

The ground suddenly became uneven and started to slope downward. It was too much for Max and he stumbled, once, twice and then he dropped into the snow.

Weak, trembling arms and legs could not push him off the ground. Soon he found that it was all he could do just to keep pushing air in and out of his lungs. Even just lying there he felt as though he was losing strength. His vision began to go gray and there was buzzing in his ears.

He remembered he still had Amanda's scarf. He had gotten it all bloody.

"mmrow?" a spicy, musky scent followed the questioning whine. Max turned his pounding head to see the Big Gray cat sitting just a foot away. Its eyes studied him intently.

"Get... the Stone..." he managed to gut out. Still the cat just stared.

"Come... on... stupid... cat. Get the... damn Stone!" The

buzzing was getting louder. Maybe the cat could not do as he asked. Before, when Max had lost the Stone, it had not retrieved the Stone but had merely led him to it. Now Max could not follow it anywhere, let alone take the Stone back from a wounded Demon.

"Guardian… right? You don't… want me… to die… do you?" he asked as the gray washed over his eyes and the cat disappeared in the haze.

"Get… it… get it…" *GET IT!* and the buzzing grew louder until it was all he could hear. The cold night air settled onto his skin, numbing it, and the burning cuts and bruises became dull and no longer hurt him. His twitching arms and legs shuddered slowly to a stop. Oddly he felt relaxed.

Maybe someone would get Amanda's scarf back to her.

He hoped that they cleaned it first.

"mmmrow!"

His hand felt hot. Not a burning kind of a hot but rather it was a strong warmth that traveled up his arm. His hand seemed to close of its own accord and he felt the Stones familiar rough edges and the twisted string against his fingertips. The gray cloud hanging over his eyes was pierced with the bright points of the uncountable stars filling the night sky. Wind blew through the bushes and the naked tree branches clattered together. There was a musky scent in his nose and a hot, heavy body on his chest.

"Took you long enough." Max ran his hand over the cats back as he lay still for another few moments. "It's dead isn't it?" he asked. Big Gray gave a long, rolling, contented purr. That was enough of an answer for Max so he took another few seconds before he got up.

The cramps and headache were gone but he still suffered from the beating he had taken that night. So slowly and carefully he walked down the snowy slope. Sooner than he thought he would, he found the beast.

It was dead. It lay some forty feet from the edge of the gorge that marked the parks true boundary. It was easy to see, the pale white scales on its skin shone brightly under the thin spots of starlight that poked through the canopy of the trees here at the edge of the park. It was almost luminescent, especially against the black pool of its sick blood that spread out into the snow beneath it. Max walked around it until he could see that the once shiny, brilliant and beautiful eyes were now dull, clouded and unseeing. Part of its face was colored. The green pattern he had seen, the ripple of color that had flowed over its body had arrested right there on its snout. It had died trying to change its color one last time.

Jasmine cut through the beast's stink. Footsteps crunched through the snow and underbrush behind him.

She walked up gun drawn until she saw that Max stood next to the creature's mouth without fear. Still she only lowered her weapon a bit and stopped a good ten feet away from its tail.

"It's dead?" she asked. Her face was tired and drawn but still alert. She bore a few more cuts and scrapes and he wondered if they would leave permanent scars. It was a big change from the impression she had first given him of the pretty tall blond who had gotten her posting as a Sheriff because of privilege or her looks. If she had not earned the job before then she had certainly earned it now.

"Dead." Max answered. He turned and saw that she was squinting at him, trying to get a better look at him. His hands were no longer claw tipped nor could he feel the points of canines in his mouth. Still, under the thick canopy trees here at the park's edge he must have appeared to be little more than a silhouette set against shadows. Only the ugly white skin of the monster stood out.

Sheriff Lynne continued to stare at him anyway and Max figured that she must know who he was, because she had not shot him any of the number of times when she could have this night.

Finally she took a breath, lowered her gun and turned her attention to the remains of the Demon. Carefully she stepped around the creature to get a closer look. When she got to its head, she raised her gun again warily and squatted to see its eyes. Two pokes, one lightly on the snout, the other a solid jab right in the eye and she was satisfied it was dead.

"Those… maniacs worshipped this thing?" she asked. Max looked down at it again. It was hard to imagine how anyone could see this thing and want to call it "master". Then a thought occurred to him.

"It wasn't… always like this… I think." he said. The sheriff looked up at him as he continued, "I think it really only recently got this big. Before it would have been… smaller… maybe the size of a man…" He remembered the attack at the Museum and the pale clawed thing attached to Jeans back. Certainly the thing could not have gotten around the campus at this size not matter how well camouflaged it was. "Maybe even smaller."

"How did it get so big so fast?" she asked.

The bones at the bottom of the elevator shaft were not all that old. "It started eating." He said grimly.

"Eating wha… never mind, I saw the bones." She stood up and looked at Max once more. "That was you… during the break-in right?"

"I…" Max started unsure of where she was going. "I tried to stop them."

"Couldn't warn the guards?"

"I…" Wait… she was talking about the first break-in, on New Year's. "…no. I wasn't there on New Years."

"Then who killed the gang members?" The Sheriff asked. "Who decapitated those two in the office?"

Max looked down at the demon. It could not have been big enough then could it? "I don't know." Maybe…a mega?

Lynne stared at him for a long moment then huffed. Turning to the body of the demon she bent and examined the whole thing, snout to tip. Then she looked to the cliff where the gorge started.

"Think we can get it the edge?" she asked him.

"The edge?"

"Yea." she said. "The Park'll take care of the body." And she began trying to grab hold of one of the creature's paws.

"You want to get rid of it? Isn't it evidence?" he asked her. "Proof of what happened at the Museum on New Years?"

"Plenty of proof is left back in that alley and in that warehouse." She said now trying to push it the body by its shoulder but not getting anywhere with the massive reptile carcass. "This thing… goes to the Park. Not my choice but probably the right decision."

Max walked around and grabbed the thing by the other paw and pulled. Now, with his strength, it moved down the slope and soon it sat at the cliff's edge. Far behind them police lights shone brightly. Lynne's radio squawked and complained with urgent voices.

"And the murders?" Max asked with his foot resting on the backside of the demon ready to push it over the side.

"Solved." Lynne said and looked Max squarely in the eye. "I put two right in the killer's chest."

"They'll never buy that. Those cops back in that alley…"

"It'll be handled. All part of the… the job." she said with an odd expression. Again Max thought of how she had looked the first night he had seen her, in that party dress, looking upset because she had to work instead of party with the cities elite. Then he thought of her on the Museum dock, with fear in her eyes as she was seeing some of the things this city had kept hidden from those who were not… "players". He recalled her interrogating him with that asshole Rogan, as she was trying to get a handle on what was going on. Now here she was this night, dirty, bruised and bloody, having just saved his life, offering to keep him out of jail.

"This is new to you too…" Max guessed.

The Sheriff looked up at him, as if noticing something for the first time.

\   "Yea", she said understandingly. "This is new to me…too." Then she looked back over her shoulder. "They'll be here soon. That blood was easy to follow."

"Just a second." There was one more thing he had to take care of. Max gritted his teeth and took a breath. Then with a little effort, he popped his claws out one last time. A few disgustingly messy seconds later he had the demon's guts spilled out onto the ground. Lynne complained and hurried him but he kept digging and rooting.

The remains of the things last meal spread out before him. Bits of bone, too crushed for Max to tell if they had been human (though he was sure that they were), a couple of wrist watches, two cell phones, an MP3 player and several sets of keys were pulled out of the viscera and examined quickly. Still; no Stones. He was beginning to think that there was nothing to be found. The thing did not have any Stones hidden inside it and he was certain it would not have left them behind when it ran. It looked like Landry was right.

"What was that for?" Lynne asked, hand over her mouth.

"Had to be sure…" He flicked guts and thick, curdled blood off of his hands. "Now the park gets it… Whoa!"

Big Gray streaked into the mass of black blood clumps and piles of entrails until it disappeared into the hole Max had gutted into the monster's belly. Lynne raised her gun again.

"What was that?"

"Wait!" Max held a hand up. The Demon's gut shook and shifted as the cat rummaged through it. After a moment it emerged slick and slimy with foul smelling blood but absolutely beaming up at Max with its silver eyes. It dipped its head and spat. Max had not seen the tiny object in Big Gray's mouth for all the blood and gore. One paw batted at the little lump until it rolled up against Max's sneaker.

"What the hell?" Lynne muttered in a disgusted tone as she watched Max pick the lump up and wipe it off. It was flat and shaped roughly like a triangle. It would have been off white, he could tell, if it had not been covered in blood. One side was blank but when he turned it over in his hand he almost gasped aloud. Etched on the other side was a half broken elliptical circle in the center of which was a similar jagged running line. This was just a pair of mountains but it was divided across its length by a slightly crooked line.

He palmed the Stone and gave it a squeeze but felt nothing. No warmth, no tingles… nothing. It felt just like a rock.

"They're coming." Lynne reminded him. She was staring at him intently again but, mercifully, she did not ask about the Stone.

Despite being tired and beaten it took Max only two shoves and the white serpent body slid over the cliff and down into the Park below, so far that its pale skin faded from sight. Breathing hard he looked at the Sheriff who stared over the edge of the ridge for a time. Then as the lights and the rising police voices grew closer from one direction he took off in another. Behind him he heard her throw up and mutter to herself.

"This job definitely isn't worth the extra five a year."

From the poorly boarded up window of an abandoned tenement just across the street Max watched the police wrap of the incident. For some reason most of the Maniacs were no longer acting… well maniacal. Large groups of listless wild haired leather clad men were easily herded by the police and crowded into wagons. Many of the cops were laughing and joking about the whole thing until the news got back to them about what had happened in the back alley. Then the night turned ugly as several Maniacs were set upon by enraged officers. None of them seemed aware enough of what was going on to even realize they were being stomped. Max looked but he did not see Jean or any of the female Maniacs. Apparently the police had not found them yet.

The beat-down was finally stopped by the harsh barked orders of Sheriff Rogan, who had been yelling at Sheriff Lynne as she was being seen to by a paramedic. He was not happy at all about not being called in sooner.

There was a small contingent of Police officials in white shirts surrounding an ambulance at the intersection where Max had fought both the Maniacs and the Downhills pack. In the center of the group, standing taller than all of them was King.

His voice boomed across the huge intersection all the way to Max's hiding spot. The big man was angry and letting the police have it about their lack of an effective response to the break-ins. Somebody, probably several somebody's, were going to lose their jobs. One of the white shirts was the Deputy Commissioner who began screaming for the Sheriff. King boomed again; this time actually giving Sheriff Lynne credit for risking her life to protect him. Why had there only been a handful of police at the Museum? Where was the Mayor? The Museum was a shambles, he ranted. Research had been lost.

But Max's thoughts were growing darker. The question Lynne had posed had been to echoing in the back of his mind. The demon was too small to have harmed anyone during the New Year's massacre. The Maniacs, even the Megas, certainly had not killed their own so…

…something else decapitated the two in Kings office. Something else… in the Museum.

The police, Max saw, were beginning to search the area for wayward Maniacs. Their searchlights were coming closer and closer. His muscles ached as he stood and moved away from the window. It was time to go home.

EPILOGUE:
The APARTMENT

The bus was one of the older ones so the heat was not very good to begin with. Add the broken side window and the fact that the only standing room was in the rear and that made for some very unpleasant passengers. That is except for Max. He and Amanda had zipped their coats together and were huddling, their faces tucked tightly against each other. Her fresh flower scent was so relaxing, it drove away the headache that caffeine withdrawal had induced and eased the aches and pains that still wracked his body. He smiled and felt her cheeks push against his as she smiled back. A quick peek out and he saw Steve frowning at them as he rubbed his hands and wiggled his hips trying to stay warm.

The Museum was actually closed so he found himself with a few days off while they repaired the damage from the last Maniac break-in. Police tape cut off most of Rebel's Keep anyway so his department was shut down. The crime scene had been bloody. Several guards and Maniacs had been hospitalized and two of the ambulances arrived at M.R. Hospital with patients that had died in transit. There would be little mourning this time as the bodies had belonged to two Maniacs. Max thought about their families, his friend Jean's family in particular, and wondered whether they could be found and notified. There were only four other deaths reported by the news. Three police officers had been killed at the Maniac warehouse when they stumbled upon a wild grizzly that the gang had been keeping in their basement. The news surmised that the criminals must have lured one out of the park before winter started. The grizzly had been put down by a Park Ranger. Another gang member had attacked a Mountary Rock Sheriff with weapons that were later found to have been stolen from the Museum. He had been killed as the Sheriff defended herself and her fellow officers. Nothing was said of the underground basement corridor which had been lined wall to wall with human bones. In particular, Max Noticed, there was no mention of any female Maniacs having been taken into custody. Perhaps they and Jean as well, had escaped.

The bus shuttered to a halt at its next stop and Max and Amanda unzipped their coats.

"This it?" grumped Steve.

"Yup."

"Nice." Amanda smiled and looked around. Chestnut Ridge was a particularly affluent part of town. Mountairy Rock was not a dirty town at all yet this upscale neighborhood looked bright and shiny in comparison to most of the city. The sidewalks were clean, the streets were well maintained and the high rise apartmnts were all shiny glass. There were a few other passengers getting off the bus as well, most were carrying their own cleaning supplies. Housekeeping employees would be the only other people who had to ride a bus out here.

"I can smell the Lake." Amanda said. The cold breeze blew across them carrying the smell and the Mountairy Rock winter cold.

"The building's over there." Max sighted the Lions crest at the buildings archway. "Chestnut Arms."

"Good. I'm cold." Steve grumbled again. Max caught Amanda making a face at him and laughed. Steve's devilish charm seemed to bounce off of her when he had first introduced them but Amanda had been pleasant. He had to give her credit; most other women either loved Steve or hated him at first glance. She was falling into the latter category however had not yet said anything to verify this.

The lobby of the Chestnut Arms was plush and beautifully decorated. Stone tiled floors, marble fixtures and leather furnishings made the trio stop and stare until the woman at the front desk cleared her throat. The three laughed at themselves and Max walked over and gave the woman the apartment number.

"I can't believe this is where you're going to live." said Amanda.

"You sure we can afford this spot?" Steve asked.

"What do you mean 'we'?" Amanda's eyes narrowed.

The woman at the desk told them they could go up and the three of them hopped on the elevator. While Steve explained to Amanda the pact the two had made in high school about getting an apartment together Max checked his cell phone.

Landry had called again, for the seventh time and for the seventh time he ignored her. He was not ready to deal with her in a civilized manner. If he had not left the Museum that night then he would have been there when the Maniacs had attacked. King would never have been kidnapped and Fatima might not have been traumatized again. Max clenched his jaw every time he thought of what she must have been going through while Landry had him running through West Oaks on behalf of all people, Prya's boyfriend.

Prya. He had not caught so much as a hint of her scent in the air since he had rescued her. Or any other Downhill's scent for that matter. Probably for the best; he was not ready to deal with them in a civilized matter either.

The elevator finally opened and they made their way down a nice hall to the farthest apartment. Amanda made nice comments about the paintings hanging on the walls. Steve talked about the party that they were going to host as soon as "they" were moved in.

"This is it." Max said as they approached the door. He knocked.

"You don't have the key?" Steve snorted impatiently.

"He has to get his key from his Uncle." Amanda informed him while stressing the word "His" twice. Steve snickered.

"Hey let's not start arguing." he said. "I mean I like you, Amanda. Really. You can come over whenever you like."

Max snickered. Luckily before Amanda launched her own counter attack the door opened.

"Wow." Steve said. It was not the bright apartment he was talking about but rather the woman who had answered the door.

"Max? Come on in." she said. She was blond with braided hair, tall and leggy. Her shape was evident as she was wearing a spandex leotard that was soaked with sweat. "I was just working out."

They followed her into the apartment which was brightly lit by the early afternoon sun. The entire west wall was one huge picture window that spanned from one end of the apartment to the other offering them a spectacular view of the Lake. The woman walked ahead of them, excused herself and promptly left the room. Steve ran right over to the window and spread his arms wide.

"The world is mine!" he said smiling ear to ear. Max laughed.

"I told you the view was unbelievable." he said.

"Oh my God. This is a dream." Steve ran back and forth the length of the room trying to see how far the view extended. "I can see the Museum!"

"Your Uncle left it furnished too?" Amanda asked with a doubtful look on her face.

"Yo… we could have the party tonight!" Steve was almost dancing around the apartment, stopping only to flop down hard on the plush furniture. The apartment looked even more amazing than when his Uncle had lived here. There was a lot more decoration and accessories now. He noticed, the huge window wall was framed by thick amber curtains, the hard wood floor was covered with a very ornate area rug, and there were fresh flowers on the oak coffee table.

Nice as it all was he certainly was not going to be throwing a party anytime soon. Despite the Museum being on lock down King was going to expect progress on the Lost Tribe research. Max had not cracked a book in almost two weeks. Because no one knew that he had been at the Museum the night of the last break-in no one was going to give him any slack on getting things up and running… again.

The young blond walked back into the room carrying a folder and a small envelope. She gave Steve an irritated glance as he whooped and hollered at the window.

"Here you go." She handed Max the envelope and folder. Keys

jingled in the envelope when it hit his palm, a very heavy set of keys. He tore it open and poured them out into his hand. There had to be about forty keys on a thick little key ring. Old keys, Max saw that some had rust on them. He looked back to the young woman and she was watching him with a hint of impatience in her eyes.

"Um…" he started.

"They're for the pad locks on the windows. But you probably won't bother with them." She said. Amanda's head jerked in his peripheral vision.

"Pad locks?" That big picture window needed padlocks?

"Yea. Wait! That's right! You've haven't seen it yet have you? I think your Uncle put the directions in here." She took the folder back from Max and pulled out a stack of papers. Right on top was a map obviously printed from some online site. It had a yellow post-it stuck to it. Steve and Amanda both crowded in behind him to read it.

"See?" she said. Max took the papers and read the note.

'I've had the place cleaned up for you but it still needs a little work so don't worry about the rent for a couple of months. Just use the money for any work the place needs done.

-Uncle David'

Max read the letter a second and then a third time. Amanda and Steve reread it too, over his shoulder.

Amanda sucked in her lips…

…Steve cursed; "All that's bullshit."

The trio hopped off the bus in Brookhaven, on the south side of Pleasant River but nowhere near the falls. It looked to be a warehouse district, with older buildings that were now being gentrified and being rented out as studio apartments.

"Oh!" Amanda's face brightened. "A lot of artists live down here."

"Yea…" Steve answered. "… but the rich ones live on the other side. This part looks deserted."

Max looked around. The bus stop was in horrible condition, probably because no one ever got on or off here. Most people were in the process of leaving Brookhaven to go to the South Hills, or coming from the South Hills to get to any other part of Brookhaven or Ivy Hills. No one stopped in the tiny little section called Spruce place.

It was another stretch of practically abandoned buildings; evidence of a failed attempt to create a dock along the river back at the turn of the 20th century. Now there was a mattress place still open, and what looked like an old Roebucks building being rented out as studio apartments. Max checked the address again and saw that the building he sought was at the end of the row.

312

Howard Night

"This is fucked up." Steve said.

"It's not that bad." Amanda argued. Max actually looked to see if she was serious. She smiled at him pityingly. "It rent free!" She tried.

The trio found the place. It sat just past the Roebucks and across from another converted to rent office building. Max could smell the river water as they approached. It stood only three stories high, or it could have been only two floors with really high ceilings. The front door was big and metal and Max saw that it had been made to slide to the side rather than to swing open. Above the door were broken metal brackets that probably once held a sign that advertised whatever the former business had been. Along the ground level the windows were all encased in barred grills bearing huge, thick pad locks holding them in place. The upper windows were all barred as well.

"It's a garage." Steve said without any hint of playfulness in his eyes.

"A car couldn't fit in here." Amanda pointed to the big front door.

"This is the back entrance," he said. "… probably built before the rest of the block. Bet there's a huge car port on the other side."

"How do you know?" Max asked him.

Steve pointed to a small plate bolted onto the base of the door frame. It read: "Walt co. 1915."

"They were machinists. This must have been one of their first shops." he speculated.

"What's inside?" Amanda had stepped up to one of the grimy windows and tried to look inside. Max pulled out the set of keys and walked up to the big door.

"Let's find out." He tried to keep his voice light but he was so disappointed that it felt like there was a bottomless pit where his lungs used to be. Everything he said came out in a whisper.

The lock set into the door was huge and so Max logically tried the biggest key and indeed it worked. He expected the door to open with a lot of clanging and grating noise but someone must have recently worked on it. Not only was it quiet but it slid smoothly into the wall on a set of counterweights.

The door opened to reveal a long vestibule. The walls here had a pair of boarded up windows set much like the windows of a waiting counter in the lobby of a doctor's office. The walls were covered in chipped paint and the resultant chips littered the floor.

"Hunh." Steve muttered. "Bet all that paint has lead in it."

Max walked to the next door which was identical to the first except it looked newer. His uncle must have had it replaced recently because the floor was swept around the door area where the workers must have cleared some space for themselves.

"This isn't an apartment building." Max said.

"What is it then?" Amanda asked.

"I mean no one else lives here." he said.

"Who would want… sorry." Amanda sucked in her lips again.

"The whole place is yours?" Steve asked almost brightly.

The lock on the second door opened with the same key as the first. It slid open easily and opened onto a huge room. Steve might have been right. The first thing Max saw was that to the far left and across the room was a big set of old garage doors. The floor in front of the doors was lower too, covered with black grime and ran all the way past the vestibule to where the back wall was. The wall beyond that was set with empty shelves.

The room in front of them was bare for the most part. The far wall had a big picture window that was boarded up at ground level and above on the second story there were barred smaller windows running the length of the building.

The three stepped into the room and looked to the right. Max's eyes adjusted quickly and he saw a metal staircase running up to what appeared to be a small loft of offices.

"Found the light." Steve announced behind them and after a loud "click" the room was flooded with bright light from newly installed lights running along the walls just above head level.

There was a stove and a small kitchen, beneath the loft in an alcove. Again these fixtures seemed to be new as there was a remarkable lack of black grime. Amanda walked around the vestibule and peered behind the kitchen.

"Oh my God." She was almost laughing. Max and Steve joined her to see a wide open room set with spray nozzles in the walls.

"A communal shower?" Max's jaw dropped and Amanda could not help but to laugh.

"I'm sorry, but this is…" she stammered.

"What the hell was Uncle Dave thinking?" Max cursed.

"Your apartment is fine Max. Just don't move." She patted his shoulder.

"I didn't renew my lease. There wasn't time." He could barely speak through his clenched jaw.

"Oh…" Amanda took another look around.

"This is great." Steve said absolutely sincere.

"What?"

"Once you get this place cleaned up… 'Shower Party'! Hey!"

HOWARD NIGHT was born and raised in the Mt. Airy section of Philadelphia which is what inspired the fictional city of Mountairy Rock. The SERPENT CULT is his first novel and the first of the MOUNTAIRY ROCK CHRONICLES

www.ingramcontent.com/pod-product-compliance
Lightning Source LLC
Chambersburg PA
CBHW061129200626
46817CB00016B/461

* 9 7 8 0 9 8 5 5 6 0 3 0 0 *